7/22

Jobs
for Girls
* with *
Artistic
Flair

Jobs for Girls * with * Artistic Flair

June Gervais

PAMELA DORMAN BOOKS
VIKING

VIKING
An imprint of Penguin Random House LLC
penguinrandomhouse.com

Copyright © 2022 by June Gervais
Penguin supports copyright. Copyright fuels creativity, encourages
diverse voices, promotes free speech, and creates a vibrant culture. Thank
you for buying an authorized edition of this book and for complying with
copyright laws by not reproducing, scanning, or distributing any part of
it in any form without permission. You are supporting writers and
allowing Penguin to continue to publish books for every reader.

All illustrations by the author.

A Pamela Dorman Book/Viking

LIBRARY OF CONGRESS CATALOGING-IN-PUBLICATION DATA
Names: Gervais, June, author.
Title: Jobs for girls with artistic flair : a novel / June Gervais.
Description: New York City : Pamela Dorman Books ; Viking, [2022]
Identifiers: LCCN 2021047701 (print) | LCCN 2021047702 (ebook) |
ISBN 9780593298794 (hardcover) | ISBN 9780593298800 (ebook)
Subjects: LCSH: Women tattoo artists--Fiction. | LCGFT: Lesbian fiction. |
Romance fiction. | Novels. Classification: LCC PS3607.E7866 G47 2022 (print) |
LCC PS3607.E7866 (ebook) | DDC 813/.6—dc23
LC record available at https://lccn.loc.gov/2021047701
LC ebook record available at https://lccn.loc.gov/2021047702

Printed in the United States of America
1st Printing

Designed by Alexis Farabaugh

For Mom
and
for Rob

Jobs
for Girls
* with *
Artistic
Flair

One

How freeing it would be—how useful, how illuminating—if a fortune-teller should walk through the door of Mulley's Tattoo.

Who else could Gina consult? For three days she'd been pacing the docks behind the shop, as if she'd catch some brilliant idea swimming in the river, just fish it out of those rainbow wriggles of oil slick. An hour ago, Dominic had said *Enough*, and he was the authority, the shop owner, the ten-years-older brother. He summoned her back inside to the shop's waiting area, where he'd set up his Olympia portable typewriter on the coffee table. *You're not wasting your life here. Time to make a plan.*

From the age of fifteen, Gina had done all her homework in this very room, while drifters and eccentrics told their stories over the staccato buzz of Dominic Mulley's tattoo machine. This was the one place on Earth where she belonged. She'd memorized every design on the flash posters, their stock eagles and ships and arrowed hearts. She'd painted that mural over the couch, the centerpiece to all their flash: a muscled mermaid leaning against an anchor, holding an artist's palette, as if she had just lettered the boldface MULLEY'S on the wall.

As of last Saturday, though, Gina was a high school graduate; she still had a nasty sunburn as a memento of the ceremony. Now began some other life.

Step one, Dominic had said. *Write a résumé.*

Résumés meant interviews meant jobs where you had to look people in the eye, and that was never easy for her like it was for Dominic. She always said the wrong thing, or the right thing in a strange way, and had to escape sometimes to the bathroom because breathing felt like sucking air through a cotton filter. It had happened when she worked at the bait shop, the movie theater, the housekeeping service, and the card store, and wherever she worked next, it would happen again.

Here she sat, though, miserably clacking out her name on the Olympia, one percussive letter at a time. If she were a typewriter key, which one would she be? The ampersand, with its crossed arms? No—a left parenthesis. The scrawny bend of her body, the shy hunch to her shoulders—

"Hey, chickie." A customer, a biker with a blond horseshoe mustache, was snapping his fingers at her. He was getting a tattoo of a blue devil from Mackie, one of the guys who worked for Dominic. "You work here?"

"She's the lackey," Mackie said, pausing to dip his needle back into a little paper cup of ink. Sweat glazed his bald head; his arms swelled out of the sleeves of his T-shirt.

"I help my brother run the shop." In truth, Gina wasn't allowed to run anything but the vacuum. She turned her attention back to the typewriter. *Hard worker seeking position as . . .* what? Leave it blank for now. *Strengths include—*

"What I'm asking is, you do tattoos? Say I wanted some artwork down here." Gina glanced over to see the biker moving his hand to his fly, giving her a sly look. She rolled her eyes. Dudes always made that joke like they were the first one to think of it.

Focus on the typewriter. *Strengths include attention to—*

"She can't tattoo," Mackie said. "And if you're that committed to decorating your dick"—he hocked a load of phlegm and bent to spit it in the trash—"I charge a hundred-dollar handling fee."

"Dammit," Gina said. She'd meant to type *detail*, and now she'd accidentally typed *dick*. She pulled the carriage release lever and yanked the paper out.

"So what are you, the secretary?" the biker said.

"I'm looking for a job."

The biker scratched his mustache. "Thought you said you helped run the shop."

"I don't take a salary." She liked saying it that way. Classed it up.

"So what kind of job are you looking for?"

And that was the question, precisely—the reason she needed a fortune-teller. She could not envision this new life she was supposed to create, much less the next step toward it, which made these orders from Dominic—*Just picture yourself in five years*—impossible. The best she could do was list all the futures she didn't want:

Not anything that required a degree. College was a foreign land with an impossible price tag.

Not any of her after-school jobs—the kind you got because you wanted to stock the neglected pantry with more than spaghetti and ketchup. The kind you quit or were fired from within a few weeks, because whenever someone talked to you, you gaped at them like a fish.

Not her mother's jobs: bartender by night, receptionist at a glass-and-mirror company by day. Not anything, in fact, that would resemble her mother's life, or keep her in that house any longer than she had to be.

But also not anything that took her away from Blue Claw, because that would mean leaving Dominic. Clearly he needed her just as much as she needed him, but in some act of pointless martyrdom, he kept harping on her to get out of their hometown and *strike out on your own*.

This is not a real list. This is just a pile of nots. You're making this difficult, Dominic had said. *Just write down your skills.*

My primary skills, she'd replied, *are doing your grunt work, managing Mom, and drawing weird pictures.* This only made him scrawl out his own list—

JOBS FOR GIRLS WITH ARTISTIC FLAIR

—and stick it next to the typewriter before stalking out of the shop on some errand.

"Hey," the biker said. "Did you fall asleep over there? I said what kind of job?"

Gina rubbed her face with both hands. "I am considering"—she picked up Dominic's list—"floral design. Window dressing. Seamstress. Candy making."

"Gina," Mackie snapped. "Less dit-dit-dit. More type-type-type." He turned to run his needle in water.

"You want to come work for me? I restore elite vehicles. I just did a Lambo for Judas Priest's drummer." This was clearly Gina's cue to be dazzled.

Did anyone actually impress women that way? If Gina were trying to get a girl's attention, she would do something legitimately sexy. Like ask the girl what she loved doing, what made her lose track of time. And then listen to the answer. Or perhaps knead a loaf of bread dough, in a casual and quietly confident way, while asking the girl what sort of sandwiches she liked and making occasional meaningful eye contact. In her dream world, she could pull that off.

Gina got up and turned the typewriter so she was facing away from the biker, toward the front window. Just as she got settled, a Dodge Tradesman van pulled up to the curb, and out climbed one of the largest human beings Gina had ever seen.

Two

Gina would struggle to explain to Dominic later why she had done it. Hadn't she heard his instructions? *I wasn't thinking.* And didn't she hate talking to strangers? *I was bored. Mackie's guy was irritating.* What she couldn't say, because it was weird: *I'd been wishing for a fortune-teller, and you never know.*

She rose and poked her head out the door. Seagulls wheeled above Midway Street. The air smelled like detergent from the laundromat next door and urine from the alley, where loiterers were still known to relieve themselves, though Dominic chased off anyone he caught.

"Gina." Mackie stopped his machine. "Dominic said you don't go out that door after dark." If Gina got mugged, accosted, or snatched into some guy's car on Mackie's watch, he knew he'd be out of a job. Apart from that deterrent, Mackie wouldn't care if the van swallowed her up whalelike and hurtled off a Montauk dock.

"It's not dark yet." The sky was smudging with orange and pink, an hour left till the street went black and blue. Gina stepped outside.

The van's driver was a bear of a man whose very appearance suggested he wanted to keep his face to himself: beard made for Viking winters, blackout shades he'd slipped on as he climbed from the van, exhales of cigarette smoke like a shroud around his head. He left the van running.

Gina stared up at the underside of that Viking beard. It was only now, getting a worm's-eye view of him, that a wave of nerves hit her. He had the earth-and-sweat smell of a gravedigger.

He took a drag on his cigarette. "Dominic around?"

"Out on an errand." Her voice sounded too high.

"Why don't he send you on the errands, Peppermint Patty?"

Rick Alvarez, the other tattooer at Mulley's, had been coaching her on how to talk to people. *Somebody intimidates you?* he'd said. *You think of one thing you can do better than they can. Change a tire. Karaoke. Rubik's Cube.*

Gina clenched her fists to hide the tremors. "Pac-Man."

"What did you call me?"

Oh, God. "I said he's almost back, man."

The driver looked her over, maybe trying to figure out if he was talking to a responsible adult. "Is Dominic the kind of guy who's going to be ticked if I leave a package with you? Because I don't want to offend a friend of the Association, but I been driving for fifteen hours and my lady is waiting for me."

"Leave it with me."

The man propped his sunglasses on his head. "And you go by what moniker?"

Muffled noise came from the shop; Gina turned to look. Mackie was rising from his chair, stripping off his latex gloves, barking her name. The Viking pulled out a delivery slip and scrawled *Left with Jenna*.

"That's not my name," Gina said, but he was already turning to jerk open the van door. He dragged out a wooden crate tall enough to hold a taxidermied vulture, with Dominic's name across the side in thick marker. Then the man heaved it onto his shoulder and carried it inside. He set the box in the middle of the waiting room, grunted something at Mackie on his way out, and peeled off.

"What the hell was that?" Mackie stared at Gina. "Give me a minute,

Jack," he said to the customer. He walked out to the waiting room, yanked Gina back outside, and pointed to the Harley parked out front. "You happen to notice my customer came in wearing a Pagans vest? Suppose that dude was Hells Angels? You gonna clean up the broken glass?"

"Why are you working on Pagans anyway? They've got their own tattooers." Her voice felt as though it was forcing its way through a straw. "Dom said no one-percenters, no outlaws."

"Don't answer that door. Unless it's a guy we know, or some hot friend of yours."

Jerk. He knew that hot girls never hung out with Gina.

Back inside, Mackie dropped the bamboo shades to block the view through the front window, just to antagonize her, and resumed tattooing. Gina collapsed into the chair nearest the crate and leaned forward, elbows on her knees, knuckles digging into her chin. The thing was clearly out of place, dingy and scuffed in a shop that Dominic tried to keep clean as a dentist's office, windows so spotless you were in danger of walking through them.

How was she supposed to concentrate on writing a résumé with this mysterious thing sitting there, begging to be opened? Gina picked up a pen and began to draw on the nearest piece of paper. She had doodles for getting through every sort of difficulty: merit badges to boost her spirits, labyrinthine spirals when she needed to disappear. Her favorite, an exotically ugly fish, was helpful for skipping over unpleasant or tedious moments. Start with the beaky mouth. Fins like fringed wings, beady eyes . . . In her mind, it even had a nature documentary voice-over: *The wing-finned trancefish— an evolutionary mystery. It can't fight; it can't flight; its lime-green glow makes camouflage impossible. Ah—but witness its clever survival strategy: in times of threat, it dims its glow and enters a quasi-sleep state—*

The bells on the front door clanked. Gina jumped, and then her whole body relaxed: there he was. Dominic was home.

His black curls were damp with the humidity. He'd always been darker than Gina, as if he'd gotten all their southern Italian genes, and she all their Irish. Now that summer had come, his skin under his patchwork of tattoos was deepening to olive as hers freckled and burned. They were ten years apart, separated by half a dozen miscarriages, and people rarely even guessed they were siblings. She was slight, he was sturdy—not like Mackie, who reminded her of a Budweiser Clydesdale; more like a quarter horse. In his clean gray mechanic shirts and black jeans—not a single rip, fray, or spot worn away—Dominic was also a better dresser than Gina. Or, for that matter, most of the people who walked into his shop.

Dominic stared at the crate in the middle of his waiting room. "Is there a body in there?"

"You want the little crowbar?" Gina stood.

"Business first. Show me how far you got." He sat on the couch next to her and picked up a paper from the stack. Then he looked at her. "Are you sure these are the skills you want to highlight?"

GINA MULLEY

Seeking position as artist's underling

Strengths include attention to dick

"Also, don't say 'underling.' And lose the fish." He picked up the one cover letter she'd managed to eke out and skimmed it. "This has no salutation. Or address."

"I don't know who to send it to." She pointed to his *Jobs for Girls with Artistic Flair* list. "We don't have all these businesses around here." Blue Claw was the county seat in name only, buffered by farms, way out east where the island forked to the sea. People came here to go to court or to go to jail or to harvest potatoes; the river mills remained only as ruins. Even the decades-old shops on Midway Street were struggling now, as malls and multiplex theaters opened farther west.

"Rick's got family in Huntington Station," Dominic said. Where *was* Rick? Everything went better with him around. "His aunt's renting out a room and it's biking distance to downtown. You'll have your pick of these gigs." Dominic ran his finger down the list.

"You want me to move an hour away?" When he'd said "outside of Blue Claw," she'd thought he meant Ronkonkoma, maybe. Three stops away on the Long Island Rail Road.

"It'll be good for you."

A little pain like a muscle spasm twisted below Gina's ribs. "Can I get the crowbar now?"

He let her go. She walked past Mackie and his customer, down the hallway to the back closet. Huntington. So he was just going to send her away, with no car of her own, like cargo shipped westward? A picture came to her: the sad wing-finned trancefish in the back of a Conestoga wagon, fishbowl sloshing water with every rut and bump. She'd draw that later.

Gina handed Dominic the crowbar and he knelt. A few little jerks and yanks and the lid splintered off. He pulled out the crumpled newspaper packed solid inside.

A trophy. A three-foot-tall trophy.

Its brassy finish had weathered the journey without a dent. On its base was a plaque:

West Coast Tattoo Association

1985 Expo

BEST BACK PIECE

DOMINIC MULLEY

Mackie put down his machine for a look. He whistled. "Look at the big man."

"About time they shipped it. It's been six months."

The golden chalice of that trophy looked big enough to pour in a bottle of pink champagne. Elation prickled up like evening stars appearing, as if the trophy had been sent not just for Dominic, but for Gina. She knew the exact tattoo that had earned it; she'd done all the research—custom work for a friend of Dominic's, a Mustang framed by a halo of exhaust clouds and spare parts, as if descending from muscle-car heaven.

Dom's friend had flown across the country with him for that convention, walking around shirtless all weekend, showing it off. Gina wasn't allowed to go. School days. So stupid. Dominic should've brought her. How many hours had she spent in the library, looking for repair manuals and coffee-table books with glossy photos of cars, even sketching mock-ups for him?

"Hey, Mack," said the mustachioed biker, his blue devil half done. "If we're taking a break, I need a smoke and a piss."

As soon as the lock clicked in the bathroom door, Mackie quietly reached to flip over the biker's leather vest, but Dominic turned and grabbed him, his knuckles wrapping around Mackie's forearm.

With his free hand, Dominic pointed to the vest's patches. He spoke under his breath. "I don't want to see this Nazi shit in my shop ever again. Get him done and out of here." Mackie nodded. "And why are my shades down? We're open for business." He pulled them up.

Dominic dragged the trophy to the most visible corner, its holographic inlay glittering. He turned to Gina; a warm calm moved through her. "Makes you want to work on the next one, right?"

"Do both our names go on the plaque next time?" she said.

Mackie snorted. "Trophy goes to the guy who got his hands dirty."

Gina lifted her hands, smeared with ink from her leaky ballpoint and the typewriter ribbon.

"Yeah, I see your grubby paws," Mackie said. "Come back and talk to me when that's tattoo ink."

There was no reason it *couldn't* be tattoo ink—no reason except Dominic forbidding it. For three years, Gina had labored at every other task in this shop: making needles, running the sterilizer, cutting acetate stencils, booking appointments . . . Of all the ways to get your hands dirty at Mulley's, there was only one she'd never been permitted to try.

And yes, she knew all Dominic's reasons. But if he was going to stand there saying *Picture yourself in five years . . .*

The bells on the door clanked again. Dominic turned to shine a smile at the pair of miniskirted young women who walked in: "Girls. Welcome."

While he was distracted, Gina took her sketchbook and slipped out the back door, into the falling darkness, where she was not supposed to go.

Three

Mulley's Tattoo, like all the buildings on this side of Midway Street, backed up to the docks of the Bifurc River. In the hundred yards of parking lot between that row of back doors and the water, the amber streetlights were snapping awake. A silver dollar moon shone on the darkening water.

Gina's thinking spot was out along the docks: a graffiti-gnarled bench, just far enough from the tattoo shop's back door to feel like a retreat. It was downwind from the laundromat and the bakery, and the reassuring smells of detergent and fresh Italian bread made her feel less alone in her troubles. A thousand times, sad or angry or puzzled or stuck, she'd come here for respite.

At this moment, though, with her stomach leaping, goose bumps on her arms, she was no longer puzzled or stuck. She saw the answer.

Whenever a customer joked to Gina, *So, are you the new trainee?* Dominic had always cut in before she could speak. *Don't put ideas in her head. She'd be a lamb to the slaughter.* This trade was cutthroat and secretive; he'd fought his way in, fought to stay in business, and his little sister absolutely would not be entering the fray, any more than he expected her to become a linebacker or a bouncer. Female tattooers were almost unheard of. In the past year or so, Gina had caught rare sightings in trade magazines, two or three at most—but those women lived in big cities, many of them on the West Coast, not in far-flung seaweed patches like Blue Claw.

But this career answered every single thing on her list of nots. She'd already mastered every mundane task Dominic would ask of an apprentice. If she could convince him to teach her to tattoo, Mulley's could become a family business. They could grow it together.

She leaned back and closed her eyes, breathing in the nighttime river smell. Her vision was so clear: Gina in the shop at twenty-one or so, strong as that Mulley's mermaid, wearing a gray button-down just like Dominic's. She had her own community of repeat customers. Her drawings were not hidden away in a ratty notebook, but crisp and bold on her own flash posters, right there next to her mural.

The machine vibrated in her hand, a living thing. On her client's calf she was tattooing a cresting wave, sky-blue as hope itself, still wet with ink. *I love it*, the girl in the chair was saying. *Gorgeous.* Gina knew exactly how to reply—and why? Because she was among her people, misfits just like her, but she wasn't the rabbity teenager in the corner anymore. Gina the Tattooer, unlike Gina the Teenager, did not panic and blurt dumb things like *I like water also—for drinking, I mean—don't drink ocean water though, that'll kill you*, wishing miserably for a pillow to stick her face in. She would reply *Thank you.*

That was all. *Thank you.* Dominic Mulley's sister all grown-up, thriving; she was never anxious, because she belonged.

Dominic had always teased her for doodling that fish again and again, but some things you could only say in pictures. She was a living fishbowl with that strange glow-in-the-dark fish inside, and if she wasn't careful, everyone would see it. She'd never belonged at Blue Claw High School, she didn't belong at her mother's house, she wouldn't belong in Huntington Station; but Mulley's Tattoo was different. A kingdom unto itself.

Something splashed in the river. Gina jolted up straight and listened. Crickets. A radio. A distant argument, two men yelling.

Then a voice. "Doofus."

She turned around. Dominic skipped another rock across the surface of the water, another splash. "That typewriter's waiting for you," he said, but he didn't sound irked, and gave her a smile as she followed him in.

This was not a good time to propose her idea, with evening ripening and walk-ins likely to wander through the door. Finding the right moment was important because with Dominic, you got one chance. When his gut feeling was *no*—whether because of intuition or indigestion—he almost never changed his mind.

Was she really going to spend her life arranging carnations and baby's breath, though? Or struggling to breathe at some candy shop job, trapped in a marzipan corset?

Given favorable conditions, Dom would see this was the answer. It was only a few hours until midnight, and two helpful things would happen. First, the shop would close. Then, at 12:12, Gina would turn eighteen. Which seemed an excellent moment to begin the future.

Four

Back inside the shop, Gina shut herself in the office and called Rick, who was due in soon. "I need your help."

"Like you helped me clean my garage last week? And brewed a batch of toxic fumes in my driveway?"

"I'm really sorry." If bleach cleaned things, and so did ammonia, it just seemed reasonable you could mix them. "Not like that. I need pizza and booze."

"They only mask the pain for so long, my friend. Listen to a man who's seen it all."

"No," Gina said. "I need them for my plan." The most reliable techniques for putting Dominic in a good mood were flattery, a can of beer plus a bit of tequila, and sausage-pepper-and-onion pizza.

Rick arrived an hour later, his black pompadour freshly combed and pomaded, but his posture wearier than usual. "You look tired," Gina said. She took the pizza boxes, stashed them in the office, and put the six-packs in the fridge.

He rolled up his sleeves, exposing the tattoos on the rich rose-brown skin of his arms, the gleaming hourglass, the beckoning virgin. "I was out at my tía's house today, cleaning her gutters." Rick had moved to Blue Claw not for the allure of Long Island, but to be close to his mother's side of the family—help a sick aunt, reconnect with his cousins. Gina sometimes wondered how long he would put up with this salt-crusted town in the sticks. Out in East L.A., where he'd learned to tattoo, Chicano tattooers had perfected a fine-line, black-and-gray style using single needles. What Rick could do bordered on photorealistic. He could've worked anywhere he wanted. "Did Dominic tell you Tía's renting out a room? Are you going to take it?"

"I'm not moving an hour away." She dug around in the closet and handed him a peanut butter jar full of coins. "For the food. Thank you."

"Pez. You are ridiculous. As of tomorrow, you're an adult and I want my debts paid in dollars." He took the jar, shaking his head.

Pez. The first time Rick called her that, she thought he'd said "pace." Then he spelled it for her and she thought he was insulting her, like she was a Pez dispenser—angular body, big head. *No, no,* he said, and pointed to the wing-finned trancefish she'd just doodled on a stray napkin. *Pez. Spanish for "fish." When you get a nickname, you know we're tight.*

"Can't I get a new name now?" Gina said. "I'm turning eighteen. How do you say 'badass'?"

"You don't pick your name, the people who love you do. Just be thankful. My cousins call me Flaco—skinny. Just to remind me I'm not." He rubbed his belly. "My other cousin's so dark we call her La Güera, white girl . . ."

"Basically you're mean."

"Pssht. That's called irony. It's all in love." He turned to walk up the hall. "Good luck tonight."

Pizza acquired, she moved on to phase two of her plan: be quietly helpful all night until closing. Gina tidied up, wiped down counters, fetched the guys' supplies before they asked. She sat down at the typewriter and composed a list:

Reasons I Should Become a Tattooer

Midnight approached. She watched for that one pliable moment between Dominic locking the front door and dropping the bamboo shades, and then she grabbed his arm. "We should celebrate your trophy." She brought the food to the waiting room.

"You bought me dinner on *your* birthday?" He whacked her lightly on the back of the head. "Making me look bad."

Rick flopped down on the waiting room couch and cracked open two beers. "Eighteen's almost nineteen," he said, handing Gina a slice of pizza along with the can.

Her stomach was quaky and her mouth was already dry; her words had to be the right ones this time, and what if she couldn't say them? She swigged the beer and set the plate aside. She'd eat when she got her yes from Dominic. Let the guys talk first.

Dom turned up the Metallica. Mackie gave his workstation a last wipe-down and joined them. Shoptalk, end-of-day commentary: Did you see that guy who muttered under his breath the whole time he was being tattooed? Full moon, every time. The chick with the unicorn tattoo—she wanted to pay in crystals. Seriously, obsidian and shit. And that guy with the real heavy eyebrows, staring at everything—didn't he look like that tattooer from Jersey? Was he scoping out their techniques?

Gina had reached the bottom of her beer and the room was getting a little wobbly. She wrestled herself out of Dominic's sweatshirt, flushed, smelling her own sweat as she pulled it over her head, and just like that—no warning, no time for Gina to think—Rick sprang it.

"Hey, Pez. Decide on a job yet?"

Gina inhaled. "I was thinking." She picked up her beer and pressed her thumb into the sharp little mouth of the can. "Why don't I work here?"

Orange streetlight seeped through the gaps in the bamboo shades. Dominic poured a tequila shot. "Doing what, exactly?"

"Being a tattooer." All at once she was a child again, trying to build words from block letters. "It solves all my nots. You've taught me everything except the tattooing part." She unfolded the new list she'd typed and extended it to him.

Dominic knocked back the shot. "No."

Just like that? "Why?"

He leaned forward, one black curl falling on his forehead. "You're getting out of Blue Claw and into a steady job. You don't start tattooing on a whim."

"I'm not a wimp."

"A *whim*. All of a sudden."

"Three years with you is sudden?"

"Stick to the plan." Dominic was rapping his knuckles on the table now. "Find your own thing."

"I thought you found your thing at the Cheshire Cat," Mackie said. "Tell me again why you quit?" Gary's Cheshire Cat: the head shop outside of town. The correct word was *fired*, but she couldn't tell Dominic that, and she couldn't tell him the reason why, or he might go over and shoot the thirty-year-old owner who'd taken such a liking to his seventeen-year-old employee. She had never been fired by a boss's wife before.

"Tattooing could be my thing," Gina said. "I'd be markiful at it."

"Remarkable?" Mackie offered.

"Shut up," Gina said.

"No, really," Mackie said. "What was that word you used?"

"Markiful, and if you don't believe me, you can look it up in the goddamn dictionary. It means marvelous, beautiful, and making marks."

"No more beer," Dominic said.

Rick was starting to shift around next to her, as if the couch cushion had suddenly sprouted thorns. Gina stared at him—*Dude, stick up for me*—but he just fiddled with his shoelace, shirt riding up to expose his lower back, where a skull tattoo breathed fire up his spine.

Mackie tossed an empty can at the wall and it clanked into the trash. "Nobody's going to take a girl tattooer seriously."

Gina looked at Dominic. "Is that it? Your lamb-to-the-slaughter thing?"

Dominic waved this away. "It's a huge investment, training an apprentice. For something you might get tired of. Rick, Mackie—there was nothing to teach them. They had portfolios already." Now he looked straight at her. "They had an education."

There it was. His real reason. Or maybe this wasn't the core objection, but at least it pointed to a way in. Dominic was so proud that all three guys had associate's degrees. Their portfolios sat on the coffee table, hefty as a trio of holy books. Gina opened her notebook and wrote two words: *portfolio, education*.

"Then I'll take a class," she said. "I'm getting my money from Billy tomorrow."

Dominic stood to pick up the empties and crumpled napkins. "That money's for your room in Huntington."

"Billy never said that." Although, to be fair, their father had never really said anything. When Gina was in preschool, he'd moved to parts unknown, sending nothing for years but the rare postcard—until the day two money orders arrived, five hundred dollars each. *Give to Dominic William and Gina Marie on their 18th birthdays. For their futures.* Dominic, a high school senior, put his toward trade school; their mother, resisting Gina's pleas to use hers for a Toys "R" Us spree, stored it for safekeeping.

Gina felt her jaw tightening. "You think I couldn't do it. Even with a class."

"You're not a bad artist." He opened the trash can and threw in all the garbage he'd collected. "You have a knack."

"Artistic flair?" she said bitterly. A single penny gleamed underneath the table. Gina bent and grabbed it, smelling the dust on the linoleum floor, the grime ground in by the long day. Tomorrow it'd be her mopping it. This no longer felt like a privilege.

She pushed the toe of her sneaker into Rick's work boot. This was the part where he was supposed to say, *I think Gina would be a fantastic apprentice, don't you?* He turned up his palms and shrugged.

The penny was hot in her hand. She took a breath to speak: eight words. A vow. "I am going to tattoo here one day."

Dominic jangled his keys off the counter. "Let's go. Mom's." He jerked his thumb toward the darkened hallway that led to the back door.

Heat burned low in her belly. Tomorrow, she would get her money and begin her *education*. Once she'd registered for a summer class, what could Dominic do? The community college would have her tuition and he couldn't ship her off to live with a stranger.

As she followed Dominic out of the room, she tossed the penny at the wide-open mouth of the trophy. It clanked in on her first shot.

Five

The Maverick was six feet shy of their mother's mailbox when Dominic slammed on the brakes.

"Sorry for the hard stop." A bottle was smashed in front of Stella's mailbox, a glittering spray of glass in the road. Gina rubbed the spot where the seat belt had dug into her shoulder. Between her hunger and the beer, she was feeling queasy.

Out the car window was the red-shingled ranch where she still lived with Stella, its paint peeling, streaks of black algae on the sagging roof. Stella's car wasn't there; she'd be working at the Crow Bar for another hour.

"Well, good night," Dominic said.

"If you won't apprentice me, then hire me for front desk and cleaning." *For now*, she did not add aloud. "It's the work I'm already doing. If I leave, you'll have to pay someone to cover it anyway. And just—"

"Gina," Dominic shifted to face her. "I can't afford to pay anyone else right now."

"So I'll live at home until you can." His silence was heavy. She pressed on. "Mom's been good with these meds. It's safe."

Out of the dark, a whippoorwill called, a looping trill. Gina held her breath.

Finally he spoke. "I'm going to take you somewhere tomorrow. You think you know what you'd be getting into, and you don't."

"What time?"

He thought. "Be ready at three. And clean yourself up. Dress like girls dress."

One step forward. Good enough. Gina got out of the car, wading through the fringe of weeds at the curb so she didn't have to walk through the broken glass. "Love you."

"Be good." His Maverick pulled off into the long darkness of Marsh Road.

Yellowed circulars piled up along the driveway. Sometimes Gina picked them up, but not tonight. One of the cats Stella occasionally fed rubbed against Gina's leg as she passed. She bent to pet it, and when she looked up, something gave her pause.

That light in the kitchen window was strange—not a nightlight glow, not from a freezer door ajar. She backed away toward the curb and stared. It seeped across the ceiling, bone-colored and spectral, and seemed to emanate from the ground up.

Was it moving? A burglar's flashlight? She could pound on the neighbor's door and call the cops. And then what? They would pull up in their cruiser, ready to shut down a criminal. Then they would find—a moth, hurling itself against that stupid lava lamp from Gary's Cheshire Cat. Dominic would be furious with her for getting the police involved, for having one more incident to associate with the name Mulley and the business he was trying to run.

Gina clutched her keys and made herself unlock the front door. She tripped over something and fell into the house.

An extension cord stretched taut across the doorway, splitting off into a tangled net of cords. Each one snaked to a halogen bulb lighting its own glass tank, a dozen or more crowding the kitchen floor. It was a colony of empty aquariums. The kitchen smelled like the showers at the county beach.

Gina knelt to look into one of them. Not empty, after all: perched on a stone, in an inch of dirty water, was a stubby little something with four squat legs, the color of a wet tire, about as long as Gina's hand. A cricket catapulted itself toward the screen ceiling of the tank. Gina recoiled and screamed.

"What the hell?" Stella appeared in the doorway to the living room, still wearing her bartender's waist apron.

For the second time today Gina's heart was racing. She was nearly sick with adrenaline, wired enough to fight a bear. "You're asking *me*? Where's your car? What is all this?"

"Come to the living room," Stella said. "I have birthday surprises."

Gina exhaled and picked her way around the cages to the doorway. The living room looked tidier than usual, their battered shag rug striped with vacuum marks, the ashtray clean. The air was sharp with ammonia window spray. A mylar balloon bobbed against the ceiling.

"Tried to make it nice for your birthday," Stella said. "Hungry? I brought dinner from the bar." She unpacked a takeout bag onto the coffee table and Gina smelled the vinegar bite of buffalo wings.

Her mother's hair fell over her eyes, softly feathered and newly dyed—her standard color, Chocolate Cherry. A good sign. She was taking care of herself. Gina should do what Dominic always said: *Focus on the good*. Look for this grounded Stella, the softer Stella. She ached for it to be like that all the time.

"Thank you." Gina collapsed onto the couch and dipped a celery stick in blue cheese. The chill on her tongue was calming, like a cool cloth to the forehead. "Are those lizards for my birthday?"

"No," Stella said sadly, as if confessing. "One of Weber's deliveries. Fire belly newts." Weber was the new boyfriend. Stella had served him at the Crow Bar and he'd left a ten-dollar tip with his business card: **Exotic Animal Dealer/Fantasy Photographer.** *Jungle Boudoir Sessions. Safari Birthday Parties. We import what the pet store won't.* "He couldn't ship them to his place, not with the baby alligator and all that."

A congested cough echoed in the hallway, followed by a voice: "I'll get them out tomorrow." A man in his midfifties with a gray-black crew cut walked into the living room adjusting his belt. "How you doing, Jean?"

"It's Gina."

"Heading back to the bar to jump your car, Stella." At least he was the helpful sort. "You girls need anything while I'm out?"

"Get me another pack of Pall Malls?" Stella twisted around to grab her purse.

Heavy fingers tousled Gina's hair, then slid to the nape of her neck. "How about you?" Weber said. "Cookies and milk?"

Goose bumps rose on Gina's arms. She jerked her head up just quickly enough to see Weber take a five-dollar bill from Stella, shoot a salute, and walk out jangling his keys.

If Gina mentioned it, Stella would say, *Oh, relax, he's harmless*—it wasn't worth the argument. Gina reached for the pencil pinning up her topknot, so her hair fell to cover the back of her neck.

Stella nudged a shopping bag toward her. "Dinner, then presents. Did you finish calling those job leads? I raved about you to Deirdre at Island Travel. She said she never heard from you."

"I called some. I'm almost done—"

Stella pulled a nearly empty pack of cigarettes from her purse. "Gina, Queen of Almost."

Gina gnawed at a drumstick. "I'm not like that anymore."

"That's your father's side. The Mulley Almost. Dominic and me—we could stay up all night to finish something. You and Billy—eighty percent along, and oh, where did they go?"

Gina frowned into the pool of Inferno sauce in the bottom of the tin.

"You know I'm just teasing," Stella said. "When we put our paychecks together, think what we can do. Fix up the house. Take a vacation. Imagine."

"I had another idea."

Stella flicked a lighter and lit her cigarette. "What's that?"

"I'm going to take a class at Blue Claw Community."

Stella took another drag. "Couple of bookkeeping classes, that's a nice bump in pay down the line. But you still need a job."

This wasn't the moment to get into the details. With Stella, like with Dominic, you had to find the right time. "I'll call your friend tomorrow," Gina said. "After I register for the class. I just need my money from the lockbox."

"Money?" Stella studied her cigarette, as if she'd just discovered writing on it.

Gina wiped her fingers on a Crow Bar cocktail napkin. "The money. From Billy. I'm eighteen today. I need it for tuition."

"Oh." Stella tapped her cigarette into the ashtray. "That'd be with all the paperwork. I have to dig it out." With her free hand, she fiddled with the balloon string. "But baby, you know that was hardly nothing. You weren't thinking that would pay for school?"

"It's five hundred dollars." A night breeze swept the trees and forced its way through the window, sounding the lonely clank of bamboo chimes. The hair on Gina's arms stood up again.

"That much?" Stella said.

"Yeah, Ma." She'd been hearing the number for years. Every time a soapy plate slipped from her fingers—*I told you, be careful. You're lucky I don't take*

*it out of your lockbox money. Five hundred goes quick when you break things
like you do.*

Stella took a nervous drag. "Well—you know Weber's dogs and all that."

Follow closely now, or she would lose the trail altogether. Gina reached
out to touch Stella's arm. "Where's the money, Ma?"

"Give me a little time." That tone—the way Stella pressed each word—
was a warning sign.

Keep it light. "Can I help you find it?"

What had she said a moment ago? Weber's dogs.

Whenever Stella started dating a new guy, Dom staged a get-together,
plied the boyfriend with a couple of beers, and got him talking. Last weekend was Weber's turn; Dominic manned the barbecue and Weber sat there
with a sweating Bud on his knee, bemoaning the woes of breeding Dober-
mans, his failed business venture. Then Weber began bitching about—
what? *Scum of the earth*, he'd said a dozen times, *scum of the earth, those guys*,
until Gina and Dominic started shooting each other looks every time he
said it, and couldn't hold in their laughter anymore and had to go inside.

Weber the Exotic Animal Dealer Fantasy Photographer. Weber Scum of
the Earth—what had he been complaining about?

Debt collectors. He was fending off debt collectors.

Gina felt cold. "Ma, did you bail him out? With my money?"

Stella's face turned hard. She ground her cigarette into the ashtray and
looked Gina in the eye. "You're accusing me of what?"

She'd pushed too far. "Nothing."

"No, go on." Stella's voice was acid. She untied her apron from her waist
and folded it sharply. "I woke up at five a.m., worked a full shift at Kowal-
ski's, spent half my paycheck birthday shopping for you—"

"I'm sorry."

"—straight to my second job, worked another full shift, brought you dinner, and—I'm sorry, did you want my tips too?" She pulled a roll of cash from the apron pocket and dropped it on the table, her voice rising. "Anything else I can do for you? Take out another mortgage, maybe? Sell my goddamn blood? How about we—"

"Mom, stop." Gina put her face in her hands. Just ride it out. A baker's dozen of *Sorry, I'm sorry.* Only in this house could she be sorry for having her own money stolen. At least Dom couldn't force her to go to Huntington now; she wouldn't have the deposit for an apartment. Still, he had to answer for this. He could've held it for safekeeping; he could've opened a bank account for her. He always said that money from Billy was his running start. Now Gina's running start had vanished.

Fingers gripped her wrists and pried her hands from her eyes. Gina tensed. Her mother's eyeshadow glittered bruise-purple in the lamplight, inches from Gina's face; the smoke was stale on her breath. "I'm talking to you," Stella said in a low voice. "Do you want your surprises or not?"

Did she want her surprises? Was she getting off that easy?

The brown shopping bag sat at Gina's feet, big markered letters on the side: *Happy 18th to my miracle baby. You and me forever.*

Miracle baby. *Angels gave you to me,* Stella said sometimes. *I lost half a dozen babies after Dominic, and you survived. We survived together.* And then the list of all they'd survived: Billy leaving. Dominic moving away. The years that followed, living paycheck to paycheck—until Dom got fed up with tattooing illegally in Coney Island and came back to Blue Claw to open a shop of his own.

Dominic had told her back then, and a hundred times since: *Listen. Some moms are like the North Shore beaches. Ours is South Shore all the way.* North Shore people had Connecticut right across the way, making a nice, protected body of water—the Sound never got too wild, you know? Stella was a South Shore beach. *We got the big beautiful Atlantic,* Dominic said, *no buffer*. And do we cry when the waves are too rough to swim? No, we do not. We watch the surf like people who know how to live on an island.

The wall clock, low on batteries, began its sour chiming, first the opening notes of *Dona Nobis Pacem*, then a tired strike of the hour: one, two. Gina felt sick.

"I'm sorry," Gina said. "Yes, let's open presents."

Six

"Train doors closing," said the conductor, voice fuzzed through the speaker. "Train to Jamaica, all tickets, all tickets please."

Dominic still hadn't told Gina where they were going. He picked her up at three on the dot, drove to Blue Claw station, and they claimed the seats in the middle of the train, the ones that faced each other.

Long Island Rail Road trains were not cushy like the Amtrak trains were rumored to be. The LIRR had faded pleather seats in brick red and navy blue, grime rubbed into the plastic armrests, and—always—somebody's abandoned can of beer, left on the floor to spill halfway down the train car. The rhythm of the train felt good, though; it always did on these rare adventures. "So this is your girl outfit?" Dominic said.

She'd had no idea what flavor of girl Dominic was asking her to be, so she'd just worn her birthday gifts from Stella, which made her look like an off-brand Madonna: purple miniskirt, blazer over bustier, funereal bow like the "Lucky Star" video on MTV. Later she would tamp them down in the bottom of her closet, along with all the other clearance-tagged items Stella had bought her over the years.

"Are we going to the city?"

"No," Dominic said. "Nassau County. Pirate Paul's."

"Paulie Napolitano?" Disappointing. She thought maybe he was taking her down to the Bowery, where all those historic tattooers worked before New York City outlawed tattooing in '61. Or maybe to see the guys who were still tattooing on the Lower East Side, underground, in basements or lofts, where you called from a pay phone on the corner and then they tossed you the keys out the window.

Nassau County was not that sexy.

Paul had visited Dominic's shop a few times, but she'd never seen his. The two men had met when Dominic was in his last year of school, tattooing in the back room of a Coney Island arcade, trying to milk advice from all the older tattooers, who'd lie to your face before they shared a single helpful word. Paul was different. He let Dominic hang around his Long Island shop and taught him how to boil down black ink to get it even blacker, and to put in a little glycerin to get it running smoother.

If Dominic had taken all that knowledge and opened a shop in Paulie's neighborhood, the friendship would've been over, but Blue Claw was no threat; they were sixty miles apart. They still got a beer once in a while.

Dominic handed Gina a package. "Happy birthday, Little G." She tore off the paper. A gold-embossed *G* gleamed up at her from the cover of a portfolio-style sketchbook—leatherbound, with pockets and pencil loops and thick creamy pages. "Thought you might want an upgrade from your five-and-dime doodle book."

She opened to the first page and smiled. He'd cartooned her as the Mulley's mermaid, wearing a hoodie instead of a bikini.

"Look in the back," Dominic said.

Business card pockets lined the inside of the back cover. Gina pulled out the cards one by one: Graham's Florist. Jaybird Signs & Neon. Molly Jane, Tailor. All Huntington addresses.

"Ten different places you could apply for a job," Dominic said. "What do you think?"

Gina fingered the stitching on the pockets. "I can't do the move."

"Gina—"

"My money is gone."

His brow buckled. "You lost it?"

"Mom gave it away."

He shook his head. "She moves things. Did you check that Folgers can in the pantry? The box under the bed?"

"The minute she left for work. Dominic, I'm telling you—she gave it to Weber. Remember some loan shark was going to break his legs or something?" Out the train window, trees snapped by in a flip book of dark summer greens. "What do I do?"

"I don't know." Dominic stared up at the train ceiling. "Break his legs anyway?"

"This isn't a joke. You need to fix this."

He closed his eyes and rubbed his forehead, which meant he was one comment away from hitting overload. If you pushed Stella too far, she'd erupt in rage; if you pushed Dominic too far, he'd switch off.

"I'll talk to her," he finally said. "But I can't do this now. Let's get through this trip."

Gina put her old sketchbook inside the portfolio, safe behind all that beautiful new paper. She traced the gold *G* on the cover. "What are we doing at Paulie's?"

"We? Paulie and I are getting a beer. You're staying behind with Eddie."

"Who's Eddie?"

"Ask him whatever you want, pay attention, and remember this one thing: Today you're not my sister. You're Mackie's."

The train lights blinked off. *Not my sister.* An odd requirement. Whenever Dominic introduced her, the first words out of his mouth were *She's my little sister*: in pride, or to establish who was in charge, or sometimes—depending where they were—to make it clear that she was under his protection.

"Oh, I see." The lights powered back on. "Today's the day you're going to scare me."

"No." He pressed the word a little too hard. "But let's say I do apprentice you. Then one day Mulley's closes, and you find yourself knocking on Paulie's door, or Joe Blow's Tattoo Peep Show Emporium, or who the hell knows. And gee whiz, it's not so cushy out there. By then it's too late, you're all tatted up like a circus freak, and the Ice Cream Cottage sure as hell ain't hiring you." Dominic leaned his head against the window, glass scribbled and scarred with etched graffiti. "Something to consider."

Her brother had just acknowledged that she *might* tattoo. There was nothing he could show her that would scare her away.

An hour later, they reached the station nearest Paulie's shop. It wasn't so different from the one they'd left behind in Blue Claw. Long cement platform, shoddy little station house, garbage crushed against the chain-link fence. A gaunt man nodded in the train shelter on the platform; at the bottom of the stairs, a pale woman in a ragged sweater gathered cans into a cart.

As Gina passed, the woman raised her head and shouted, "You! I told you not to come around! You murder slut, you steal from me again—"

Gina's shoulders tensed.

"Friend of yours?" Dominic said.

Pull it together. Keep walking. Hadn't she seen plenty of yellers on the streets of Blue Claw?

"I'm fine." Gina straightened her skirt. "My first tattoo's going to say Murder Slut."

They walked several blocks, arriving at a door wedged between a storefront church and a video store. It was shadowed by a red awning, printed with PIRATE PAUL'S TATTOO PARLOR.

"You first." Dominic motioned toward the door.

Gina walked into a room dim with yellow light like aging plastic. It smelled of gritty, cigar-bitter smoke. A greasy golden retriever with scabs behind its ears wheezed on the floor by the chairs. A hundred sheets of flash were thumbtacked to battered wood paneling, old cellophane tape shining in the gaps.

Where were the tattoo chairs, the massage tables? This wasn't like Dominic's shop, with its open layout; this one had private rooms with doors. Muffled behind one of those doors, a man was shouting words that sounded like, but could not possibly have been, "Toucan sucker Botticelli paper fascists, Donna!"

"Oh, get off it!" a woman snapped. "You and your—"

The man again: "I'm out. I'm out." One of the doors opened and there he was: potbellied and mustachioed, wavy hair to his shoulders, receding hairline. His T-shirt sported Freddy Krueger flexing metal-clawed fingers. As soon as the man saw Dominic, his face changed. "The great Dominic Mulley!"

Dominic lit up. "Paulie, my Obi-Wan, my Yoda—"

"Call me Vader and you're out on your ass." After a moment of aggressive embracing and backslapping, Paulie cut out of the hug and opened another door. "Eddie," he said. A man in a swivel chair turned himself around.

Eddie was younger—twenty-five, maybe, one arm sleeved with a Japanese dragon. He had wavy hair, too, but wore his pulled back into a ponytail. A takeout container was balanced on his lap. Good-looking guy.

Paulie rapped his knuckles on the doorway. "Grabbing a beer with Dom. This is the girl I told you about. Macchiarolo's sister." Paulie turned toward the room he'd emerged from. "Crystal," he barked. "Let's go."

A woman with a wild perm, presumably Paulie's sparring partner, stalked past Gina and out the front door without a word. Paulie followed, pointing at Gina on the way out: "Do whatever he tells you."

"Within reason," Dominic said, just before the door slammed behind them.

Eddie and Gina were alone.

Seven

eg?" Eddie said.

What did he want with it? Gina, puzzled, extended her sneakered toe.

Eddie snorted. He lifted his takeout container and held out a chicken drumstick. "Would you *like* one."

Gina flushed and shook her head.

"So you want to be a tattooer." He rose from the chair, strolled over to the sink, and lathered up like he was getting ready to perform brain surgery. He rinsed his hands and snapped the water off them. "I don't know any girls in this line of work."

Gina pointed to a flash poster of fine-line wildcats. "That's Kari Barba flash." Mulley's had the same poster. Barba wasn't just tattooing; she'd opened her own shop in Anaheim.

"I said I don't *know* any. New York ain't California." Eddie returned to his workstation, where his tray was already set up. He picked up a needle, bent it with his thumb, and began to slide it into a tube. "So what do you want to know?"

Dominic hadn't told her to come prepared with questions. Gina shifted in her stiff sneakers. "If I wanted to be your apprentice, how would I . . . apply?"

Eddie paused with the needle halfway into the tube. What was that face supposed to mean? He was staring as if she'd asked him to shine the silver because the Queen was dropping by.

He broke into a full-bellied laugh. "Let me find our application form for you." He leaned back in his chair. "Wait, we might be out. Let me run up to McDonald's and see if they have any." He rubbed his eyes. "You are green, girl."

Glow-in-the-dark green, ugly-fish green. Gina turned away and walked to the counter, out of his field of view, hating herself, hating Dominic. This trip wasn't meant to scare her out of tattooing; it was meant to humiliate her out of it. She flipped open the portfolio on the counter, all the pictures a blur, nothing to see but her own scrawny hands gripping the edge of the page, trembling.

Eddie followed her. "You got to toughen up and expect the comments. People will grind you down until you quit." He leaned his elbow against the counter. "I mean, I'd be skeptical of a girl trying to tattoo. Like—look at your hand, look at my hand." He flexed his fingers. "You just don't have the musculature. It's not your fault, it's nature. Machines are heavy, you know? Some days you work for a ten-hour stretch. Can you handle that?"

Gina's breath was getting tighter, her torso fidgety: her energy for this conversation was dwindling fast. She needed to get out.

Or did she? She could crumble right now and walk away. Or she could rise to meet this day, and this guy, and this dive bar of a moment, and all the ones to come.

"Watch." Gina stuck her palm out at Eddie, straight and flat, like a cop stopping traffic. Then she pulled the pencil out of her hair and, using only one hand, snapped it in half.

Eddie laughed again, more warmly this time. "I could be wrong. I should tell Mackie to keep an eye on you. You might beat him out." He held her gaze a little longer than she was used to, as if contemplating a puzzle. Normally she'd avert her eyes, fiddle with that broken pencil, but now it was a challenge. She refused to blink first.

"Let me see your drawings," he said finally.

Gina pulled her old sketchbook out of the portfolio and handed it to him. "Skip to the middle. The first part is just copying." Whenever she was anxious in high school, she copied out all of Dominic's classic flash, over and over—flags and crosses, roses and skulls. Then she'd begun to wonder: Why did those posters always have the sun and moon, but never Saturn? Why a praying Mary and a pinup Marilyn, but never an aviating Amelia Earhart? Gina had seen crosses in every style from Gothic to gory crucifix to solid simple black. But she had never seen a cross made out of, say, vegetables. She had never seen a Star of David made of circuitry, an om of lug nuts. What if you were a religious grocer, electrician, mechanic?

Eddie paged through all of it and more: Hybrid animals like seagull-phoenixes and octo-foxes. A full back piece inspired by a pizzeria menu, from garlic knots to spumoni Italian ice. Alternative merit badges for unsavory Scouts: Pole Dancing, Ass Kicking, Hell-Raising.

"This stuff is pretty weird," Eddie said, with no derision.

Her hands weren't trembling anymore. "Nobody makes the flash I want to see. So I draw it."

"Got any of these on you?" Eddie looked her over.

"No tattoos yet."

"None? And you want to be a tattooer?"

If he was going to keep sizing her up like that, then she'd take the liberty of doing the same. Gina studied him. He was built lean, but his arms looked ready to move some furniture, like they'd be happy to do it. He was smiling with just one corner of his mouth, as if he and Gina were coconspirators.

After a long moment, she realized they had gotten a few inches closer, and she was no longer thinking about anything else.

"Whoa, girl," he said. "You eighteen yet?"

"It's my birthday today."

Eddie tugged the lapel of her blazer. "Here, take this off."

If Dominic were here, he would've come over and wordlessly, firmly moved her away. But what if she didn't want to move away?

"You came to watch me work, right?" he said. "So why don't you get some work done?"

He gave her that half smile again. Gina decided she liked it.

Ten minutes later, Gina was leaning forward in his chair, hair secured with a new pencil in a languid pile on her head. Heat radiated off Eddie's body on the stool behind her. He rubbed the back of her shoulder with a cool slick of Vaseline and pressed the stencil against her skin, leaving the charcoal outline of a crescent moon.

A thousand times she'd heard customers ask, *Does it hurt?* She wouldn't lower herself. She was ready. Eddie pressed the foot pedal and gave the machine a few little test runs, the dits and dahs before that lusty buzz began.

Just as the needle made contact, the front door swung open.

Dominic hurried into the shop. He looked over at Eddie and Gina; his mouth dropped open; he leaped, as if propelled by an invisible force, into the doorway of their private room. "Eddie! Hold up there." He was short of breath. "That's Macchiarolo's sister. She can't come home with a new tattoo."

"Why not?"

"Because—Mackie was a wrestler, man, and I just wouldn't, if I were you." His eyes were locked on the far wall, on Eddie, anything except Gina in her bustier.

Gina sat up taller. "It's my skin." Eddie's hand was still warm on her shoulder.

The dog roused from its sleep, scratched its scabby neck with its back leg, and loped over to a water dish. It began to lap loudly.

"He's really going to care?" Eddie said.

"She doesn't have the money to pay for that."

"That's between me and her, right?" Eddie smiled at Gina, and it became clear what he was doing: screwing with Dominic just for the fun of it. He'd already told her the tattoo was a birthday freebie. What a pleasure to watch Dominic squirm for a change.

"Gina, get your clothes on." Dominic enunciated every word. "We're going out with Paulie. You're coming, too. Because I've got my wallet now"—he picked it up from the floor, where it had fallen—"and if you spring this shit on—Mackie, he might not let you back in the shop, Gina."

She looked apologetically at Eddie. "I'll come back." She wriggled her blazer on. "Do you have a business card?"

Eddie pulled off his latex glove and handed Gina a card, which she stuck into the pocket of her brand-new professional leatherbound sketchbook.

Eight

It was late afternoon by the time they caught the train back to Blue Claw. Gina slid into the seat, opened her sketchbook, and began to draw. An arc became an oval became the mouth of a gleaming trophy. "Paulie was nice."

"Nice? My friend is a hundred things, but he is not nice. He threatened to punch the bartender."

"He said he'd apprentice me." She felt a rush of glee.

"He was joking. Or drunk. Probably both."

The train horn cut him off, squalling long and loud as it raced past a crossing gate. Gina raised her voice. "Eddie said I could crash on his couch until I find another place. I don't even have to wait on the money from Mom."

Dominic slumped back into the seat. "That was not supposed to be the lesson today."

She didn't especially want to work at Pirate Paul's, with all its stale air and yellowed light. Paulie's shouting would be jarring, and although Eddie was fun, his couch would surely host pork rinds and roaches. The map of the possible world, though, had just grown; she could get by in that town. It was Blue Claw's gruff cousin.

Most important, though: a successful tattooer, a complete stranger, thought she could do this job. And Dominic had heard him say it.

"Forget Paulie. I'm going to make some calls." He fiddled with his watch. "We'll find you a better situation."

"What about the money? When are you calling Mom?"

A piece of faux leather flaked off Dominic's watchband. He picked at it unhappily. "Let's get you hired first."

B ack at Mulley's, Dominic disappeared into the office. After Paul's shop, Dominic's felt pristine with its milk-white walls and meticu-lously framed flash. It should've been busy tonight, with the summer season warming up, but it was quiet as a library.

Rick was sitting on the couch, flipping through a white book embossed with a gold cross. If it weren't for the Reuben sandwich next to him, he could've been posing as some saintly icon; the comb lines in his pompadour shone like the carvings in a lithograph plate. Gina flopped down across from him. "What the hell? Why didn't you stick up for me last night?"

"Buenas noches to you, too," Rick said. "My day is going beautifully, Pez, thank you for asking."

She made a face at him. "Happy birthday to me, too, if we're getting sar-castic."

He only laughed. He took an orange from the coffee table and started peeling it; a zing of mist needled the air, a sweet citrus smell. "It was be-tween you two. If I jumped in, he just would've dug in his heels."

Gina pointed to his book. "Since when are you religious?" Rick once told her he was raised Catholic but converted to science fiction. His bookshelf was an altar to Ray Bradbury and Octavia Butler; his high holy day was the yearly *Twilight Zone* marathon.

"It's for a client." He lifted his drawing pad, where he was lettering words in Latin. "Pax Domini sit semper vobiscum. There you go. Your birthday benediction."

She might have found it beautiful on some other day. "Benedict me something useful. Some good luck. Dominic changing his mind."

He bit into a segment of orange and sucked at the juice. "Pez. Do I look like some abuelita, handing out endless blessings to her nietos? I'm not here to save you. But I think you'd be good at this job. If I can help you once in a while, I will. Don't give up."

"Did I say I'm giving up?" She stood and began to pace.

"How about I bless you an orange. Vitamin C sit semper vobiscum." He made the sign of the cross in the air and tossed her a slice. "And one more present." He flipped to a new page in his drawing pad and drew a word, swooping the letters, looping the swashes. "You asked for a new nickname."

Gina stared at it. "What is this? Señorita Fish?"

Rick snorted. "One of my cousins was trouble from the time she could walk. Full of spirit. Pura PITA, pain in the ass, going to rule the world. You call a girl like that Pesadita—little heavy." Rick handed her the paper. "From this day forward you are *Pez*adita. Go get it, little fighting fish."

"Thank you." Gina looked at the word. "Sorry I was cranky." She bent to give him an awkward hug and ended up mashing her ear into his face.

"Now go be a pain in someone else's ass," Rick said. "I got work to do."

In the quiet, Gina could hear the frustrated rhythms of Dominic's voice through the office door. He was wasting his time. She'd worked for half of his friends already, and it was a running joke that Gina Mulley quit jobs like she was bolting out of a haunted house.

Maybe she'd end up doing the same thing if she worked at Pirate Paul's.

No, that was Stella talking. *Gina, Queen of Almost.*

Given the right conditions, people could change, just as places could. Five different beauty parlors failed in this very storefront before it was reincarnated as Mulley's Tattoo. It still held remnants of its past lives; just look at those workstations—aquamarine cabinets, hair-washing sinks. But you never noticed it, because those glamour-bulb mirrors where old ladies used to check out their perms were now a happy ruckus of rebel art and tattoo Polaroids and rude bumper stickers. Change was possible when the time was right.

Dominic stuck his head out the door, his curls damp with sweat. "Gina. If you're just sitting there, make me some needle bars for tomorrow? I'm going to be on the phone awhile."

She opened the supply cabinet, reached for the soldering iron, and then stopped. She was still clutching Rick's drawing: *Pezudita.*

Either she worked here or she didn't. This in-between, this free and friendly labor, had felt cozy for so long. Today it felt painful. Dominic couldn't have it both ways.

"Not tonight," Gina said.

Dominic shrugged. "It's been a long day. Listen—"

What if she said the words out loud? *Either I work here or I don't.* Was that ungrateful, though? Dominic had spent his day trying to get her life straightened out. *Either I work here—*

"Gina." He was waving at her. "Back to planet Earth."

"Sorry."

"We're going to the diner in the morning. Dress professional this time. Not this 'Like a Virgin' thing." He waved his hand at her clothes. "Go on and bike home. I have to wrap up a few more details. But I solved it. Just show up tomorrow, don't say anything batty, and I think I got you a job."

Gina stood at the supply cabinet, feeling sodden as waterlogged driftwood.

"What is it?" Dominic said.

"Can I stay with you tonight?" she said. "I don't want to see them."

He paused. "You'll be fine. Head straight for your room. If you see them, hello goodbye."

"Please."

"One problem at a time. Go. I'll see you in the morning."

Nine

The kitchen still smelled like beach bathrooms, but the lizards were gone. Gina heard voices in the living room, Weber's coy, Stella's delighted. She walked quietly toward the hallway, staying close to the wall, where the floor squeaked less.

"Do I hear my girl?" Stella's voice called. "Come join us."

Gina's stomach dipped. "Bedtime for me. Long day."

Stella appeared in the living room doorway, cheeks flushed, hair mussed, wearing a tiger-striped robe Gina had never seen before. She smiled and tugged Gina's sleeve. "Five minutes. Come on."

Hello goodbye, Dominic had said. Gina edged into the room.

Weber lounged on the couch, two shirt buttons undone, gray chest hair crinkling out. "Have a drink with us." A fifth of whiskey was sitting on the table. He poured some into a paper cup.

Stella grabbed it from him. "Don't give her that straight. She'll keel over." She cracked open a can of Tab, poured it into the whiskey, and handed it to Gina. "Go slow with that."

"Salud." Weber raised his own.

Gina took a sip. This could eat the rust off her bicycle fender.

"Two things." Stella took Gina's hand and tugged her down to the carpet, next to a suitcase painted with Weber's logo: *Island Exotic Photography*. Another suitcase gaped open, spilling animal print attire; Stella pulled out snakeskin pants and a feathery jacket. "First of all—Weber wants to know, will you and me do a photo shoot? Mother-daughter, just for fun? He got some gorgeous parrots. You always wanted a parrot."

Exhaustion hit Gina, as if she'd just gotten the bill for the past twenty-four hours. She moved toward the door. "I don't like having my picture taken."

"I told you," Stella said to Weber.

He shrugged. "Que sera, sera."

Stella turned to Gina again. "One last thing before you go to bed. Close your eyes and put out your hands."

Gina gave in. Something papery dropped into her hands. She opened her eyes and her heart jumped; it was a wad of bills.

"All my tips from yesterday," Stella said.

Gina counted them, and when she was done, her heart kept beating fast, as if it hadn't gotten the message: This was not five hundred dollars. It was barely twenty-five.

Stella already felt guilty; laying on more guilt now wouldn't get the money back. "Thanks, Ma."

"You got some nice mom," Weber said.

Hello goodbye. Hello goodbye. Gina downed her drink and put the cup on the table. "I need to sleep. Really."

"Well, this'll get you there," said Weber. He tipped a little more whiskey into her cup. "One more for the road."

Gina woke to the sound of her door bursting open, doorknob cracking into the wall, and the lights flying on. She sucked in a breath and sat straight up in bed, dizzy.

Stella stood in the doorway, shaking.

"What?" Gina's tongue was sticking to the roof of her mouth. She was clammy with sweat, woozy from the whiskey, not all the way sober yet.

Stella's breath was heavy with liquor. She slapped a Polaroid on Gina's bed. "Disgusting. But you let him and that's worse."

Gina stared at the photo. It was her. Splayed across her bed, eyes closed, braless in her tank top and underwear.

The hair stood up on the back of her neck. "Oh my God, Ma! I didn't—"

"So you don't like your picture taken. And the minute I go to sleep, this is what you do."

"Ma, *I* was sleeping. Does that look like I'm posing?"

"You wake up if I drop a pillow. You don't hear a *camera*? Where the hell did he go when you two were done? He drove off wasted, forgot half his trash in the driveway."

Gina wobbled out of bed, pulled her jeans on, and stumbled to the window. In the pale predawn light, one of Weber's suitcases was splayed open in the driveway.

"Don't you dare ignore me."

Gina leaned on the window frame, trying to steady herself.

Stella grabbed her by the back of the shirt, threads tearing with a *crick*, and Gina sucked in a breath. She pulled away. "Stop."

Stella grabbed again, her shoulder this time. "Are you even sorry?"

Do we cry when the waves are rough? No, we do not. Dom's words were swimming in her head, and he was right; if she just apologized, tomorrow Stella would be stricken with shame and bring another peace offering, another bag of gifts—

Gina glanced down at the photo again. It looked like a crime scene: unconscious woman, mouth half open, hand hanging off the bed.

"No." Gina shook herself loose, scooped up the rest of her clothes, and pushed past Stella.

"No what?" Stella followed her out of the bedroom, tripping over the doorframe. Gina locked herself in the bathroom and dressed, dizzy, as Stella pounded on the door.

"Not sorry." Gina slipped out of the bathroom. She threw her wallet and her new portfolio in her backpack and made for the door.

"Running away? That's cute. Should I give this to the cops for your milk carton photo?" Stella waved the Polaroid.

"When you're eighteen," Gina said, "it's called moving out." She snatched the photo from Stella's hand and slammed the door on her way out.

Stella clicked the lock behind her.

Gina took three steps away from the house, leaned on her bike, and was hit with a wave of nausea. The leopard-print lingerie dangling out of that suitcase in the driveway was soggy with rain. Just the newest addition. New company for the cigarette butts, and smashed glass, and cracks sprouting crabgrass, and the dead mockingbird the stray cat had dragged to their doorstep.

She climbed on her bike and headed up Marsh Street.

She willed herself not to think about the click of that lock, or what she'd miss on the other side of that door: the flannel blanket she clung to as she fell asleep, the comforting smell of the cedar sachet in her pillowcase, the frozen bagel she'd saved for today's breakfast.

Don't think about it. Don't think at all. Listen to the whistle of the waking chickadees. Look at the sky, lighter by the moment—sunrise soon. Better yet, eyes on the road. Five miles to Dominic's apartment, where she could lie down on his couch, warm and dry in his biggest sweatshirt. He would know what to do.

Ten

Dominic lived in a tired Victorian carved up into apartments. Its wraparound porch was cordoned off with jump ropes and handwritten signs: **DANGER—ROT—KEEP OFF**. Gina's sneaker broke into a decayed spot in a board as she climbed the steps to ring the bell.

He'd be dead asleep at this hour. She leaned her head onto the doorjamb, flaky paint scratching her cheek, and rang it again. Finally Dominic opened up, still in boxer shorts, rubbing his eyes. "What's going on?"

Gina handed him a folded piece of paper and sat down with her back against the shingles. "Read."

Halfway to his house, tired and ill, she'd sat down on a concrete parking block in a 7-Eleven parking lot. What if she tried to tell him what happened and she couldn't say it out loud? She'd pulled out her sketchbook and started writing. If she got it out on paper, maybe there'd be less of it in her head.

God, let him finish reading already. Gina pulled her knees to her chest.

Dominic cleared his throat. He looked almost as ill as she felt. "This was last night?"

"You want to see the photo?" She reached for her backpack.

He put his hand up to stop her. "I believe you."

After all these years of *Look, don't swim when the water's rough*—the relief of *I believe you*.

"I need to lie down," Gina said.

Dominic closed the door behind him. "I'm so, so sorry." He sat on the porch next to her. "This is terrible timing. Someone's here."

What the hell? She lifted her face from her knees.

"How about this," he said. "I drive you to the shop. It's quiet and safe. Sleep on the couch for a couple hours. And then we go to the diner."

"Who slept over?"

"Someone."

Today, of all days? One more person showing up to muddy the Mulley waters?

Gina was too tired to press him with questions. She climbed into Dominic's Maverick, tinted gold by the early light, and slumped her head back into the headrest. Dominic ducked inside his apartment and returned wearing pants. He started the ignition.

They drove in silence. Within minutes, they were approaching the shop, the gilt letters on the Mulley's Tattoo sign blinding in the sun. "When was the last time you ate?" Dominic said.

"Pretzels with you and Paulie at the bar."

The Maverick rolled past the shop and continued down Midway Street.

"What are you doing?" she said.

"Heading to the diner."

She was still in her dirty jeans. "You told me to dress for an interview."

"But you're hungry," Dominic said. "Let's just go."

I f someone said to Gina *Draw me a picture of Abundance*, she would've drawn three words on a neon sign.

You couldn't throw a bagel without hitting a diner on Long Island, but here in Blue Claw, in the crotch of Paumanok, was the most miraculous specimen of them all. Twelve different cakes and pies floated in dreamy circles in their rotating display case. Silver streamlined, railway-car slim, the building was wedged on the corner of Midway Street, and those narrow quarters stocked enough ingredients to maintain a twenty-four-page menu.

They settled into a booth and ordered. Gina sipped ice water. "This is a bad morning for an interview. Where am I sleeping tonight?"

"You don't have to talk. Just listen." Dominic looked at her seriously. "There are some situations I haven't told you about. Things are a little sticky right now."

Sticky had been Dominic's word when Stella was admitted to the hospital for that episode when Gina was fourteen. But sticky could also mean *The ceiling's leaking* or *Well guys, this is awkward, we're out of beer.*

"What kind of sticky?" Gina said.

"I don't know if you've noticed," he said, "but I'm fairly shitty at running a business."

"That's ridiculous. We've been open three years."

"The first six months, I was barely solvent." The waitress brought coffee. Dominic sipped it gratefully. And then he recounted all the things he'd never told Gina.

Those early days were so bad that he almost called it quits in '83. Dom thought he'd have to pack it in and go back to Coney Island before the shop's first birthday. But he went to one last convention and met a tattooer who did the most brilliant fine-line black-and-gray work that Dominic had ever seen. And, as it happened, he was looking to move to the island.

Rick Alvarez was a shot in the arm for Mulley's. Year two: They picked up the pace. The shop was attracting people all the way from the city.

By year three, business was so good, it just made sense to bring another guy on board. Dominic knew Mackie from trade school, and when he heard Mackie had been tattooing out of his apartment on the weekends—

"I *knew* he was a scratcher," Gina said.

"Let's not get sidetracked," Dominic said.

This year, though, business slowed to a crawl. At first Dominic chalked it up to winter and figured there was going to be a summer uptick; it hadn't happened. Now Dominic and Rick were limping along, even with their client base and word of mouth. Mackie—still dependent on those walk-ins—was barely making enough money to justify his time. And the expenses of running the shop were stacking up.

"Could it be Keith Yearly?" Gina said.

Yearly was a second-generation real estate agent in Blue Claw. He'd bad-mouthed the tattoo shop from the time it opened, predicting it would lower property values, but he was mostly an annoyance until he was voted president of the chamber of commerce. Lately he'd been using the position to settle his grievances one by one.

"Yearly's probably a factor. He left us off the new business directory. Maybe there's more I don't know." Dominic looked weather-beaten, licking already-chapped lips. "The point is, though—"

The waitress brought her toast, and Gina wished she could hide her stringy hair and ratty shirt. The two of them must look like hell.

"I'm already stretched thin," Dominic said. "It's a huge investment, training an apprentice. You're killing me, pushing this right now."

"But that's exactly why you should bring me on." She dumped cream into her coffee. "What if I was a shot in the arm, like Rick was?"

"Even if I could afford the time to train you, you'd end up poaching Mackie's business. It's not good for anyone."

"Then why are we even talking about this?" Gina crushed the empty creamer cup in her fist.

Dominic placed a manila envelope on the table. "Open this."

She opened the flap and pulled out a piece of typewriter paper.

TATTOOING APPRENTICESHIP AGREEMENT

She sucked in a breath—just as the waitress arrived with Dominic's Hungry Man Deluxe, as if Gina were astonished by the wonder of Canadian bacon.

"You threw me some curveball at Paulie's." He doused his pancakes in syrup. "I wish you'd just trust me—you're not going to be happy in this line of work. Three months from now, you'll agree. But if you're going to be stubborn about it, I'd rather you waste those months at my place than Paulie's. At least I can look out for you."

"What about all that business stuff? I thought you couldn't—"

"Read the names at the top," Dominic said.

> Between Gina Mulley, Dominic Mulley,
>
> and Jeraldine Harrison
>
> on behalf of Harrison Entertainment Inc.

"We have an investor," Dominic said. "Jeri's been working with her family business since she was sixteen. She's brilliant. She helped her dad turn it from this rinky-dink Staten Island carnival to a very slick, very successful company. As of last month, they're investing ten thousand dollars in us."

"Ten thousand? When do we pay it back?"

"We don't. They get a part of our profits now. Harrison Entertainment owns twenty percent of Mulley's."

Gina picked at her toast. "What does that mean, they own part of us? Like, could they repo the furniture?"

Dominic smiled. "You're worried about our crap furniture? Don't be scared." He dug into his pancakes. "But they have input now. I called Jeri last night and asked if we could use part of the money to give you a stipend."

"You're *paying* me?" Apprentices didn't get paid; you had to get a side job. He pointed to the agreement.

> Harrison Entertainment Inc. will furnish stipend of
> $100/week but NO OTHER EXPENSES. Gina is responsible
> for the cost of her equipment, drawing class, etc.

Gina laid the paper on the table. It was happening. What to do with this flood of energy? She drummed her fingers under the table in a fierce hallelujah of tapping.

"Don't get excited. Stipend is just a fancy word for 'not enough to live on,'" Dominic said. "You can stay with me for a couple nights, but after that you need to rent a room and that'll be another expense. Not the greatest time to leave Mom's."

She fingered the dial on the tabletop jukebox. That photo—the rumpled sheets, herself half naked. Waking up to the door flying open.

"I'm not going back. I'll get a side job." She looked down at the paper, which was dense with print. "You wrote all this last night?"

"I typed. Jeri dictated."

Initial term: Three months. If Gina meets all benchmarks
and requirements, term may be extended quarterly, up to
ONE YEAR MAXIMUM of training.

Gina skimmed the page. *All skills taught at Dominic's discretion . . . under Dominic's exclusive mentorship . . . Gina may not progress to new skills without specific consent of Dominic . . .* "Was she supposed to be at the meeting this morning? Is that why you told me to dress like a professional?"

"Yeah," Dominic said. "She wasn't real keen on getting up at sunrise, though."

Gina put down her toast and looked at him. "Oh, man." She bit her lip to keep from smiling. "That was her in your apartment."

"We . . ." Dominic hesitated. "Look, she came out to do some work. It's a three-hour drive from Staten Island, and every hotel around here is a flea circus."

"And then," Gina said, "things got sticky."

"Enough," he said.

This apprenticeship was real. Be cool—don't betray all this joy welling up—but it failed. Gina laughed out loud.

"Listen." Dominic pressed his hands to the contract. "Assuming you actually stick it out an entire year—by next July, Jeri thinks you'll be tattooing real skin for real cash. That pace feels dangerous to me. But she's the one with the money."

The waitress refilled his coffee. He wearily tore into a sugar packet, stirred the coffee with a knife, and downed half the cup. "Before you tattoo people for money, you tattoo people for free. Before *that*, you tattoo grapefruits and pigs' feet until I say you're ready. You learn to draw twice as well as me, because you'll have to, to be taken seriously. Even then, some guys will never take you seriously."

Dom still saw her as the shop mascot, with *artistic flair*, not *talent*, and *a whim*, not *ambition*. But with time, with work, that could change.

Gina leaned forward. "I know you think this is just something I have to get out of my system. And I know you think you don't need me." Dominic opened his mouth to speak, but she waved it away. "I'm in for the whole year. I'm going to be useful. I'm going to come up with ideas and help pull us out of the hole."

"For now," Dominic said, "I'd just like you to eat something."

"Last question." She looked straight at him. "Can I get a tattoo now?"

He rolled an ice cube around in his mouth. "If I do it. No one but me. Yes?"

Yes. *Yes.*

Eleven

By the time they got back to Dominic's apartment, Jeraldine Harrison was gone, headed home to scenic Staten Island. A powder-blue note was stuck to the fridge; he pocketed it before Gina could read it.

For all its hazards, she liked Dominic's strange apartment, a high-ceilinged parlor converted to a studio. The oddness of the place made it feel like a cousin to the tattoo shop. Instead of a closet, it had a massive walnut bar with built-in cabinetry, probably added in the fifties when cocktail parties raged through suburbia. Its glory days were over; on the shelves that once displayed spirits, Dominic kept his boxer shorts and undershirts.

"Make a list of what you need from the house," he said. "I'll go get it and check on Mom."

"Check on Mom? Really?"

"She's going to be a wreck, you moving out. It's just—a situation to deal with, now." He cleared his throat. "I'm not saying you did the wrong thing."

He also wasn't saying she'd done the right thing. A familiar stirring of guilt began.

No. Maybe, one day, she would figure out how to take care of both Stella and herself. At this particular moment, she could only handle one.

Gina lay down on Dominic's corduroy couch, the sunniest spot in the room. A garland of pine-tree air fresheners stretched above her from one side of the windowsill to the other—Dominic's answer to the apartment's periodic mildew. "You said you had a lead on a place for me?"

He flipped through his address book. "Mackie's cousin Connie was renting the top floor of a house with her friend, but there was some kind of drama, I don't know, the other girl split, and now she's scrambling to sublet the room. It's cheap and I could *maybe* spot you the first month's rent. But Connie is— her own special person. If I had my pick of roommates for you—"

"You got time to hold a Miss Roommate pageant?"

He sighed and spun the rotary dial.

Gina closed her eyes. Breathing the chemical evergreen smell of the air fresheners, she could almost imagine they were in the forest, with the purr of the phone dial for crickets. Sanctuary. Rest.

She'd left home. She'd gotten the job. Tomorrow, she would sit in Dominic's chair at the shop, get her first tattoo, and everything would begin. From this point on, maybe life would begin to unfold as it should.

The next morning, Dominic and Gina pulled up to a split-level ranch on Quarter Street with its grass crisping brown in the July heat. A sign hung from a gangly locust tree: VIOLIN LESSONS FOR CHILDREN AND ADULTS. Dominic popped the trunk.

Gina carried her cardboard box to the door, grateful her hands had something to do. Dominic led her inside to a landing with two doors, one labeled NO ENTRY, OWNER ONLY, and one ajar. "Come on up," a young woman called. "I can't touch anything."

They walked through the open door and five steps upstairs to a living room. Clear plastic covers encased the furniture. What person their age would do that? There was Connie, though, on her plastic-covered sofa, painting her nails white. Her mascara made her eyelashes look thick as cricket legs; her hair had clearly been through a disciplinary regimen of bleaches and heated devices.

"Sorry I can't shake your hand," Connie said, waving her wet nails.

Gina took one hand off the cardboard box to wave back, and its bottom immediately gave way. Art supplies rained onto the floor, crayon shavings speckling Connie's skim-milk-colored rug, pencils rolling under the couch.

Connie gave Dominic a look. He retreated down the stairs. "Going for another load."

Gina knelt to the floor, mortified, fumbling to reassemble the box. "I'm sorry."

"You can vacuum later. The disinfectant is in the kitchen." What did Connie think she did with those pencils? "I'll show you the room." Gina followed her down the hall.

The walls smelled newly painted, with not a scuff or dent in sight. A light fixture glowed softly, both bulbs working. What an odd, fresh feeling.

In the middle of the room stood two folding chairs with music stands. An end table in the corner was stacked with sheet music, a bulletin board propped atop it.

"I'll move all this for you." Connie picked up a music stand in each hand. Apparently her nail polish was only at risk from human touch. "Usually I teach in the living room, but otherwise we won't see each other much." She started toward the door. "Leave me a note if you need to reach me. I'd appreciate if you'd use your own pens, though."

So Connie wasn't going to be the kind of roommate she'd stay up watching movies with. Or whatever girls did together. Rooming with someone had seemed like such a handy shortcut to a social life.

Fine. It didn't matter. She had work to do, anyway.

Gina collapsed the folding chairs and followed her into the hall, but Connie stopped her. "I'll take care of it. I have a system."

As soon as Connie left, Gina bent to read the bulletin board. She had a new fascination with business cards, now that she'd gathered a collection in her sketchbook, and Connie's board was plastered with them—instrument repair, sheet music distributors, record stores.

One card stood out. It was slightly larger than the rest, deep lavender, silver embossed letters:

NICOLAS EGGLI-PFISTER
House of Mystical Delights

PSYCHIC | TAROT

CLAIRVOYANT GUIDANCE

Connie didn't seem like the New Age type. Interesting.

When Connie returned, Gina pointed to the purple card. "What's the deal with the—"

"Can we bring her mattress up yet?" Dominic called.

"Come on up," Connie hollered back. She carried the bulletin board away, purple card and all.

Twelve

All the way to the shop, fireworks popped in broad daylight, and as Gina stepped over the threshold of Mulley's Tattoo, she was flooded with happiness: the arcade of flash, the Ramones on the radio, the buzz of machines. Rick and Mackie were tattooing matching broken hearts on a punk rock couple, and even without knowing them, she loved them, too: the guy with his Mohawk dyed like a parrotfish, the girl with pink hair wild as a Seussian Truffula Tree. These were her people. This was her place. This was her initiation.

Dominic waved at the flash on the wall. "What's it going to be?"

She'd been ready to accept a crescent moon at Paulie's, but when she'd imagined her first tattoo, she'd always secretly hoped she could design it. Until recently, she'd been picturing some aquatic creature, maybe—a bay scallop, a blue crab. The town of Blue Claw didn't feel like home, but the ocean always did.

Lately, though, she'd been poring over the *National Geographic*s on Dominic's reference shelf, engrossed in the flora and fauna, and she'd stumbled on a photograph that made her pause.

It was a close-up of a woman's hands, slicing a kind of fruit Gina had never seen before. The fruit's skin was a stormy blue-black, flecked with dots like distant stars, halved to reveal crimson middles and a swarm of seeds. *Lunch of figs, bread, and cheese. Delphi, Greece.*

She'd never known figs looked like that. She'd only seen them in Newtons, reduced to gritty paste. This was the real thing, luscious color from five thousand miles away. She'd spent the afternoon drawing figs.

But as she reached for her sketchbook, Dominic shook his head. "Nothing crazy. Not for your first tattoo."

"It's going to be hidden under my clothes." He'd made that rule right off the bat, citing her future employment prospects. "Just look before you say no."

She opened to the page.

"That drawing's not terrible," Dominic said. "But if you think I'm giving you a tattoo with five thousand little dots—"

"However you want to draw it, then." She pulled the *National Geographic* off the shelf and showed him the page. "This is what I want."

He studied the photograph. "Let me see what I can do."

———

As Gina watched him take the transfer out of the hectograph machine, it came to her: this was the blueprint of a thing she would wear for the rest of her life.

The evening was cool for July, and Dominic propped the front door open for fresh air. The breeze carried in the smell of frying arancini from across the street and the chant of girls playing double Dutch. How strange to be the one straddling Dominic's chair, draped forward, baring her skin.

"Ready?" he said.

She raised her eyes just in time to see, out the window, the distant pop and sparkle of fireworks over the roofs of Midway Street. "Ready."

He pressed the foot pedal, set the needle buzzing, and carved the first line into her back, between her shoulders. It was like being scratched with the broken-off tine of a plastic fork; a hot vibration, like putting the tip of your tongue to a nine-volt battery.

"You doing okay?" he said.

"It's not bad." A few minutes later, the needle passed over a vertebra, a sharp little bolt of pain. She pressed her lips together and took a breath. "I remember your first tattoo."

"You weren't even there."

"But you came straight home to show me." It was Dominic's first year out of high school, off to trade school, living in Queens. Gina was eight and missed him so much it felt like being hungry all day long.

One weekend, he went to a carnival with some buddies and stumbled upon an old guy tattooing out of a trailer. And on that guy's ratty old flash posters, Dominic spotted a design he knew from their father's arm.

Gina barely remembered her father's tattoos, but Dominic used to sit on Billy's lap tracing their outlines with his finger, memorizing them. Years later he could still describe every one. He loved the classic anchor with the SINK OR SWIM banner, tattooed a thousand times by the legendary Sailor Jerry, still toiling in the Honolulu shop where Billy Mulley, seaman third class, had gotten his.

"You had him change the words across the anchor," Gina said.

"'Hold fast,'" Dominic said—the words tattooed across their father's hands. The old tattooer mocked him for it: *That's for knuckles, not biceps. If you're trying to grip the rigging, you don't stop and admire your Popeyes.* But for an extra five bucks, he did it.

Dominic drove all the way home from the city just to show Gina. She'd come screaming out the door to see that anchor, bathed in the patchy flush of all new tattoos, still speckled with blood. Old men at carnivals didn't bandage tattoos; they sent you out like a man (*like a moron*, Dominic would later say) without a single instruction for what to do with the open wound.

Then, in marker, on Gina's shoulder, he drew her an anchor to match his own. HOLD FAST. She'd felt so protected, so cared for.

Quiet filled her now, a silence that was safe and full. Time melted; she couldn't see the clock, and it didn't matter. She'd been so irritated the other day when Dominic practically yanked her out of Eddie's chair, but this was the way it should be. They belonged together, doing this. Billy Mulley didn't hold fast, but Dominic and Gina Mulley always would.

"G," Dominic said. "Gina."

Her eyes fluttered open, vision blurry. "Was I sleeping?"

"It's break time." He set his machine down and poured her a cup of apple juice from the fridge. "Drink this. You're pale."

The juice was sweet and cold; she blinked until her vision sharpened. She was back in the room, with the shiny silver bullet of the autoclave and the crisp edges of the countertops.

Dominic stepped out for a cigarette, and Gina wandered over to her apprenticeship agreement, taped behind the counter.

At the diner, it had glimmered like a list of charmed ingredients in a fairy tale quest: *One year. Ten skills. One hundred gold coins . . .* Up on the wall, it looked more like a legal document, stark and rigorous. *Take one class.* If her lockbox money was never coming back, that would be a feat—to save the tuition and find the time, with two jobs, with rent to pay. *November/December: Begin small tattoos on friends.* She had to make friends, too?

Dominic walked back in and saw Gina frowning at the paper.

"Don't worry about it now. Jeri wrote one for me, too, but it's ten times longer. I'll explain on your first day."

She knotted her fingers together. "It's weird to have another person involved."

Dominic shuffled through some papers until he found a Fotomat envelope.

"Don't you think?" she pressed. "After so long of just you and me?"

"She's been a good thing for me." He fished around in the envelope. "For the shop, I mean." He handed Gina a photo. "Meet Jeri."

Jeri Harrison was sitting on the counter of a carnival airbrush booth against a backdrop of tacky T-shirts. She looked older than Dominic, but she was perched like a big-eyed doll on a shelf: ink-black hair and teeth white as Chiclets and a dainty rounded chin.

This wholesome woman was going to rescue a tattoo shop? Look at those baby-blue cowgirl boots—she was like a flash pinup girl come to life. This person didn't look like she had an ounce of toughness. LUV HURTS, said her airbrushed T-shirt.

Gina dropped Jeri's photo on the counter. "Hey, I'm good to keep going."

"Right. Of course."

She put Jeri out of her mind, back in the photo where she belonged. Dominic switched to his shader, filling in color. They didn't talk.

He worked, wiping away blood and ink as he went. Time blurred again. And just as spots began to appear in front of Gina's eyes—just as she was about to mumble *Are we there yet?*—Dominic wiped her skin one last time. "Look in the mirror."

Dots of her blood welled up in a surge of green: two lobed leaves, palmate like hands. And then the pair of figs in the middle—one whole and one halved, scarlet at its core, seeded, wild.

After eighteen years of quiet load bearing, Gina's skinny little shoulders were speaking.

"Holy . . ." She stared in wonder.

"Holy first prize." Mackie leaned in. "That's outstanding."

Dom just stood there with his hands behind his head, watching her marvel over her new tattoo. "What do *you* think?" Gina said, but she already knew—just by the ease in his body—that he was pleased with his work and delighted by her reaction.

"You look so grown-up," he said.

She raised an invisible glass. "Cheers."

Dominic smiled and raised an air glass of his own.

The bells on the front door clanked. Gina didn't turn around. If Jeri showed up now, or Stella—which would be worse?—this day would lose its shine in her memory, and she wanted to keep it like this, flawless, radiant. If she had just one memory like that, maybe she could make more.

"Hey, do you take walk-ins?" Just a customer, someone she'd never met and didn't need to. It woke her up, though. She should leave.

"I'll bike home," Gina said. Connie's apartment was only a mile from the shop.

Dominic smeared the tattoo with ointment and bandaged it. And then their goodbye, same as always. Gina: *Love you.* Dominic: *Be good.*

T he bike ride was quiet, smelling of cut grass, pink with sunset light. A silver flower of fireworks exploded in the sky as she turned the corner onto Quarter Street.

Gina held her breath as she walked through the apartment door. She didn't even notice she was doing it until she got to the top of the stairs, when a thought came to her: she didn't have to hold her breath walking into her own house anymore. She was not checking for pill bottles or small creatures. She was doing a simple thing: coming home.

When she got to her new room, she reached to lock her door, and then it came to her that she didn't need to do this, either.

She stood for a moment, aghast at all this freedom. Then she turned her back to the tall mirror on her wall, pulled off her shirt, and peeled the bandage off her tattoo. She angled a hand mirror so she could see.

The figs glowed with a warm wet darkness, brimming with ink. Their color would never be this rich again. Below the tattoo, the long slim pour of her back, pooling into hips she rarely gave thought to, the seam of her spine like the crease in a milky envelope. Whose back was this? What foreign woman? It almost frightened her. She hadn't known this was possible: for something to be so beautiful that it hurt you to look at it.

Thirteen

At sunrise on the first day of Gina's apprenticeship, she biked to her new side job at the traffic circle gas station, and although the world might not know it from her gunmetal-gray jumpsuit with the Shell Oil insignia, *today she was a tattooer*. Almost a tattooer. A giant leap closer to being a tattooer.

After a morning that lasted approximately 102 years, filling tanks and running squeegees over windshields full of stubborn seagull crap, she finally clocked out. At the shop, Dominic was at the counter, frowning at a ledger, red pen behind his ear. "Apprentice," he said. "You're late." He walked to the bathroom and pointed at the orange ring on the inside of the toilet. "As of today, this is all yours. And so is that"—the mop bucket, the crumb-littered counter—"and so is that."

"Was I supposed to pick up grapefruits on the way?"

"Why? Somebody got scurvy?"

"For tattooing practice."

"Pull up a chair," Dominic said. "Let's talk about your summer."

He brought out a copy of her apprenticeship agreement.

Summer Quarter: Benchmarks & Requirements
_____

TO BE COMPLETED by Check-in Meeting #1,

FRIDAY, SEPTEMBER 27

***Daily completion of shop cleaning, administrative tasks, and drawing practice.

***Pass test of safety/hygiene/sterilization procedures, administered by Dominic, with grade of 90% or higher.

***Secure second job and save money for equipment to be purchased in Fall Quarter.

***Register for one drawing class to be completed in Fall Quarter. Tuition to be paid by Gina. No assistance provided by Harrison Entertainment.

"I don't see any grapefruits," Gina said.

"Right. Your summer boils down to three things," Dominic said. "Be useful. Practice drawing. Save money. Jeri says if you prove yourself, the fun stuff starts in the fall."

"I didn't prove myself these past three years?"

"She wasn't around, and she's got the cash. Listen, I told you—she stuck me with a list, too. You think I'm all horny to learn VisiCalc on the Apple IIe? We suck it up."

Gina picked up Jeri's photo from the counter, irritated. "Is this woman going to show her face at some point? Or does she give all her orders through you?"

Dominic handed her a note, powder blue, tidy as a tea party invitation.

> *Hi, Gina!*
>
>   *Congrats on your apprenticeship. I was hoping to meet you, but it's peak season and I'll be tied up in Staten Island for a while. Our first check-in is scheduled for September 27. But feel free to join Dominic when he visits, if you're feeling brave! I'll treat you to a snow cone at the carnival.*
>
>   *Cordially,*
>   *Jeri Harrison*

"If I'm feeling brave?" Gina said.

"I told her you get nervous around people," Dominic said.

Oh, God. Gina hurled the note onto the counter. It turned out cardstock didn't hurl well; it was more of a gentle flutter. Now she looked like a weak-armed pansy in addition to a frightened recluse. "Did you also tell her you're afraid of objects with tiny holes?"

Dominic ignored this. He opened the cabinet at his workstation and took out a jar of soapy water, where he soaked the used needles and tubes after each tattoo.

"So every night, you scrub these with bleach and a toothbrush. Then—"

"I know how it works." Gina took the jar.

"No shame in turning back," Mackie said. "If you stop now, you can still be a preschool teacher."

She turned to him. "Is this your normal jackassery, or are you scared I'll steal your customers?"

"Gina," Dominic said. "No need to say everything that comes into your head."

"No offense taken," Mackie said. "I'm not scared. You're going to quit this job in a month like you always do, and in the meantime we have a much cleaner bathroom."

"Macchiarolo. We're meeting here." Dominic turned back to Gina. "Bottom line—we pay our summer dues, things get better in the fall. If you want to try something new when you finish cleaning, I can give you an idea or two. But most days, get your thrills on your own time."

She looked over at her mural. That Mulley's mermaid had not earned her biceps sitting around complaining. A summer of grunt work at Dominic's shop was still better than equivalent grunt work at the bait shop or movie theater. Gina got the mop.

Dominic's post-cleaning idea turned out to be attaching a pencil to their junkiest tattoo machine and having Gina draw with this contraption. "Two dozen identical roses," he said, and went back to work. Was she training to tattoo a busload of flamenco dancers? She set to it. Five roses. Ten. Her hand ached and she was woozy from hunger. But she would not give up.

The volume in the shop had steadily risen, and now the radio was yammering a Yearly Realty commercial, that loathsome jingle that hell's tour buses surely played on repeat. She'd promised Dominic she would come up with ideas to pull Mulley's out of its slump, but it was hard to imagine anything working if Keith Yearly really was after them.

Gina had paid attention to the stories Dominic's clients told from the tattooing chair. Lamar Phillips's was the most recent, but not the first: He'd owned Phillips Electric for fifteen years, and when he wanted to expand into new office space in east Blue Claw, Yearly Realty blocked him at every turn. Lamar Phillips was Black; the east side of town was almost wholly white, and Keith Yearly's bread and butter was the people who wanted to keep it that way. When Phillips filed a complaint with the state, Yearly spent the next six months retaliating—preventing Phillips Electric from working on any property Yearly bought or sold, slandering their workmanship to other Blue Claw businesses. Meanwhile, Lamar Phillips's complaint went nowhere. Yearly got off unscathed.

How did you fight back against a guy who got away with everything?

Gina put the machine down and massaged her temples, trying to ease the headache away. Rose number nineteen. One more spiral.

She had the sudden feeling that she was being watched.

She looked up. A middle-aged man and his daughter stood in the waiting room. It was hard not to stare at the young woman, who was quite a bit taller than her father, looked about twenty, and was unlike any Long Island girl Gina knew. Italian, yes, with plumes of thick brown hair—but then there was that crimson kimono jacket, the Joan Jett T-shirt, the black leather pants clinging to legs that were several miles long. Leather pants. Like, who was July to tell her what to do?

Whatever Gina had been fretting about now seemed very far away.

The young woman was talking in an animated way with Rick, gesturing at the sketchbook Gina had left open on the counter. The shop was so noisy that Gina couldn't hear anything beyond the rising and falling of her voice. And then, straining to hear, a thought bobbed up inside her:

My flash is for a person like that.

The thought appeared fully formed, matter-of-fact, as if it had been hovering over the threshold of the shop all along, just waiting for this long-legged rock-and-roll girl to walk through the door.

My flash is for a person like that. All those nights drawing—she'd never realized.

The middle-aged man took a few steps toward Gina, stopping before he actually crossed into their workspace. He wore linen pants, a Nehru shirt, and leather thong sandals; the guys would probably mock his clothes as soon as he walked out. The way he locked eyes with Gina, you'd think they had an appointment.

"I know you," he said.

Gina tilted her head. "From where?"

He smiled and held her eyes for a moment. Finally, he shrugged.

"The information that eludes us"—what was that accent?—"is sometimes revealed with the passage of time." *Ze passage of time.* She couldn't possibly know this man if he wasn't from around here.

"Where are you from?" Gina said.

"Baden bei Zürich. Switzerland."

Dominic was watching, holding a large bottle of black ink as if it might double as a murder weapon. The Dire Straits cassette had snapped to a stop. Only Mackie's tattoo machine buzzed on, but the shop suddenly felt expectant as an empty stage.

"My card." The man dropped a business card on the front counter. "Do call us. My assistant could use a friend." He gestured out the window at a silver convertible, parked in front of the shop. The girl had already slipped out of the shop and into the passenger seat, red running shoes propped on the dashboard. Not his daughter, then. Assistant in what?

The man made a small bow and walked out.

Rick picked up the card. "Nicolas Eggli-Pfister. Psychic."

"You're messing with me." She pulled it from his hand. It was the same deep lavender card from her roommate's bulletin board. "Connie has this card. Mackie, how does your cousin know this guy?"

"Who cares?" Mackie stopped tattooing his customer for a moment, leaving the bird on his forearm temporarily beakless. "You're not going to call them."

"I might." Gina flicked the card with her fingernail.

"As if you've ever called a guy." Mackie resumed his tattooing.

"Don't call this guy." Dominic took the card from her hand and dropped it in the trash. "He's too old for you."

"Rick, was that girl asking about my drawings?"

"She liked your weird vegetable crosses. She wants to think about it." The phone rang; Rick picked it up. "Mulley's."

Dominic turned back to his work and called over his shoulder. "Gina, setup includes green soap, razor—"

She slipped over to the trash can and rescued the purple card. She opened to the back of her portfolio and slid it into her collection.

When Gina got home, Connie was already in her pristine pajamas, watching *Miami Vice* and doing a paint-by-numbers during the commercial breaks. Not a drop of paint had fallen on her.

Gina sat on the love seat, the plastic cover stiff under her legs. "What's the deal with that psychic card on your bulletin board?"

Connie yawned. "This girl Anna—she was the psychic's assistant, I think?—I gave her violin lessons for a while. Why?"

"They came into the tattoo shop today. Kind of strange, right?"

"Not really. I'm the one who gave her the address." Connie fluffed her hair, like a bird making itself look bigger. "I told her my cousin was a tattooer and she got all interested."

"Are they—nice?"

Connie shrugged. "Quirky. But probably harmless." She turned her attention back to the screen, where a landscape of pink stucco and palm trees erupted into machine gun fire.

If Gina didn't call them now, she might lose her nerve. She went to the kitchen and picked up the phone. The dial pad glowed a weak green. She dialed and waited, coiling the phone cord around her finger.

"Good evening," Nicolas said. "House of Mystical Delights."

Her breath caught in her throat. She slammed the phone back down.

What had she expected to happen? You called someone, they answered. And then, if you were normal, you said, *Hello, my name is—*

Her conversational skills were no better than they'd been last week, when she blurted *Pac-Man* at the Viking delivery man. If she miraculously made it through the phone conversation, they might invite her to get together; the psychic had said, *My assistant could use a friend.* But then she'd have to admit she was car-less. Even if she *borrowed* a car, she had no money for going out for pizza or however people socialized. And even if she *had* money, she was back to the problem of small talk.

She'd been too hasty, picking up the phone like that. She would call another day. When she'd settled into her apprenticeship. And practiced conversing with customers. And saved up a little cash, and figured out the car situation, and practiced saying whatever came after *My name is Gina*. It couldn't take more than a few weeks to pull all that together.

Fourteen

JULY/AUGUST

G oddamn Mackie, with all his predictions of *You're not going to call them*; so far, Gina was proving him right. Day after day, she woke and saw the purple business card on her bedroom windowsill, but Dominic had said, *Your summer boils down to three things*, and she wasn't taking that lightly.

So every morning (*save money*, because there'd be a class and equipment to pay for) she pumped gas.

Every afternoon (*be useful*) she scrubbed tattoo equipment and toilets.

Every evening (*practice drawing*) she worked on whatever old-school warhorses Dominic assigned her, repeating the same flash until she was outlining clipper ships and pinups in her dreams.

Stella began to call the shop, looking for Gina, but the thought of facing her mother for the first time since their blowup was paralyzing. Avoiding Stella became another job in itself. Gina's days felt like an endless contortionist's act, twisting herself around to finish this, dodge that, and by the time all the work was done, she was too tired or too chicken or it was too late at night to call the psychic and his long-legged assistant.

July slid by, humid as the steam rising from Gina's mop bucket. From time to time, they wandered into her thoughts, the young woman especially—the way her hands moved like a flame darting up from a lighter, and the realization she'd caused to appear: *My flash is for a person like that.*

After a few weeks, the pit bull on the calendar page began to stare at Gina with macho disdain, as if Mackie's voice had taken on animal form: *You're not going to call them.*

The hell she wouldn't.

After three rings, an answering machine picked up.

Grüezi, bonjour, and thank you for calling the House of Mystical Delights. For the duration of the summer holiday, we will be operating from our Switzer-land location—

Gina's shoulders dropped.

Clairvoyant guidance is still available for US clients via international call with director Nicolas Eggli-Pfister, or by mail with his protégé, Anna Roche, at—

Gina jotted down the address and hung up. She stared out the window, thinking, as a ragged mat of clouds passed over the sun, dimming the street and then brightening again.

She'd probably make a better impression on paper than in person, anyway.

Dear Anna,

> *I work at Mulley's Tattoo in Blue Claw, where you and Mr. Eggli-Pfister came in last month. He recommended that I contact you. In case writing to this address is like a calling a 1-900 psychic hotline, I just want to say that I'm not seeking any*

clairvoyant guidance, so please don't send me a bill. I'm just reaching out in a friendly way.

How do you like Switzerland? Are you both from there? What are your other interests, besides travel, prophecy, etc.?

I noticed you were looking at my work in progress. If you're interested in a custom design, please let me know. I'm not religious, but my colleague mentioned you appreciated my crosses, so I'm enclosing a new one for you, just as a token of Hello.

Sincerely,
Gina Mulley

"Gina," Dominic yelled. "Have you seen an envelope around? Says *Past Due* in big red letters?"

Gina flipped over the envelope where she'd scrawled the address. "From LILCO?"

"New York Telephone."

"How many bills are we late on?"

"That's what Jeri's asking. Can you bring it to me?"

She copied down the Switzerland address and dropped the envelope on Dominic's desk, where he was staring at the screen of that new Apple IIe computer, furnished by Harrison Entertainment. Gina was gaining respect for this mysterious investor woman, despite her powder-blue stationery and cutesy airbrushed T-shirts; she appeared to be a hard-ass in the most helpful way. Dominic's sudden concern about *past due* was new and, honestly, refreshing. In the past, whenever Gina heard him on the phone with billing departments, he was leaning on charm to buy time on final notices.

He was so lost in the green-and-black chambers of that VisiCalc spreadsheet that he didn't even notice her. She retreated to the couch to begin her drawing for Anna.

Dominic's voice startled her. "Gina? How's it going saving up for your class and equipment?"

"Seventy-three bucks."

"Hurry it along, okay? We got a lot of boxes to check off."

Hurrying seemed unlikely, unless Gina could hurry more tips out of her gas station customers. "I'll get on it." She turned her eyes to the paper—the first drawing she'd done in weeks that required any imagination.

Nothing stuffy or tired for this adventuresome woman. If Gina was going to draw a cross for Anna, it should be made of something like . . . tropical coral. Forest berries. Parrot feathers. Something ripe and vibrant as Gina's figs.

In the second week of August, an envelope arrived with red-and-blue edges: international mail. The center of Gina's chest flipped like a fish tail. She sank to the couch.

> *Dear Gina,*
>
> *Can I tell you how bitchin' it was to get a just plain friendly letter for a change? Don't ever work for a psychic. Your heart starts to hurt. Everybody wanting star-crossed loves back and missing their dead so much they'll believe anything just to hear from them again.*
>
> *That was intense and I apologize. In answer to your question, I was born and raised in Bensonhurst, Brooklyn, and lived there most of my life, except for three semesters at SUNY Stony Brook and then this past year at the House of Mystical Delights. So far Switzerland is incredibly beautiful (enclosing photo) and the*

chocolate is oh my God. Nicolas loves to take us out to dinner and introduce me to his Swiss friends. They're kind of eccentric, but according to my family I'm in no position to judge.

To answer your other question: My interests are radical politics, rock shows, and baking. I'd love if you designed a tattoo for me. I was in junior high when Janis Joplin did that Rolling Stone cover with her wrist tattoo and I just fell in love.

I don't go to church anymore, so I'm going to pass on the crosses, but your parrot-feather drawing is riveting and I can't stop looking at it. As a kid I dreamed of having a parrot and everything I'd teach it to say.

We'll be back sometime in September. Do you want to swap letters till then?

Warmly,
Anna

The words vibrated on the page. *Your parrot-feather drawing is riveting.* This world-traveling rock-and-roll girl was right there with her—a trace of melted chocolate on the cuff of her leather jacket, incense clinging to her hair from all those tragic but hopeful séances. Gina could imagine the clink of restaurant glasses, the crisp fold of Anna's newspaper as she perused international headlines and said words like *perestroika* on purpose.

The envelope held something else: a snapshot of Anna in a meadow, mountains towering behind her, wearing punk-rock bracelets and a black smock dress. A crown of wildflowers ringed her head.

Gina sat down with her sketchbook. *Dear Anna. Out of curiosity, what kind of tattoos WOULD you like to get?*

"Can I have the rest of the mail?" Dominic said. "Or did you want to sit there smiling at every piece one by one?"

She handed the pile to him. "You know that flash poster I always talk about making? Where can I hang it when I'm done?"

"The wall above the crapper is available," Mackie said.

"You're making this poster on your own time, right?" Dominic said. Gina nodded. "Show me when you're done. If you do a good job, we'll find a spot."

Just like that, the long, boring expanse before September 27 was transfigured into a gift. The sooner Gina finished her daily chores, the more time she had to work on her poster. Anna hadn't replied yet about what sort of tattoo she might want, but given the photograph, flowers seemed like a good place to start.

At the library, Gina found a book of botanical photography and another about floriography, which was—fascinating discovery—a secret flower language invented by tongue-tied Victorians to send messages to each other, saying everything they couldn't speak aloud. *WILD ROSE: Pleasure and pain. YELLOW MARGUERITE: I shall arrive soon.* Anna seemed like someone who might be interested in secret languages.

Each day, when Gina was done scrubbing toilets and blood-specked metal, she tried, again and again, to draw convincing petals and pistils.

Rick peeked over her shoulder. "You never struck me as the frilly type."

"Rude," Gina said. "Someone didn't read the captions."

POPPY: I am not free.

PEACH BLOSSOM: I am your captive.

WILD TANSY: I declare war against you.

"Pez. Intense." He tapped a drawing. "Is this one the war flower? Because my landlady just planted one outside my apartment."

"No, that one's hydrangea," Gina said. "It can mean 'Thank you for understanding' or 'You are heartless and frigid.'"

A metallic clank outside: the mail carrier depositing their daily pound of catalogs and bills into the box. Gina walked over to check, although there'd been nothing for a week. Today, though, there it was: a red-and-blue international envelope.

Dear Gina, I found this postcard at an antique shop and thought of you. A young woman in a black-and-white photo stood confidently on a boardwalk, sporting a short white dress.

Tattooed with flora, fauna, and Americana,

BETTY BROADBENT

appears in the first televised beauty
pageant, 1939 World's Fair, New York

Gina had heard the song about Lydia the Tattooed Lady, but she had never seen a woman so thoroughly tattooed as this—covered shoulder to ankle—and so self-possessed. It was the most thoughtful gift Gina had received since Rick calligraphed *Pezadita* on her birthday. From a person she'd never even met.

Don't you love how free and happy she looks? Anna wrote. *In other news, you asked how I got into this situation. That's a story for when I get home.*

Between the dazzling details of her Switzerland tales, Anna often sounded tired. Not world-weary: actually tired. That seemed strange, given that her jobs were dispensing advice by mail and amusing strangers over Zürcher Geschnetzelte, but Gina knew what sadness sounded like, and she felt it dwelling quietly in the shadows of Anna's letters.

Gina couldn't do much from four thousand miles away, but maybe she could create a moment of happiness for Anna upon her return.

So when Anna wrote, *I'm getting into herbal tea,* Gina added to her poster: *SPEARMINT: Warmth of sentiment. PEPPERMINT: Virtue. CHAMOMILE: Patience in adversity.*

When Anna wrote, *Did you know sunflowers are a symbol for nuclear disarmament?* Gina added one, thickly seeded and strong in stalk.

Confession, Anna wrote. *I can't eat one more bite of cheese. Craving a cold tomato salad. Or a fresh clementine.* Gina drew an orange slice.

And when Anna wrote, *Nicolas says we'll be home on the autumn equinox,* Gina went to the calendar and circled September 23.

Before the Great Quarterly Check-in of September 27—*when the fun starts,* as Dominic put it—there'd be a brief, ripe window when Gina could meet her new friend in person. Anna would walk through the door of Mulley's Tattoo. She would stop to look, really look, at Gina's flash poster. And despite whatever was making her sound so troubled and weary, maybe she would see the drawings Gina had made for her and feel understood, and seen, and known.

Fifteen

SEPTEMBER/OCTOBER

The voice on the answering machine was crisp and sweet as a slice of honeydew. "Dom, it's Jeri. That storm is coming up the coast and I'm moving the Friday check-in to tomorrow. Getting on the road now. Let's go over your reports for Dad tonight, and I'll meet with Gina in the morning. See you in a few hours."

"Shit." Dominic paused his tattooing. "I didn't finish my checklist. She's going to be pissed."

"How many spreadsheets till she's happy?" Lamar Phillips's voice was muffled, facedown on Dominic's table. Today he was adding cherry blossoms to the koi pond spilling across his back.

"I finished the spreadsheets. I didn't do the Yearly meeting."

"Why don't you get the two of them in a room?" Lamar said. "Yearly versus Harrison. I'd pay to watch that fight."

Dominic and Lamar met when Mulley's first opened and Lamar did the electrical work. He casually said he'd always secretly wanted a tattoo; his father had a koi on his chest from his time stationed in Japan. That was all Dominic needed to hear. The banter went on for weeks. Dominic: *Just a little one. In honor of your dad.* Lamar: *I'm a professional. I can't walk into people's houses looking like that.* Dominic: *We'll make it discreet! Your chest. Your back.* Lamar: *Talk to my wife.* Dominic: *Just get her flowers, man.* Lamar: *Right. You let me tattoo you sometime, and then we'll talk.* Dominic: *For real?* He was desperate for new customers in those early days. Lamar thought Dominic was joking, right up until Dom handed him the machine and let him ink a couple of wobbly lightning bolts on Dominic's leg.

When Lamar finally got that koi on his shoulder, he was hooked. It turned into their mutual pet project, session by session—an entire back piece, rich blue wave splash and currents swirling across his deep brown skin.

Gina loved to eavesdrop on the back-and-forth during these tattoos. Sometimes, the men just trash-talked each other's baseball teams, but other days, Dominic forgot she was sitting there, and Gina learned the kind of things he tended to keep from her.

"When do I meet your lady?" Lamar said, his voice still muffled in his arms.

"She's not my lady," Dominic said.

"Just the occasional steamy night on Staten Island," Lamar said.

"Come on, man," Dominic said. "My sister's here."

"Too late," Gina said, but it wasn't really news anymore. Ladies generally *were* fond of Dominic—even hardheaded investor ladies trying to keep things businesslike—but usually these liaisons petered out into friendships. You could learn a lot eavesdropping.

"Gina," Dominic said. "You heard the message? You're meeting Jeri tomorrow. Do you have your boxes checked off?"

Safety/sterilization test: 100 percent.

Register for drawing class: Paperwork done, deposit ready to go.

Save money: Nearly two hundred dollars.

Practice drawing: A hundred pages to prove it.

Be useful: Every damn day.

Besides all this: Gina's first original flash poster was now approved, framed, and hanging right next to the Mulley's mermaid.

According to Anna's last letter, her plane should've arrived yesterday. She'd promised that as soon as she got over her jet lag and unpacked, she'd come by the shop. It could be today. It could be any moment.

"Everything's checked off." Gina looked over at Dominic. "Can I pack up this stuff yet?" She'd been making needles for two hours. If Anna arrived right now, she'd find Gina sitting with a mess of bug pins and needle bars, solder and flux.

He kept shading the cherry blossoms on Lamar's back. "Did they give you a receipt for your drawing class? Jeri's making me document everything."

Gina unplugged the soldering iron. "I'm handing in the forms tomorrow."

Dominic stopped and looked at her. "You didn't go yet?"

"You said I had until the twenty-seventh. The class doesn't even start until October first."

"The twenty-seventh is Jeri's deadline. Check the *college* deadline." He set the machine down.

Gina paged through the course booklet from Blue Claw Community. The last day for late registration was yesterday. She looked up at Dominic, heavy with dread. "Crap."

"Feels like break time to me," Lamar said, getting up from the table and heading toward the watercooler in the back, leaving Gina and Dominic alone.

Dominic pulled off his gloves. "You've had all summer. This was a soft-ball. It was *right there.*"

"It's that big of a deal? One box out of four?"

"The Harrisons' favorite word is *discipline*," he said. "You signed on for three months. If you don't meet your benchmarks, they sure as hell ain't keeping you on for three more."

"What should we do?"

"The question is what do *you* do," Dominic said. "I can't fix this. I'm slammed today finishing *my* list."

This was 100 percent fair, true, and terrifying.

"All right. I'll figure it out." Gina packed up the needle supplies in silence and looked at the clock. The registrar's office had closed. The best she could do was go to campus in the morning and ask if there was *any* way she could still get in.

"Maybe if you have dinner with us tonight," Dominic said. "Try and charm her. Bond over girl stuff. Maybe you can just tell her the truth and ask for help and she'll show some mercy."

Gina's stomach jumped as if Jeri had actually appeared in the doorway. Charisma was Dominic's fallback; it would never be hers. She couldn't meet their investor like this, in a ketchup-stained Oingo Boingo T-shirt. "I said I'll figure it out."

Dominic drummed his fingers together. "Dinner's a good idea. We make it nice and casual."

"I can't." Gina's mouth felt dry. "I have plans."

"With who?" He crossed his arms.

She turned back to the counter and began to fiddle with the bug pins. "My friend."

"You can't reschedule?"

"She's in crisis," Gina said.

"How about you call her?" Dominic said. "I bet she's doing better now."

Lamar returned from the back. "You're brutal, man. Let the girl go."

She reached reluctantly for the phone on the counter. She knew the number by heart—she'd been staring at that business card for seven weeks.

Nicolas Eggli-Pfister answered. "House of Mystical Delights." He had a deep drawer of a voice.

"Hey, it's Gina—" *From the tattoo shop*, she almost said, but you wouldn't need to tell your friend where you were from. Please, let him remember the name.

"The famous Gina! Anna's correspondent! I sensed you'd call soon." Lucky break. "Perhaps you're interested in a reading, at our friends-and-family rate? It would be an utter pleasure."

Oh no. She hadn't thought of this. She stretched the phone cord as far as it would go, to the coffee table in the waiting area, where someone had abandoned a Hostess Fruit Pie. She picked up a pencil and began to stab nervous holes in it.

"Or can we entice you to join us for cocktails at home?"

"You mean—now?"

Nicolas let out a sudden shout. "Anna!" He yelled a stream of words in a language that sounded like German. A woman broke into wild laughter. "My God," he muttered, "always a little creature roaming free—Anna. It's the young lady from the tattoo parlor." Gina heard her voice, the same buoyant rise and fall from the day they'd walked into the shop.

"Little creatures?" Gina said.

"What kind of crisis is this?" Dominic said.

"Anna's darling müusli, not to worry," Nicolas said. "You'll need directions." She grabbed a ballpoint and began to write on her hand. All these turns—they must live in the woods. "See you soon. Ciao." A click. Nicolas was gone.

Gina looked at Dominic. "Yeah, she's in bad shape. She can't even drive. Can I borrow your car? She's in Shoreham."

"Shoreham! Well, well," Lamar said, facedown on the table again, voice muffled in his arms. "She could pay for your taxi."

Dominic dug around for his keys. "I don't have time to argue. Just go. When you're done with her crisis, see if she can fix yours."

Sixteen

Gina drummed agitated fingers on the steering wheel for fifteen miles of darkening farmland. When she saw the Shoreham nuclear power plant silhouetted in the evening sky, she knew she was almost there, and her anxiety kicked up another notch. What if Nicolas and Anna expected her to be good company, and then realized who they were dealing with? She wasn't affable like Dominic or well traveled like Rick. She couldn't even provide an array of recreational drugs, like her old friends at the Cheshire Cat.

She turned onto a wooded side street of prim colonials until she found the one Nicolas described as "the color of a mourning dove, with an alluring porch." Ivy twisted around a gilt-and-wood sign: EUROPEAN CLAIRVOYANT GUIDANCE. She parked Dominic's Maverick at the curb.

At least she'd found a better shirt to change into. Jeri must've left her dry cleaning in Dominic's backseat last time he went out to Staten Island.

Gina stood in the yellow halo of the porch light. A smaller sign hung next to the door: HOUSE OF MYSTICAL DELIGHTS. Somewhere in the perfectly trimmed rosebushes, a lone cricket creaked.

The door swung open without warning. She jumped. Nicolas Eggli-Pfister extended his hand, smiling warmly. The sleeves of his linen shirt were rolled up, revealing tanned and untattooed forearms. "Grüezi."

He led her into a room resplendent with built-in bookshelves, embroidered draperies, a silver-and-sepia animal skin rug. The air was thick with the smell of baking bread and cedar incense. "Have a seat on my reindeer hide. You'll find the energy is especially good on the floor today." He disappeared through the kitchen doorway.

Was that a joke? She sat, just in case. Funny that the energy preferred a dead deer over the velvet sofa across the room, or the person-sized wicker birdcage in the corner, or—

"Gina."

She looked up. Anna stood in the kitchen doorway, wearing those leather pants and an angora sweater, downy as a vintage pinup angel. She held a tray piled with steaming bread, an assortment of jams, and a large bottle.

Maybe it was just the lighting in here, a trick of the lamps, but she had some of the most luminous skin Gina had ever seen. It was soft-looking, deep olive, like Dominic's in summer. Everything about Anna was generous—her broad, soft build; her height; the look on her face, open like a curious child's.

"You look just like your letters sound," Gina said.

Anna laughed as if Gina were delightful, which was exactly what a generous person *would* do upon meeting an awkward person, and Gina was filled with gratitude.

She set her tray on the coffee table, joined Gina on the reindeer hide, and looked her in the eye, smiling. "A pair of teeth?"

Gina hesitated. An occult reference, maybe? "I'm sorry?"

"A pair of teeth." Anna pointed at the bottle, which contained a whole pear suspended in clear liquid.

"A *pear* of teeth?" As if that made any more sense. Gina's face was growing warm.

"My fault," Anna said. "Nicolas is always telling me to enunciate. A-P-E"—she began to pour three small glasses—"R-I-T-I-F. From Switzerland. It's called Williamine."

"A drink," Gina said.

"We'll have to wait for Nicolas. We toast the Swiss way. He'll say *Proscht*, and then you look into each person's eyes as you clink glasses." She spread a piece of bread with preserves. "But you can sneak a bite to eat while we wait." She gestured for Gina to help herself.

The bread was crusty, creamy, like nothing Gina had ever tasted. She suddenly noticed her shoulders relaxing, her hands no longer locked together.

Nicolas appeared in the doorway. "There is nothing so sweet as the vibrations of women." Gina thought she saw a twitch of annoyance on Anna's face, but it was gone by the time he sat down. "What an elegant blouse." He touched the gauzy sleeve of Jeri's shirt, stolen from Dominic's backseat.

"It's okay." Gina was not used to being complimented on clothes. Or anything, really.

"To new companions," Nicolas said. "Proscht." As he clinked her glass, he looked her in the eye, just as Anna had said. Gina had already been dreading this compulsory moment of connection, but her actual reaction surprised her: she felt welcomed. When Anna's turn came, she winked at Gina.

Gina took a timid sip of the mystery elixir in her glass. If a pear could harbor secret risqué thoughts, they would taste like this.

"Do you remember yet?" Nicolas said. "Where we met?" Gina shook her head. He shuffled a deck of cards in a leisurely way, then offered it to her.

"Here. Pick one. Gratis." Grat what? Her face must look idiotic. He smiled. "Free, that means."

She drew a card. It had six branches on it, one of them brandished by a man on horseback, wearing a wreath.

"Six of Wands! Victory. Honor. If you're working toward a goal, expect a breakthrough. Soon." He was looking at her the way he had in the tattoo shop, as if she were the only thing in the room.

The feeling that came over her then—she didn't know what to call it. A jolt of fear alongside a ripple of desire. She hadn't known those things could go together.

A twitchy movement edged into Gina's periphery. She turned to see a sleek white rat waddling along the floorboards. Anna jumped up. "Ghost escaped again. Let's bring her home. I'll give you the tour." She scooped up the rat, started up a flight of stairs, and gestured for Gina to follow.

Gina hesitated. Was it rude to leave Nicolas behind? He reached out and gave her hand a friendly squeeze.

"Go on," he said. "No need to fear."

Gina followed Anna upstairs into a windowless hallway of doors, all closed, their outlines visible in the glow of a nautilus-shell night-light. Anna pointed them out one by one without opening them. "Library. Divination room. Nicolas's bedroom. Bathroom—I'll show you the clawfoot tub sometime. And this one's mine." She opened a door and clicked on the light.

Anna's room was remarkably like Dominic's apartment—old-fashioned radiators, high ceilings, clearly built years ago by someone with money—but unlike Dominic's, it was well preserved. A brass candelabra glowed above them, polished and formal. Anna's bed was the homiest thing in the room, a mess of books, a rumpled quilt of a city skyline that looked well loved.

"All this belongs to Nicolas?" Gina gestured at the ornate furniture.

"He lets me put a few things up. That's mine." She pointed to a framed poster of a woman in a star-scattered robe, haloed and levitating over the ocean, STELLA MARIS lettered on a thin banner above her. *Mary, Star of the Sea.*

"He has nice digs for a part-time psychic," Gina said.

"The psychic business is how he amuses himself. His aunt left him pretty comfy." Anna carried the rat to an ornamental cage and gently dropped her in, latching it shut. "He lets me stay here for free, as long as I do the psychic show."

"You said in your letter that you'd tell me how you got here," Gina said.

"Oh. Right." Anna shook out the rumpled quilt and began to make her bed. "At Stony Brook, I used to pick up cash as a drawing-class model. Nicolas was auditing the class. We got to talking and realized we were both going through a rough time. His aunt had just died, I had some stuff going on. Anyway." She tucked the corners of her bedspread and smoothed the pillows. "I needed a place to crash. He tells me, *If you can assist with my aunt's share of the business, I have a room for you, gratis.*" This sentence she intoned in Nicolas's accent: *my ahhnt's share of ze business.* "So now I put on the mysterious purple veil of Tante Anna Roche"—she pointed to a gauzy shawl hanging on the wall—"wave some incense around for readings, and answer her clients' letters. When I'm not being mystical, I waitress on the side. So there you go."

Gina walked over to examine the shawl. It was embroidered with beads like cats' claws. "He makes you pretend you're his aunt?"

"He used to. Now he's started calling me his protégé." Anna wiggled her fingers as if conjuring a cloud of stars. "Lucky me."

Gina watched Anna straighten the knickknacks on her nightstand, lining them up by height: antique alarm clock, Russian nesting doll, fossilized shell. "You just happen to have his aunt's name?"

No, she didn't. Gina knew it, suddenly. Something about the way Anna was pausing with that Russian doll in her hand.

"What's your real name?"

Anna twisted the doll's two halves without pulling it open. "Are you just here for curiosity's sake, or are you coming back?"

"I'd come back."

Anna looked Gina in the eye for the first time since they'd come upstairs. Her eyes were the plummy brown of olives. "Marianna Dellarocca."

Something happened to the air—no, not exactly the air. The space between them. It filled with an aerated weight, potent-dark like a mouthful of stout. They didn't know each other, really, but it suddenly felt as if they did. Gina, afraid to break the moment, didn't move.

Then Anna looked away. "Marianna—it's not so different from Anna. It wasn't such a big change." She put the doll back on the nightstand and faced it neatly forward.

Those two names, *Anna Roche* and *Marianna Dellarocca*, were not at all the same thing. "You don't want me to call you Marianna?"

"Nah."

"Are you in love with him?"

Anna laughed. "We are not remotely in love."

"So, between you guys—there's no—"

"Are you asking, have we slept together?" Anna said. "Because that's a different question. But yes."

Gina felt herself blushing. "I just wondered. He's older."

Anna shrugged. "I'm almost twenty-one. He's thirty-nine. Maybe that's weird to you—"

"I'm not judging."

"—but this is our arrangement. So he wants to fool around sometimes. I'm not uptight. It's fine."

It's fine: She wasn't telling the truth. It was right there, in the jerky movement of Anna's hands. Gina had never met a single person before, other than Dominic, whom she could so easily read—as if Anna were a book in a language she was fluent in. After eighteen years of eyestrain over cryptic sigils, here, finally, was someone written in her native tongue.

Downstairs, the phone rang.

"Let's go," Anna said. She clicked the door shut behind them and they headed down thickly carpeted stairs to the living room. By the time they arrived, Nicolas was already hanging up.

"Your violin teacher called." He stretched out on the couch and put his bare feet up on the armrest. "Small world. She's Gina's roommate now."

Anna started to speak, but Nicolas was already talking over her. "She said your brother wants you to call him at the shop, posthaste."

Not now. Not while she was having, possibly for the first time in her life, a pleasant social engagement. But Nicolas was pointing her toward a rotary phone on a spindly end table. She spun out the number on the dial; the answering machine picked up.

"Are you guys there?" She tapped her fingers against the receiver.

Anna sifted through a pile of records, sliding one out to drop onto the turntable, as if deliberately giving her privacy, but Nicolas was still watching Gina. He pushed the Six of Wands card across the table toward her and winked. The odd new feeling, the one she didn't have a name for, rippled through her again.

"Dom. Rick. Mackie. Pick up." Nothing. She hung up.

"Something wrong?" Anna said.

Gina closed her eyes and squeezed the bridge of her nose. "I have to go."

"Oh." Anna looked disappointed. "Really? Why?"

Because Dominic had pressed the Unspecified Crisis button, its power in its withholding of information. The chance of actual disaster was slim, but still real: maybe Dom had found Stella blacked out on her kitchen floor. Maybe a drunk driver had crashed through the shop's window. Dom could've provided a clue and saved Gina the worry, but he hadn't. And even if it was a lesser crisis—Jeri demanding to see her tonight—Gina had begged for this apprenticeship; she would do almost anything to keep it.

"Family." Gina said. "I'm so sorry. I'd really like to do this again."

Regretful goodbyes all around. Outside, in their quiet neighborhood, nothing but lonely crickets. Gina yanked Dominic's car keys out of her pocket, furious, feeling like she'd just pulled the pin on a grenade.

Seventeen

Gearshifts should have a setting for "speeding resentfully." Someone should invent a method of parking your car so people understood they'd better have a good reason for interrupting your evening.

Gina had to do the next best thing, which was slamming the car door and clipping up the sidewalk toward Mulley's Tattoo.

She walked in to find an unusually large man standing in the waiting room. Blackout shades, beard made for Viking winters: it was the guy who'd delivered Dominic's trophy back in July. This time, instead of a crate, he had a cardboard box.

Rick looked up from his customer's biceps. He was tattooing one of those rip-out pieces, making it look like the skin was torn open with a skeleton hand poking out.

"Where's Dominic?" Gina said. "Is everything okay?"

"Everything's fine. Just take a look at the box. This gentleman . . ." Rick paused and looked at the Viking. "What's your name?"

"Sally," the Viking said. "Salvatore. You want to discuss it?" An Italian Viking, then.

"No, dude, I'm good," Rick said. He turned to Gina. "Sally's unloading some supplies. Dom thought you might be interested."

Gina peered into the box. A bunch of tubes and needles, bottles of ink, bags of pigment, and two machines. Sally handed one to her. "These are Paul Rogers irons. Run like a dream." Other than the coils, gleaming carnelian, they looked clunky, nothing special.

Rick nearly jumped at the counter, leaving his client sitting there like an awkward piece of furniture. Gina handed him the machine and he whistled. "Man, you're going to let this go? Why?"

"Frankly"—the guy pulled his hair into a ponytail—"I got busted for dealing blow. I'm going to be away for a while. Just trying to liquidate."

"How much?"

"One-fifty for the whole box."

Gina looked at Rick. "Is that good?"

He looked at her over his glasses, callused fingers cradling the machine's frame, and she knew what he was thinking.

"Well, I got three minutes," the Viking said. "I'm stepping out for a smoke and then I'm gonna need a yes or no." He walked out.

As soon as the door clanked shut, Rick put a hand on her arm. "Pezadita, buy this. This is what you call divine intervention."

"What were Dominic's exact words?"

"*Gina should take a look.*" Rick washed his hands and returned to his client. "This kind of machine isn't going to walk through the door again. That's me talking, not him. But it's true."

She picked up the machine again. It felt good in her hand—one step closer to her vision. Her own workstation, tattooing her own designs, machine vibrating against her palm like a living thing.

She had the money. Two days ago, Dominic would've said *Use it for the class*, but at this point, even if she dragged herself down to the registrar's office tomorrow and pleaded all morning, that class would still be closed. Her apprenticeship agreement specifically required her to buy her own equipment this fall. If Jeri Harrison came down hard about missing the deadline, this purchase would prove that Gina was still committed and serious.

Six of Wands. Victory. Breakthrough.

With Sally on his way, Gina rummaged through the box, dazed. She held an ink bottle up to the light. Purple? What magic potion was this? Even Dominic didn't have purple, and she'd thought he had a lock on all the secret supply sources in a hundred-mile radius.

Rick kept his head down, tracing the jagged crags of the skeleton hand on his customer's biceps. The man moaned.

"Sorry, man. Inner arm's a bitch. . . . Pezadita, when are you taking that beauty for a test run?"

"Dom said I could try pigs' feet after the Jeri meeting tomorrow." She turned the machine over in her hands. So many things to adjust: contact screw, tube vise, spring tension. If Rick was right, she had a Cadillac in her hands. What if she broke it?

"Paul Rogers," Rick said again, and clicked his tongue.

The back door opened; Gina heard a woman's voice lilting *Byyyeeee*. The door slammed, and Mackie strolled into the front room, thumbs in his pockets. His face was unusually relaxed, radiating goodwill, like his clothes were light as sheets hung in the sunshine. He surveyed Rick's work, then walked over to Gina and said, with great cheer, "What's that piece of shit?"

"My new machine," Gina said.

He reached for it. She held it against her chest.

"Okay, Miss Paranoid." He put his hands up. "I'm not gonna steal your secondhand whatever. I got a Jonesy I'm very happy with. So if you want to breastfeed that for a while . . ."

She handed it over. The way he studied it made her feel that she herself was under inspection. "This isn't going to run right. It's going to cut in and out." He gave it back.

She felt deflated. "Rick said it was a good machine."

"It's a fine machine, but it's not going to run right, and you won't know why."

"Okay. Tell me why." No way she was going to have a conversation in this position, craning her neck to meet his eye, him looming over her. She stood.

"First of all"—Mackie leaned in far enough that she could smell his fresh sweat and the Jägermeister on his breath—"this contact point is oxidized. That's going to mess up your circuit. Second, these binding post screws should have rubber washers to insulate them from the frame. Do you understand how current works?"

She knew what he was baiting her toward: an embarrassed *No*, or a defiant *Of course I do*, in which case he'd quiz her until he found something she didn't know. She wasn't playing this game tonight. "Fine. Show me how it works."

"I'm pretty busy." He sauntered off to shuffle through the mail pile at the fourth workstation—the one that Dominic still wouldn't let her clean off and claim for herself. "But I just got lucky and I'm in a good mood. If you want me to sand up that contact point for you, tune it up . . . leave it and I'll try to squeeze it in."

Gina turned toward Rick, who felt her watching him and glanced up. It was getting humid in the shop and a light dew of sweat was starting to shine at his temples. Gina tilted her face toward him and raised her eyebrows, and he seemed to understand what she was asking: *Can I trust him?*

Rick shrugged.

Gina turned back to Mackie, who was squinting at an envelope. "Could you teach me how? So I could do it myself next time?"

"I don't have time to dick around giving you lessons." He sliced open the envelope with a letter opener.

"I won't get in your way. I just want to watch."

"Go on and use Dom's old machine, then."

When Dominic saw her tattooing for the first time, she wanted him to be glad he hired her, to see something new in her. It would be stupid to use a finicky machine if she had something better available.

"Fine." Gina brought him the machine, the clip cords, the power supply.

"Did I see a bottle of Jose Cuervo in that box?" Mackie said. "Some people might include that as a thank-you."

Gina rolled her eyes and brought it to him. "Don't drink and tinker."

Eighteen

Maybe it was the long day of surprises or maybe it was the satisfaction of acquiring her own equipment, but when Gina went to bed that night, she fell dead asleep. Nine hours later, she woke with unusual energy and peace.

For three months, she'd worked with all her heart, and prepared the best she could. Today, with luck, Jeri would agree to keep her on for three more.

When the time came for their meeting, however, there was no Jeri. There was no Dominic, for that matter. Gina waited, watching school buses rolling down Midway Street; their tailpipes coughed exhaust, sunlight knifing off the back windows.

Finally Dominic arrived—alone. Gina told him the story of the night before, how she'd bought the machine. When she mentioned shelling out the cash, he looked concerned. And his voice was somewhere between dismay and disbelief when he said, "You bought it with your school money?"

"I had to decide fast," Gina said. "Didn't you want me to?"

"You didn't tell me that was all the cash you had."

"Why does it matter? I missed the deadline. I thought if I got the machine it would make up for the class." She began to clean off the coffee table, strewn with chewed-up pencils and a Coke can. "Or did you literally mean '*Look* at the machine'? As in, 'Gaze at it lovingly'?"

Dominic stared down into her new box of gear as if peering into a murky pool.

"Where is Jeri, anyway?" Gina said. "When's our meeting?"

"After dinner last night she checked the forecast, turned around, and went back to Staten Island."

"You're kidding."

"She's worried about Gloria."

"Gloria who?"

"That tropical storm coming up from the Bahamas."

"Jeri tracks the weather a thousand miles away?"

Dominic rubbed his scalp with both hands, fingers disappearing into his curls. "You would, too, if your business was outdoor events. Look, I'm driving out tomorrow afternoon to help her prep for the weather. If she asks about your progress, what am I supposed to say?"

"How about—Gina is impressing the hell out of me, working overtime at two jobs! An incredible deal came along, and she snapped it up! So savvy. That's how we do it in the Mulley family. Not everybody has infinite cash flow from their parents."

Dominic stared at the ceiling. She'd hit his wall.

"You really have to go out there?" Gina said. "And drive home in the storm?"

He rolled his eyes. "It's TV hype. I'm only going because she's freaking out. Every year the sky is falling, we all buy flashlights, and then we get a day of hard rain. I can drive in the rain." He opened the fridge, reached for the milk, and stopped. "Are these pigs' feet yours?"

She'd stopped at the grocery store on the way. "I was excited to start."

"I can't teach you today. I've got back-to-back appointments."

"I know," Gina said. "I looked at your book. So I penciled us in for tomorrow at noon."

Nineteen

Today was the day.

Gina daydreamed through her gas station shift, barely conscious of the tanks she was filling. By the end of the afternoon, those pigs' feet would be covered with perfect roses. Dominic would be amazed; Rick would be proud; Mackie would realize that she wasn't going anywhere, and that it would be wiser to accept her as a colleague than waste his energy antagonizing her. Each day she would continue to create ephemeral wonders on animal parts and tropical fruits until Dominic forbade her to tattoo anything but people anymore because it was a shame to discard such beauty.

She would go back to Anna and Nicolas and tell them their tarot card was right: Six of Wands. Breakthrough on a goal. Honor. Victory.

One hour into Gina's lesson, the visions of victory had somewhat dimmed. "Hand's getting tired, isn't it," Dominic observed. "You should've started with grapefruits."

"I told her that machine's too big for her." Mackie swiveled in his chair. He had the nerve to sit there eating popcorn—from a movie theater bucket, no less.

"I'm feeling fine," Gina lied. Her palm ached from wrestling with the machine, her back hurt from hunching over, and with the toughness of the pigskin, she was starting to worry she'd damaged her needle. Nothing looked right.

"Speed up your machine and it won't snag so much," Dom said. "See that double line you're getting?" Gina lifted the needle, tried again.

"She's overcompensating." Mackie leaned in close enough to cast a shadow on the pig's foot. "Because she doesn't have the hand strength. Look how light her lines are."

She kept her head down. "Shut it."

"Did you set up your machine right?" Mackie said.

Gina took her foot off the power supply and stared. Mackie leaned back into his swivel chair, barely holding back a smile, and propped the popcorn bucket in his crotch.

"Let me look." Dominic examined the machine. "G, you know better than this. Look at this gap between the points. This is only supposed to be the depth of a nickel. You've got an eighth of an inch."

"Didn't I say?" Mackie picked at a kernel stuck in his teeth. "That machine's too nice for somebody who doesn't know what she's doing."

He'd sabotaged her. The perfect detail: too subtle for her to notice, but enough to waste her session and make her look careless. He'd banked on the fact that Gina wouldn't tattle on him, too embarrassed to confess she hadn't set up her own machine. And he was right.

"Let's call it a day." Dominic looked at his watch. "I have to get on the road."

Mackie grabbed his cigarettes off the counter and ambled down the hallway toward the back door.

Gina stuffed the pig's foot in a garbage bag, cleaned up quickly, and followed him. She found him by the dumpster, sucking on his cigarette in cool puffs. He stared her down as she heaved the bag in.

She wiped her hands on her jeans. "This time I protected you. Next time I'm telling him."

"Telling him what? That I did your homework, and you still managed to screw it up?"

"Just stop." She looked up at the thin blue sky, where hungry gulls wheeled. "You ruined my one chance with him today."

"You don't need me for that. I heard you blew your registration deadline."

She put out her hand. "Can I bum one?" Mackie handed her a cigarette. The least he could do. She flicked his lighter, inhaled, blew the smoke upward. She hadn't had one in four months, not since she added up how much it was costing her. "What do you think about Jeri?"

Mackie shrugged and took another puff. "Haven't met her yet. If she makes us rich I won't complain. Not thrilled about the dress code idea."

"What dress code?"

"You'll see."

A gull lit on the dumpster's edge, swiped a soggy roll in its beak, and flew off again.

"Let her find someone else to rescue," Gina said. "We're a family business. She's a stranger."

"You know what happens if your wish comes true, right?" Mackie took another drag. "Your paycheck goes away."

For another moment they both stared out at the water, saying nothing, smoking. Gina began to feel ill—the way she had when she smoked her first cigarette. Maybe she'd gotten used to functioning lungs. She dropped it and ground it out with her sneaker.

"Doesn't feel good, does it?" Mackie said. "Thinking your income might dry up?"

She felt a flash of guilt. She'd never been close with Mackie, but their back-and-forth needling used to be play; now it felt real, like he was trying to draw blood. He really did think she was out to steal his job. "This doesn't have to be a competition."

"Everything's a competition. Welcome to the world."

"Why couldn't we bring in business for each other?"

"Kumbaya."

Her empathy turned to irritation. Was she supposed to be sorry for wanting this job? Let him rise to the challenge, then. She went back inside and slammed the door behind her.

Twenty

"Qué onda, Pezadita?"

In the time Gina had been standing by the dumpster, Dominic had left, Rick had shown up, and the air-conditioning unit had begun to leak again. Water dripped down on a stack of Rick's drawings. "Rick, your stuff." She rescued them and grabbed a maintenance bucket to put under the leak.

"Thanks." He dabbed the drawings with a paper towel. "How'd your practice go?"

"Aborted. I am so pissed." She grabbed the nearest rag to wipe up the puddle.

Every muscle in her body had been ready to leap forward today. She had to redeem this afternoon.

She walked over to her apprenticeship agreement, taped behind the counter, and stared at the requirements. *Drawing class to be completed in Fall Quarter.* Gina picked up the phone and dialed.

Anna answered. "House of Mystical Delights."

Gina fiddled with the phone cord. "I have a crazy idea."

"That's the best kind," Anna said.

"I need to get art lessons somehow. You said the other night you modeled for drawing classes. Do you remember anything they said?"

"Sure," Anna said. "Plenty."

"Do you think you could teach me? And be my model, I guess?" Silence. This was worrisome. "Just once maybe. To try it." It made so much sense a minute ago. Did Anna think she meant nude? So awful. Dominic should take away her phone privileges. "Please don't hang up. I'm not creepy."

Rick started scribbling a note on the counter. He handed it to Gina; she clutched it without reading it.

Finally Anna spoke. "How about we start by getting a hot dog?"

Gina made a noise of relief.

"Did you just laugh? What's so funny?"

"Nothing. Hot dogs. Are not funny, I mean. What I mean is I like them."

"My friend has a hot dog truck down by Smith Point, on William Floyd. Maybe we get a bite, hang out at the beach for a while? Before we start, you know, getting naked?"

Oh God, Anna *did* think she meant nude. Gina could feel her face flushing. Rick tapped her hand, but she turned away. The phone cord twisted around her body.

"You want to come get me?" Anna said.

"I don't have a car. I'm stranded at the tattoo shop—"

"I'll pick you up." Anna sounded amused. "See you in half an hour."

After Gina hung up, she stood there, dazed, until Rick said, "You're a dork. I mean big time."

"Why were you bothering me on the phone?" She whacked his bare arm.

"Ay! Take it easy." He was putting ointment on a new tattoo on his wrist, one she hadn't noticed before, Spanish words she couldn't decipher. He wagged a shiny finger at her. "And see what you miss when you don't read?"

She uncrumpled the note. *Buy grapefruits. I'll teach you.* She stuck her face in her hands, groaning. "I didn't even think of that."

"No, you just attack me with that brutal golpe." He sneaked a sly look at her, cradling the arm she'd whacked. "God, I hope I live."

"Will you be around in the evening?"

He shook his head. "Going to the movies with my cousins. I have a life, you know. But for the next three hours I'm here."

Something inside her leaped. This sudden opportunity, this brief window— it felt like a gift from on high. She could reschedule her hot dog date with Anna. She looked over at Dominic's workstation, out of habit, as if he were there to confirm permission.

Then she stopped. Why did she feel sad, suddenly? Water dripped from the air conditioner down to the dirty bucket. She leaned her elbows on the counter and looked at Rick again. "That means so much. But—"

"You want Dominic, don't you."

Gina bit her lip.

"You know you don't have to ask his permission to breathe?" The playfulness was fading. Rick straightened up, no longer clutching his arm. "You love Dom, I love Dom, we all love Dom, but you're waiting on a guy with his head in the clouds. You've got another brother right here."

"It just feels like—that's the way it should go."

Rick threw up his hands and turned away. "Your call."

Twenty-one

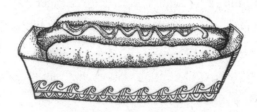

Gina shifted foot to foot on the sidewalk in front of the shop, waiting for Anna. A drill whined, plywood clattered: the owners of the shoe store across the street were boarding up their front window. Another business closing on Midway Street. Gina didn't want to think about it.

Within a minute, Anna rolled up in a beat-up Buick. Her hair was pulled into two pigtails just beneath her ears, wound with crimson ribbon, like some gorgeous Mediterranean version of the Sun-Maid raisin girl.

"Hop in quick," she called. "Rainbow Warrior's been finicky. Sometimes when she stops she doesn't want to move again."

"Rainbow Warrior?" Gina climbed in, and they were off.

"I just renamed her," Anna said, patting the steering wheel. "After that Greenpeace ship that got bombed this summer." Gina nodded as if she knew what Anna was talking about. "Ruined my dreams. In high school I used to imagine I'd join the crew and save seals, and . . . all the stuff you think you'll do when you're fifteen."

What had Gina dreamed about at fifteen? She couldn't remember. Until this moment, she hadn't even known seals needed saving.

She should ask Anna questions. Rick always asked people about themselves, and they seemed to like him for it. Ask about that dashboard ornament, maybe: a pillbox hat hanging on the passenger side, red as a box of Valentine's chocolate, with a spray of feathers and a bit of black netting. It seemed attached by magic.

Gina took a breath to ask, but Anna was speaking again. "Why do you need art lessons? Your drawings seemed good already."

"I'm a million miles from where I need to be. And my contract requires it." Rules were a dreary subject. Anna wouldn't care. If Gina didn't say something worthwhile, Anna would wonder why she'd bothered with this excursion.

"When we get back, I have something to show you," Gina said. "A project I did this summer."

"Can you tell me now, or is it a surprise?"

Gina thought. "Are you the kind of person who *likes* surprises?"

"That letter you wrote me in August," Anna said, "was one of the best surprises I've had in a long time."

Twenty minutes later, they arrived at a hot dog truck on the expressway service road, whipped by the highway wind, awning flapping like the wing of a startled seagull. A hand-lettered poster was duct-taped to the side: *Back to School Special! Dog + Chips, Just $1.*

"Be right back." Anna hopped out. "Let's hope she moves again when we're ready to go."

Gina sat in the Buick, drumming her fingers on her knees, staring at that pillbox hat until curiosity drove her to pick it up. It wasn't magically attached, but hung on a hook screwed into the dashboard, the tiny word *DAD* painted beneath.

Maybe Anna's father had disappeared, too. Maybe her mother was as unpredictable as Gina's, and she'd just needed to get out of the house, and then along came a guy offering free rent and a job all in one. Would Gina have turned down an offer like that?

DAD. She was about to replace it when Anna slid back into the front seat with a paper tray of hot dogs.

Anna stared for a half second. That tense, startled look—Gina had trespassed. Then the look softened. "You can try it on."

Gina did, clumsily, not sure what to do with the feathers and netting dangling over her eyes. She looked in the rearview mirror. The hat made her look even paler and more skittish than she normally did—like an orphan dressed up for a train journey alone.

"Pretty," Anna said. "But not you."

Gina put the hat back on the hook. There was an uncomfortable silence that hadn't been there before. "Did it belong to your father?"

"Did your father wear pillbox hats?" Anna's voice was a little spiky, as if warning Gina off.

"He left when I was little."

The spikiness disappeared. "I'm sorry. I was being a wiseass. I'm sorry." Anna put her hand on Gina's. Her fingertips were smooth as a sun-warmed stone. "Eat."

Within five minutes Anna's Buick was speeding across the drawbridge to Smith Point. They crossed the narrows between the Great South Bay and Moriches Bay, the inlet below them restless and choppy; the wind was picking up. Gina rolled up her window. "Are you sure you want to—"

"Yes." Anna sailed past the shuttered guard booth, parked in the empty lot, and they climbed out.

Down the footpath, through the tunnel, through the dense seagrass of the dunes, the ocean beat at the shore with the barrel rumble of thunder. It churned into yellow foam, skimmed up the sand, and retreated, leaving iron-brown seaweed like bundles of unspooled cassette tape. Except for a middle-aged woman smoking a joint on a boardwalk bench and one old guy pacing with a metal detector, the beach was theirs.

First Life Drawing Class, Gina scrawled in her sketchbook. *Smith Point, September 26, 1985*. Anna stripped down from a hoodie to a halter top. "The drawing instructor used to say"—she lay on her side in the pale gray sand, head propped on her hand—"'Hold up your pencil. Now make a line across my shoulders . . . '"

"You look chilly." Gina rubbed her palms together.

"I'm tough. Just draw."

Gina drew. Once in a while she caught a whiff of the woman's joint or the beeps of the metal detector, but mostly the wind swept away everything but the sound of Anna's voice.

How long did she draw? An hour? More? Gina was in a trance, sketching the dip of Anna's waist for the fifth time, when out of nowhere she was seized by joy. Her machine had been sabotaged, her mentor was distracted, her money was gone, but she'd taken back her day. Her socks were gritty with sand and her eyes were watering in the wind, but she was close to euphoria.

Breakthrough. Victory.

After a few more minutes, Anna heaved herself to sitting and shook the sand out of her hair. "Should we call it a day?"

Gina slid the pencil into her sketchbook. "I hate to leave."

"I know. This was fun," Anna said. "You want to do it again?"

"Yes." What a gift. Gina felt expansive, like stretching out in the sunshine. "Listen. Do you guys have letterhead for the House of Mystical Delights?"

"What for?" Anna pulled her hoodie back on.

"I need a document saying I'm enrolled in lessons with you. Something official-looking. Do you think Nicolas would mind if we used it?"

"He'll probably volunteer to teach you himself." Anna yanked her hood strings tight. "So far he's had me taking violin lessons, corrected my taste in chocolate, and made me watch *Pygmalion* and *My Fair Lady* so we could compare them over raclette."

"No one's ever paid that kind of attention to me," Gina said.

"It's really something." Anna's voice was flat.

Gina felt a twinge of . . . something. Regret? Guilt? Rick had offered his attention today, and she'd run off to the beach with her pretty new friend. She was making the best choices she could; Dominic was so insistent about the drawing classes. Maybe this was adulthood—every yes was a no to something else, leaving you to worry you'd chosen incorrectly.

"I just realized—usually you get paid for modeling," Gina said. She had a little money left over after the equipment. "Can I give you cash?"

"Don't be silly," Anna began. Then she leaned in to touch Gina's arm. "How much is a tattoo worth?"

Another jolt of joy. "You want to barter?"

"Deal." Anna had a very firm handshake.

"I just started my apprenticeship, though. They don't let me work on people yet."

"That's okay." Anna smiled. "I'll get to be an artist's early work." Her eyes didn't look brown today, as they had the other day; in this cloud-dimmed light, they were black as grackles. "I don't see any tattoos on you."

"It's on my back." Gina pulled off her sweatshirt, trying not to strip away her tank top in the process, and turned around.

Anna made a noise of delight. Soft fingertips traced shapes on Gina's skin. "Figs. Beautiful."

The hair on the back of her neck stood on end. The ocean suddenly smelled sweeter.

Anna's fingertips were still resting, spots of soft heat, on Gina's back. "Do you like poetry?"

Gina tried to remember even one poem from English class. "I guess I liked 'The Raven'?"

"I mean, *come-hither*-type poetry."

Thank God Anna couldn't see her face. "Uh."

"In high school, I had to choose a Bible passage to memorize," Anna said. "Go home and look this up." She pulled a felt-tip marker from her purse and wrote on the back of Gina's hand: *Song of Solomon 2:10–13*.

Gina looked at the ink on her hand, Anna's breezy handwriting, and realized that she was—for the second time in an hour—perfectly happy. This was so new, contentment this pure, with no hovering unease.

A voice rasped behind Gina. "Girls."

Gina startled and turned. The old man with the metal detector stood ten feet away, skinny as a clothes rack in his fraying Mets jersey, waving one wiry arm.

"Earth to girls," he yelled. "Go home."

Twenty-two

Gina glanced at Anna, who looked as startled as she was.

The man walked closer and tapped the transistor radio on his belt. "They just issued a hurricane watch."

"We know," Gina said. "Down south."

"It picked up speed. Landfall on Long Island tomorrow." The man clicked on his radio. It hissed with static; he tweaked the dial until a broadcaster's voice came through.

. . . expected to issue hurricane warnings for the entire Atlantic coast from Virginia to Massachusetts. Locally, residents of Fire Island are urged to evacuate—

"It wasn't supposed to get past the Carolinas," Anna said.

"You girls better get over that bridge." The man zipped his jacket and reached for his radio.

"Wait." Gina strained to hear. *New York City schools will be closed tomorrow. The World Trade Center will also close, with dangerous vibrations possible in elevator shafts due to wind tunnels. Staten Island ferry will be closed to cars beginning at midnight—*

Gina's breath caught. "My brother's in Staten Island."

"Well, I hope he's got the radio on," the man said. "He better turn himself around."

B y the time they got back to Blue Claw, a dozen cars were lined up at the gas station where Gina worked. Across the street from Mulley's, the shoe-store owners had finished boarding up their windows, and now half the shop owners on Midway Street were doing the same. The street vibrated with the stutter of drills, the whine of circular saws, the roar of a chainsaw lopping off weak branches.

"This is the fastest I've ever seen this town move," Gina said.

Behind the shop, along the river's edge, county workers in orange vests heaped sandbags along the wharf. Anna whistled. "Do they always sandbag the river?"

Gina shook her head. "Never."

"Are you worried?"

A hundred yards separated Mulley's back door from the water. That was a lot of pier and parking lot. But as soon as Anna said *worried*, it became possible: the river rising, spilling over the asphalt, creeping toward the only place she'd ever wanted to spend her days.

Gina snapped her portfolio shut. "It won't flood," she said, with more certainty than she felt.

Anna pulled up to the shop's back door. "It was supposed to be my first day back at the diner tomorrow."

Gina, only half listening, was searching the parking lot for a white Maverick. If he wasn't in the shop, she would have to call Jeri. This would be their humiliating first contact: Gina needing something.

Anna was looking at Gina as if waiting for an answer to a question.

"I'm sorry," Gina said. "What?"

"Call me later?" Anna raised her eyebrows. "So I know what to type on your enrollment papers?"

"You're a lifesaver." Gina reached for the door handle, then stopped. What was the protocol for goodbyes? She put out her hand. "Have a nice day."

Anna started laughing. "Okay, colleague." She pulled Gina in for a hug; Gina found herself with her face in Anna's beachy tangle of hair. "Have a nice hurricane." Anna kissed Gina's cheek and gave her a gentle shove. Gina stumbled out.

She wobbled her way into the shop, her body feeling oddly light. In the dark hallway, she paused, leaning up against the wall to catch her breath.

"Dominic," Mackie yelled from the front. "That you?"

That collision with Anna's body was so brief, and so surprising, that it was only now sinking in. She should have hugged her back. Anna's hair smelled like incense and peppermint. Did Gina's skin feel that soft, too? She ran her fingers across her cheek, trying to imagine what Anna had felt.

Mackie called again. "Who's back there?"

She walked up the hall. Dom's portable Zenith TV flickered on the counter, a weather map menaced by a blob of orange. One of Mackie's regular customers, a skinny redheaded guy with hair teased into a cloud of metalhead glory, watched from the chair. "Yesterday it's in the Caribbean, and now it's our storm of the century? Somebody's trying to sell generators, man."

Mackie, who was smearing Vaseline on the guy's new tattoo, glanced up at Gina. "Have you heard from Dominic?"

"Oh, sure. He called my secret shoe phone." Gina watched the weatherman sweep an urgent arm up the East Coast. "How would I hear from him? And where's Rick?"

"Split." Mackie stretched plastic wrap over the guy's arm. "Five minutes after you left, the landlord called and said turn on the TV. Rick calls his aunt, tells me la familia needs him, packs up his machines and leaves." Mackie stood and yanked his gloves off. "Then Barry DiMangelo calls back. He wants to know if I'm boarding up the windows. I'm like, uh, isn't that your job? He wants to know where the hell Dominic is. I call Jeri three times . . ."

Gina left him there ranting and opened the back door. The thick gray sky was starting to tinge pink; the flagpole clanked a steady rhythm in the breeze. The wall of sandbags along the wharf was already a layer taller.

Back inside, she flipped through the Rolodex and found the number. Four rings and an answering machine. "You have reached Harrison Entertainment, the family carnival! Our events for this weekend . . ."

After the beep: "This is Dominic Mulley's sister. He needs to call the shop. It's urgent." She shoved the phone back into the cradle and stared at the ceiling, the seam that sprung a leak in every heavy thunderstorm, the heating vent that stayed cold every winter till they called DiMangelo five times. This landlord wasn't going to board up his own windows. If a branch smashed through that glass, it would be their problem. The rain that whipped into the shop would soak their equipment, the wind would tear the flash from the walls, and no insurance check would make up for the weeks they'd be powerless to work.

If she wanted this to be a family business, she had to carry it when Dominic wasn't here.

"I'm packing up." Gina lifted the lockbox with her machines onto the counter.

"Packing what?"

"My stuff and Dominic's and anything else I can carry."

"And biking it home?"

"No. You're going to drive me."

"I am?" Mackie raised his eyebrows and waved at the redheaded kid, who was still admiring the new Elvira on his arm. "Danny, that'll be fifty for today. Cash. Come back in a few weeks, we'll do the rest."

"Unless your shop floats downstream."

"Not my shop," Mackie grunted. He pocketed the cash while Gina snapped open Dominic's travel case.

She packed up Dom's machines, piece by piece, delicate as surgical instruments. "Next we're taking money from petty cash and going for plywood."

"Ain't your shop either, kiddo."

"If Dominic were here, he'd tell me to do it."

"I've got three more appointments today. I'm not leaving money on the table."

"You think people are showing up with a hurricane coming?"

The bells clanked on the front door and a woman in her fifties swaggered in. Between the long gray braids and the bandanna, she looked a little like Willie Nelson. "You ready for me, Mack?"

"Give me ten, Penny. Just setting up."

Gina clicked the travel case shut and looked at him. "We should board it up now. It's going to be twice as hard in the dark."

Behind her, the cowbells clanked again. What kind of lunatics got their jollies being tattooed on the brink of a natural disaster? Gina opened a filing cabinet and ran her fingers along all the documents that Dominic had spent the summer straightening out. "Mackie, come on."

"If your brother cared that much," he said, "why didn't he tell his girlfriend good luck and stay here?"

"She's not his girlfriend," Gina said. "It was a couple of one-night stands."

"I don't care what they call it. He's obviously not worried, or he'd stop thinking with his joystick and drag his ass home."

"Fair point," a woman's voice said.

Gina stopped. That voice wasn't the Willie Nelson lady. She turned to see a woman with a brown cloche hat and feathered hair, holding two steaming cups. She looked so much calmer and steadier than the woman Gina had been avoiding for three months.

Mackie spoke first. "Thanks, Stella."

Twenty-three

Stella must have just come from work; she was still dressed for her daytime receptionist job, in buckled oxfords, everything oaken brown, as if she'd purposely chosen a grounded and trustworthy color. She lifted one of the cups to Gina, speaking quietly. "Can we take a walk? I brought hot cider."

"Ma, the weather."

"Just give me five minutes. I need to ask you something." Stella glanced at Mackie. "Outside." She'd never been comfortable in the shop. Tattoos were for dirtbags, junkies, and filthy sailors like their father.

Stella held out the cider; Gina took it silently. Stella touched the gold pelican pin on her coat, as if the wind might rush through the shop door and blow it off.

"I'm not going to rehash everything. I'm here to start fresh. Just five minutes."

Funny, the things you learned after years with a person. *I want to start fresh.* Fresh, as in: *I don't want to talk about what I did, or how you felt, or why it hurt you.* Fresh, as in: *Let's hurry through a "sorry" so it's over and done.*

Why bother saying any of that? It was a futile, exhausting exercise. "Fine. Five minutes."

They headed out the back, toward the boardwalk, where orange-vested workers were still piling sandbags. A gust of wind roiled the trees along the river. Empty cans clattered along the docks.

"I came to ask . . ." Stella paused. "Do you want to stay with me during the storm." Her sentence was quiet at the end, no lift, as if it was afraid to be a question.

Gina looked out at the restless water. "Let's not do this."

"I just want you safe. I know the part of town you're in and it's all trees waiting to come down. I'm not asking you to move home again. A night or two, that's it."

It had been a long time since Stella had spoken to her with such gentleness— the way her voice had sounded when Gina was little, waking from night-mares, and Stella said, *Come on, climb into my bed.*

Gina glanced back into the shop, uneasy. "Dominic could be back any minute. He went out to—"

"I know. He's with Jeraldine, a hundred miles away. You and I are going to need each other if this year goes the way she's planning."

Cider seeped over the lid of Gina's cup, burning her hand. She hadn't even realized she'd been squeezing it. "You talked to him? They said the Staten Island ferry's shutting down at midnight."

"Gina." Stella rolled her eyes. "That ferry goes to Manhattan. He takes the Verrazzano Bridge." As if she should know that. As if Stella had ever taken her out of Blue Claw to see anything. "But he's going to be stuck if he doesn't get out soon. He said he's not leaving till Jeri's taken care of. Come stay with me to wait out the hurricane. No other guests, I promise. Just you and me. I already fixed up your room. I have a pantry full of food."

Gina's gut feeling was that Stella was speaking the truth, just as she could detect when she wasn't. A full pantry and a clean house were acts of contrition.

They said *I love you. I want you to be safe and happy.* They were often the first things Stella did when she came out of a bad spell, shaken with remorse for whatever had happened. And if Stella assumed that Gina did *not* have a pantry full of food right now, she guessed correctly. Gina had nothing to get her through the hurricane, in fact, but a banana, a package of ramen, and some barely expired cottage cheese she'd rescued when Connie was about to toss it.

Stella reached out and took her hand. For a split second Gina was disoriented; time shifted and she was her mother's Gina again. Not *Queen of Almost*, not *Gina, wake up I'm talking to you*, but *my miracle girl*, following Stella across this very parking lot to pick out a new dress at Sweeney's or get an Italian ice. It froze her for a moment.

Stella was right about the trees in her neighborhood. Connie's apartment *was* surrounded by those gangly locusts that creaked with every breeze.

"We need to talk," Stella said, with more insistence. "I found out some things about that family, the Harrisons."

Gina tensed. "What does that mean?"

"That'll take more than five minutes." Stella gestured at the choppy river, the wind beating the water into little peaks. "We don't have time."

If she went to Stella's, how long would she stay? A night, maybe two. It could be the closure they needed. Her mother looked entirely lucid right now.

But Gina had promised Dominic: *I'm going to be useful. I'm going to help pull us out of this slump.* That was meaningless if she ran back home when things got hard.

"Dominic's going to need me here," Gina said. "I'll call you later. I promise."

Stella raised her eyebrows. "Phones might be dead later. But go ahead, try your luck. When you change your mind, I'll be home."

Twenty-four

Dominic never called, or if he did, he surely got a busy signal. Mackie—still unmoved by the hurricane warnings, insisting they were media hysteria—tied up the phone for half an hour talking to his girlfriend.

Gina did what she could.

She duct taped giant X's on the windows. Anything valuable went on the highest shelves, in case of flood. With nothing but her bike for transport, she could only carry her own equipment, snug in a lockbox that barely fit in her backpack. Balancing would be difficult, especially with the wind, but she couldn't leave it here; it was the most important thing she owned.

Sunset burned a fleeting orange stain into the clouds and then faded into darkness. Time to leave, before the rain began. Maybe the smartest thing would be to bike to Dominic's apartment, use the spare key under the gargoyle statue, and wait for his return. If he needed her help prepping the shop, she'd be ready to go. If he said not to worry, then she could sleep soundly.

"You'll close soon?" Gina said to Mackie, pausing in the doorway. "And call me at Dom's apartment if he shows up?"

"Sure." He didn't even glance at her, focused on the shipwreck he was tattooing on his client's arm.

Gina climbed on her bike. For five miles, the corner of that lockbox dug into her back; what a relief to finally pull up to the battered Victorian. She walked her bike inside, massaging the spot; no doubt there'd be a bruise tomorrow.

She turned on every light. She picked up the phone on the bar and called Harrison Entertainment one more time. Again, no answer. Then she wriggled under the afghan on Dominic's couch and looked up at the crooked electric chandelier, flickering a little as the house creaked in the wind.

He'd promised he'd never do this again—disappear to the city and leave her to manage a crisis alone. If they didn't ward it off together, later on they'd have to clean it up together.

They had learned that lesson when Dominic was living in Brooklyn, tattooing in the back room of a Coney Island arcade. Gina was left behind, lost in the shuffle of Blue Claw Junior High. And Stella was Stella, cycling through her moods like she always did.

Wintertime Stella: morose, calling in sick to work, crying in the living room while Gina did homework over lukewarm SpaghettiOs.

Heading into summer, Stella was at her best: buoyant, irritable on and off, but it was a good time of year. *Let's go for a drive. Let's go shopping. How about we paint your room?*

June 1981, though—Stella's energy went into overdrive. Gina woke the morning of the solstice to find her mother sitting on the floor, surrounded by hundreds of old photos, sliding them into albums. She was wearing day-old clothes, blouse a sunburn pink, as if she'd been oversaturated with noonday glare.

"You think photos can have bad energy? That maybe there's a reason we put them in plastic?"

"Were you up all night?" Gina said, unnerved.

"We should take a road trip and let this place air out. It's ten years today. If he ever comes back it'll be now and I don't want to see his face. Or his slut common-law wife."

Gina's stomach dipped. Things were bad when she started talking about Billy.

Stella pointed to a mess of brochures. Las Vegas, Great Lakes, Ocean City. "Just two weeks. Just enough to clear the air."

Gina snuck into the bedroom to call Dominic. He sounded tired or hungover or both. "I'll be home this weekend. Just steer clear till she gets over it."

"I need you."

"I can only do one thing at a time. I have to work tonight. Can't you sleep over at a friend's house?" She hated sleepovers, even with the few friends she had back then. It felt so vulnerable, sleeping and eating in an unfamiliar house, the humiliating risk of panicking and needing to call home.

Gina hung up the phone, hopeless, and went to school.

By that evening, Stella had accelerated, darting from thought to thought, quick as flipping channels. "Come to the living room. Do you smell that? Like rotting meat?" Gina smelled nothing; Stella swore it was getting stronger. "Where did this blood on the wall come from?"

"That's a water stain."

"Gina, come on. You don't smell a dead animal? He *would* do that. Let things crawl into the attic and die. I'm not sleeping with a carcass in the walls."

Again Gina called that backroom tattoo shop in Coney Island, whispering:

"Dom, come home. Something's really wrong." From the living room came hammering and cracking.

Gina was afraid to go in, but Stella was crying; she couldn't leave her mother like that. She found Stella standing with her back to a ragged hole in the drywall, voice shaky. "I can't even look. God knows what Billy left in there." Gina took a deep breath, went to the hole, and looked. No dead animals. Nothing but wooden studs and wiring.

It was two long hours before Dominic got home and took Stella to the ER; he was the one who spoke to the doctor when they transferred Stella to the psych unit, where she spent three days, but it took both Dominic and Gina to clean up the house the next day. "You shouldn't have to do this," he'd said. "But I don't have anybody else." He bought a piece of drywall. He taught Gina how to measure properly, how to cut it, how to use a drill. And then, as soon as Stella was discharged, he went back to Brooklyn—as if repairing a wall set everything right again.

When Dominic didn't pay attention to the signs, they both ended up with the wreckage.

Now Gina stood and looked out the front window. His car was still missing from the driveway. The wind was holding steady; heavy boughs swayed in the amber glare of the streetlight. It felt unbearable to be alone anymore.

She picked up the phone on the bar and dialed Stella.

"Where are you?" Stella said. "Are you safe?"

"Dominic's," Gina said. "He's probably on his way. What did you want to tell me?"

"I'll come get you—"

"Just tell me. Before the phone cuts out. Please." She sat on the barstool and leaned her elbows on the bar, ear pressed to the receiver.

"Last week," Stella said, "I met the Harrisons."

Twenty-five

irst of all," Stella said, "that beefy boy at the shop is correct. Jeraldine Harrison is in a capital-*R* Romantic Relationship with your brother. Let that sink in and then I've got a furthermore."

Gina had forgotten this feeling: the familiar comfort of gossip with her mother, like an old sneaker that always fit just right. In these moments, it almost felt like they were close.

"Furthermore," Stella said, "Dominic dragged me to Staten Island to meet her and her father."

"He took you and not me?"

"I'm not here to explain what goes on in your brother's head," Stella said. "I'm just telling you what happened. Dominic's serious about this woman. *Nice* Italian restaurant. She's all eyelashes and sugar. Her father is Mister I'll-Have-the-Ribeye-Black-and-Blue. One of those."

If Dominic had taken *her* to a restaurant, Gina wouldn't have wasted her time nitpicking the Harrisons. She would've shut up and enjoyed her garlic bread. God, she was hungry. A bowl of navel oranges sat on the bar; Gina began to peel one.

"Daddy pays the check but he's not done with his Scotch, so Dom and Miss Jeraldine go outside for a smoke. He chats me up like we're old friends. And he tells me—not even ashamed!—that Jeri's last boyfriend was a married man. With kids. Can you picture the look on my face?"

Yes, Gina could.

"Jeri was going to move to Vegas for this guy. Daddy was all in favor. *People* should *have the guts to find someone else if they're not happy*, he says. That's what *he* did when Jeri's mother turned out to be a pain in the ass. *But that bastard in Vegas didn't have the balls to go through with it*, her daddy tells me. *And honestly, thank God. We'd be lost without Jeri.*

"Then he gets talking on Dominic. He likes the potential there. He's *so glad* Dominic isn't tied down, and free to move, instead of his daughter making all the sacrifices, because maybe she'll finally get married and settle down on Staten Island."

"Her dad sounds crazy." Gina ate a slice of orange. "Dominic would have to commute four hours a day if he lived out there."

"You want my prediction? A year from now, if things go Harrison's way, Dominic's married in Staten Island and there *is* no commute. Because there's no more shop."

Gina looked out at the oaks bathed in streetlight, still flush with leaves, the autumn shedding not even begun. Early fall was usually a good season for Stella—a lucid, healthy season. In a bad time, she'd get locked inside the dots she connected and you couldn't reason with her. This didn't feel like one of those times.

"Nobody's closing the shop," Gina said. "The Harrisons just invested ten thousand dollars."

"Think," Stella said. "Jeri's thirty at least. If she wants babies, it's now or never. They're going to make it so Dominic can't run the place without her. And once she's got a ring on her finger—suck him into her family business, and off they go."

"Ma," Gina said. "You think Jerald Harrison invested all that money to help his daughter catch a man?"

"Anything for princess. Ten K for a tattoo shop? He'd buy her a castle if she wanted. He's one of those who used to be a drunk, a bad one, and now he's cut down and he's making up for all the years he missed."

Gina dug her thumbnail into the discarded orange peel. "Is that such a bad thing? To repay your debts?"

Silence on the other end. She'd surprised both of them; it was the kind of thing she wouldn't dare say in person.

She heard the cellophane crackle on a pack of cigarettes, then the flick of a lighter. An inhale, an exhale. "I said I wanted to start fresh."

Gina opened her lockbox, phone receiver still pressed between her shoulder and her ear. She unfolded a paper napkin on the bar and laid her machines on it, piece by piece. Equipment like this would belong to the kind of person who could wait on the phone with patient strength and not rush to fill the silence.

"It's not easy raising kids alone," Stella finally said. "I had to borrow from those envelopes a hundred times."

Gina felt a whip-flick of anger. "You used my savings for petty cash?"

"You think I'd let five hundred dollars sit in the closet, all the times the oil tank was empty, or electric was due? Would you rather we freeze? Or sit in the dark? I always paid it back. Always. This time—your birthday just crept up on me."

If Gina picked up her machine right now, she could set it buzzing with the electricity in her body alone. "You weren't filling the oil tank this time."

"One day, I promise, I will pay you back."

"Don't say things like that. I'd rather just think it's gone."

"Help me keep Dominic here and I swear we'll find a way to get your money."

"We don't own him," Gina said. "He's going to do what he wants."

"Go to his bookshelf. Look for a bright yellow photo album."

Gina's stomach was starting to hurt. "Why?"

"Just look."

She put the phone on the bar and went to the shelf. She pulled the album and returned.

"Now open to the first page."

Christmas 1966. Her own family, the year before she was born, in a sillier mood than she'd ever seen them: ten-year-old Dominic, fierce in a Santa hat, thrusting a turkey baster at the camera. Stella waving a spatula, belly newly round under an untied apron. Billy at the center, wiry in rolled-up sleeves with arms covered in tattoos. He was pale like Gina, with a bristle of rusty stubble on his face, Irish to Stella's Italian. He held a plucked turkey by the wings, as if making it dance.

You think photos can have bad energy? Stella once said, but if this photo had energy, it was nothing but apple cider and flannel pajamas. This snapshot family didn't look the way Gina had always imagined them, like boards of a shoddily strapped raft, about to split off into driftwood. They looked like three people who belonged together.

"The week before this was taken," Stella said, "Billy was going to leave us. You want to know why he didn't? I fought for you."

"He was going to leave you *pregnant?*"

"I could tell you stories. Someday I will. The point is you had a provider for the next four years because I didn't give up."

So what happened after four years? Gina wanted to ask, but it wasn't a good idea to get her started.

"Imagine Dominic marries this woman," Stella said. "He leaves town. The shop closes. What do our lives look like?"

"*Our* lives?" Gina said, wary, not sure where this was going. It wasn't like Dominic paid Stella's bills or drove her to work every day. Yes, she'd lose the little ways he helped her around the house—emergency repairs, maintenance—but Stella used to do those things herself. "Your life doesn't change."

"You're not a mother," Stella said evenly. "You don't know."

Gina was quiet. For Stella, a person showed they loved you by never leaving. Those odd jobs meant Dominic loved her. *Worrying* about Stella meant he loved her.

It was occurring to Gina for the first time: this was more than just a craving for love, or a fear of loneliness. If *both* her children abandoned her—Gina moving out, then Dominic moving away—Stella feared some essential part of her might disappear.

Stella broke the silence. "You realize," she said, "you wouldn't just be losing your job."

"But we wouldn't lose Dominic." Gina didn't know if this was true, actually, but her job right now was reassurance. "He'd still be in the family. A couple hours away."

Maybe Stella assumed Gina felt as she did. That if her brother left, some part of Gina couldn't function. Obviously that was ridiculous; Gina wasn't like that. She was entirely her own person. And Dominic leaving was speculation, anyway.

"You'll feel different," Stella said, "when you see the taillights on that moving van."

"I shouldn't tie up the phone," Gina said. "Dominic might call."

Stella would be rolling her eyes right now, grinding out her cigarette. "Think about what I said."

Gina hung up. She picked up another orange and held it to the light, examining its dimpled skin. If you could tattoo on grapefruits, what about oranges? She set up her machine at Dominic's tiny dining table.

What would our lives look like? Imagine.

It would be just Stella and Gina again, the way it had been in the hard times. Gina had never felt so alone as the months after that episode in '81, when kids at school said *I heard your mom went crazy*, nobody wanted to come over, and if Gina had ever known how to make friends, the knack withered away.

Until Dominic got sick of Coney Island, that dirty back room, the drunks and brawling, and moved back to Blue Claw to open Mulley's Tattoo. Suddenly Gina had a place to be, an endless river of fascinating people moving in and out, who were almost always friendly to that scrawny, tangle-haired kid in the corner. They didn't mind that she was quiet. They liked having an audience for their stories: bike runs in the desert and acid trips in Acadia, surviving foster care or winning a game show grand prize, and whether it was true or not, she liked *being* the audience.

The tattoo shop had saved her life. She had grown into the shape of it like a vine on a trellis, a topiary on a frame; there was no other place on earth where she'd belong.

If her mother was right and Jeri meant to take Dominic away, that one and only place would disappear.

Don't think about it. Attach the clip cord. Press the foot pedal.

The machine shot sparks, buzzing in her hand like a metallic hornet. Gina screamed and jerked her foot away.

Breathe. Drop shoulders. Adjust power supply.

This time, no sparks; calmer buzz. She began to freehand a spiral on the orange skin. The needle ran smooth and clean, so much easier than the laborious toughness of pigskin.

There was no plot to spirit Dominic away, just as there had been no animal carcass in Stella's walls. If that was Mr. Jerald Harrison's daydream, he should stop and read Dominic's tattoos. People got tattooed with the mottoes they lived by. *Death Before Dishonor. Laugh Now, Cry Later.* Dominic's arm said *Hold Fast* because their father hadn't. You couldn't forget something written in your skin.

—

At midnight, Dominic still wasn't home. Gina tried sleeping on the couch, but she felt exposed, right next to the window. Finally she got up and made a sleeping nook behind the bar, as Dominic used to do for her when she was younger, arranging a heap of couch cushions and blankets until it felt sheltered and snug. But every time the wind surged against the house, the change in pressure creaked the basement door open, then sucked it closed a moment later, as if the storm had woken ghosts.

She stared into the darkness of the empty wine rack, breathing the faint smell of turpentine, and then closed her eyes. She'd never seen the Verrazzano Bridge, but she knew the sea at night, how the black Atlantic went violent with white peaks, and how ocean wind felt when it rushed land, strong enough to knock you off balance into the dunes.

In her mind she threw a glowing lasso out into the universe, grabbing Dominic and tugging him home.

Twenty-six

Gina woke to a faint whirr and the clacking of plastic. Her eyes snapped open.

Above her was the purple-hooded face of Skeletor, its yellow jaw snapping—Dominic's alarm clock. A metallic laugh echoed from the speaker. *How unpleasant it is to see you, you sniveling coward!*

"Bet you're sorry for that Christmas present now," Dominic said.

She couldn't see him, could only hear him; she was still curled up on the floor behind the bar. Gina stood, yawning. "What time is it?"

"Noon, and we might not have power for long. If you want your shower hot, I'd do it now." Dominic looked like he'd been awake and dressed for hours, smelling like Irish Spring soap, T-shirt flawless white, his dark curls sprung up tight in the humidity.

"Is it hurricaning?" Rain coursed down the windows.

"Look outside."

Gina opened the door a crack. Immediately it swung fully open and a rush of wind doused her in mist. Trees writhed like tide-twisted seaweed;

the road was a mat of green leaves spiked with broken branches. Someone's garden saint lay headless in the road.

She jumped back in and slammed the door. "You're crazy." He was still laughing as she dragged her duffel bag down the narrow stairway to the bathroom.

When she came upstairs after her shower, the coffeemaker was percolating. She poured a mug. "When did you get home?"

"About one."

"I needed you," Gina said. "The whole street was boarding up. I was alone, putting everything on shelves and duct tape on the windows. Even Mackie wouldn't help me."

"Jeri had work for me." Dominic shrugged. "Harrison's company is the mother ship now. If they go down, we go down."

"We also go down if *we* go down."

"The shop's going to be fine." He topped off his coffee. "Jeri sent me home with a truckload of supplies and a ten-thousand-watt portable generator. Worst-case scenario, we sustain a little damage, DiMangelo's got insurance for the building, I have a policy for our equipment. We're fine."

"What if the river surges and the shop floods?"

Dominic paused. "Let's not think about that one."

"But what if?"

He sat down at his tiny dining table. "Me being here wasn't going to hold the river back."

Gina gripped the handle of her coffee mug. "Why won't you worry with me?"

Dominic laughed. He turned to the table, where three thoroughly inked oranges sat in a neat line, and picked one up.

"Did you tattoo yourself a gang last night?"

She said nothing. He glanced up and frowned. "What are you upset about?"

How was he so oblivious? "I just told you."

He tilted the kitchen chair back. "Six months ago I gave the worrying job to Jeri. All I want is the business to stay afloat. I don't care a hell of a lot how we get there. If Jeri tells me something's a problem, I believe her. If she gives me a job, I do it. Everything's black and white, cause and effect. Basically"— he tossed one of the oranges in the air and caught it—"it's the opposite of dealing with Mom. And it's a relief."

"What if Jeri doesn't want to keep the business afloat?"

"Are you high?" Dominic said. "Her money's on the line. She's tackling all the stuff I shoved under the rug." He tossed the orange up again. "You think I'd go out and fight Keith Yearly if she wasn't making me?"

"You finally confronted him?"

"We're going to, after the storm. It's like . . . boot camp," he said. "You don't like it but it toughens you up."

Gina sat down, opened her sketchbook, and began to draw an aimless spiral. Abruptly she stopped and looked him in the eye. "Mom said she met the Harrisons. You and Jeri are an item now? Like, in a serious relationship?"

"You saw Mom?"

"You didn't answer my question."

Dominic balanced the orange on the crook of his elbow, rolled it down to his hand, and caught it. "I told you we were dating."

"No, you didn't. I'm not stupid, all the overnights."

"You zone out, you miss things," he said. "Why the interrogation today?"

Because she hadn't zoned out. He'd kept this one close to his chest, like the business troubles he'd hidden, like the investment deal he'd concealed until July.

"You scare me when you hide things," Gina said. "I never know what's coming."

A gust of wind slammed the house, and the walls groaned like the wooden bones of a ship at sea. The lights flickered.

"Nobody ever knows what's coming in life," Dominic said. "Maybe I just want a piece of my life for myself."

Quiet as a paper cut, that one.

Gina flipped back a page in her sketchbook, tracing her finger along Anna's lovely waist. If she'd known Dominic had no intention of protecting his own shop, she could've spent this hurricane at the House of Mystical Delights. For all she knew, Anna might've invited her on the ride home, and she was too busy worrying.

And she'd forgotten to call Anna last night, like she'd promised. If she didn't pay better attention, she was going to ruin this chance at having a friend.

Another wallop of wind hit the house; something shattered behind Gina. Her body tensed. A panel of glass from the electric chandelier had smashed on the floor.

"Stay away," Dominic said, as if Gina were stupid enough to go and stand directly under it. They both stared up at it.

A sudden cracking sound outside rattled the window. The lights cut out.

Gina jumped to her feet and looked out the window. Across the street, an oak had toppled onto a garage, splintering the roof. Roots broke sidewalk slabs in half. A power line dangled between two poles, now tilted toward the earth at forty-five-degree angles.

Dominic came and stood next to her.

"Well." He took a deep breath. "That's not ideal."

"*Not ideal?*" Gina said. "Is that the new *sticky?*"

Sheets of rain snapped against the house. They stood by the dim light of the window, the room in shadow. "Jeri sent me home with candles," he said.

"Well, that solves everything," she said. Outside, the wind whipped dirt from the base of the fallen tree. Newly naked roots dangled over broken concrete.

—

After Dominic swept up the glass, with Gina keeping an eye on the chandelier, they settled into an uneasy peace: Crazy eights by candlelight, cold Pop-Tarts, checking the news on the hand-crank radio. Gina showed him her drawings, told him she'd secured private lessons. *Good girl,* he said. *I knew you'd solve it.*

When he stretched out with a magazine, she called Anna, who was not only forgiving of Gina's failure to call last night, but apparently just happy to hear from her. What a curious person. They talked for an hour.

"Holy crap," Dominic said when Gina got off the phone. "Does she always make you laugh that hard? Or just when she's in crisis?"

"The crisis got better." She felt her face warming and poured some more lukewarm coffee. "Listen. I had an idea while I was talking to my friend." *My friend.* "What if we found a way to milk the hurricane?"

Dominic looked up at the ceiling. "I'm not familiar with that expression."

She sat down with him and opened her sketchbook to a banner she'd sketched while she was on the phone.

She'd promised to come up with ideas, and now she had one.

Even if the shop made it through the storm intact, nobody on Long Island was getting a tattoo tomorrow. They'd be busy with repairs and cleanup. If the power stayed off, though, people would be dying for coffee.

With Jeri's generator for power, Mulley's could provide it. Not for profit— for public relations. If Keith Yearly was running a smear campaign against them, most people would never walk into the shop to discover he was wrong. Coffee would lure them in, even for five minutes, which was enough to see that the staff at Mulley's wasn't shady, strung out, or dangerous. Maybe they'd even come back.

The wind was getting louder, whistling like they were whipping down the expressway with the windows cracked.

"Well," Dominic said slowly. "That's an idea."

"People will need electricians," Gina said. "We could put out Lamar's business cards—"

He didn't meet her eyes. "Let's see what Jeri says."

"She'd have a problem with free coffee?"

"Don't stress over this," Dominic said. "There's nothing for you to do. We'll get through the hurricane and she'll figure out our next step."

"I'm really confused right now," Gina said.

He drummed his fingers on his knee. "Jeri has a vision. Big changes coming. And you'll be a lot happier if you can just roll with it."

"What changes?"

A metallic clatter outside startled them both. They looked up to see a lawn chair lodged in the crook of a tree, seesawing violently.

Dominic took a deep breath. "One thing at a time."

"That's what you said about getting my money from Stella. It's starting to feel like code for *drop it*."

The wind ripped the chair loose and sent it flying down the street.

"I'm just saying let's take it easy today." He turned away from the window. "Tomorrow we'll find out if we have a shop at all."

Twenty-seven

Gloria rolled north and Saturday in Blue Claw dawned clear.

"Let's go," Dominic said.

Maybe it was the wailing sirens and the whiff of smoke in the air or maybe it was all the fallen trees in the light of day, but his voice sounded less cavalier than it had at the storm's beginning.

Gina got dressed by flashlight in the bathroom, then climbed into the passenger seat of the Harrison Family Carnival loaner truck. Dominic navigated out of the neighborhood, steering around broken boughs.

Down a side street, a fire engine had just pulled up to a downed pole shrouded in smoke. He gestured at it. "We're going to be dead for a month. People don't suddenly put down their chainsaws and say, 'Gee, I'd like to spend some money on a tattoo today.'"

Gina turned toward him, irritated.

"What's that pissy look?" Dominic said.

"I think I said that. Yesterday."

The closer they got to the shop, the harder Dominic drummed his fingers on the steering wheel. "I've never worked this kind of generator before."

"We can read instructions."

"If the building's flooded, it's not the end of the world. I'll get a regular job."

"Oh my God, stop." Gina put her hands to her temples. "Can you please not give up before we even see it?"

They rolled up to the back parking lot, which separated the river from their back door. Dominic stopped the car. "Holy crap," Gina said.

The sandbags were dingy with silt where the river had surged over them. She had never before seen the water such an opaque brown. It had crept up toward the row of buildings on Midway Street, sweeping garbage along the asphalt—and then it had stopped. Halfway up the parking lot was a ragged line of debris, the place where the river had peaked and receded.

"No flood," Gina said, relieved.

Dominic exhaled. "No flood."

She looked at the shop. "And no trees on the roof."

The air smelled fishy from the thousand little silversides the river had dragged up. Gulls dive-bombed the asphalt, screeching and feasting.

Dominic parked. "Let's go in."

They went in through the back. The floor was dry, but the air felt damp, as if they'd descended into a cellar. Dominic's flashlight beam swung across the walls and floor, and as they approached the front of the shop, it illuminated a mess of papers littering the ground. It smelled of wet cardboard. Gina realized she was clenching her jaw. A slight breeze cooled her skin, raising goose bumps.

As soon as they got to the work area, she looked out into the waiting room and saw the source of the breeze.

The front window was shattered—nothing left but some dangling duct tape and a jagged parapet of glass clinging to the edges. The wall—soaked. The furniture—soaked. Framed flash, knocked to the floor, lay facedown in a slick of dirty water and glass shards. A long piece of steel gutter had crashed through the window and lodged in the wall—straight through the neck of the Mulley's mermaid.

Gina walked over to the mural, boots crunching on glass, and touched the wrecked drywall she'd once spent hours painting. She grasped the gutter in both hands.

"Wait. You'll hurt yourself." Dominic grabbed her by the sleeve. "Let's clear the glass first." He handed her a pair of work gloves, embroidered *Harrison Entertainment*, and flipped the useless light switch. Nothing. "Maybe we hook up the generator first."

Gina spied a particular flash poster facedown on the floor, smaller than the others. She turned it over. The glass was cracked on the diagonal, making a jagged stripe where water had seeped in, blurring the drawings she'd worked on all summer.

She hung it back on that battered wall. Then she sat on the stool at the counter and slumped forward onto the damp Formica.

Dominic examined the damage. "I think it missed the studs. It's just drywall. We can replace drywall. This window must've broken at the tail end of the storm or the pressure from the wind might've . . ."

He could have prevented this. If he'd bothered to give five minutes of thought, twenty bucks' worth of plywood, and an hour's worth of preparation, then she wouldn't be standing here with her ruined work, hands pressed against her eyes to hold back tears.

"Can you get the big broom?" Dominic said.

Gina kept her head in her hands. She wasn't ready to be useful.

"Everything's going to be okay," he said. "Jeri was planning renovations anyway. All this means is the insurance will pay for it instead."

"My artwork," Gina said.

He put his hand on her arm. "We can paint another mural. You can draw another poster. The way you'll be drawing next year, you won't even want to look at your old stuff anymore. It's wet paper, okay? But if we don't dry this place out, the mold is going to be a nightmare."

She kept her head down. "I need a minute."

Dominic rubbed his face. "I'll give you five. I have to call DiMangelo. If the phones are even working. But then we've got to move." He walked off to the dark office, flashlight in hand.

Gina used her shirt collar to dry her eyes. She looked up at her mermaid, impaled on that steel gutter splitting her head from her body. Her painted skin had already begun to wrinkle and bubble from the moisture.

She looked down at her marred poster. *PURPLE HYACINTH: Sorrow.*

T he day passed with the whirr of fans, the smell of rotting fish, and dustpan after dustpan of broken glass dumped into contractor garbage bags. The old couch, drenched, was condemned to the dumpster.

Gina and Dominic yanked the gutter out of the wall and returned it to the pizzeria across the street.

The generator worked, but it made an endless grating noise and intermittently smoked, which was also true of Dominic. *We were so lucky*, he kept saying. The computer, the equipment, the portfolios that Gina had stashed on the high office shelves: *All the important things are safe.*

Around lunchtime, Gina finally said: "It wasn't luck. I prepped for the storm."

"Lucky you stopped by, I mean," he said, absently, as if she'd just happened to waltz in that day and noticed a few things askew.

If Gina was waiting around for appreciation, she'd only make her day worse. There was work to do. She was mopping the floor with bleach when she heard a cautious voice: "Hello?"

The door creaked open. When Gina saw Anna poking her head in, she felt a little lift of relief, like the first April day warm enough to leave your jacket home.

"Okay to come in?"

"Probably better if I come out," Gina said. "Fumes. Let me wash the bleach off my hands."

Anna came in anyway, wearing a maroon waitress dress and sneakers. She walked around the destroyed waiting room and stopped at the mermaid. "Oh, Gina, I'm so sorry," she said. "You must've worked on that forever."

"How did you know I painted it?"

Anna pointed at Gina's initials, still intact and hidden in the mermaid's tail. Nobody ever noticed those.

"It's been a hard day." Gina dried her hands and followed Anna out the front door. The sun blazed off all the unbroken windows up and down the street, newly freed from their plywood and cleaned by diligent hands.

"Did you guys make it through the storm OK?"

"Nobody has power, but it looks better than here. Nicolas called the hurricane *flaccid*." Anna pulled a copy of *Newsday* out of her purse. "*Storm Less Than Media Predicted*," she read aloud. "*If it all seemed a bit like overkill by yesterday afternoon—followed by a perverse feeling of letdown for some . . .*" She looked up. "Those let-down perverts were us."

Gina snorted. "Are you heading to work now?"

"Turns out the diner doesn't have power either. My manager let me take food before it spoiled. I brought you some chicken pot pie."

It was not possible for someone to be this thoughtful.

Anna reached through the open window of her Buick and handed Gina a shopping bag. "And while I'm here—you never showed me your project."

Gina looked up at the iris-blue sky and shook her head. "It's a wreck now."

"As in, gone?"

"Ruined. Like the mermaid."

"Show me anyway? Please?"

Gina went inside, took the fractured frame off the wall, and carefully carried it back to Anna, who set it on the hood of her car to study it. Gina watched her. She was reading every single flower, looking close to read the water-blurred ones in the middle. Gina wondered if Anna would remember how many of these plants she'd named in her letters.

Anna finished, looked up at Gina, and put her hand to her heart. "Don't tell me you were going to trash this."

Gina nodded.

"Can I have it?"

Gina laughed. "You want my wet paper?"

"It's not just wet paper. You don't know what a gift this is," Anna said. "I don't meet a lot of people who pay attention like I do."

"Thank you," Gina said.

Just _thank you_.

Twenty-eight

THE BLACKOUT: AN INTERLUDE

Two weeks.

It took two weeks for the Long Island Lighting Company to restore power to the whole island, nose to tail. Some towns got it back in three days; Blue Claw suffered for seven. People began to heckle the repair crews and call for the death of LILCO.

Gina, meanwhile, quietly kept her secret: she was content to live in the dark for as long as possible. When real life returned, Jeri was coming to talk about her Vision. Gina suspected this would not be the kind of Vision where one suddenly understood important things about the nature of the soul or one's true purpose. But in the meantime—as if the ordering power of the universe were granting Gina an astounding consolation prize—there was Anna.

BLACKOUT DAY ONE

After helping Dominic clean up the worst of the wreckage at the shop, Gina got a frantic call from Sam, her manager at the gas station. "We got cars lined up for a mile to fill up gas cans," he said. "Tomorrow I need you here an hour early."

She was already biking to work at sunrise each day. One hour earlier would mean waking at four thirty to bike a winding road with no streetlights in the dark.

"Just tomorrow?" she said.

"No. Going forward. Until it eases up."

What would she have done in the past? Sucked it up. Then, after a few days, she would've quit.

When Gina told Anna about it on the phone later, she wasn't expecting actual help with her problem. But Anna said: "Could they lend you a car?"

In Gina's experience, bosses just issued demands; they didn't give you resources to actually meet them. Although, she recalled, Sam not only had an extra car around, but griped about it; his brother had moved to Alaska and abandoned his old Plymouth in Sam's garage.

Could you even ask for something like that? *Can I borrow a car?*

Amazing, the things people would say yes to. O, freedom!—this 1972 Plymouth Cricket, with its tail end sloped like a bee's back, and its honey-gold paint! Even the spots of rust were auspicious as lucky coins.

BLACKOUT DAY TWO

As it turned out, Anna had a gift for asking that kind of question—for seeing possibility where there was none.

By the end of day two, Gina's gas station job had become a living hell. She'd chosen this work for its minimal conversation with strangers—*Leaded or unleaded? Windows?*—but Gloria exploded this bland ease. Customers were now livid about hour-long waits and jacked-up prices on gas, ice, and bottled water. They unleashed it on Gina, and Sam expected her to know what to say.

"What if you treated it like a social experiment?" Anna said over the phone.

"You lost me already." Gina, who'd been washing dishes with the receiver wedged between her ear and her shoulder, rinsed the suds off her hands.

"If you try different responses, what do they do? Then, if they yell at you anyway, you're just a scientist, observing them."

"You're crazy," Gina said. "I'll just say a hundred wrong things and they'll curse me a hundred different ways."

"Just more data!" Anna said.

BLACKOUT DAY THREE

G ina tried it, primarily because she wanted Anna to think she was gutsy. Most people were just as rude as they'd been before.

One thing changed, though: Gina noticed that she feared people a little less. And the less she feared them, the more she was able, in small ways, to connect with them.

A woman who pulled up in a station wagon looked ready to lose it, snapping at Gina for not getting to her fast enough. Gina began to tense up and avoid eye contact, waiting for the tirade to begin.

Then she remembered Anna's suggestion. Five seconds of observation revealed that this woman's backseat was a maelstrom of children, yelling and whipping each other with Twizzlers.

"You look like you could use a break," Gina said. Then an idea came to her. "Let me give you my employee discount."

The mother began to cry.

This was awkward, but better than yelling. When the woman pulled herself together and paid up, she slipped Gina a three-dollar tip. "You're the first person today to help me with anything," she said.

If something new could happen in a situation like *that*—a scenario Gina had suffered through a hundred times, feeling powerless and stuck—what else was possible?

BLACKOUT DAY FOUR

Shoreham had its power back already, and Gina and Anna were lazing around in Anna's room at the House of Mystical Delights. They were watching a VHS tape labeled *PBS Nature—Faves* in Anna's handwriting that she had popped into the VCR.

To our naked eye, said a narrator, *the cinquefoil is a humble flowering herb with little to distinguish it.* There it was on-screen—five plain yellow petals.

But here is the cinquefoil as perceived by a bee. The flower paled to white with a bull's-eye center of red.

"What!" Gina said.

These markings point bees to the bonanza of pollen on each blossom. Under ultraviolet lights, the patterns fluoresce and reveal themselves to us.

That's what it was like knowing Anna. She saw things in ordinary days, even terrible days, that Gina had never thought to look for before.

BLACKOUT DAY FIVE

At first, Gina wondered why a person like this would spend time with her. Then it occurred to her: Anna also saw hidden qualities in people. Including Gina.

Perhaps Gina actually was gutsy, and not just pretending.

"Hey," Sam said. "You seem happy with that car. And I hate the thing. Do you want to buy it? A hundred bucks. Pay in installments. I like having my garage back."

Although Gina did have extra cash from working overtime, the very idea of car ownership was intimidating—insurance, registration, baffling legalities. If she went to Dominic for help, he'd be all-or-nothing, depending on his mood, jumping in and handling it for her or snapping, *Gina, I can't arrange everything for you.*

Anna's approach was so simple and effective that it struck Gina as nothing short of magic: She drew the answers out of *you*. She listened. She shared basic information without patronizing. And later that day, she'd delight in your story of going to the DMV on your own for the first time. Even the part where the employee stared at your license for ten seconds and said, "You look like you're channeling demons in this photo."

Anna would belly laugh as if you were a gifted comedian, instead of a loser with a creepy ID. And then she'd climb into your ugly wreck of a new car and absolutely love it.

BLACKOUT DAY SIX

f Anna could find hidden gifts in her days, perhaps Gina could, too.

In this in-between world of the blackout, for example, Dominic had time to teach her. He explained mechanics, drew schematics. She would never need Mackie to tune up her machine again.

Rick gave her an Alvarez original on her hip—hidden under her clothes, so Dominic couldn't complain. *Pezadita*, in that swooping script that made Rick the most coveted artist at Mulley's for name tattoos. Every time she looked at it, she felt strong. *Little heavy, full of spirit, going to rule the world. Go get it, little fighting fish.*

Stella started dropping by the shop, calmer than usual, less complicated. As if there was sufficient chaos right now and she could afford to relax, bring Gina a buttered roll, and gossip for a bit. She'd never done that before.

All the while, Gina tattooed a sackful of oranges. The sweet zing of their smell became the aroma of the blackout for Gina: unexpected brightness in a time of no lights.

Looking for these gifts was not the same as *cheering up*, which is what

Dominic kept telling her to do. *Cheer up*, on day one, when Gina helped him remove the damaged drywall, her maimed mermaid crumbling to the linoleum. She kept waiting for him to say *I hate to see this go*. Instead: *Maybe you'll paint a new one. That'll be fun. Let's see what Jeri says.*

Soon enough, Gina *would* see what Jeri had to say. Rumor had it that in the next day or so, LILCO would finally get around to Blue Claw.

BLACKOUT DAY SEVEN

Gina was ready. By the final day of the blackout, she'd nearly given up on sharing her ideas with Dominic.

He was fretting about getting customers in the door again, so she did the obvious thing: design an ad. It was a drawing of a woman's behind in Daisy Dukes, a heart tattoo peeking out from the bottom:

We Tattoo the County Seat . . .
and Other Places.

He didn't even crack a smile. "I know you're sick of hearing this—"

The list of things that were not part of Jeri's Vision was getting longer. First, free coffee; now, cute butts. Tomorrow, who could predict?

"Hey you," said a voice. "Lady at the counter."

Gina's heart jumped. She turned, and there she was: scarlet lipstick and wild waves of hair. Anna hugged her, smelling fresh, like grass and lavender. "Can I steal you away to the beach?"

Gina looked at Dominic. "Do you need me for anything?"

"Nah, the spackle's still drying. Have fun."

The expressway was all theirs, the evening golden and clear as some honey-eyed elixir. The hurricane had ripped away the beach stairs, so Gina and Anna sat on the boardwalk eating hot dogs as dusk fell.

"Did you ever look up that poetry?" Anna said.

Gina had read the verses so many times by now that she'd memorized them. "Lo—" Immediately she felt embarrassed, like she was channeling some ren faire bard. Too late now. "Lo, the winter is past, the rain is over and gone."

Anna's face lit up. "The voice of the turtledove . . ." She stared into space. "Damn. Maybe I did forget the words."

"The fig tree puts forth its green figs," Gina said. "The vines with the tender grapes . . ." Anna's smile was pure delight. Gina felt like she'd won something.

Time to change the subject. These glimmers of heat she was feeling around Anna—that was something to keep to herself, like pearls found on a secret beach. People backed off when you were too fascinated with them.

"Hey," Gina said. "I need some clairvoyant guidance."

Anna snorted.

"How do you guys do that? Is any of that real?"

"You pay attention to what people say, how they say it. Which makes me think people could find their answers if they just paid a little attention to themselves." Anna licked relish off her thumb and leaned back on her elbows. "But tell me what's on your mind."

"My mother thinks Dominic's investor wants to kidnap him to Staten Island."

Anna laughed. "What's your gut feeling?"

Gina picked trash out of the sand: a plastic bottle cap, a Bazooka Joe wrapper. "Who'd waste their time with a hole-in-the-wall tattoo shop in

Blue Claw? Maybe she wants to turn us into a carnival outpost." She leaned back, too. "She's coming to tell us the Vision once the lights are back on."

"Don't those wrappers have fortunes on them?" Anna said. "Probably just as accurate as anything I'd come up with."

Gina picked up the wrapper. "*You will make the team if you do not fail.*"

"That sounds like a wait and see," Anna said.

POWER RESTORED

On the morning of October 5, Blue Claw woke up to alarm clocks blinking *12:00*, light switches that worked, and three thousand coffeepots ready to percolate.

Gina was toweling off after her first hot shower in days when the phone rang. "It's happening," Stella said.

"What?"

"Dom told me Jeri's coming. You need to be ready."

"Mom, he's not leaving us," Gina said. "You saw the repairs."

"Would it hurt to mark your territory? Take over one of those workstations. You have to be ready to fight," Stella said. "Do you think your father took off because he loved the seven seas? He left me for a woman down south. Gina, listen to me. Jeri *is* your woman down south."

"We're not married," Gina said. "He's just my brother."

"And your employer, and your best friend, and the one person who looks out for you—"

Though they had started out with such grief, these blackout days had held so many consolation prizes: the long talks with Anna. The focused lessons. With the smell of fresh primer and the whirr of drills, there were even brief moments when it felt like the shop's early days, taping their first dollars to the counter for luck and prosperity, believing the future would be good. Believing the rain was over and gone.

"I don't want to worry about this," Gina said to Stella. "Let's wait and see."

Twenty-nine

S o this is the sidekick I'm always hearing about!"

The voice was lemon-zest bright, so startling that Gina almost dropped the spray bottle. She had been lost in thought, wiping down the shop's new front window, and hadn't heard the back door. Now Jeri was coming straight at her, arms wide, with Dominic trailing behind. Gina found herself in a crushing hug, her face curtained in perfumed hair.

When Jeri stepped back, Gina took stock of the woman in front of her. Stella would've called her *Sears catalog pretty*, like a mom in a back-to-school sale circular. She had porcelain-doll hair, a little scar on her cheek—a mole removed, maybe? Also, kick-ass work boots. Those were unexpected.

Dominic gestured to the folding chairs, and the three of them sat down.

"I brought goodies." Jeri cut the red-and-white string on an Italian bakery box to reveal bland cookies dressed up with sprinkles. She set it on the coffee table, which had swelled with the rain until the laminate split. "So that was some storm! Thanks for holding down the fort while I took care of the mother ship."

Gina made her mouth smile.

"First of all, this is not bad luck." Jeri waved at the reconstructed waiting area, fresh spackle still visible. "We had renovations on the docket anyway. Mother Nature just did our demolition for us. Everybody can cheer up." Ah. The source of Dominic's new favorite phrase.

Jeri clasped her hands. "To make this real quick—we have big, beautiful dreams for this studio. I'm going to paint the picture, assign some roles, and then we'll ring the bell on the fall quarter and off you go."

"Studio?" Gina said. "You mean the shop?" She looked at Dominic, who'd somehow squeezed in a haircut while returning the generator to Staten Island. His curls were shorn close to his head, his gray work shirt replaced with a white one. He smiled at her.

"When my family took our business next-level," Jeri said, "we identified a gap in the market. Did anyone really want another seedy carnival? Barkers with no teeth and freak shows, you know? Families don't want that."

"Depends on the family, I guess?" Gina said.

"Enough families wanted our carnival, honey, that we currently net a quarter-million dollars a year."

The eye contact was getting uncomfortable. Gina looked down at the bakery box—all those dry, golden cookies—and then saw an Italian rainbow cookie peeking out from the bottom, layers of rich almond cake held together by whisper-thin films of chocolate and raspberry jam. She dug it out and nibbled at it, one layer at a time,

"You've heard the phrase 'upwardly mobile,'" Jeri said.

"Yuppies?" On TV, they read *The Wall Street Journal*, joined health clubs, and wore Rolexes.

"Smart girl. If you want to attract those people, we need to make this shop feel like a studio. It's already hygienic, it's producing high-caliber work. All you need is a higher-quality clientele."

"Are we low quality?" Gina said. "How do people get quality rated?"

Dominic leaned forward. "That's not what she means."

Jeri's earrings dangled in the light, clusters of pearls like petrified soap bubbles. "I'm saying, you're on the doorstep of the Hamptons."

That was a considerable doorstep. In summer traffic, an hour at least.

"I don't think those kinds of people get tattoos," Gina said.

"Maybe not like this wild man, sure." Jeri ran her hand affectionately along Dominic's densely illustrated forearm. "But did you know tattoos were in vogue with Victorian aristocrats? Gentlemen got the family coat of arms."

Gina sat mute. Stella had no idea what she was asking when she said *Help me keep Dominic here.* This woman's attention probably made Dominic feel like he'd boarded a gilt-and-glass elevator to the top of the world.

"It's logical," Jeri said. "They have party planners, interior decorators, they sculpt their bodies with personal trainers. We are offering tasteful custom artwork for those bodies."

Gina looked up at the wall above them, as if the painted mermaid were still there, a seaborne saint who could help her. *Mer-guardian, salty sister, give me strength.*

"We're for misfits," Gina said.

Jeri's smile could've been cut out of a magazine. "That's the world you're used to, yes."

"People who feel at home here," Gina said, "don't feel at home other places."

"Do you mean you?" Jeri said dryly.

Gina, stunned back to shyness, could not answer. She folded her arms across her chest, tucking her hands into her armpits.

Jeri's voice softened. "The bottom line is, honey, this is not a nonprofit." She gave Dominic's knee a pat. "I mean, technically I suppose it's been nonprofit. But it's time to make some money." She put her hand on Gina's. "Nobody's hanging you out to dry. You're going to help us."

Gina bit another layer off her cookie. Her stomach hurt. This was not just a business. This was her sanctuary, her home, her house of worship. The world held one safe place, and this was it.

"Dominic says you hit all your summer benchmarks. Very nice," Jeri said. "Let's talk about your drawing class. It starts when?"

"I started already," Gina said.

"Excellent!" Jeri said. "And it's where?"

"I'm taking private lessons in Shoreham."

Jeri frowned at her copy of Gina's apprenticeship agreement. "If I were to ask you the difference between 'class' and 'private lessons,' what might you say?"

Was this a trick? "Number of people?"

"Spot on," Jeri said. "This class wasn't just for your personal enrichment. You were supposed to be a studio ambassador. Connecting with people, educating them, helping to change our image. That's going to be hard to do with nobody else around."

"Oh," Gina said. "The paper didn't say any of that."

"Orchestrating the big picture is not your job," Jeri said. "Your job is sticking to the plan. So. What would you do in my position?"

Gina shrugged. "Give me an extension on the class, until winter session comes around?"

"If you go rogue on another requirement," Jeri said, "we will be docking your pay."

Gina sat silent, humiliated, her face growing hot.

Jeri picked through the bakery box and found herself a treasure, a mini cannoli. She scooped out a bit of sweet ricotta with her finger, licked it, and smiled. "Anything else before we move on?"

Thirty

Gina walked fast down Midway Street, past all the businesses lit up as if nothing had happened last week. The laundromat's neon sign blinked its usual ice blue. All the TVs at Royal Discount Electronics crackled their synchronized pictures, seven Michael J. Foxes swaggering up to seven Pepsi machines.

When Jeri sized her up, she saw a kid sister on a stipend. But Gina's fingerprints were all over that shop; she had helped install the tile Jeri walked on. Stella was right. Gina should have claimed that workstation. If Dominic wouldn't speak up and say his sister mattered, then the physical space would have to do it instead.

Fifty cents at Goodwill bought her a brass picture frame, cast to look like nautical rope. She got back to Mulley's two minutes before the cowbells clanked and Keith Yearly walked in.

"Mr. Mulley." A tall man in a camel-brown suit stuck out his hand. "Glad we're finally having this discussion."

Keith Yearly's voice had the same resonant bounce as his radio commercials. His wide gold tie was patterned with lighthouses—the same tie he wore in his newspaper ads.

Jeri had changed into patent leather heels. She put her hand on Gina's arm. "Honey—coffee, please."

Gina walked to the back as their voices batted back and forth down the hall. Coffee percolating, she went on a hunt for the toolbox.

By the time she found it, their voices were rising. Gina poked her head out of Dominic's office into the darkened hallway, where she was invisible.

Keith Yearly was sitting with legs splayed, one arm stretched along the back of another folding chair as if he intended to reserve both for the day. "I get News 12 down here—hey, look at Blue Claw, back to business!—and guess what they film? The eyesore tattoo parlor with the busted window. For a week straight you run a generator so loud that Midway Street sounds like a bike rally, you use that machine to help exactly nobody, and I'm supposed to like you why?"

"So we're a big family now?" Dominic said. "I didn't get that impression when you left Mulley's off the directory."

Gina smiled in the dark of the office door.

"People don't want to open up their nursery school on a block with a scab merchant," Yearly said. "My best deal just fell through because the buyer took a drive down here at night. And what do you think he saw?"

"You think everybody on the sidewalk is my client? Do I make the druggies come out at night? Three years, Keith, I've been a team player. You remember when I opened up, we went door-to-door, every shop on Midway Street, how you doing, bottles of wine—"

Gina had carried those bottles. Dom used to smile his charming smile at the other business owners and point at her: *If I'm keeping my little sister around, you know we're keeping it clean.*

"Gina?" Jeri called. "Coffee, please?"

Gina carried three cups to the front.

Jeri leaned forward, voice silky. "This is a great time to talk about our new business vision."

Dominic was revved up now. "I got the No Loitering sign outside, I try—"

Yearly barely looked at Jeri, fixed on Dominic. "Who's bringing in the bikers, then? The sewing shop?"

"So do you blame Diana for the drunks?" Gina said.

Keith Yearly looked at Dominic, as if to ask who this interloper was.

Gina's mouth was dry. "Diana Barry bought the Blue Clam the same year we opened up. Do you blame her for every drunk on the street, just because the clam bar serves beer?"

Dominic spoke in a low voice. "Gina," he said, "how about you get the sugar."

She'd made a good point. She knew she had. Heat began to rise in her chest. "Diana keeps her place emasculate and so do we."

"Immaculate," Dominic said. "Gina—" He pointed to the hallway. She pressed her lips together and walked over to the counter.

Yearly stood and adjusted his belt, elbows out, taking up space. "Well, this has been illuminating. Fair warning—people are saying you're a liability. You'll hear from the board of health."

"We'd welcome that," Jeri said calmly, but she'd lost him, and she knew it. She reached out to touch his sleeve. "Can I tell you about some exciting changes we're making?"

"I've got an open house." Yearly lifted his wrist to display his gold watch. "Call my girl. She'll try to squeeze you in." He shook Dominic's hand like he was trying to jerk his arm out of the socket, gave Jeri's a limp squeeze, and walked out.

Dominic unbuttoned his cuffs and shook out his hands, as if releasing every profanity he'd balled up in his fists.

"We're subject to board of health inspections?" Jeri said.

"No. Nobody gives a shit about tattoo shops. But all they need to do is find one person who tests positive for hepatitis and claim they got it here." Dominic drowned a cookie in his coffee. "Even if it's a lie, we die by the rumor mill." He turned to Gina, voice cold. "And are you crazy? I have to handle that guy delicately."

"But I was right." He couldn't be proud of her for speaking up?

"I'm going for some fresh air." Jeri slipped out the front door.

"Did it occur to you," Dominic said, "that mentioning Diana isn't going to win us points with this guy?"

"She's making better money than we are. All summer her parking lot's packed."

"When Keith Yearly says *the new face of Blue Claw*," Dominic said, "he's not picturing Diana."

Gina stared. "I'm sorry—what?"

Dominic looked up at the ceiling. "Gina, please don't make me spell it out."

"I can't believe you right now," Gina said. "I wasn't supposed to mention Diana because she's Black?"

"I'm not saying I agree with him—"

"But you're catering to his bullshit. When Lamar's around, you call Yearly a racist and act like you care. Then Yearly comes around and I can't mention a business if a Black woman's running it? That's so two-faced."

Dominic put his hands up. "I didn't create the world we live in."

"No, you're just making a nice comfy couch for it, so it can put its feet up and have another beer."

"Talk like a normal person," he snapped.

Gina's hands were trembling; if she didn't find something for them to do, she was in danger of hurling that coffeepot against the wall.

She turned and yanked the drop cloth off the fourth workstation. This morning, she'd draped it there to hide all the guys' garbage: Dominic's junk mail, Mackie's dying cactus, Rick's pulp sci-fi novels. The communal box of condoms.

Gina removed it all. Starting today, she would have a space of her own.

She began to tape up her things around the mirror, just as the guys did: Anna's Betty Broadbent postcard. A 1940s photograph of Millie Hull, *New York's Only Lady Tattooer*. She slid a photo into the new brass frame: Dominic and Gina at the Mulley's Tattoo grand opening. This needed to be prominent, a thing you wouldn't dare remove. She dragged the stepstool over and began to hammer a nail into the wall next to the mirror.

The bells on the front door clanked. "I forgot to mention," a man's voice said. Gina glanced over her shoulder; Yearly was back. Dominic walked over and they were at it all over again.

Mackie—who had snuck in the back door as the meeting wrapped up—looked up from *Wrestling Revue*. "Aren't you making yourself at home."

She spoke under her breath. "I need a place to work."

"But that's where we keep the mail." He kept his eyes on Gina but raised his voice, loud enough for Dominic to hear. "And are you leaving those wang wrappers on the counter?"

Dominic stopped drinking his coffee mid-sip. He looked behind him at the box of condoms, bright as a punch bowl, emblazoned with DUREX FIESTA.

"Goddammit—" He turned and saw Gina on the stepstool, still holding the hammer. He stared at the cleaned-off workstation, at Gina's picture frame and Millie Hull and Betty Broadbent. "Gina," he said sharply. "Get down from there."

Her anger was rising, arms tense, but she stepped down.

"Put the toolbox away. Workstations are my call. Not yours." As Gina picked up the toolbox, Dominic looked at Yearly. "Excuse the interruption. She's gotten a little big for her britches."

Everything went white—a snow-blind burn all across her scalp, behind her eyes. The toolbox hit the linoleum with a metallic clatter. It sprang open, a hundred brackets and bolts jingling on the floor and scattering, an explosive commotion of metal across the tile floor. Then, as the rolling washers fell flat like coins, she looked up at Dominic.

His move.

The look in Dominic's eyes was blistering. "That's going to be a lot to sweep up."

"Well," Gina said, "best of luck." She left the hammer on the workstation, wiped her hands on the back of her jeans, and stalked out the front door.

Thirty-one

Gina spent her afternoon slapping paint onto the wall.
Connie had been asking for a mural over the couch: something "uplifting, like a beach sunset." Gina had never been more ready to set a sky on fire. She dragged the couch away, smothered it in a sheet, and draped the floor. She shot a quarter tube of ultramarine directly onto the wall, smooth as hot mud, the base for a churning sea.

Half an hour in, as the anger died down, a hollow feeling came over her, a half-sick numbness. She couldn't undo this. Months of proving herself— she'd smashed it to the floor in three seconds. And in that nerves-firing, lightning-hot whiteout, she'd been Stella.

The phone rang. It rang without stopping for five minutes and then, after a brief pause, began again. Gina switched the ringer off.

Soon Rick showed up at her door, sucking on a Tootsie Pop. "Heard about the toolbox. I'm in your corner, but that was stupid."

"If he fires me, I'll go to Paulie's." She tried to work up her anger again, to sound as if she didn't care. "People do get out of Blue Claw."

Rick stepped inside and shut the door behind him. "I don't want to crush your dreams, but if you apprentice with anybody but your brother, you're going to be working a lot of nights on your knees." He stuck the lollipop into his mouth.

"Really?" Gina stared at him. "I'm used to the bullshit comments from everyone else. But you, too?"

"I'm not saying let everything slide, but come on. What if I threw a toolbox every time somebody said something asinine to me?"

"Dominic would never talk to you like that. Here, give me your jacket. Come upstairs." She hung it by the door. "Jeri's making him spineless. Did Mackie tell you what he said when I brought up Diana?"

"You think that attitude's new?"

"That's not the Dominic I know."

"Boy, is love blind." Rick snorted. "So you've never seen a customer come in, take one look at me, and say to Dominic, 'I don't want the Mexican.' And Dom says 'You want *this* Mexican. This is the hardest-working Mexican you'll meet in your life.'"

"At least he's standing up for you."

Rick leaned in to look her in the eye. "Really, Gina? If that don't make you cringe—" He followed her up the stairs to Connie's living room, tossed his lollipop in the trash, and sat back on the couch, foot propped on one knee. She curled up on the other end.

"How about this one. Customer casually refers to me as a spic." His jaw was tight. "And Dom pretends he doesn't hear. Now, if it's so obvious he can't ignore it, maybe he fires a little warning shot, but if the guy shuts up after that, Dom lets him stay. Better to keep the peace, right?" Rick stretched his arm along the back of the couch. On the inside of his forearm was La Virgen de Guadalupe, black and gray, her perfectly shaded robe an expanse of stars. "Have you ever seen him demand an apology from one of those guys?"

Gina shook her head, achy inside, heartsick. He was right. She leaned her head against the couch pillow.

"Or wait—here's one. Your brother's got somebody in the chair, I'm across the room, the customer yells over"—he affected a gruff Long Island accent—"*Where you from, man?* I'm from California. *No, but where your people are from.* CALIFORNIA. Where I was born." Rick looked up at the ceiling, fingers on his temples, as if channeling the conversation. "*Man, you speak great English. Like, you know more words than I do.* Like he's surprised I'm not sitting there wearing a zarape, sombrero, and leather chanclas made from tire treads. Dominic says, *Well, no shit, this hombre reads more books in a week than you read in your life.* I hold my tongue because I'm not wasting my energy telling every idiot off the street I grew up speaking English. And yes, I probably have read more books than that guy, by a long shot. Now the customer checks out that picture of my cousins. *Those your sisters? Those Hispanic girls are fiery, right?* Or—"

"Okay. Okay."

Rick stopped and turned toward her. "Really? Okay?"

"Not okay. I mean—" Gina's body felt heavy. An hour ago, she could've painted the whole apartment on the power of pure rage. Now she slumped into the couch, exhausted. "I'm so sorry. For not seeing. For not thinking. God, I am so sorry. Why don't you talk to him?"

Rick gave her a look she'd never seen on his face before: *You are so naive.* "First of all, you're sure I haven't?" He rubbed his Guadalupe tattoo, just above his new wrist tattoo, words Gina couldn't read. "And what about you? Do *you* tell him everything? How you don't like it when you come into the shop and Mackie's got porn going on the VCR? You ever tell him it's obnoxious when you come up with an idea and he ignores it—"

"And then the next day he's got this brilliant new idea," Gina said. "And it's mine."

"Or have you ever told Dominic"—Rick fixed his eyes on her—"that you don't like the way he talks down to you?"

"I told him today."

"Why not before?"

"What am I going to do, point out every little thing?" She pressed her thumbs into a couch pillow. "Pretty soon it's *Oh, Gina can't hack it. Gina's so sensitive.* If I stopped to protest every stupid thing, I'd never get any actual work done." She had never thought about this before; it was just how you got along. How much energy did that take every day? Absorbing a thousand sideways putdowns, acting as if they hadn't happened, so she could do the work she wanted to.

Rick held his palms up. "Then we understand each other."

She stared over at her half-finished mural with its smears of pearl red and alizarin crimson. "Fine." She looked him in the eye. "You want me to point things out, I'll start with you."

"Go on."

"You said nobody's going to hire me unless I put out. And I just want to say—" She took a breath. "That was some super-obnoxious, Mackie-quality disrespect."

"Eso, tell it like it is." Rick grinned. "So throw a toolbox at me."

Gina got to the gas station the next day as sunrise broke, weak red on pewter gray. An hour into her shift, Dominic drove up in his Maverick.

She turned toward his gas cap and spoke in a flat voice. "Leaded or unleaded?"

When Dominic didn't answer, she glanced back at him. His lips were set in a hard line. He looked like hell. His eyelashes were crusty with sleep gunk and his newly short hair was all flattened on one side. Not used to waking up at dawn like she did. "You will never, ever do that again. What the hell is wrong with you? Got your period or something?"

"Don't you dare talk to me like that."

"Then don't pull shit like that. I can't have people talking about some crazy girl throwing fits at my shop. Especially when everybody knows about Mom."

"Big for my britches?" Gina said. "Really?"

"People need to see discipline. You were purposely undermining me."

"I'm not putting on a show for Keith Yearly. Jeri was supposed to come out here and confront him. Now we're kissing his ass? Is that the new policy?"

"Gina!" Sam appeared in the gas station door, gesturing at the cars pulling in.

She straightened up. "You buying gas, or what?"

Dominic jerked his wallet out of his pocket and gave her a five. "Leaded."

She put the nozzle in the tank. "Are you even going to apologize?"

He stuck his head out the window. "*Me?* For what?"

"Humiliating me in front of a total stranger, maybe?"

He rolled his eyes. "I'm sorry you felt insulted."

At least Stella apologized for the actual awful thing she did. Dominic only apologized for your regrettable sensitivity. *Sorry you felt so threatened*, she wanted to say. "Fine. I'm sorry I dropped your toolbox. Now what?"

"Jeri says you're on probation. If her dad was there, you'd have been fired."

"I hate these people," Gina said.

"If you want to do serious work, you need clients who can pay for it. Nobody wins trophies tattooing a thousand little Tasmanian devils." A Jeep behind Dominic beeped its horn. Dominic craned out the window, lifted his hands in a *what do you want* gesture, and turned back to Gina. "Dress code starts tomorrow."

"What?"

"Your new uniform." He handed her a bag out the window. "In November we're hitting a conference in California—"

"We who?" Gina looked him in the eye. "You and Jeri?"

"Of course me and Jeri." The Jeep driver leaned on his horn. Dominic gave him the finger.

"Remember when you said you'd take *me* to a convention?"

"And one day we will." He scratched his stubble. "You're so convinced this'll turn out bad for you. You can't see the future."

"Can't I?" Gina said.

Thirty-two

Fall Quarter: Benchmarks & Requirements

TO BE COMPLETED by Check-in Meeting #2,

FRIDAY, DECEMBER 20

***Create NEW flash poster of TASTEFUL, CHIC designs to be used for free practice tattoos (i.e. no pizza toppings, merit badges etc.).

***DECEMBER: Begin small practice tattoos on friends and other volunteers for free.

Discipline.

In the weeks after Jeri's Vision meeting, Gina assembled and disassembled her machine with military precision. She attacked her tattooing practice, all those roses and sailor stars, as if failing to render them perfectly would mean an Earth barren of flora, heavens bare of constellations.

She wore the uniform issued by Harrison Entertainment, which looked suspiciously like a beautician's tunic paired with the kind of pants her mother called "slacks." The guys, spared the tunic, were provided with button-downs—everything freshly embroidered with the new logo for Mulley's Fine Art Tattoo Studio.

With her considerable discipline, Gina even refrained from calling the shop MulleyFATS—occasionally extended to Mulleyfatter's—in front of Dominic, as she did privately with Rick; nor did she act on her strong impulse to answer the phone with these new names.

She worked hard. She behaved. And every night, when the tattoo shop's brand-new art deco wall clock chimed nine times, Gina promptly drove away.

This disciplined precision allowed her to arrive at the North Shore Diner just in time to meet Anna at the end of her shift, at which point they went back to Nicolas's house, avoiding the creaky boards so they wouldn't wake him, and talked in Anna's room for hours. Gina always pretended not to hear the clock striking midnight, because she never wanted to leave.

Showers weren't part of the routine, but tonight Anna had a braid full of maple syrup, so Gina found herself trying not to stare at Anna's silhouette, blurred through the frosted glass shower door, as she kept her company.

The rush of the water made a wall of white noise. Gina raised her voice. "They said I can't repaint the mural."

Anna turned the water off. The door slid open a crack; her arm emerged and grabbed a towel. "I don't want to wake him," she whispered. "What?"

Gina lowered her voice. "A crew repainted the entire shop today. The whole place is escrow."

"In escrow? They're selling it?"

"No. Escrow, the color. Like beige if it got scared."

"Ecru?"

"Yeah, that." Gina twisted the rug fringe, making a tiny rope. "And Jeri said we're not doing murals because we need the negative space."

Anna wrapped her hair in the towel and stepped out of the shower, smelling of peppermint soap. Gina's face began to burn. She should've been used to bare skin, working at a tattoo shop. But it felt different when the naked person was your intensely attractive friend, and she was all wet, and not in a terrible hurry to put her clothes back on.

Was it her imagination, or did Anna do these things on purpose? Greeting her *Hey, beautiful,* or letting her hand linger at Gina's waist just long enough to seem meaningful?

Anna nudged Gina with her toe, gesturing toward her bedroom. Gina scrambled up and closed the door behind them as Anna wrapped herself in a wine-red kimono.

"They painted the bathroom mauve." Gina's chest had been aching all week. "The whole place feels wrong."

"That agreement you signed—is it legally binding? Could you quit?"

"I wouldn't even if I could. This is the only job that takes care of all the nots."

"What knots?"

Gina opened her sketchbook to a bookmarked page.

REASONS I SHOULD BECOME A TATTOOER

#1

I already know a lot. You barely need to train me.

Just the actual tattooing.

#2

This job solves my whole pile of Nots, such as:

Not boring

Not like Mom's jobs

College not needed

"If those are your only criteria," Anna said, "you might as well come work for Nicolas."

"Read number three," Gina said.

#3

I belong here. I could be so good at this.

We could make this a real family business

and I could help you.

"Maybe you still will," Anna said. "Maybe they'll break up and Jeri will cut her losses and go. Wait it out. Focus on this."

She took a pencil and circled *I could be so good at this.*

"Let work be work," Anna said. "Don't expect so much of it. And if you need a place to belong, come over and belong with me."

"That means a lot," Gina said. "More than I can say."

Anna was studying her. Gina met her eyes, dark and alert, and felt a tingle along her arms. It was so quiet she could hear their breathing.

Abruptly Anna looked away. She gave her hair one last tousle and threw the towel across the room. "I'm thinking of moving out."

"Did something happen?"

"The anniversary is coming up." She stood and turned the dimmer on the wall; the chandelier light sank to a dim glow. "It's making me think about life. And this is a strange life."

"What anniversary?"

Anna opened an ornate cabinet painted with Japanese birds and took out an open bottle of wine. "You remember how I ended up here?"

"You dropped out of school," Gina said. "You needed a place. He had a room."

Anna poured two glasses of wine and brought one to Gina. "I dropped out because my sister died. Two years ago in December."

What to say, except the things people always said? *Sorry for your loss?* So thin, so insufficient. "What was her name?"

"Daniela Alma Dellarocca. That hat in my car, with the initials—that's hers." She pointed up at the Stella Maris painting. "That, too. She was such a troublemaker in church, but she had a thing for Mary. I haven't set foot in a church since her funeral. If I heard one more person say *She's in a better place* I was going to scream. She liked *this* place. Earth. She wanted to travel. Collected all these knickknacks." Anna picked up the Russian nesting doll. "You drink wine?"

Gina didn't, generally, except when Stella insisted, but she took a sip. The wine was velvet red, sweeter than she'd expected. "What happened?"

Anna opened the nesting doll. "She had a heart defect. We didn't know."

"How come you didn't tell me?"

"Didn't know if you were safe yet." Anna opened the next doll, and then the next, lining them up on the nightstand. "Anyway. After the funeral I finished out the semester, but I was a zombie. I didn't really know Nicolas; we'd talked on class breaks, just casual, here and there. But after the last class, we ended up in this deep conversation. I told him, *I don't know how to move home if Daniela's not there.* Finally she came to the tiniest of the dolls—no bigger than a bean. Anna held it in her palm, as if protecting it.

"And this was really generous of him." Anna gestured up at the room. "And for a while it was fine." Her voice did not at all sound like it was fine. She took a long drink. "But I keep thinking, I'm about to be twenty-one. In five minutes I'll be forty. How you spend your days is how you spend your years is how you've spent your life."

Anna put the bean-sized doll at the end of the line, all those pear-shaped wooden women in a row. "I think I need to go."

"When?"

Anna shrugged. "I start to plan, and then I worry about money. And get overwhelmed by the classifieds. Next thing you know, my mind's going a mile a minute, and somehow Nicolas knows it, and he's saying, *Vould you like to smoke a bit viss me?* And I put it off again."

"Smoke what? Weed?"

Anna laughed. "No, cigars. Yes, weed. Do you smoke?"

"Socially, I guess?" If she counted her tenure at the Cheshire Cat. Right now she couldn't imagine wanting anything stronger than this wine. Already she was feeling pleasantly buzzy.

"Well, we're very social. If you want to join us." Anna crossed the room, flopped down on her bed, and patted the space next to her.

Gina joined her. "I'm kind of on call the next two weeks. My brother's traveling." Dominic and Jeri were leaving tomorrow, Wednesday, to spend the Thanksgiving weekend with her family in Staten Island; then flying out to California for the tattoo convention, then a road trip to some tattoo shops Dominic wanted to see. This afternoon, he'd sat Rick, Mackie, and Gina down for a meeting. *No drama while I'm gone. No ammo for Yearly. If you get a problem customer, deal with it quietly. If something catches fire, try your damnedest to put it out because I don't want so much as a fire truck showing up.* She was supposed to work almost every night Dom was gone, two straight weeks, keeping *everything buttoned up.*

Gina took another drink and was surprised to find her glass empty.

Anna smiled. "Slow down, girl. That's not fruit punch." She put her glass on the cedar chest and played with Gina's hair.

"Maybe I can get a night off this week."

"Nicolas would like that. He's been asking after you." Anna gathered a section of Gina's hair and began to braid. "No pressure, though." The braiding felt heavenly. "I like having you to myself."

That kind of remark wasn't an accident. People didn't talk like that unless they meant something by it.

Gina's scalp tingled under Anna's fingers. Somehow, she managed to speak. "That feels so nice."

Anna curled the braid around her finger. "*You're* so nice."

Gina snorted. "Is that your pickup line when you go out? *You're nice?*"

Anna laughed and tugged Gina's hair. "Shut up."

Gina tugged Anna's hair back.

"Oh, you want to start something?" Anna took hold of Gina's hoodie strings and pulled her closer, closer than Gina had expected, and she wasn't quite sure who started it, but suddenly they were kissing.

Just as quickly, Anna pulled away from her. She rose from the bed, wobbly. "This is trouble."

What trouble? Trouble seemed an impossible thing right now. Gina stood, too. She looked up at Anna's dark eyes, close enough to smell the peppermint soap on her skin. "Do you want me to go?"

Anna looked away. "Maybe. I don't know. Sober up first. I'll be normal tomorrow." But she just kept standing there, a handbreadth away from

Gina, and didn't seem to be going anywhere. And there was Anna's warm soft mouth, and then they were kissing again, Gina sliding her hands up the satin folds of Anna's kimono. Anna's fingertips were traveling along the back of Gina's neck and her skin tingled like sparkles on water; every atom of her was fizzing, dizzy like the whirl of the Zipper at the carnival, that feeling of flying face-to-face with the sky—

"Wait," Anna breathed, but she kept one hand in Gina's back pocket, as if making sure she couldn't leave. "Wait."

Gina stopped. "What?"

"I had something to ask you tonight." She collapsed her forehead onto Gina's shoulder. "And this would make it complicated. I was going to ask you to be my roommate when I move out." After a moment, she pulled away and sat down on the bed. "I don't know. Think about it."

Think about it? Gina could have coffee every morning with someone who actually liked her. A place that smelled like cedar and bread, with Anna's curios crowding the windowsills like good luck charms. Snow days watching movies on Anna's VCR, a bowl of butter-wet popcorn between them, on a couch with no plastic. Never having to leave when the clock struck midnight.

"We could get a parrot." Anna paused. "Parrots are expensive. We could get a parakeet."

Five minutes ago, getting a parakeet together would've sounded like a lot of fun. But if she had to choose between whatever *this* might become and a bird . . .

"If we just rewind five minutes and start over," Anna said, "then we can get a place and it's not weird. It can be fun and simple, and . . . doesn't that sound good?"

"It does sound good. But the past two minutes were . . ." Ecstasy. A revelation. "More than good." Gina took Anna's hand. "We can't have both?"

Anna turned away, picked up the nesting doll on the nightstand, and snapped its halves back together. "This is a friendship I don't want to mess up."

"So we pretend this never happened," Gina said. As if that were possible. Those ten seconds of kissing would ruin her concentration for days.

"People do impulsive things, right? It doesn't mean anything. We just— stay cool."

"And then what? I get to kiss you again one day? Or we just get a couple of boyfriends?"

Anna started laughing. "Do you need to know the future? Maybe we're nuns."

"We are not nuns," Gina said.

Anna propped her head on her hand. "Says Saint Regina, who can't even hang out this week because Dominic said *Behave*."

"Not a saint," Gina said. "Just disciplined."

Thirty-three

On the way home that night, Gina accidentally drove five miles past Blue Claw and had to make a U-turn, just thinking about that kiss.

When she got into bed, she rested her head on her arm and caught a lingering scent of Anna—peppermint and incense and something else that was just Anna. With her eyes closed, it was impossible to think of anything but that soft mouth, her fingertips on the back of Gina's neck.

So this was what desire felt like. So tense and so full that it almost hurt.

People do impulsive things, Anna had said. *It doesn't mean anything.*

But sometimes people did impulsive things that told the truth.

The tattoo shop was tense the next night. Dominic's warning—*no trouble*—felt so present that it might have been spray-painted across the ecru wall. *No trouble*, but it was the night before Thanksgiving, a night of booze and brawl second only to St. Paddy's Day. *No trouble*, but it was also a full moon, which always brought wild cards through the door.

Gina was supposed to be on alert. Instead, all day, her thoughts kept straying back to Anna's room.

Should trouble come, Rick was good at defusing it, but he'd been occupied for two hours tattooing a spear-wielding angel on a big, solid arm. "Did you know," said the owner of the arm, "that Saint Michael is the patron saint of law enforcement?"

"You got family on the force?" Rick said.

"I'm on the force."

Rick gave Gina a sideways look. *Trouble* would be especially troubling if it included the phrase *police involved*.

Sunset was darkening to twilight, and all Gina wanted was to strip off the MFATS tunic, get in her rusty Cricket, and drive away. She had to find something to drag her mind back into her body.

"Rick. I'm going to tattoo myself."

She was supposed to start practicing on actual humans when Dominic got home, and although she'd tattooed a crate's worth of citrus fruit and pigskin, she'd never tattooed herself. It was overdue.

Rick didn't blink. "Go for it."

"Where should I work?"

"Dom's space. Be careful."

Gina pulled one of their old acetate stencils. Nothing elaborate: a classic star. She changed into a pair of cutoffs she had left in the back office so she could work on her leg—easy to reach, and the tattoo would be hidden.

Maybe it was the adrenaline kick, maybe the fearful concentration, but this, finally, did the trick. Unlike with grapefruit flesh, she had to coordinate two hands, one to tattoo and one to stretch her skin, all the while trying to make the straightest lines of her life. After half an hour, the fog cleared.

She finished just as Rick was ringing up the cop. "Law enforcement discount," he said. The cop gave him a friendly slap on the back. As soon as he was gone, Rick's shoulders dropped.

"Nice touch," said Mackie, who had shown up for an appointment with Danny, his metalhead friend.

Rick wiped his forehead. "I'm starving. Running out to the deli."

With the cop's departure, it felt like a fever broke. Her post-tattoo endorphins were kicking in; she felt calmer, and when she looked down at the new star on her thigh, she decided it wasn't terrible. She settled into a chair and watched Mackie add color to Danny's newest Elvira, shading the scarlet blot of her mouth.

Tires crunched on crumbling asphalt. Gina looked up, out the front window, expecting to see Rick parallel parking at the curb. Instead, she saw a convertible, black and sleek as a shined shoe, swerving to stop suddenly in front of the shop.

"Is that Jeri's dad's car?" she said.

It jerked toward the curb at an angle so sharp that Gina tensed, waiting for its headlight to smash against the lamppost. At the last second, it wobbled itself straight.

Mackie glanced up. "Yuppies off to the Hamptons. Maybe they got lost."

Two young men climbed out of the car. The passenger wore khakis and an Oxford shirt; the driver, dark chinos, a broad-shouldered blazer.

"Gina," Mackie said. "Go tell them we're closing."

"You're turning down business? You?"

"They look like trouble."

Gina shook her head. "They look like money."

The khaki guy gaped at the scuff on the bumper. The driver—windburned across the cheeks, with a boyish sweep of sandy hair—didn't even notice. They stared through the Mulley's window for a minute, as if at a zoo exhibit, before the driver took the lead.

"Evening, gentlemen," he said. "We'd like to browse the gallery."

"Gallery's closing," Mackie said sharply. "Gina, can you give these guys a card and merrily they roll along?"

The khaki friend had already wandered over to shake Gina's hand. "Morgan Kenning."

"Gina Mulley."

"Preston, look. They have *Jaws*." Morgan pressed his finger to Gina's sea creature flash, which Jeri had deemed acceptable because it was "Contemporary Nautical."

"That's a night shark," Gina said. "I drew it."

"You are *so* talented," said Morgan. Was he mocking her? "Preston, you get this shark and I guarantee Blair's all over you tonight." Was he slurring? Shop rules said no tattoos under the influence, but there were no rules against browsing. They were polite, at least.

"Blair with the baby face?" Preston said.

"She's freaky, that girl. Be the man with"—Morgan paused dramatically—"the *night shark*."

"I am a night shark." Preston tripped over the coffee table and managed to catch himself before he fell headfirst into Dominic's trophy.

Morgan, still standing unsteadily by Gina's flash, smiled at her. He had an underbite, with canines slightly cockeyed; she'd expected perfect white teeth, like an actor's. "Just driving by. Up for some fun."

"Buffy," Mackie growled. "You dropped your flask. It's leaking on my floor." Preston looked down. Gina had never seen anything like that flask: a luster like silver, an intricate monogram on the side.

"Did you know," Gina said, "Victorian aristocrats got tattooed with their family crests?"

"Gina," Mackie said. "For the seventh time—give them a card. We're locking up."

She handed Morgan a card and then looked at Mackie, shrugging. What else did he want? Nobody was getting rowdy. Dominic didn't grant him the authority to close the shop because he was irritated.

Preston took the chair nearest Gina and leaned in. "If you like the flask, check out the car. BMW Three series. Two months on the bond-trading floor and those are my wheels. After Yale—"

"Gina. Show us your classics," Morgan interrupted. "Show us what you give the tough guys."

Gina hesitated, but got up. She felt his eyes on her as she walked over to the traditional flash she'd hand-colored, the venerable anchors and eagles. When she turned around, Preston was half smiling. "What?"

"You're charming, that's all. They ever let you out of this hole-in-the-wall? Baby, are you corgi Zen—" Preston paused, staring up at the ceiling. "Corgi Zen . . ."

"I'm no religion in particular."

"Cognizant. Cognizant that . . . Forget it. Baby, do you know they throw tattoo parties out in the big city? Hush-hush, like a speakeasy."

Morgan clapped his hands. "Sondra." He pawed at his pockets until he found a slim silver case. "My girlfriend throws a rooftop soiree every summer." He handed Gina a card. "She could plan the Macy's parade, she's that good. This year it's a circus. Preston, wouldn't she love a tattoo lady?"

"Gina can't tattoo," Mackie snapped.

"Of course she can. Call me around New Year's."

She felt a hand on her waist. Preston leaned in closer. "It's my birthday, you know." His cologne smelled dark and woodsy, like fermented pine sap. Her body tensed.

"Want to give me that tattoo"—he pointed to his biceps—"and tag along for some fun in Montauk?"

Mackie abruptly put his machine down. He pushed past Gina's chair, the rough denim of his jeans scuffing her arm, and pulled Preston's hand away.

"We do tattoos only. That's it. No bonus shit on the side. And you talk to me, not her."

"Relax, chief. She can't speak forself?" Preston paused. "Didn't you rednecks get women's lib yet? Out here in the shticks?"

"Time to go."

Preston rose out of the chair so his face was a brick's width away from Mackie's. "I said relax, my friend."

"And I said get the hell out or I'm going to escort you."

"Mackie," Gina breathed. "Not in here. Dominic."

"Get the door," Mackie said. She darted outside to hold it open. The temperature had dropped; she shivered.

Mackie steered Preston by the shoulders, walked him to the doorway, and shoved him out onto the sidewalk. Preston turned, grabbed Mackie by the shirt, and pulled him out along with him.

Mackie fell forward. Gina's stomach turned. Preston took a crooked swing at Mackie's face, but he only managed to graze his ear. Mackie was already getting his footing, grabbing Preston by the wrist, hooking his foot around his ankle. He swept it out from under him and in a split-second Mackie had him on the sidewalk, flat on his back; he was straddling him, landing punches, and then there was blood—

Everything happened so fast. Somewhere beyond the ringing in her ears, there was faraway shouting. The world was a blur except for the blood running down that guy's mouth and his head straining to turn away from Mackie's fist, trying to roll to the side. Mackie pinned him facedown on the sidewalk.

"Maybe this wasn't the best plan, boss," Mackie said, his mouth next to Preston's ear. "How about you get back in your Bimmer and run off to Daddy's summer house before this gets worse."

Heads were poking out of doors on Midway Street. This fight would be tomorrow's gossip. At least a dozen people watched the men stumble into the BMW and peel out, eastbound, and as the red rectangles of the tail-lights shrank to a distant blur, two more men came running.

One was Rick. One was the cop Rick had just tattooed. Within a minute, another cop car had arrived. A minute more and Mackie was in the back of it.

G ina watched the silhouette of Mackie's head staring stoically forward, as police lights threw choppy flashes of blue and red across the front of Mulley's Tattoo.

Gina shivered. Rick pressed his hand on her shoulder. "Go inside."

"Wait," said the cop. "Tell us what happened."

Gina twisted her hands. "The drunk guy who started it—his name was Preston. It was a BMW. I didn't get the plates."

The second officer ducked into the car and began to talk into his radio. Even when the crowd filtered away and they let her go inside, they still hadn't released Mackie. Soon, another car pulled up and a woman got out to take pictures.

Gina couldn't watch. She filled a bucket with steaming water and mopped the floor, filling the shop with the smell of pine.

After a while, Rick came inside. "They radioed to Southampton. They'll look out for the car. Mr. Laundromat got the plates."

Gina stopped mopping. "Did they arrest—"

Mackie was right behind him. Her shoulders dropped in relief.

"Hermano," Rick said to Mackie, "you are so damn lucky that cop liked me."

They were still shivering. Rick had goose bumps on the tattooed roses that bloomed thick as a garden around the Lady of Guadalupe. Mackie grabbed his jacket.

"I think Dominic would call this 'not ideal,'" Rick said.

Gina pressed her fingernails into her palm. "Do we have to tell him?"

"If you want to, knock yourself out," Mackie said. "I'm going home, killing a six-pack, and passing out."

Gina turned to Rick. "You?"

"We could call him at the Harrisons' right now and ruin his Thanksgiving." Rick rubbed his arms. "Or call him Friday and ruin his California trip. Or wait till he gets home."

Gina used the mop scrubber to grind miserably at a stain on the floor. "Three, I guess. Let's do option three."

Thirty-four

Gina called Anna to tell her the story; Nicolas picked up in the other room and chimed in, making sympathetic noises. *Come, come. It would be a delight.*

Gina changed out of the MFATS tunic and cutoffs into her own comforting jeans and slouchy shirt, and headed for Shoreham.

She felt a tug in her chest when Anna opened the door. Her thick waves were pinned up on her head, eyes done up with kohl, and she was wearing a flowy shift dress that Gina had never seen. "You look beautiful."

"Fresh from a reading," Anna said, and Gina knew, because they could read each other now, that this was not true; Anna had gotten made up for her, which was wonderful and terrible, because she was not allowed to say anything else.

Anna's hug was brief and friendly, a hug for a sister-in-law. And when they got to Nicolas's room and he beckoned them to the floor to sit on huge cushions—big enough to share, like sliced plums from a giant's orchard— Anna waited for Gina to settle in, and sat six feet away.

What did Gina want from her, really? Anna was doing what they'd agreed on: putting the kiss behind them. On a train wreck of a night like this one, she was lucky to have any kind of friend to turn to.

Nicolas's room was high-ceilinged like Anna's, with a four-poster bed between two tall windows, sparsely adorned. Anna shuffled through Nicolas's record collection. "Your brother's not really going to blame you, is he?"

"He told me a hundred times Mackie and Rick were in charge," Gina said. "Mackie said close up shop. I didn't do it. We ended up with a big scene. The worst thing you can do to Dominic is publicly embarrass him."

"Why talk of troubles? Relax." Nicolas lit the candles arrayed on his bureau. "And Anna, good God, choose a record."

Gina leaned against the wall, eyes closed. The record player crackled, a throaty woman's voice warbling in French. She felt a tap on her hand; Nicolas was holding out a lighter, along with an emerald-green glass pipe. "Go on," he said. "Have it."

"Take it, you mean," Anna said. "*Have it* means *keep it*."

He shrugged. "English. Take it and have it, if you like." He smiled. "We are generous in the House of Mystical Delights."

Gina held the flame to the bowl, drew in a lungful, and managed not to cough. She handed it to Anna. "I should've called Dominic. It's going to be worse if he hears it from Mackie first."

Anna exhaled a gentle cloud of smoke. "Will Rick back you up?"

"Anna, müusli, shhh." Nicolas handed Gina a chocolate in gold foil. "Gina, try. Zurich's star chocolatier."

The quiet was coming on fast, the gentle unraveling of the edges. This was better stuff than she'd ever smoked in her life. The chocolate was velvet on her tongue. "Nicolas. Give me some clairvoyant guidance."

"Only happy things tonight." He flexed his fingers in a slow wave, as if radiating energy only he could see. "Tell me about yourself, Gina Mulley, star of the Cheshire Cat."

She opened her eyes. "How do you know about the Cheshire Cat?"

"Give me a break," Anna said. "That head shop is his candy store."

Nicolas unwrapped a chocolate, fingers languid. "I used to see you making incense in the back. Eyes down. Such focus. I thought if I dared pay you a compliment, I might scare you to death."

Gina flicked the lighter, inhaled. "That was my longest job ever."

"You were good at it," Nicolas said.

"I was." It was the first job she'd ever felt good at, in that renovated barn with its door painted electric tangerine, rafters dripping with colored beads. Jim Morrison on the record player crooning *People are strange*—but when she was there, she never felt strange.

"This is so weird." Gina watched the incense spiral into the air, curlicues in space. "My words are speaking me."

Anna's laugh was rain on the surface of a pool, splash and ripple, and Gina was immersed in it. She tried to speak, but now she was laughing, too, falling apart in laughter; who would want to leave this?

"It was a good place for you," Nicolas purred. "They understood you there."

How stupid of her, actually, to treat Mulley's like it was the only place she belonged. She never would've left the Cheshire Cat if it weren't for the thing with her boss. Gary: a chubby guy with a baby face, who recited *The Hitchhiker's Guide to the Galaxy* from memory, and left work every day saying *So long, and thanks for all the fish.*

One night, the whole crew went out for drinks. The bartender was Gary's buddy, which is how Gina ended up drinking Long Island iced teas when she was still more than a year away from the legal nineteen. The drinks were sweet as cola, Gina and Gary were the last to linger, and as she was trying to tie a maraschino cherry stem into a knot, he'd said, "Time is an illusion."

Gina, who had been listening to his *Hitchhiker* recitations for eight months at that point, answered: "Lunchtime doubly so."

Gary smiled. "You know what you are?"

Sober Gina would have kept silent and thought: *Beanstalk? Stray cat? Old balloon tied to a mailbox?* Drinking Gina said: "Sleepy?"

"A connoisseur of hidden talents." Gary took the cherry stem and knotted it for her. "Ready for mine? I can remove earrings with my mouth."

Gina started laughing. "No, you can't."

"I'll prove it," he said. "Come out to my starship *Heart of Gold.*"

He seemed about twenty—not thirty, as she'd later discover—and too dorky to be a womanizer, let alone a married one. But they'd been in Gary's van for about ten minutes, and he'd removed a few items of Gina's clothing along with her earrings, when an angry woman threw open the door.

Were those Nicolas's fingers in her hair now? He was speaking low and gentle. "It wasn't your fault."

Had she just told that whole story out loud? The room was warm and drowsy. "I shouldn't have gotten fired. Nobody said—about the—I didn't know he had a wife." Words were effort. He knew what she meant.

"You can't be held responsible. It wasn't you who broke the rules." Exactly. Gratitude washed over her. If she weren't so sleepy, she'd smile at him.

Leaning her head back into some comfy lap, eyes closed, she heard Nicolas saying something else. Maybe it didn't matter what. Her shoulders were softening. Limbs melting. On the window above Nicolas's head, the frost made a net of glass—astonishing.

Thirty-five

When Gina woke, alone on Nicolas's four-poster bed, the candles were out. No noise but the soft tick of a clock.

Woozy, thirsty, she got up, untangling herself from Nicolas's blanket. Except for the glow of the nautilus shell nightlight, the hallway was dark. She paused at Anna's doorway; Anna and Nicolas were sleeping, sprawled across opposite sides of the bed.

She felt a twinge, seeing them there—Nicolas, allowed to be in Anna's bed, allowed that closeness. Anna, who gave that to him.

Gina turned away.

She felt her way down the stairs to the kitchen, filled a mug with water, and took it to the living room, steadying herself on the wall. The room tilted dizzily. Did she remember a bottle of wine? Something stronger, maybe? She slouched on Nicolas's violet brocade couch.

The floor creaked upstairs, followed by the click of a door, the faucet running. Bare feet padded down to her.

"Hello, night owl." Nicolas wore fresh linen pants. His eyes were bright and his hair tousled, as if he hadn't been sleeping at all, but out for a walk in a refreshing breeze. He reached for her mug and looked at the painted design, a hawk perched on a falconer's hand. *"With empty hand men may none haukes lure. For wynnyng wolde I al his lust endure . . ."*

It was too late at night for this. "I don't know German."

"Middle English. Don't they teach Chaucer anymore?" He sat down next to her, unlatched a wooden box, and turned it over onto the coffee table; a snowdrift of tarot cards tumbled across the surface.

"I can't pay you—"

"Gratis. Let us delve into the mystery of Gina Mulley."

Nicolas turned over a card. *The Moon.* A somber moon frowned down on a wolf and dog trapped together on a narrow island. A lobster crawled out of the sea.

"Fantasy, distractions, illusions. You must decide what you want and take action. You need a vision."

Gina yawned. "I already had a vision."

He put his feet up, looking amused. "I love a good epiphany. Go on."

"The night before my birthday—"

"What auspicious timing."

"I was sitting by the river, and I saw myself working at my brother's shop. I was a real artist, making people happy with my tattoos. I belonged there." She sipped the water. "That's it."

Nicolas pointed to the bottle of Williamine on the table, the one Anna had brought out on Gina's first visit. *A pair of teeth. Aperitif.* "Do you know how they got that pear in there?" She'd never noticed—the pear was far too large to fit through the narrow neck of the bottle.

"They put the bottle over the branch when the fruit is small," Nicolas said. "By the time it's grown, it's trapped inside." He held the pile out to her. "Take the top card."

The Star, it said. A naked woman poured rivers of water from two pitchers. Above her, a many-pointed star blazed brilliant, with little white stars all around it.

"Inspiration. Hope." Nicolas took her hand and uncurled her fingers. He drew a pen from his pocket and wrote a word on her palm: *Sternli*.

"Little star," he said. "You can't imagine the potential I see in you." He opened a drawer in the table and took out a calendar. "I'd like to make a tattoo appointment with you."

Gina shook her head. "Go to a professional. I'm just starting."

"Experience isn't everything." He reached into the drawer again, pulled out an ornate money clip, and handed her a crisp bill. "My deposit. I'd wait six months for the chance, if you'll agree."

She looked at the money in her hand and dropped it, stunned. A hundred-dollar bill. "Seven or eight months, at least. I'm not allowed to charge yet."

"Artists need to eat." He put the money back in her hands and hovered his pen over a calendar square. "I'm choosing a date. Unless you're really going to turn me down?"

If Jeri docked her pay, she was going to need this money. "Okay."

He marked the date and sank back onto the velvet brocade of his couch. "Relax," he said, nudging her head onto his shoulder. "Sternli, with the future ahead of you, a man like me will be—how does one say it? A little potato?" He tapped his temple. "Small potatoes."

She smiled. "You're just trying to make me laugh now."

He wrapped a strand of her hair around his finger. "Why not? You should laugh more." He moved his hand to her lower back and spoke in a low voice. "Is your offer still open?"

Gina paused. "What did I offer again?"

"You said you and Gary didn't get very far. I asked if you were curious to go farther. Signs pointed to yes."

A quiet shiver, suddenly, like standing at the edge of a canyon.

"I won't press if you've changed your mind. But if you're worried about Anna," Nicolas said, "she's not possessive."

That much was obvious. Anna seemed to be tiring of Nicolas quickly, and had no interest in Gina at all.

Her mouth felt dry. "I'm not that interesting." Gina, walking aquarium for the grotesque wing-finned trancefish. Gina, who'd allowed herself the stupid risk of kissing Anna one time, which was enough for Anna to realize she'd had enough.

"I'd like to show you otherwise." Nicolas's breath was warm on her neck.

She hesitated. So strange, to be spoken to like this. It was hard to believe he meant it. "How far do you want to go?"

She couldn't see his face, but she felt him smile.

"Well," he said. "Let us embark and see."

G ina didn't enter his bedroom planning to lose her virginity. She didn't exactly plan not to, either. But one thing began blurring into the next, first his kisses on her neck, then her lips, and then her shirt was on the floor. The thought came floating *Maybe I'll go*, but then he started murmuring, *I want this for you*, and she felt something like a flicker of desire and let the thought go. Her jeans were being wriggled off her and she was letting that happen, and when the thought came again—*I could go*—he muttered, *Gina, you enchanting little creature, you perfect little thing.*

And with one swift move, he was flipping her onto her stomach, gripping her wrists, the bed pressing painfully against the new tattoo on her thigh, and breathing: "Let me have you." It was so surprising that the words stopped up in her throat. She could leave now, she could say, *No, that's enough, thank you—*

"Say *have me*," Nicolas said, low in her ear. "I want this for you." Dominic would say *Get the hell out of there*.

But she was only halfway in her body now, dizzy, thinking of anything else, even her car, the little Cricket, and she saw it in her mind rusted fender to fender, frightening. Look at the wall clock, then. 4:37, 4:38—*I'm fine, I'm fine, I'm fine.*

Thirty-six

Gina knew this about the timeline of her jeans:

She pulled them back on around 4:45.

At some uncertain hour before sunrise, when she got home to her own bed, she worked them off again.

They lay on her bedroom floor until she woke up at noon.

You should go before she wakes up, he'd said when he was done. *More soon.* Then he disappeared to some other part of the house. She stumbled out of his bed. Pressed her face against a cool wall.

She pulled on her underwear and saw a smudge of blood on her palm, sweat smearing the ink of the word he'd written, *Sternli.* She felt queasy. As fast as she could, she wiped her hand on his black bedspread and knelt to the cold wood floor to find her jeans.

Why did she just go along with that?

She could have taken five minutes, before she ever set foot in his bedroom, to lock herself in the bathroom and decide what *she* wanted.

She could have left when he flattened her against the wall and kissed her in that oblivious way.

She could have said the words that came to her—*No, that's enough*—instead of the ones he gave her.

The first time Anna hugged Gina—in the car behind the tattoo shop, the day before the hurricane—she'd thought about it for days. Now she'd gone to bed with someone for the first time and she didn't want to think about it at all.

She'd never planned to save herself for some far-off wedding night, or even necessarily for true love. Pleasure seemed a perfectly good reason for sex, too. Last night, though, had not been much of a pleasure. And if she couldn't even have that, then at least she wanted the words to be true, for someone to believe those words: *You can't imagine the potential I see in you.*

Aching and sore, Gina pushed her jeans and everything else into Connie's washing machine. One hour, a couple of Tylenol, and a piece of toast later, when she moved it all to the dryer, she discovered her jean pockets had been holding one more secret.

At the bottom of the washing machine sat a hundred-dollar bill and a tarot card. Gina picked up the card. It was wet, edges softened, but the image was still perfectly clear. The star above the woman's head looked like a seal of good fortune that would follow her everywhere. Abundance beyond imagining.

She should give the money back. The picture on this card, though, felt like the purest thing about the whole night.

G ina ate a bleak Thanksgiving dinner with Stella, hoping she'd come home to a message from Anna. Nothing.

She called the diner on Friday, when she knew Anna would be back to work. "Could we drive to the beach and talk?"

The clink of plates in the background, the clipped chopping of a knife. Anna's voice was cool. "I'll check my schedule and call you back."

All evening Gina waited for the tattoo shop phone to ring. At 9:57, it finally did.

"Sternli," Nicolas purred. "Recovered from our revels?"

"Oh," Gina said. "Well."

"A curious thing happened today," he said. "I kept trying to give readings, but a fascinating young lady kept coming to mind. Everything worked out with your brother?"

She twisted the phone cord around her finger. "We haven't told him yet."

The conversation she was avoiding with Dominic was getting worse by the day. On Thanksgiving, Mulley's Tattoo debuted in the Crime section of the paper; *Newsday* reported on the fistfight and Preston Tripp's DWI arrest.

"I'd like to see you more often," Nicolas said.

Gina paused. "For what?"

"Guiding you," he said. "Helping you manifest your vision."

She had words to speak, and she couldn't get them out. They were simple words, too: *I need to give your money back. I can't do your appointment.* But then he'd ask why, and the answer was *I just don't want to. You want something from me, and I don't want to give it.* Why was it so hard to say those words?

Thirty-seven

So began the phone triangle between Gina's apartment, the North Shore Diner, and the House of Mystical Delights.

Anna kept putting her off. *I'm not feeling well. My car's in the shop.*

Nicolas kept calling, leaving messages on Connie's machine, or catching her at the tattoo shop, where she wasn't allowed to ignore a ringing phone. *I've never encountered energy like yours. When can I see you again?*

Anna, meanwhile: *Can't get together, working double shifts.*

Gina finally drove to the diner one night and asked for her. When Anna walked out of the kitchen, still holding her order pad, Gina's heart jumped. Anna's face went flat.

"Can we talk?" Gina said. "Outside?"

Anna paused, pulled her woolen coat off the rack, and followed her out.

"Five minutes. I'm on the clock." The parking lot lamps made sharp wedges of light in the darkness, bare traces of snowflakes shivering down through them.

"Are you mad at me?" Gina, freezing in her hoodie, wrapped her arms around herself.

Anna was silent for half a minute. "I don't meet a lot of people I can trust." She looked up at the black sky, the stone-faced moon. "You were such a breath of fresh air. Then I wake up Thanksgiving morning and he tells me you two were going at it while I slept across the hall."

Gina was stunned silent. She couldn't even defend herself.

Anna's hair, braided into a tight bun, began to glitter with snowflakes. "You never said you were interested in him. Not once. So how do I read this? Were you hiding it? Did I miss the signs? Or is your self-esteem so low that you'll just sleep with any guy who—"

"That was my first time," Gina said.

"Yeah, I'd hope so. If you were screwing Nicolas on a regular basis and I was so stupid I didn't notice—"

"My first time," Gina said. "Ever."

Anna looked down at the pavement. She folded her arms across her chest, saying nothing.

"I know you have to go," Gina said. "But—"

"Were you attracted to him this whole time?"

If she said *No, not at all*, she'd be lying. The little jolts of desire. How Nicolas made her feel like the only person in the room. But it wasn't even the same category as what she felt for Anna.

"I don't know," Gina said.

"You have some personal stuff to work out." Anna smoothed the snowflakes out of her hair. "And I'm not the one to help you." She turned and walked back, the silver-edged diner doors closing behind her.

——

Parcels arrived from Nicolas. *Sternli, I trust I'll see you soon. In the meantime, a little gift. Hematite—wear this next to your heart. Rosewood oil— for anointing at new moon.*

Every time Gina called the diner now, Anna was *unavailable.*

Unavailable for good? Could they see each other again if Gina "worked out her personal stuff"? She didn't know what that was; she was the same glow-green mess she'd always been. Unfixable, maybe.

Being lonely was even lonelier than it used to be.

"Do you need help with anything?" Gina said to Rick. "Like, outside the shop?"

"Órale, you got plans tonight? Want to help me hang my Christmas lights?"

It was exactly what she needed: easy, cozy, comforting. They warmed up with mugs of Abuelita, creamy cinnamon chocolate.

"You want to stay for the *Star Trek* marathon?" Rick said.

Maybe it was the cold, dark days, or the loss of Anna's presence, but she fell asleep after one episode, and woke up two hours later to Rick poking her arm. "We've got to find something that'll keep you awake," he said.

A few days later, they spent an evening at the mall, blowing through quarters at the arcade. They laughed so hard she snorted her Orange Julius out of her nose, and it was fun—uncomplicated fun—and she was grateful. But there was a certain kind of awake that she only felt with Anna.

The calls from Nicolas had started out playful. Now they began to change: *People pay for my guidance, Gina. I'm offering it to you gratis. You don't seem terribly grateful.* When the phone rang at the tattoo shop, she let it go to the answering machine, though Dominic would've killed her if he knew.

Nicolas sent one final note: *Did I ever tell you, Gina?—Many years ago, I had a protégé. I invested in her and built her up. She took everything I gave her and disappeared. I didn't think you were that type, Sternli. Did I read you wrong?*

After Mulley's Tattoo appeared in the *Newsday* crime report, the *Blue Claw Monitor* ran an op-ed from Keith Yearly, on behalf of the chamber of commerce: "NYC Banned Tattooing for a Reason. When Will Long Island Wise Up?"

The shop's landlord followed up with a six-word message on the answering machine: *Mulley, it's Barry. Call me immediately.*

"Pez," Rick said. "We have to tell Dominic."

"I don't want to be here when you do."

"Not even to tell him your side of the story?"

Gina shook her head. She went home, slept for an hour, hid miserably under the blankets for another hour, and took the long route back to the shop. "What happened?"

"He made us read him the articles," Rick said. "He got really quiet, he took down Barry's number, and then he hung up."

"He didn't yell?"

Rick shook his head. Mackie shrugged.

The phone rang. Gina—distracted by worry, forgetting she'd been letting the machine pick up—answered it. "Mulley's Tattoo."

"Gina. It's Dominic."

Her stomach dropped. "Hey."

"I'm going to ask you three questions," he said evenly. "Is it true that Mackie told you to get those guys out of my shop, and you kept talking to them?"

"Yes."

"You remember you were on probation?"

"Yeah."

"And do you have my calendar there?"

"Yes."

"Open it to next week. Find the date where we have your first tattoo penciled in." She did. "Now cross that out."

Gina felt a sharp pain beneath her ribs. She put the pencil down and pressed her eyes into her hands. She would not cry in this tattoo shop. She would not.

"When I get back," Dominic said, "expect some changes."

Thirty-eight

How helpful it would be—what relief, what comfort—if a fortune-teller should walk through the door of Mulley's Tattoo. Not the kind of fortune-teller who called you Little Star to get you in bed. A genuine seer. One who could tell Gina if Dominic and Jeri planned to fire her when they got home, or just withhold her pay and make her sit through another humiliating lecture about discipline.

Did it matter? Was one much better than the other? Did she want to work at a tasteful beige skin-art salon where her own brother saw her as a constant source of possible trouble?

Gina opened her portfolio to the back and pulled a business card out of its pocket.

Two rings later, a man's voice was yelling, "When you clean your goddamn milkshake off my dashboard, maybe . . . Pirate Paul's, Eddie speaking."

Gina managed to rasp out her name and some other words.

"The girl from Blue Claw!" Eddie said. "Did you end up working at Mulley's?"

"It's not working out." She picked at the stitching on her jeans. "I was wondering—does Paulie still have an opening for an apprentice?"

Out the window, across the street, gulls flocked to a ripped-open trash bag, diving, stretching open their shell-sharp beaks.

"You should've called a month ago. We just took on a guy." Eddie raised his voice. "Although he's pissing me off right now. So who knows?"

"Will you call me if something opens up?"

Eddie said he would. Gina hung up and rubbed her eyes. He wouldn't.

She arranged every business card from her portfolio flat on the counter, a brick wall of jobs, erected by Dominic. Assistant to candy maker, florist, seamstress. *Jobs for Girls with Artistic Flair.* Even that seemed lofty now. *Jobs for Screw-ups with Rent Due Soon and No References.*

When Rick arrived at the shop, he found Gina sitting in his favorite spot—just where she'd found him on her eighteenth birthday, with his mass book and his Reuben sandwich. More than five months had passed, but that picture was still clear: his Latin benediction. Her new name.

"Pezadita. What are you doing?"

"Deciding if I should quit before they fire me or humiliate me."

Rick came over, with his easy walk and his fresh-combed pompadour, and leaned against the counter. "You can't quit before your first tattoo. See how it goes."

"I told you, he canceled. He won't supervise." Gina couldn't get comfortable on this furniture Jeri loved, a bench that resembled a leather-wrapped casket. She missed the old plaid couch. She missed the roving storytellers and wild things and Calamity Janes who used to come in.

"I could supervise," Rick said. "You got a victim lined up?"

"Linda, this girl I used to work with at the Cheshire Cat." They might've become friends, if Gina hadn't been fired and Linda hadn't gone off to college.

"Linda! What's she going to get?" He began to sing. "Una guinda linda, for la Linda . . . Un tatuaje homenaje for la Linda . . . See if she'll come today. I have a little time."

Gina pushed her glass of water into the sunlight, trying to conjure a rainbow. "I had this vision."

"Pezadita, I know. But if you don't find another reason to do the work, this fight will own you forever. Who's winning, you or her? Does he respect you or not?" Rick sat down across from her and leaned forward, elbows on his knees. "Did I ever tell you about sine proprio?" Gina shook her head. "I used to be friends with some Franciscan friars. They're like monks—"

"You have the weirdest life."

"They take a vow of poverty. In Latin, they call that sine proprio. *Without grasping.* Without grasping at anything for yourself." He opened and closed his hands. "There are things you have to hold lightly or they'll make you miserable."

"But think of 'Hold Fast,'" Gina said. "The sailor tattoo. Families are supposed to hold fast."

"Look, you know what family means to me. Of course, hold fast. But if you grip somebody like a rope ladder, you strangle them. Put it like this: Forget the shop. Why do you want to tattoo?"

You can't quit until you tattoo me, Anna had said. In Gina's vision, there'd always been a young woman in her tattoo chair, so thrilled with her work: *This wave, it's gorgeous, I love it.* At Smith Point beach she'd made Anna a promise.

Suddenly Gina missed her keenly.

She opened her sketchbook and handed Rick the list she'd typed for Dominic. *Reasons I Should Become a Tattooer.*

"The day this arrived"—Gina touched Dominic's trophy—"I thought, I could win one of these. If I worked hard enough."

"And that's enough to keep you going on the hard days?" Rick said.

The penny she'd tossed back in July was still sitting inside the trophy, coated with dust. She rescued it and polished it on her shirt. "Fine. Why do *you* do this job?"

Rick rubbed his belly. "Feeds the panza and pays the landlord. Homeboy's got to eat."

"But you could do other jobs."

"Ha. If my parents heard you say that, they'd light a candle to thank San Juditas for bringing you into my life."

"Why, what do they do?"

"Mamá, she's a nurse. My father teaches high school. Puro middle-class respectable."

"They still get on your case?"

"They ask the same question as you, 'Ay Diosito, Little Ricardo, you could've been a famous painter or an architect! Why are you doing this dirty job? Puro mugrero that tattoo shop.'"

"What's your answer?"

Rick stretched, shirt riding up, and the tattoos on his lower back peeked out: the skull exhaling fire, a swirl of lettering she couldn't read.

"My answer is another question." He pointed to the tattoo on the inside of his wrist. "¿De qué sirve? What does it serve—to what good, in other words. A question from the great Archbishop Óscar Romero. Maybe they'd understand if I threw a priest in the mix."

"Like, what good does it serve in the world?" She massaged her palms. "Does it?"

"I've been asking that question a lot lately." He looked down at his wrist. "Life is short, and the world is wide. Wider than my parents realize."

Gina stared at the ceiling. The new light fixture cast a shadow like a misshapen shamrock.

"Well, Pezadita?" he said. "You gonna call the lovely Linda?"

"Only if you let me do something for you. Clean your car or something. You're always helping me."

"Deal," Rick said. "I got a date Friday with the Waldenbooks lady and my Chevy needs some love."

Gina found Linda's number and dialed.

An hour later, the door swung open. A young woman with stringy strawberry blond hair entered the shop as if busting through the double doors of a saloon and dropped her army-surplus rucksack on the leather bench. "Girl!"

Rick walked toward the back while Gina did the necessary How Have You Beens. While Linda made her selection, Gina slipped over to Rick and spoke under her breath. "Do you have last-minute advice?"

"No matter how it goes," he said, "you're going to wake up in the middle of the night, panicked that you messed it up."

"You suck."

"Pezadita," he said, "I am a truth teller."

At least Linda's choice of design provided some minor comfort. At this point, Gina could tattoo roses in her sleep.

She picked up her machine. As angry as she was with Dominic, the voice in her head was his. *When the needle enters the skin, it should choke down. Vibration gets a little muted. If it doesn't do that, you're giving the machine too much juice, you'll turn the skin to chop meat.*

Linda's muscle twitched when the needle made contact. "You okay?" Gina said, as she'd heard the guys say a thousand times before.

"So amped," Linda said.

Up from the bottom of the stem, toward a crown of petals yet to appear, Gina drew a small but steady line.

———

When Linda had thoroughly admired her new tattoo, declaring it *bitchin'*, *bad*, *bodacious*, and *radical*; when Gina had snapped a picture with Dominic's Ricoh FF-90 Super and sent her off with ointment and thanks; when everything was broken down and put away—at long last, Gina flopped down on the long leather bench.

She felt high. She felt like she'd been hang gliding.

"What do you think, Pez?"

Gina covered her face. "You made me try it and now I love it. Just in time for them to fire me."

He grinned. "Better to have loved and lost."

"When should I wash your car?"

"I thought of something better. I've got a private appointment coming up. An important client who wants something I've never done before. I could use an assistant."

"The great Rick Alvarez needs no one."

"Captain Kirk has Mr. Spock and I got you. This is the most ambitious thing I've ever tried. Cross your fingers the client even lets you in the room."

Thirty-nine

DECEMBER 12

Jeri Harrison was shaking sleigh bells. She jingled through the front door, wearing one of those cherry-red Princess Di coats, and said, "You know what this shop needs? A Christmas tree." She walked over and touched Dominic's arm. "Why don't we cut down a fresh one?"

That luxe coat seemed impractical for felling timber, but fine. "Have fun," Gina said.

"The three of us," Jeri said. "No need to have all our big talks in a stuffy shop."

Big talks. Dominic had already told Gina, *We're moving up your quarterly check-in. We need to discuss Thanksgiving.* Here was the plan, then, for her tongue-lashing and/or sacking: dress it up as a merry holiday expedition.

"Dom?" Jeri said. "Ready?"

Tree farms patchworked the North Shore. Jeri, diligent researcher, had found one with cider and doughnuts in a party tent. Dominic turned in to a dirt lot and Jeri pulled a brand-new bow saw out of his trunk. She smiled. "What first? Chop or talk?"

You don't chop with a saw, Gina wanted to say, but her desire to get this over with was stronger. She headed over the ruts of iced mud toward the cider tent.

The air was wisped with woodsmoke, the sky swollen with gray clouds. A boom box on the checkout stand crooned Bing Crosby. Dominic bought three doughnuts, Gina claimed a table, and when they were all settled in, Jeri snapped open her Tiffany blue Filofax.

"So, Gina." She pulled out the apprenticeship agreement. "Up until this Thanksgiving incident, how would you say you've been doing?"

Gina brushed the sugar off her fingers. "Markiful."

Jeri tilted her head. "Come again?"

"Tattooing jargon," Gina said. "You wouldn't know. It has to do with marvelous, beautiful—"

Jeri cut her off. "Dominic. How would you evaluate Gina's performance before the incident?"

"Hard worker. Ambitious." It was freezing in this tent. Dominic exhaled a fog cloud of breath. "Means well." Just had to add that last part.

"Just struggles with the chain of command, would you say?" Jeri said.

"Sure," Dominic said.

"So I think we agree," Jeri said, "that we don't need to have Gina read the *Newsday* article aloud to us, or the Yearly op-ed, or the chamber of commerce censure, or the landlord's letter, or some other ideas that might have been floated. We don't need to get all eye-for-an-eye here, right? Regarding public embarrassment? We've all calmed down."

"Right," Dominic said.

All morning, Gina had been repeating to herself: *Sine proprio*. Hold this meeting lightly. Don't cling to this job with a stranglehold. You could find another mentor. You don't need to win any fights or score any points.

But irritation was a hard habit to break. "Is Mackie having one of these meetings, too?" she said. "About punching potential clients in the face?"

Jeri put her hand in the middle of the table. "Those are separate discussions. Gina, nobody likes to split up a family and I'm racking my brain here. If we found a way to move forward, what would it take for you to get on board? Like, really get on *board*?"

Gina breathed into her cold hands and rubbed them together for warmth. Then she said the first thing that popped into her head. "Hope?"

What the hell? How long had that word been lurking in there, and what did it want from her? God help her if Jeri asked her to explain *hope*.

"Hope," Jeri said thoughtfully. "Well, it's the season of hope, isn't it."

A tractor pulled up outside the tent, engine at full rumble, towing a hay wagon decked with jingle-bell garlands. A riot of children piled on board, followed by their parents and a hysterical sheltie.

When the wagon rolled away, Jeri gave Dominic a meaningful look. "And isn't that a great segue to part two. Dominic?"

Dominic pulled a drawing out of his pocket and put it on the table.

Gina stared. "I don't get it."

And just like that, Dominic was smiling. Smiling like he'd been dreaming of playing Santa in the pageant, and by God, he got it, *he got the part.*

"Gina," Dominic said. "She's pregnant."

He started laughing. Jeri started laughing. They squeezed each other's hands.

Gina dropped her doughnut. Holy snow tornado. Holy mushroom cloud of what the hell.

In a miracle of appropriate behavior, she found the right phrase. "Wow! Congratulations!"

Jeri grinned and tipped sideways to put her ear on Dominic's shoulder. "I'm due in August."

It was getting oddly warm for a tent in December. Gina unbuttoned her coat.

"A little sooner and the baby could've been born on your birthday," Dominic said.

"Imagine!" Gina put her hands up, trying for jubilation, realizing too late that it looked like she was surrendering to a stickup.

"This is great news for you," Jeri said. "Not just because you'll be an auntie. You probably thought we were going to ream you out today—"

"Boy," Gina said. "You really got me."

Jeri reached out and squeezed Gina's hand. "We could all use a fresh start. And when that baby comes, we want to get all we can out of you." She clicked a pen and wrote *Helping Gina* on a clean sheet. "Number one—let's get you that workstation you wanted."

Yes, she had wanted the workstation, but something about this felt weird as hell.

"Number two—I hear this drama with your mom owing you money has been a big energy suck. She's going to call and say she has a surprise."

Gina looked at Jeri, puzzled. "Did you give her the money?"

"Details not important," Jeri said. "Act surprised. And very happy."

"Will she call me in time to register for the next semester?"

Jeri paused. "Let's put the drawing class on hold, actually. I'm thinking studio ambassador is not your thing."

"Is Dominic still giving me lessons?" Gina said cautiously.

Jeri and Dominic looked at each other.

"The scope of your job has been a little broad," Jeri said. "So let's carve out your niche."

In fact, they'd already done the carving, and Jeri just knew Gina was going to excel under their new plan. When that sweet baby came, time would be so precious. Efficiency would be everything. And Gina was so faithful with the little things—all those fundamentals that kept the place running! And did they really need four working tattooers at a studio that was still finding its legs?

This didn't mean Gina would *never* tattoo. To the contrary, she had a vital role. What MFATS needed to break into this new market was a kind of gateway drug, a *chic starter tattoo*, for the intrigued but hesitant. Had Gina seen those L.L.Bean catalogs, with the monogrammed boating bags? She was going to master the monogram lettering tattoo.

Yes, they'd absolutely still permit Gina to create that flash sheet of apprentice tattoos! Jeri already had the concept: a set of mix-and-match design elements called the Trendy Twenty. Hot items like checkerboards and triangles. Perfect for clients living in the now, who didn't waste time fretting over the future.

Would Gina be tattooing anything *else* eventually? Would her lessons ever resume?

No need to hash that out now. This year had been so full of surprises already. When the studio started turning a healthy profit, they'd revisit all of this. Right now, everyone should just celebrate this victory—that Gina was staying on at all. Considering everything.

But—was this still an apprenticeship?

"Stop looking so worried." Dominic tickled Gina's shoulder with a sprig of pine needles. "Permission to be happy."

"Really, though," Gina said. "Is this still an apprenticeship?"

"So exciting." Jeri snapped her Filofax shut and handed the saw to Dominic. "And now, love—let's go slay a tree."

Forty

Back at the shop, while Jeri and Dominic wedged a Douglas fir into a tree stand, Gina slipped out to the river. The freezing air burned in the back of her throat; goose bumps rose on her arms. When she got to her bench, she opened her sketchbook to her list from last July— *Reasons I Should Become a Tattooer.*

When Jeri asked *What would it take for you to get on board?* what a strange word to appear—*hope*—but now she understood. Hope that all this was going somewhere. Hope that any part of her vision was still possible.

Gina looked at her list, with one item already crossed out.

~~I belong here.~~

She yanked out a pen and swiped two more lines.

~~I could be so good at this.~~

~~We could make this a real family business~~

and I could help you.

I could be so good at this: not without real guidance. Gina would make guesses in the dark and develop bad habits and end up doing the kind of tattoos that people came to Mulley's to cover up. Rick might teach her here and there, but she couldn't lean on him for everything; he had his own work to do.

A *real family business*, but the family was Dominic's and Jeri's now.

What was left? *I could help you.* She could have the satisfaction of supporting their vision. How lucky for them.

"Gina." Jeri's voice, calling from the back door, across the lot. "Grab the box from my trunk on the way in."

Gina could hear Stella already: *Didn't I tell you what Jeri was after?* She'd been right about the baby part. At least Jeri hadn't mentioned marriage, or moving away, or shutting down the shop.

That's phase two, Stella would say.

Gina didn't need to sit here having imaginary conversations with her mother.

She walked stiffly through the cold and retrieved a large box from Jeri's car. Dom held the door as Gina staggered down the hall with her arms wrapped around it.

"By the way," Dominic called from behind her, "your friend is here." Gina looked up.

Anna was hovering nervously by the mirror, with her wild brown hair and that downy angora sweater that made her look like an angel. Gina lit up with nerves, crackling like sparks in a crystal ball. She clutched the box in front of her body, shielding herself.

"I like your Christmas tree," Anna said.

"I helped kill it." Gina's mouth was dry. She set the box on the floor. "What are you doing here?"

"On my way to the DMV," Anna said carelessly. "Just walking by." She pulled a lipstick from her purse, turned to the mirror, and smudged her mouth cranberry red. Then she looked over the room: at the weird new coffee table, like a hovering glass kidney; the countertops, tiled in black pearl—at everything in the shop, in fact, except Gina.

"Do you go to the DMV a lot?" Gina said. "I thought I saw you walk by the other day."

Anna reached for the door. "You look busy."

"I'm not." Gina could barely swallow. "Stay."

Anna leafed through Dominic's portfolio, pausing on a tattoo of the Virgin Mary. Finally, quietly, she spoke. "I missed you."

Gina glanced behind her. Dominic and Jeri had disappeared into the office; Mackie had stepped out; Rick was absorbed in tattooing a four-chambered, realistic heart on his client's chest. She spoke in a low voice. "Why'd you come?"

"To apologize." Anna picked up a fallen clump of tinsel and pulled the strands out one by one.

"I'm the one who messed up."

"But I kind of knew he'd try it." Anna paused. "Maybe there was a part of me that wanted to see what you'd do. And I'm sorry."

"I'm an adult," Gina said. "My choices are my own."

"He makes his living swaying people's choices. And I left you alone." She wrapped a strand of tinsel around her finger. "Did he call you?"

"A dozen times. I kept blowing him off and he finally stopped. I feel guilty for ditching him."

"Don't."

Gina glanced behind her again. Rick was still focused, Jeri and Dom still in the office, out of earshot. "He kept saying he believed in my potential."

Anna kept her voice quiet. "That's his favorite line."

"It's a stupid reason to sleep with someone." Gina began to untangle a knot of Christmas lights.

Anna shook her head. "When you never hear it, it's like a drug. I was a *remarkable girl*, I was so *unusual*, he was *captivated by me*. And then he started saying—" She frowned. "*I love to feed on your energy*. And I don't know what the hell that means, but I always felt drained. Or dazed, like I wasn't in my body. I didn't sign up for that job, letting somebody feed on me." She looked away, smoothing her hair, as if to reset herself. "I'm moving out for real this time. I put a deposit down on a place."

Gina stopped untangling lights. "Does Nicolas know?"

"He's in Switzerland for Christmas and won't be back till January. I'll call him when I'm gone."

"Where are you going?"

Anna gathered her hair in her hands. "I found a place in Blue Claw."

Gina laughed. "You just happened find a place here."

"The rent's cheap. They were hiring at your diner."

Gina bent to pick up a stray pine cone from the floor, so Anna wouldn't see her smiling.

"I was wondering"—Anna fiddled with the tinsel again—"if you still wanted to be my roommate."

Well—that was an intriguing and frightening offer.

It had only taken one mistake for Anna to stop calling her. It had taken only one moment of remorse, apparently, for her to change her mind and propose moving in together. Gina had spent most of her life with a capricious woman, and having switched to Connie, there was something to be said for a cranky but predictable roommate whose rules—*flip-flops in the shower please*; *disinfect your doorknob*—never changed.

How would a flower-fluent Victorian put it? *LARKSPUR: Fickle. BEGONIA: Beware.*

But also—the prospect of something happy erupting in Gina's life right now was enticing, and happiness was the one thing she'd always felt with Anna. Not just happiness—the feeling of belonging, being understood.

Things were not looking so sunny at Mulley's Fine Art Tattoo Studio; Anna had always helped her see possibilities when she thought there were none.

SAFFRON CROCUS: Mirth. FERN: Fascination. FLOWERING AL-MOND: Hope.

"What's it like?" Gina said. "The place?"

"A bungalow near the bait shop. It's tiny but it's in good shape." Gina didn't mind tiny. Less to clean. "You'd have your own room."

Gina started untangling lights again, thinking.

"Tell me what would convince you," Anna said. "I'm so tired of living in a heavy, dark house. I just want some joy."

"Could you commit to a thing with feathers?" Gina said.

Forty-one

Connie made half-hearted noises about how she'd miss Gina, but they were both in an excellent mood on the afternoon of January 1 as Gina roped the mattress to the top of her Cricket, hoping never to live in a perfect white apartment again.

At the far end of Midway Street, a mile down from the shop, stood a tiny sea-green bungalow sheltered by walnut trees. Gina pulled up, heartbeat like a revving engine. Anna leaped out the door without a coat even though it was twenty degrees. "You're here!"

They carried armloads inside. The wood floors were worn but clean; in the corner was a small brick fireplace where tealight candles flickered. Milk crates of miscellany, still to be unpacked, lined the wall, but the record player was spinning, and already—Anna had been there all of twenty-four hours—the air smelled of baking bread.

"It's no House of Mystical Delights," Anna said. "Maybe a Cottage of Good Sandwiches."

Gina didn't care if sandwiches were all they ever ate.

Anna had already hung her posters above the fireplace: *Free Nelson Mandela*, Siouxsie and the Banshees. "Are those new?" Gina said.

"No," Anna said. "I'm just finally allowed to hang them."

Gina's botanical flash poster was there, too—water-wrinkled, but framed, like a valuable antique unearthed from an old library. She felt elated all over again.

"Notice anything else?" Anna pointed to the coat tree where her leather jacket hung. An electric-green parakeet was perched on one of the hooks.

"My coworker's birds keep making more birds," Anna said. "But I haven't figured out how to get it back in the cage. So watch your head."

After they brought everything in, they spread a picnic dinner on the living room floor: chicken salad sandwiches, salt-and-vinegar chips. "I haven't unpacked my card table yet," Anna said.

"The floor's fine." Gina looked up at the parakeet. "I always thought if I had a bird I'd name her Maud Wagner. She was the first known female tattooer in the US. And an aerialist and contortionist."

"That's an amazing skill set," Anna said. "I'm fine with Maud Wagner."

Maud Wagner had already fallen asleep, head tucked in her wing.

"So what now?" Gina said.

"Pie?" Anna said. "Unpack?"

What Gina wanted to ask was, *Are we still settled on being nuns?* The room had a couch, but Anna hadn't joined Gina in leaning against it; she was about as far away as you could get in a room this small, as if she expected Gina to pounce on her.

Too soon to talk about that. Gina might never summon the courage, in fact, to talk about that. But in the meantime, there was the big picture *what now.*

"Can we talk about life?" Gina said.

"Deep," Anna said.

"What I mean is," she said, "you have a new job at a new diner. I have a new demotion at the same tattoo shop. But I don't want to be the shop lackey forever and you said you don't want to waitress forever. I mean—" The needle on the record player was circling mutely on the innermost groove. Gina reset it to the beginning. "I used to be able to picture my future. Now I can't."

"I never had a clear picture of my future," Anna said. "I went to Stony Brook because my parents said I'd be a good nurse."

"Do you want to be a nurse?"

"No," Anna said. "Not even a little."

Gina opened her sketchbook and pulled out Dominic's old list. *"Jobs for Girls with Artistic Flair.* I still don't want to do any of these jobs."

"The title's a little dated," Anna said. "Can I edit this?" Gina handed it over. Anna crossed out the words and wrote something else. "I think this is what you're looking for."

Jobs for Artists.

Gina smiled.

For now, this was the plan: They would not sleepwalk through their days. They would keep their eyes open for opportunities.

Each night, they would report back with something that had piqued their curiosity, made the day more satisfying, stimulating, purposeful or fun or otherwise life-giving.

Presumably, when they'd gathered enough observations, all those little inklings would start to form a picture. And that picture would be a map to their futures.

Forty-two

Winter Quarter: Benchmarks & Requirements

TO BE COMPLETED by Check-in Meeting #3,

TUESDAY, APRIL 1

***Continue free practice tattoos on volunteers, using flash sheet created in Fall Quarter.

***Begin work on portfolio, an album with 40 photographed tattoos, due at exit interview, July 1, 1986.

O n January 2, the first official workday of the year, Gina walked into Dominic's office and put her apprenticeship agreement on his desk. "Are we still doing this or not?"

"Doing what exactly?" He reached for a travel bag and started pulling out film canisters. "I need you to run these to the Fotomat today. California pictures."

"*This.*" Gina put her finger on the winter requirements. This densely typed piece of paper, which she had come to loathe in the fall, now seemed like her only remaining chance of being trained—properly trained—at the shop. "*Can* I tattoo with the flash I created. *Do* you want me to work on a portfolio." Her questions felt more like declarations.

"It's not up to me," Dominic said.

Gina stared at the frames on his wall—his diploma from art school, his plaque for supporting the local Little League team. "Remember when everything *was* up to you?"

"Gina, I have things to do."

"The Harrisons own twenty percent of this shop. You own eighty. Make a decision."

Dominic looked away. "If I can't get our profits up by April—that percentage might be more like fifty-fifty."

"What? Why?"

"Because we burned through our cash on these renovations and we're still not turning the profit we need. Harrison wants to know how I'm going to support his grandkid. And he said he's not pissing away any more money on this shop until he calls the shots on how we spend it." Dominic looked up at the window. The sky had darkened to deep gray, threatening snowstorm, already spitting sparse white flakes.

"If I can help—"

"You can't."

Gina looked down at the agreement in her hands. *Practice tattoos. Portfolio.* This was all she had control over.

"Half my life, Mom's been calling me Queen of Almost," Gina said. "I don't want to leave a single thing undone. I'll do everything Jeri said, okay? But if it turns out we don't attract all those high-quality people who want to get monogrammed or look like sticker albums—I want to work on this. My actual, original requirements."

Dominic's expression was closing up. He didn't want to get into this. "Stuffy in here." He opened the window and cold drifted in, stray snowflakes disappearing in the warm office air.

"*Dominic.*"

"Fine," he said. "If it doesn't interfere with your other work. Use that flash you were banging out on pigs' feet, or those sea creatures Jeri approved. I'll tell her this is what we're doing. But you have to find your own people. Don't poach Mackie's walk-ins and don't charge."

"Final question," Gina said. "Are you going to be teaching me at all?"

"Take these, please?" Dominic pushed the film canisters toward her. "Jeri doesn't want me spending time on lessons. I'm supposed to be ramping up advertising." He flipped through a copy of the *East Hampton Star*. "If I'm not around, Rick or Mackie can supervise."

Gina put the canisters in her hoodie pocket and stood there, feeling heavy.

"What?" Dominic said.

"I miss the days when you cared."

He looked away. "You have no idea what I care about."

"You could tell me."

He rubbed his face. There it was: the wall.

"Fine," Gina said. "I miss *you*." She walked out before he could answer.

G ina set to work on a flyer. She went up to Blue Claw Community College and left a stack: FREE TATTOOS FOR STUDENTS BY APPRENTICE ARTIST. When she got back, a woman with a backpack was already waiting for her. An hour later, a young guy showed up; later that evening, he returned with a friend.

Gina set to work.

For years, she had heard the guys talk about "good skin" and "bad skin." Good skin was buttery, easy to run the needle across. Bad skin was fragile or tough, or quickly went spongy, unable to hold up under all those tiny holes. Suddenly it felt like she'd been assigned a survey course in bad skin.

The woman, who wanted "just a little heart with wings" on her shoulder, bled so much that Gina could barely see what she was doing.

The guy picked a lighthouse, then went pale and dizzy and wanted to stop after the outer outline. "I would recommend you stay for the detail," Gina said. "It looks a little phallic." He declined.

A lanky guy in his fifties—"I'm a nontraditional student," he kept saying—wanted a snake slithering up his foot, biting his ankle. It was a bony location, scant fat; it would be tough for her, likely painful for him. "I'm just learning," Gina said. "Probably not a good idea."

"Think positive," the guy said.

"Seriously," Gina said. "How about your arm?"

The toilet flushed; Jeri stepped out of the bathroom, looking ill. She'd already thrown up twice this afternoon and was still managing to monitor Gina's customer service through the wall. "Gina. We cater to the client. Give him what he wants."

Gina white-knuckled her way through it, trying to keep his ankle perfectly still and not let the needle go too deep. Suddenly his leg moved. She looked up to see him tugging Nicolas's tarot card from the corner of her mirror. "You into this occult shit?" he said.

She stopped the machine, pulled off the gloves, and yanked the card from his hand. She shoved it in her back pocket. "Are you serious? You don't go grabbing people's things." Now she'd have to wash her hands again. Asshole.

Jeri stuck her head out of the office door. "Gina. Courtesy."

Gina bit her tongue and turned to the sink. As she turned off the faucet, the man said, "Why's the tattoo blurry like that? Is that a bruise?"

Worse than a bruise—a blowout. Maybe she'd been too heavy-handed or maybe it was his wiggling, but the needle had jabbed past the dermis to the subcutaneous layer, where the ink had nothing to hold it in place. The snake looked bathed in an evil fog. Face hot, quiet with dread, Gina looked over at Mackie.

Mackie walked over and examined it. "If it's a bruise, it'll fade. If it's a blowout, it won't. Tattoo on the ankle, that's the risk you run."

"What am I supposed to do?"

"Enjoy your free tattoo. Next time listen to the nice lady and don't move around."

The guy begrudgingly accepted Mackie's answer; Gina finished the shading in silence. When he left, Mackie tapped her on the arm and spoke under his breath.

"Don't listen to Jeri next time. If you think you can't do something, don't do it. I'll back you up."

"Thanks," Gina said. This kindness felt suspect. "Why are you being nice?"

"Because Jeri annoys the hell out of me." Mackie walked away.

Gina put on her coat and walked out back for a breath of fresh air. Night was falling. The last bit of light on the river's black ripples was going dull and dark.

Dominic was letting her drown. This wasn't just about the two of them anymore. She was being trusted with people's bodies, and tonight she'd left somebody with a permanent mess. For the rest of that guy's life—for every beach trip and summer barbecue, and eventually to the morgue—he would carry her crappy tattoo.

What would Gina have said to that guy if Mackie weren't there? No one had taught her how to explain mistakes to clients. No one was even teaching her how to avoid them.

Her hands went to her pocket. She pulled out the tarot card—that illustrated woman pouring water like it would never run out, with the beacon of the star above her. Gina didn't have a beacon and a flowing stream. She had a streetlight and the Bifurc River.

Those gulls over there, settling down to roost on the ice—they were scavengers. That's what she would have to be.

A scavenger's apprenticeship, then.

Every single time Mackie, Rick, or Dominic said to one another, *How does this look to you?* or *Would you put more shadow here?* listen up hard.

Watch for lulls when she could grab five minutes of teaching. If she could wring anything out of Dominic, take it. It she could beg time from Rick, beautiful. If she caught Mackie in a generous mood—gulls didn't turn down anything.

She had to pay attention and be present for every moment, because it might have a stray crab leg for her.

And maybe, even though Jeri wasn't requiring it anymore, even though Gina wasn't cut out to be a studio ambassador, it was time to get registered for a class.

It felt so good to pull up to the bungalow that night and see Anna's Buick in their dirt driveway. The kitchen window was fogged up, glowing a warm yellow, and as soon as she stepped out of her car, Gina could smell bacon frying.

Anna was in the kitchen managing a crackling skillet, a cutting board full of fat tomato slices and a head of iceberg lettuce. "How many BLTs can you eat?"

What a beautiful question to come home to.

Gina wiped down the card table and laid out the silverware they'd just bought at Goodwill. Anna brought their plates, golden BLTs with pickle spears on the side. "Was your day fun?"

"No," Gina said. "But I had some useful epiphanies about my job."

"I talked politics with the diner manager." Anna relaxed into the folding chair, and Gina recognized her expression: the particular relief of sitting down after being on your feet all day. "It reminded me of my poli-sci class. I liked it. That's my observation for the day. What's yours?"

"I realized," Gina said, "I need to be more like a seagull."

T he wonderful thing about these dinnertime check-ins was realizing— despite the terror and anxiety—how much she enjoyed the actual practice of tattooing. Nowhere on Gina's list of *Reasons I Should Become a Tattooer* had she thought to write *It sounds like fun*. But lo and behold: tattooing was fun.

The only downside of answering questions like *What was the best thing about your day?* was realizing that she couldn't always speak the whole truth. Her favorite moment, when she felt most alive and present, was often being with Anna.

Surely that couldn't last. Some terrible secret about Anna was bound to come out. Any day now. But so far, all her faults seemed to be of the ordinary kind: dirty dishes in the sink, crankiness before her morning coffee. When Gina confessed she was dreading their first argument, Anna jokingly saved the wishbone from one of their roast chickens, saying they'd use it to settle the issue then. But their uncanny peace continued, the wishbone remained uncracked, and weeks passed with nothing more difficult than stubborn discussions about whether it was okay to feed sandwich crusts to Maud Wagner.

Even the precoffee surliness had its upside. "Oh my God," Anna muttered one morning. "You keep going on about that drawing class. When are you going to do it?"

"Alas," Gina said. "Money." Despite what Jeri had promised at the Christmas tree farm, Stella never called to say *I have a surprise for you.* Gina still had the hundred dollars Nicolas had given her, but if she spent it, she'd be stuck giving him that tattoo one day. She wanted to return the money, but she hadn't figured out how.

"What's one class, maybe a hundred or so with fees?" Anna said. "If we pooled our tips and each chipped in twenty bucks a week—"

Gina was taken aback. "I can't let you do that."

Anna spooned sugar into her coffee. "Why not?"

The day Gina walked into her first session of Drawing I at Blue Claw Community felt like a dream. She was a *student.* She hadn't known she could feel so at ease, just standing in a big room sweeping charcoal across a page with twenty other people doing the same thing.

At home, still giddy, she sat on the floor in front of the couch. Sometimes when she did this, Anna would wander over, sit behind her, and braid Gina's hair, the way she used to. Gina was too shy to ask, but when it happened, the pleasure of those fingers on her scalp softened every bit of tension in her body.

Anna joined her and began to brush her hair. "How was it?"

Gina closed her eyes and let her shoulders drop. "I never thought I could love school so much." She told Anna every detail, even the campus center: an airy greenhouse of a place, high ceilings and skylights, the ambitious smell of coffee.

"You belong there." Anna tied off the end of Gina's braid. She tugged her closer and kissed the top of her head. "I knew you would."

Gina ached. It was all she could do not to turn around. But this was their unspoken rule: only Anna was allowed to approach. If Gina sat too close, Anna would move away.

She wished they could lounge around talking until midnight, the way they had in Anna's room at the House of Mystical Delights. Instead, each night, Anna had taken to flipping on the eleven o'clock news, letting the world invade the bubble of their cottage with bleak words like *Chernobyl, apartheid, immunodeficiency.* It was the last thing Gina wanted as she was winding down for bed, but more often than not, she joined her; it was the one time of day Anna didn't seem skittish about Gina's presence on the couch. And once in a while—just before bed, usually—Anna would let her guard down, and things felt the way they used to.

On the last night of January, they sat watching the memorial service for the *Challenger* crew. Everyone had seen the disaster by now: the tunnels of smoke as the space shuttle split in the sky, pieces flying off in separate twisting arcs. The president delivered his remarks: *Sometimes, when we reach for the stars, we fall short. But we must pick ourselves up again and press on despite the pain. . . .*

"Those words sound so hollow next to what they lost." Anna stood and switched off the television.

Gina watched the picture collapse into a bar of light, shrink to a dot, disappear. "Like a poster in the guidance counselor's office."

Anna returned to the couch, looking pensive. She began to rearrange her handful of knickknacks, now displayed on their coffee table.

"You're thinking about something," Gina said.

Anna fingered her sister's nesting doll. "It reminds me of all the useless things they said at church when Daniela died."

Just like that, even from the far end of the couch, Gina felt it again: the magnetic field between her and Anna, some invisible ether where thoughts passed back and forth without words.

"When you talk about church," Gina said, "it feels like they broke your heart. Like the way I feel about the shop. You used to belong there."

Anna put down the doll. "I never stopped believing God was real. But I didn't believe anymore that God was *good*." She paused. "I hope this doesn't freak you out. But when I'm with you—I feel it again. The generosity. The goodness."

"I don't think I believe in God," Gina said. "But that's beautiful."

Anna met Gina's eyes. She looked so soft in the evening lamplight, close enough for Gina to smell the honeyed tea on her breath, and for those three seconds, it felt like they might kiss again.

Then Anna broke away. "Going to brush my teeth." A moment later, she called out through her closed bedroom door: "Good night, roommate."

That one stung.

Gina opened the cage and let Maud Wagner climb onto her finger. Was the bird anxious, clinging to Gina's hand, grinding its beak? "Shhh," she whispered. "You're home." Mary Star of the Sea watched from the poster above, with her star glow and ocean-grazing toes.

Gina should be grateful. She was lucky to share a house with Anna; it was enough to have her nearby. She'd tell herself that until she believed it.

Forty-three

Gina opened up her lunch bag to find a box of candy conversation hearts.

Technically she was not supposed to be eating on the black pearl countertop, but Jeri and Dom were gone for the day. Gina shook a handful of hearts onto the counter, wishing for a hidden message. CUTIE PIE. FAX ME. She ate MY GIRL. It tasted like peppermint chalk.

Rick walked up and poked through the hearts.

"What are you looking for?" Gina said. "'Beam me up'?"

He nudged them aside one by one, building his reject pile. Finally he made a selection: ASK ME.

"Ask you what?" she said sourly.

"Ask me what she said."

"You proposed to your girlfriend already?" Rick was getting serious about the Waldenbooks lady. Mackie was seeing some fire department woman. Everybody else's romantic life was going beautifully.

Rick leaned on the counter, eyebrows raised. "My important client. The one with the private session." He pointed to his wrist: ¿De qué sirve? "She said you can assist."

Gina crushed KISS ME into green crumbs. "Who is she?"

Rick put his hand over the hearts until she looked up. "This is an incredible privilege, Pezadita," he said. "Tomorrow at two. Don't be late."

Laughter echoed up the hallway from the front room. Rick's client was already there. The blinds were drawn and Rick was turning on floor lamps when Gina arrived at the threshold of the work area; he beckoned Gina in.

"Tía, this is the apprentice I told you about. Gina—my aunt Andrea, my cousin Victor."

Sitting in the swivel chair was a woman on her way to being grandmotherly, soft lines in her forehead, relaxed blouse with buttons like rubies. A man of about Rick's age stood next to her, at ease, Wayfarer sunglasses propped on his head. They had the same playful mouth, skin a shade lighter than Rick's, rosy golden.

Andrea looked at Gina. "Are you helping? You're a baby!"

Gina sat down across the room in Mackie's chair. "Just watching. It's nice to meet you." Rick waved her closer.

"Tía, this is what I worked up for you." He grabbed his largest sketch pad.

Andrea touched his wrist, stopping him. "Remember—I don't want that prison style."

"They call it something else now. Black-and-gray fine line."

"I'm a nice old lady, not some torcida."

Rick started laughing. "Yes, nice and proper for my tía who's never been in the pinta. A church lady tattoo."

"Shhh, callese mi'jo. I'm not joining a gang and I don't want to look like an old-school chola. I can't believe I'm doing this. Just make me beautiful."

Rick looked up at Gina. "She's fishing. My tía knows she already is." Andrea gently slapped Rick's arm and punched air through her teeth. He opened the drawing pad. "You want colors? Look."

A watercolor peacock lit up the page. Its tail was draped behind it in a slackened fan, gold and green; its breast glowed blue. He'd been working on this all week, starting each version with the same peculiar lopsided arc.

Rick ran his finger along the arc. "Here's the scar. The tail drapes across here. The body and neck"—he traced a vertical line in the air, midway between Andrea's armpit and collarbone—"and the head looks off this way." He touched her shoulder.

"How much can you cover?" Andrea bit her lip.

"All of it."

Rick's aunt sat up to look down at her chest, trying—as Gina was trying—to picture how the peacock would sit. Then Gina noticed the hollow in her shirt.

"Make it feminine," she said.

"My beautiful tía." Rick's voice was gentle, reverent. She could imagine him as a little boy, bringing Andrea a fistful of dandelions and nuzzling his face in her dress. "Tía, when I'm done, they're going to call you an Aztec queen."

"Mi'jo," Andrea said, "the Aztecs didn't have peacocks." Victor laughed.

"I'll draw it with a marker first, right on the skin to follow the shape of your body. If you like it, I'll make the stencil." Rick gestured toward her body as if it were a piece of museum art he was about to restore. "Cuando estés lista."

"Take this off?" Andrea tugged at her shirt collar.

Rick went behind the counter for his markers. "No need, Tía. Just unbutton."

Victor settled down in the waiting area, facing away from Andrea.

"Do you want Gina to turn around, too?"

"After all those medical students walking in and out?" Andrea's laugh was nervous, but Gina had already turned away. She set up Rick's machine and condiment cups for the ink, laid out the spray bottle and petroleum jelly and razor. She was afraid for Andrea. How fresh was this scar?

When she looked up, Andrea was sitting with her shirt half off, and Rick, wearing latex gloves, was drawing on her shoulder with a pink marker. Where her breast would have been was a pale brown scar curving out from her armpit. It was like a seam; the flesh puffed out above and below.

Gina looked away again. "Do you want music?"

"We brought some." Victor handed her a cassette, *Chavela Vargas* scribbled on the label. She put it in the tape deck and a woman's throaty voice began to sing over acoustic guitar.

Andrea sank back with a great exhale.

Every step of Rick's process today seemed even more meticulous than usual. Finally he took his machine in hand.

"Do it like your IVs," Victor said to Andrea, over his shoulder. "Take a deep breath. Tranquila."

"Thank you, boss," Andrea said. But she did, and as Rick dipped his needle in black and began to draw the long pod of the body, her eyes watered and she bit her lip, but she didn't cry. No one spoke. Over the buzz of the machine, Chavela Vargas sang *Volver, volver* in a voice like a crimson banner weathering the wind.

An hour later, as Rick layered tail feathers over the scar, Andrea finally spoke. "When I was little, I dreamed I'd be a world-famous dancer and travel the world, and I'd have a costume with peacock feathers."

Rick smiled. "You never told me that."

"You just chose a peacock out of nowhere?" Gina couldn't take her eyes off Rick's work, each careful teardrop in the tail, each flourish and fringe.

"We have a connection," Rick said. "This one and me, we are like uña y mugre. It means dirt and fingernail, connected forever. But I didn't know you wanted to be a dancer."

"Your mother was the angel girl santita and I was the wild one, the girl without shame." Andrea started laughing. "If she could see me now. Her sister the sin vergüenza getting a tattoo."

The outline of the peacock bloomed across her chest. Rick had planned well: The seam fell naturally in a hollow along the tail, and the flesh above swelled the crest of the feathers.

"Rick," Gina breathed. "It's amazing. You're doing so good."

Rick lifted his foot from the pedal. "Mother Teresa does good. I do well."

"Sea bueno with Gina. Don't be mean to her," Andrea said, eyes still closed. "You're also doing good." She began to hum along with the music. "Ponme la mano aquí Macorina, ponme la mano aquí . . ." After a while she opened her eyes. "Gina, do you know Chavela?"

"No."

"She caused a scandal in ranchera music because she sang love songs to women."

Gina waited to see if there was more, but Andrea just closed her eyes again, relaxing more deeply into the chair.

She didn't look grandmotherly anymore. Her belly rolls were bolts of fawn silk; a flush appeared in her face like an aurora.

When Rick was nearly finished, Andrea became quiet again. She turned her cheek to the chair and began to breathe more deliberately, as if counting the length of each breath.

"Tía, you want a break?"

Andrea murmured something, eyes closed. Rick stopped the machine. "Gina, could you walk up to the store for me?"

"What do you want?"

"Oh . . ." He wiped blood from his aunt's skin. "Cold juice. No hurry."

Understood. They were kicking her out for a while. She left her car behind, walked a mile in the cold to Rick's favorite deli, and brought back a half gallon of Hawaiian Punch.

When she came through the back door again, she stood in the dark hallway for a minute, letting her eyes adjust. The machine had stopped; the tape was over.

Then she heard voices, a click, a whir. She carried the juice to the front, where Rick was photographing his aunt's tattoo. Andrea was lounging like the Queen of Sheba. Her eyes were as pink and swollen as the skin around the tattoo.

After she'd been bandaged up, Andrea patted her nephew on the arm. "Mi'jo, give me a minute with Gina." Rick and Victor went out back, saying they'd walk by the docks, stretch their legs.

Andrea looked through her purse. "My Ricky said you ask a hundred questions a day. He thought you might have some for me."

"We were talking the other day about whether tattooing does any good. And I wondered . . ." Gina paused, too shy to finish.

"Ricky said your tattoo is beautiful. Can I take a look?"

Gina unzipped her hoodie and slipped down her tank top straps to expose the figs.

"Breathtaking," Andrea said. "So, you tell me. Did it do you any good?"

"I don't know if I've grown into it yet." She sat down, letting the hoodie fall to the bench. "I don't think I could be half as brave as you. Sitting there like that in front of my nephew. That was—very personal. Why did you go to Rick for that tattoo? Wasn't that awkward?"

"Who else was I going to go to? Can you see me walking into some tattoo parlor full of big tough boys? Hey, the old lady's here!" She blotted her lipstick on a tissue from her purse.

"You're not old."

Andrea waved her hand. "My little corazón, I'm old enough to not belong in a tattoo parlor. I nursed babies with that breast. You cry and cry over it, what you lost and can't get back, but I was tired of crying. And I'd seen what my Ricky could do, and I asked him to make something beautiful."

She started to tear up again. Gina handed her a tissue and Andrea blotted the corners of her eyes.

"See now, Gina—if you were a full-fledged artist here, I would've said to Ricky, *Let that girl do it*. Wouldn't you, if you were me? At a moment like that? Corazón, you could make a lot of women feel whole again."

A fter Andrea and Victor left, Rick and Gina sat in the waiting area drinking the fruit punch. A couple of kids on battered Schwinns flashed past the window.

Rick fanned himself with a folded-up newspaper, eyes closed. His temples were damp, body slack and tired; he looked like he'd pulled an all-nighter. "Thank you for being there."

"You didn't need me." She'd done nothing but get him a fresh rubber band when the one on his machine snapped. A few times he'd asked her what she thought about this or that, as if her opinion meant anything.

"Sometimes you give someone a gift just by being in the room," Rick said. "We didn't know how it would go. She had the surgery a year ago. She still gets tingling from the chemo. She was glad you were here." He looked at Gina. "And so was I."

She pointed to the tattoo on his wrist: ¿De qué sirve? "Is she your answer?"

"I love her so much, I'd take a bullet for her. But this kind of tattoo—that's not my calling." He drank the last of his juice. "Women like her could be your answer, if that's what you wanted. That tattoo reminded her she was beautiful."

Gina picked up his drawing pad. "You really came up with this peacock out of nowhere?"

"You listen to the person, you get a feeling. And then sometimes you find out it was exactly what they needed." He leaned back and rested his hands on his belly. "Look, Pezadita, tattooing is like being a bartender or a barber. People want to tell you their story. Somebody survives something, they want to mark it. It's like the teddy bears cops keep in their trunks to give to little kids when they answer a domestic call—do they do that around here?"

Gina shook her head.

"Well, you'd see it in the hood. And people think it's to comfort the kids, but it's actually a memento. So the chiquitos can remember and process it and be stronger after. And I think—if you want to have a mission in life, that's not a bad one, to be a listener. But we also get to be a part of the story. Maybe even a part of their healing."

Gina stretched out on the leather bench and looked up at the wall where her mermaid used to be. She'd gotten so tired of looking at that ecru wall that she'd snuck a couple of prisms onto the windowsill, flecking the blank space with rainbows.

"I wish I was your apprentice," she said. Back in September—that day she went to the beach with Anna, instead of accepting Rick's offer of a lesson—would she do the same thing, if she could go back in time?

He reached out and patted her sneaker. "Nah. I'd just yell at you all the time."

Gina smiled.

"When you picture your work in five years," he said, "what do you see?"

"If I ever got trained properly?" She hugged her knees to her chest. "I like the stuff you do. Realistic. But not just black and gray—color, like you did for your aunt." She pointed to the flash on the wall. "Could I get so good that I could tattoo a flower on someone and make it look like you could pick it right off them?"

Rick leaned back in his chair and put his feet up. He looked tired, but content.

"Why are you smiling?" she said.

"Because I see where this is going." He winked at her, then closed his eyes. "And it's fun watching you fall in love."

Forty-four

FEBRUARY 13

A rickety disco ball sent diamonds of light jerking across wood paneling. The airbrushed banner above the bar, presumably gearing up for Valentine's Day, said LOVE IS IN THE AIR, although Gina would've described the aroma as something more like stuffed sole and boozy pink lemonade. Everyone wore their Thursday best. All the drunken cousins danced.

It was party time at the Blue Claw community hall.

This scrubbed stucco landmark was the place for local weddings and retirement parties. It wasn't the sort of expense you'd go to for a birthday party, particularly the non-milestone of thirty-one; but Jeri wanted to bring her Staten Island friends and family out to see her remodeled tattoo studio and her hometown-to-be. She'd been giving tours of the shop all day.

Stella's first words when Gina introduced her to Anna were, "Well, you're a tall drink of water," and Anna was gracious enough to laugh. Stella steered them over to her table and headed to the bar to fetch everyone spiked lemonade.

"I'm surprised she came," Anna said when Stella walked away.

"She really warmed up to Jeri," Gina said. "She's not calling her the succubus anymore." After the pregnancy news, they all waited to see if an engagement would follow, but so far it had not. Dominic and Jeri were looking for an apartment in Blue Claw, not Staten Island, and Jeri had been patiently earning Stella's favor—taking her for manicures, airbrushing a WORLD'S BEST GRANDMA T-shirt.

Stella set three cups down and settled in next to Gina. "Listen. I have a surprise. When can you come over?"

It had been two months since Jeri's promise: *Your mom's got a surprise for you.* Gina poked the ice in her cup with a cocktail sword. "What's the occasion?"

Stella smiled. "Jeri helped me put together a little something for you."

Act surprised. And very happy. There was no way Stella still had that money, two months later. Gina wasn't putting herself through that again.

Stella was already turning to Anna, asking what part of Brooklyn she was from; Gina began to play with the confetti on the table. It was a relief when Rick walked over. "Pezadita. My client sends her love." Rick swigged his beer. "She said you're a beautiful soul. She'd love to see you again."

Anna looked up. "Who's this client?"

He winked. "Gina can tell you."

Rick slipped off into the crowd; Stella left to find Dominic. They should seize the moment. "Let's get some air," Gina said. She and Anna grabbed their coats and snuck out to the rear of the building, where hedges grew, away from the road.

"So many mysteries today," Anna said. "When are you picking up your mom's surprise?"

"It won't be the money. It never is. It'll be a weird lawn statue, or a bag of underwear, or she repainted the kitchen."

"I don't know," Anna said. "She doesn't seem like a bad person."

"She's not. She's a scared person, and even if she wins the lottery, she'll never give back that money, because it keeps me tied to her. It was a button she could push. And the only way I can disconnect the button is stop hoping for it."

"That's sad."

"At first it was sad." Gina tipped back the last of her drink. "Now it's freeing."

Anna leaned against the wall and sipped her lemonade. "So who's this celebrity client who loves you?"

Gina smiled. "Jealous?"

Anna picked a few crimson leaves off a mostly bare hedge and sprinkled them in Gina's hair.

"Rick's auntie."

Inside, the band launched into a new song. *Like a fool, I went and stayed too long . . .*

"I love this song." Anna reached for Gina's hand. "Dance with me?"

Gina rolled her eyes. "No."

Anna took Gina's cup and set it in the cold dirt. She put one arm around Gina's waist and took her hand with the other, singing, "You got my future in your hands . . ."

Gina pulled away.

Anna stopped. "What's the matter?"

Gina wished she could channel Chavela Vargas, who sang to women when it was forbidden, to be that bold, just for five minutes. To have the courage of Tía Andrea, who turned her scars into art at sixty. Sin vergüenza, a girl without shame: Gina knew that phrase wasn't a compliment, but what would that be like, to feel no shame? To make something happen instead of letting something happen?

"That night in November"—Gina's breath made cold clouds in the air—"you didn't kiss me like you were just drinking. You kissed me like you meant it. But if you just want to be pals"—she pointed at the door—"let's find you a nice guy to dance with."

Anna looked away. "That night— I'm sorry. I went too far." She pulled more leaves off the hedge, collecting them in her hands like rose petals. Anything, it seemed, not to look at Gina.

"No," Gina said. "The opposite. But I guess I repulsed you, because you treat me like I'm radioactive. Except when you feel like cuddling. I don't know what you want."

"You don't repulse me," Anna said.

"Gosh, thanks." Gina put her hands up in a gesture of surrender and started to walk away.

Anna grabbed her sleeve. "I can't *have* everything I want."

"Is this some religious thing? Because it didn't stop you with Nicolas."

A flare of anger in Anna. Gina had never seen that before. "You're the only friend I have here. If we go down a road and mess it up, that's it. And it's lonely in Blue Claw."

"You're telling me? I don't know why you're here. You belong in the city."

"Do I? Or do I belong out in Mattituck at a vineyard? Or down in DC at an antinuke march? I spent a year of my life with an older guy trying to steer my future—"

"Forget the future. I'm asking what you want now. With us." A crow swooped from the roof toward the pine tree, cawing.

"I don't know," Anna said.

"You really don't know?" Gina said. "Or it's scary to think of getting it?"

Tears came to Anna's eyes. She looked up at the sky, trying to blink them back. "I need a minute to think."

Gina stared at the ground. If she had a stick, she would draw the trancefish in the dirt. Instead she knelt, knees cold, to see what these tiny stubborn plants were, still green in winter. She rubbed one between her fingers: wild mint. It smelled like Anna's skin. Please, let omens be real.

When she glanced up, Anna was looking around them. There was nothing to see but twiggy hedges.

"This winter shrubbery," Anna said, "is terrible cover."

"Cover for what?"

Anna pulled Gina to her feet and then behind the towering pine tree. Her face was inches away. It was all Gina could see, snow on her lashes like glitter, wet red lips, cheeks pink from the cold.

"I can't believe you'd say you repulse me." Anna spoke under her breath. "Gina Mulley, you are sexy as hell. You walk around in that tank top, with those *arms*, and then you put up your hair all casual like you don't know how sexy the back of your neck is."

Holy ambush, what was happening? Gina could hardly speak. "What?"

"This." Anna pulled Gina into a kiss.

After the one-two punch of shock and elation came terror. Someone could walk out the side door any moment. Anna's face looked like she'd surprised even herself.

"What are you doing?" Gina hissed. "But please do it again. But not here."

"Can we leave?"

Gina peeked around the corner of the building. "We have to make it through cake or Jeri will notice. But as soon as we sing 'Happy Birthday,' you get horrible cramps and I'll pull up the car."

"Why me?"

"Because you started it."

Gina never imagined it would be this difficult to eat a free meal. Anna's bare leg was so close under the table that Gina could feel the heat radiating from it. She barely picked at the antipasto. Each course felt like an endurance test until finally the last plates were taken and Anna made her best attempt at looking stricken.

"You're really leaving?" Stella said.

"We'll come back if she feels better," Gina promised. In the safety of the Cricket, as Anna fumbled with her seat belt, Gina saw she wasn't the only one with shaking hands.

Three minutes driving back to the sea-green cottage. Three hours of giddy blur.

Beeline to the couch, then Anna's futon; making out, talking and laughing, making out again. Bootleg Fuzzbox tape on Gina's cassette deck, joyful crunch of electric guitar and punk-rock shouting.

"I feel like I just embarked on the best road trip ever," Anna said, "but it might be going somewhere weird."

Maud Wagner came swooping through the doorway and landed on the windowsill, bobbing her head, warbling.

"Are we really doing this?" Anna hit rewind on the cassette. "Are we each other's girlfriends?"

"We don't call it anything. We keep it to ourselves. This isn't a good town for stuff like that." This wasn't the time to talk about those two boys who got beat up in the woods, or the lockers spray-painted with DYKE or FAG, and the fear that maybe people could see into your thoughts and you'd be next.

"*Is* there a good town for stuff like that?" Anna said. "You think Bensonhurst was better?"

She had a point. Gina rolled onto the floor and stretched. It felt so good to be out of those party clothes.

Snow had started falling, white flakes blowing past the window in bursts. Water rushed through the cottage's old pipes. The radiator clanked.

"Can I ask one thing?" Gina said. "Can we drive slow?"

Anna propped her head on her hand. "How do you mean?"

"I went too fast with Nicolas. I went too fast with the Cheshire Cat guy. I didn't think and I let things happen. And for the next few miles . . ." Gina paused. "I want to take our time. Is that okay?"

"Of course," Anna said. "We make the rules at the Cottage of Good Sandwiches."

Forty-five

W as there a way of savoring time like peppermints, holding each
round little moment in your mouth as long as you could?

Waking up was joy now. Talking on the couch, feet up on
Anna's cedar chest, the house fragrant with her challah or a honey-wheat
loaf. Dressing for work while the record player crackled Sonic Youth. Anna
applying eyeliner, singing badly. Kisses goodbye. Every little thing quotidian
and thrilling, achingly good.

Anna started covertly distributing Gina's FREE TATTOOS fliers at work,
and several times a week, she'd show up at Mulley's with a fellow waitress or
busboy or adventurous customer ready to bare their shoulder or leg. Just
having her there to watch, calm them down, draw their life stories out of
them, made the studio feel more like the shop Gina missed.

Whether she was tattooing or not, Gina threw herself into her scavenger
education. One slow Monday, nobody was around but Rick, so she ran

across the street to pick up an extra-garlic pizza to share. "Question," she said, folding the slice in half and taking a bite. "How do you get your shading so subtle? I watch what you do with your hand and it's—wispy somehow. I can't figure it out."

He stood to wash his hands. "Want me to show you?"

This became a treasured routine:

Slow Monday.

Yeah. Pizza?

Sure. What do you want to learn this week?

Sometimes the most riveting moments came from watching Mackie and Rick solve problems. One afternoon, Mackie was almost done with a tattoo when Rick stopped him, pulled him aside, and whispered that the second word of "good riddence" was traditionally spelled with an *a*. Mackie looked like he might punch a wall.

"Blast out the lines on that *E* with white ink," Rick said quietly. "It's going to be a scabby mess, but if he comes back when it heals, you can make it a boxy *A*."

"That works?" Gina said.

"Don't even try it, rookie," Rick said. "You'll gouge a hole in them. Use a dictionary." Gina wrote it down in her notebook anyway, under *Emergency Measures*.

Dominic, for his part, seemed badly in need of Emergency Measures. The upscale clients the Harrisons wanted were not materializing, even with his ads in *Dan's Papers* circulating throughout the Hamptons. He managed to get one wealthy client—an orthopedic surgeon from Sag Harbor, who became a repeat customer—but to Jeri's frustration, all he wanted was pinup girls in discreet locations, nothing particularly chic; and despite his thriving practice, he did not spread the word about MFATS as hoped.

The Past Due notices were starting to show up again. Behind Jeri's back, Dominic even tried advertising to their old clientele, posting fliers in bars, running ads in local music rags and even *Pennysaver*, but every time they started to get a bump in business, Keith Yearly lobbed another grenade at Mulley's. A flier appeared under windshields, in libraries, and on supermarket bulletin boards, first in Blue Claw, then beyond:

 EMERGENCY PUBLIC HEALTH WARNING!
READ THIS BEFORE YOU GET A TATOO

The Harvard Journal of Medicine reports there is a <u>flood of deaths relating to TATOOS.</u> The Surgeon General has discovered the source is nationwide batches of <u>Contaminated Tatoo Ink</u>. Ink tested in laboratories THIS YEAR has been found to contain Dran-O, crack-cocaine, and even mutent strains of syphilis.

The CIA believes these contaminations may be a form of covert Soviet Germ Warfare being funneled into the United States through campus Communist Groups, so-called "anti-nuclear Activists" and <u>other "US citizens"</u> <u>seeking to undermine the United States of</u> <u>America</u>. Not every tatoo parlor is knowingly participating in the Conspiracy, they are at risk nonetheless as the contaminated ink has been detected in 37 (thirty-seven) states and Puerto Rico. So even if you "trust" your Tatooist, BE AWARE that NO tatoo ink is currently considered safe until further notice from The Surgeon General.

NOTE!! Even children are NOT SAFE! BE AWARE
that some local Tatoo Parlors WILL tatoo
minors after hours without their parents
consent.

PLEASE SHARE THIS EMERGENCY NOTICE with your
loved ones, local civic groups, all concerned
citizens and especially those At Risk of
Getting a Tatoo.

It was ridiculous and effective. The phone calls began: Did Mulley's tattoo children? Were they aware of the conspiracy? A board of health inspector sprang a visit. Given the lack of actual regulations, it wasn't clear what he was looking for—excrement on the floor? people bleeding all over?—but after poking around their indisputably clean shop, he said *You pass* and looked irritated about his wasted afternoon.

This should've been good news, but Keith Yearly had still won a victory. Dominic was knocked off balance, was deeply anxious, and spent the next week puttering around wiping things down.

If we went back to our roots, Gina wanted to say, *if we could keep all of Jeri's good accounting practices, but ditch the makeover and just be ourselves, we could fight our way back.* She knew it. She'd already said it, though, and they hadn't listened.

At least she went home each night to someone who did listen.

Just as the night was cooling, Gina pulled into the driveway to the smell of chicken roasting, zucchini frying, and hugs from Anna when she walked in the door. While Anna finished cooking, Gina cleaned up runny eggshells and bread crumbs. After all the cleaning she'd done in her life, never had it occurred to her that it could be such a willing act of love.

Over dinner they wrote down their observations from the day, anything that felt like a clue to a satisfying future, and a funny thing started to happen: they were not just looking for their separate big pictures anymore. They were trying to see if those pictures could fit together.

"Peace Corps?" Anna said.

"Tattooing is traditional in some countries," Gina said. "But I'd feel like an intruder."

"I'd have to finish college anyway," Anna said. "How about this: Have you heard of the Nevada Test Site? It's the most bombed place on the planet. We move to the desert, I throw myself into antinuclear activism, and you tattoo in Vegas."

"And how are you going to make money?"

"Work at a bakery."

"Okay, then. How about *this*," Gina said. "You help me stage a mutiny at Mulley's so I can run the place, and you open a bakery next door. All of the bread, none of the nuclear fallout."

Anna covered her eyes. "We have to get your mind out of Blue Claw."

But all this was leisurely play, no more stressful than the thousand-piece jigsaw puzzle they were putting together: night after night, an undersea paradise coalescing, fins and pirate coins and a hundred impossibly colored corals. "Aren't you sick of my puzzle yet?" Anna said. "I need to drag you out to CBGB some weekend so you don't get bored with me."

"I'll never be bored." Gina forgave Anna for not understanding why it was so miraculous, doing a thousand-piece puzzle. It meant you lived in a house where things stayed in their place. The pieces wouldn't be swept to the floor in a rage. All your work would still be there tomorrow.

"You don't draw that fish much anymore," Anna said.

"I guess I don't need to." These days, there was nothing that Gina wanted to skip over. The fish was how she'd felt when she was alone: like a glow-in-the-dark creature who didn't belong in this town. But the funny thing was, she didn't think much about the town anymore. Anna and Gina had made a little fishbowl world all their own.

It was 10:58, but sometimes Gina could make Anna forget the eleven o'clock news. She slid over on the couch and kissed Anna's neck, that soft hollow where Anna dabbed a drop of jasmine oil each evening. *SPANISH JASMINE: Sensuality. CAPE JASMINE: I am too happy.* Anna purred and pulled Gina closer.

I n this way, the weeks passed. February, March, and then the brink of April: things-are-stirring season. The soil drank up the snow. The fields outside Blue Claw greened one by one, crisp with asparagus, tender with grape shoots. On the last night of March, as they settled in for bed, Anna cracked open her bedroom window and the breeze was so fresh it could've swept off the ocean.

Gina was changing into her pajamas in the dark. Six weeks in, she was still too shy to let Anna see her naked. *Can we go slow?* she had said, and Anna had said *Of course*, but there was only so much you could do with all your clothes on—and so much Gina *wanted* to do with Anna, if she weren't so afraid of doing it wrong.

"Have you seen the farms?" Anna said, wriggling under the covers. "It's amazing. They're alive all of a sudden."

Gina climbed in next to her. "I grew up here, city mouse. That's how spring goes. Next comes spinach, then strawberries . . ." A startling thought arrived. "By the time we have sunflowers, my apprentice contract will be up."

Anna high-fived her in the dark. "Then you attract your hordes of paying customers, and we buy our house in the country."

It was too dark for Anna to see, but Gina smiled at the thought.

"Good night, Maud Wagner," Anna called. Across the room, in her cage, Maud made her new laughing sound.

We buy our house. Such an adult dream.

Once in a while, Gina still found herself wishing for something akin to a crystal ball, any indication that it was safe to trust all this—that it was actually possible for this kind of happiness to last.

Maybe the only thing to do was enjoy the peppermint in her mouth right now. Do good work. Fall in love. Stop worrying about whether it would end, and just say *thank you.*

That was hard. But it came easiest at bedtime, because for the first time in her entire life, Gina curled up at night with someone's arm around her.

Forty-six

Gina, Queen of All the Things on the List, was sitting alone in the MFATS waiting room, 100 percent prepared for a quarterly check-in that nobody else had remembered.

Jeri was five months pregnant while juggling her father's business, advising Dominic, and coordinating a ninety-mile move.

Dominic, freaking out that he wouldn't be able to provide for his kid, had been consumed with desperate efforts to boost the shop's profits before his own quarterly check-in with Jerald Harrison.

When Mr. Harrison, on a whim, demanded that meeting a week earlier than expected, it got shoehorned into today's schedule. He was in the office at this very moment, grilling Dominic as Jeri chirped her positive takeaways and tried to raise the vibes. And now Gina sat alone in the waiting room, breathing the uncomfortable cocktail of Harrison's Aramis cologne, Dominic's morning of stress-smoking, and large amounts of anxiety Lysol.

Was all this a bit depressing—no one remembering Gina's quarterly evaluation? Yes. Was this lonely? Yes. But was Gina a scrappy seagull of a woman who would choose to thrive even in neglect? Also yes.

So she took out her agreement and checked in with herself, swiping green highlighter over her accomplishments. She had now done eighty free tattoos—Anna was a gifted recruiter—and deemed twenty of them worthy of her portfolio. If Jeri had bothered to look, she'd even see a monogram and a sprinkle of pop-art geometry.

High marks. Gina, Queen of All the Things on the List. Just try and derail her.

Rick walked in and sat down. "Pez. I need confirmation on something." He opened his hands to reveal a pile of fake cockroaches. "This isn't the year for April Fool's jokes, is it."

"He'd stab you," Gina said.

The office door swung open. Dominic gave them a tense look and stepped outside for another cigarette.

Gina followed him. "How's it going?"

He took a long drag, exhaled, and rubbed his face. His curls were sweaty at the hairline. "He's not happy with anything. The accounting, the advertising, he doesn't even like our awning. He wants to know how I'm patching it up with the chamber of commerce. There's nothing I can do; Yearly is an asshole. Okay, he says, what else have you done for your public image? And I'm like—"

"Breathe," Gina said.

Dominic just continued smoking, which involved breathing, at least. "He keeps saying, *Take control, you need to take control.*" He held the cigarette in one corner of his mouth, closed his eyes, and rubbed his forehead. "How do you tell a control freak there are things you can't control?"

The door opened gently. Jeri came out in a white maternity blouse, lace at the collar, fingers at her temples as if she had a headache. "Let's finish up so we can get lunch."

Dominic gave Gina a defeated wave and followed Jeri back to the office.

Gina came back inside to find Rick at the drafting table, getting out his drawing supplies. Might as well do the same.

She'd been drawing for five minutes when Anna walked through the door in pajama pants and a sweatshirt. "You forgot your lunch."

"Why aren't you lounging? It's your day off."

"Took me two minutes. How's it going with the meeting?"

Gina gave her the thumbs-down. The office door burst open, hinges squeaking. Harrison stepped out, gave them a skeptical look, and went into the bathroom.

"I think we got the stink eye," Anna said. "I'm going to go." Gina squeezed her hand, their public substitute for the impossible kiss goodbye.

By the time Harrison came out of the bathroom and returned to the office, Anna was gone, but Gina had just barely settled into her drawing when Anna pushed open the front door again.

"Everything okay?"

"Those fliers are back," Anna said. "They're all over the pharmacy parking lot." She handed Gina a neon-green paper.

"Flashy stationery this time," Gina said.

"I'd collect them for you but I've got bread in the oven. Are you—"

The office door burst open again—perhaps Harrison could traverse doorways only by bursting?—and this time, Jeri and Dominic followed. "We're going to lunch," Dominic said, but Harrison paused when he got to Gina.

"What's that you've got?" he said.

She didn't even have a chance to answer. Harrison took it from her hand and started reading.

Dominic looked stricken. "That's nothing. April Fool's joke. Was that in our mailbox?"

"The pharmacy lot," Anna said.

Harrison looked up from the flier. "What's this about viral risk?" He couldn't possibly be that stupid. *Tattoo* wasn't even spelled correctly.

"Sir, that's a hoax," Dominic said tensely. He looked down at Gina and Anna. "Girls, go round these up."

Gina gave him an incredulous look. "She doesn't work here."

"Then why is she sitting here?" Dominic's voice was sharp. "I'm not running some hippie college coffee shop."

Anna looked stunned. She stood, gave a stiff wave, and walked out the door.

Gina jumped up and ran down the sidewalk after her, squinting in the harsh noon light. "Anna. Holy shit, I am so sorry."

"Yeah," Anna said. "That was no fun." She wrinkled up her nose—her reset maneuver when she was near tears.

Gina took her hand. "I'll talk to him later."

Anna shrugged. "You want advice from a veteran waitress? Walk back in there, put in your day's work, and bitch about it when you get home." She extended her arms for a hug.

Gina held her a moment longer than she normally would have, in broad daylight on Midway Street. Behind her, the bells tinkled on the studio door.

"Gina," Dominic said. "Let's get in the car."

"Just go," Anna whispered. "We'll talk later."

Forty-seven

Gina and Dominic spent twenty minutes yanking fliers off windshields in the pharmacy parking lot. Neon-green paper sliced between Gina's finger and thumb; she shook it off and kept going.

They drove away with a stack of fliers in the back. Dominic cruised the next few lots. Pelican Plaza strip mall: nothing. Off-track betting: a scattering. High school parking lot: everywhere. They collected them silently, working from opposite ends of the lot.

Finally Dominic decided they were done, and started up the Maverick with the growl of the speedsters at Blue Claw Raceway. It drove like a pat of butter sliding across a hot pan, sizzling up Route 25, flying eastward.

"Aren't you going to lunch?" Gina said.

"Skipping it. We need to talk." The road stretched before them, empty. Dominic gunned the engine and the car leapt forward. The farms flashed by. "Do you have any idea why?"

"Well, gee," Gina said. "You could thank me for running around getting paper cuts just now. Or maybe you want to apologize for disrespecting my roommate?"

He drummed his fingers on the steering wheel. "Funny."

"If it weren't for Anna, a hundred people would've taken that flier home while you were out to lunch, clueless."

He kept speeding along. "We're not even up to the flier yet. What were you doing chitchatting with Anna during that meeting? Harrison had *finally* shut up about control. Then he comes back from the bathroom and you know what he says?"

"I don't really care, honestly."

"*Prime example out there, Mulley.*" Dominic made his voice deeper. "*I walk in and see your kid sister yakking away with her girlfriend stinking like patchouli and BO, I'm not thinking upscale studio, I'm thinking lesbo college coffee shop.*"

Gina's stomach jumped at that word. She'd never said Anna was more than a friend, and Dominic never asked.

"Boy," she said. "That guy's got a fancy vocab."

"That's your whole rebuttal?"

"Yup." She stared out at the ragged edges of the farms, all those chicken wire fences and gray abandoned barns.

"That hoax flier." Dominic leaned on the gas again; the fields whipped by even faster. "I've been trying to put that fire out for three weeks. I was working on it. But you know who didn't need to be involved? At all? Our investor."

Gina looked out the window. A cloud broke open, shooting a slant of light down into the turned-up soil.

"Do you have *anything* to say?"

"Nope," she said.

Do we cry when the waves are too rough to swim? No, we do not. We watch the surf like people who know how to live on an island. Mulley's Tattoo used to be the safe harbor where she didn't have to be on her guard all the time, where she could breathe freely and just be.

"I don't want Anna hanging around anymore," Dominic said.

Gina stared at him.

"We're not a social club," he said. "You don't like the way Harrison puts it, fine, but he's right."

"My roommate—"

"Your roommate? Please," Dominic said. "You're transparent as hell. The first time Harrison met you at Jeri's party, he said to me later, *Your sister's not a dyke, is she?*"

Gina's chest felt hollow. *Your sister's not a dyke, is she?* That sentence wanted to take the best thing in her life, light and sweet as lemon meringue, and curdle it into an offhand slur. Whatever else she might hate about herself, she refused to hate herself about this. She shot those words through the ether to Mr. Jerald Harrison, a message to land in his lunchtime scotch like a bomb detonating a warship: *I refuse.*

"I don't care what that walking mustache thinks," she said. "And deep down, you don't either."

"Guess what," Dominic said. "Business owners who don't care what people think go bankrupt." He slowed and made a U-turn in the dirt lot of a shuttered farm stand.

Gina was two feet away from her only sibling, and she was completely alone. The longer he spoke, the more he felt like a stranger, and if she couldn't get him to shut up right now, everything might fall apart. Maybe it was too late already.

She opened her window to let in some fresh air, the crackle of gravel under tires loud in her ears. The Maverick surged back onto the road, hurtling home.

"I don't want to see you guys around town together."

"Give me a break. We're not holding hands, we're not—"

"I'm tired of dealing with rumors. Any rumors. Enough. And I need a promise," he said. "She can't hang out at the studio anymore. She cannot walk through that door."

Forty-eight

Gina paused at the curb, leaning back against her Cricket. The metal was warm against her back; Anna's baking made the whole yard smell honeyed and buttery; reggae rolled easy off the turntable inside the cottage, Bunny Wailer lilting *Jump little figs into your tree, and say you are free.* . . . If it weren't for the past two hours, this would be pure peace.

Anna's face appeared in the window. "Are you coming in? I have a surprise for you."

Gina opened their battered storm door and wrapped her arms around Anna, who returned the hug for just a moment before taking her impatiently by the hand. "Close your eyes and follow me."

Anna led her down the hall; Gina's bedroom door opened with its particular stubborn creak. "Now look."

Usually, Gina's mattress sat matter-of-factly in the corner with a limp blanket tossed across it. Now it was the centerpiece of the room, wrapped in a midnight-blue bedspread, atop a wine-red rug heaped with pillows. A gauzy canopy draped from the ceiling, making an enclave dusky as summer plums. "A bed for a queen," Anna said. "Regina."

Gina's mouth dropped open. "I don't deserve you."

Anna squeezed Gina's hand. "The morning sucked and I wanted to cheer us up. It cost me twenty bucks at Goodwill and eight quarters at the laundromat."

"My name's not even Regina—"

Anna disappeared down the hallway, calling, "Try it out."

Gina wriggled between the bed curtains to stretch out on the bedspread, light and soft and freshly laundered. A moment later, Anna returned with a plate of stuffed grape leaves. "From the diner."

Gina shook her head. "You know you don't have to be so good all the time? I can't keep up."

Anna smiled. "Eat."

Gina picked up a grape leaf. Then she put it back down.

Anna noticed. "You're not hungry?"

Gina exhaled. "I had a fight with Dominic." She twisted her hair into a knot and reached for a pencil to stab through it. "He's so terrified of Harrison. He said you can't come to the shop anymore. He doesn't even want us hanging out in public."

Anna rolled her eyes. "Did you tell him his authority stops at the door?"

Gina looked down at her lap.

Anna sat up to face her, her dark hair mussed from the bed. "Did you?"

"My agreement says they can fire me for anything. He's my boss." An ache was spreading up the back of her skull. "There's nowhere else for me to work. No tattoo shops for fifty miles."

Anna stared at her, dismayed. The magic was draining away fast. "So what do you want to do?"

It was the same question she'd pressed Anna with, outside the hall at Jeri's party, and now she understood why it was terrifying. If you said what you wanted, out loud, you might have to trade away something important to get it.

"You were scared, too," Gina said. "Did you already forget what that's like?"

"You think I never made a choice that scared me?" Heat was rising in Anna's voice. "You think it was easy to move out of Nicolas's house? To start living on diner wages again?" She twisted the corner of the bedspread as if wringing her hands. "But when I decide something, I do it. Not almost. All the way."

"Almost? Did you just whip out an insult from my mom?"

"You don't think it applies right now? When you're basically telling me we're housebound now?"

Gina felt short of breath. "I've never seen you act like a bully."

"And I've never seen you act like a coward."

It all pressed in so fast, so stifling and close. All she wanted was to get out of the room. Gina picked up one of the grape leaves and threw it at Anna.

It fell to the bed. Anna looked stunned.

Gina stared at the oily spot on Anna's strappy camisole, radish-red satin, and only now did it occur to Gina that Anna might have worn this for her.

"What the hell was that?" Anna looked down, her lips parted, eyes wide and furious.

"I don't know." It felt like a power surge, like her body acted without her.

"You're mad at the wrong person." Anna rolled off the bed and walked toward the doorway. "And I'm not your punching bag."

Gina leapt up and grabbed her shoulder. "I'm sorry. You're right."

Anna pulled away and disappeared to her room. The camisole came flying into the hallway and Anna's door slammed.

The oven timer trilled. Gina slouched to the kitchen, numb, Anna's camisole over her arm, and pulled a pan of baklava out of the oven. She dabbed at the oil stain with a sponge, but it was only making it worse.

She went back to Anna's door and spoke softly. "Can I come in?"

Long pause. "Fine."

Anna sat cross-legged on her futon. Outside, bamboo chimes clinked hollowly.

"I panicked," Gina said.

Anna shifted, saying nothing. The futon creaked.

"I will never let that happen again." She stopped. Could she really make that promise? She'd thrown a toolbox the same way. "How come you never freak out?"

"I just freak out differently."

"You disappear." Gina paused. "Like those weeks you stopped talking to me."

"That's how we do it in my family." Anna ran her finger along a seam in her bedspread. "You gave me another chance, though. I didn't know if you would."

"It's hard to be different from your family." Gina slid her hand across the blanket. "But I don't want to treat you like that."

Anna took it, her palm warm against Gina's. "Do-over?"

"Maybe . . ." Gina hesitated. "You could put that pretty thing back on?"

Anna looked at her roguishly, her hair full of late-afternoon light from the window. "Troublemaker. Take off your own shirt for a change."

Before she could chicken out, Gina went over to the window, lowered the shade, and stripped off her T-shirt. She stood there with her back to Anna, hugging her arms across her chest.

"Why aren't you turning around?" Anna's voice was playful.

If she could summon the Gina she'd seen in the mirror, on the night when she'd gotten her tattoo—the ripe figs, the curves of her back—maybe she'd be brave enough.

Fingers grazed her shoulder. A drizzle of something ran down her collarbone. She yelped and whipped around. Anna was holding a glass flask of olive oil and grinning. "Oh, did you get some oil on you?"

"You—devious—wench! I only hit you with a grape leaf!"

"At least I let you get your shirt off first."

Gina smeared the oil off with one hand and reached out to wipe it on Anna, but Anna jumped away, laughing.

"You better put that bottle down or you're going to get another shirt ruined."

"Do I look scared?" Anna held out the flask, still open, and shook it so another splatter hit Gina.

"Oil's expensive!" Gina said. Anna looked close to falling apart in laughter.

Gina leapt at her, but Anna darted away again just in time to shove the flask onto the windowsill, and Gina toppled onto the futon. She grabbed Anna's ankle and pulled her off balance until she came tumbling down, but Anna was quick and had her pinned to the mattress in three seconds. "You cannot win this, Regina. I'm stronger than you."

"Not a fair fight. I'm shirtless and you're not."

"Irrelevant," Anna said, but she did pull her own shirt over her head, with a motion so casual that she didn't appear to know she looked like a dream right now, every curve a wondrous invitation, skin that glowed like sandalwood polished soft.

While Anna was off guard, tossing her shirt aside, Gina wriggled free, tackled her, and whispered into that glorious skin: "I win."

"No." Anna's hand slipped between Gina's thighs. "I win."

"Whoa," Gina said, and then blurted, "Do you know what you're doing?" which surely was on a universal list of worst things to say in bed, but it only made Anna laugh. She slid her mouth down to kiss Gina's neck, then her chest, then just below her navel, her hair spilling onto the blanket in a raucous tangle of coffee-dark waves.

If Anna didn't know what she was doing, it didn't take her long to figure it out. A wave went through Gina, up through her torso, crashing over her head. She was clutching handfuls of the blanket, eyes closed, breath shaky, until her arms lay helpless at her side and her breath fractured into laughter again.

After she caught her breath, Gina looked at Anna, woozy with wonder. "That—never happened to me before."

"So," Anna said. "I won."

"Guess what." Gina sat up and leaned in close to Anna's ear. "The game's not over."

W hen they were both spent and blissful, sprawled on Anna's futon, Gina laid her head on Anna's chest.

"This is too much happiness to give up," Gina said. "Tell me what to do."

Anna shook her head. "You've got to make this call yourself. You want to be Dominic's lovely assistant? Or do you want your own life?"

"I want tattooing and I want you."

Leaving now was out of the question. Her exit interview was July 1, three months away, and she had to check off everything on that list—not just for the sake of learning to do her job properly, but for herself, to see this through.

"You think about that," Anna said. "I'm getting some baklava." She came back with a honeyed, flaky square on a plate.

"I just don't have any leverage right now," Gina said. "After July first, I will. Harrison won't be paying my stipend anymore, so either I start making money for the shop, or I leave. I don't think they'll *want* me to leave, because they'll need me when the baby comes. Three months. We just suck it up for three months."

Anna had brought two forks, but she had yet to surrender one to Gina. She did not look thrilled. "So for now we're just caving in to his paranoia. And for what? Let's say July comes and it all works out with your job. There's still nothing for me to do around here. What then?"

"Then we leave," Gina said. "We both need to be happy."

"It wouldn't be that easy. Your heart's still there. By the way, do you re-member you made me a promise? On the beach?"

"I will give you that tattoo." Gina took Anna's hand. "Three months, and we get some freedom."

"I'm free *now*. If I want to meet you for bagels by the river, I will. So if Dominic comes in one day going *Roar, roar, boo-hoo, I saw you and Anna outside existing in public—*"

"Then Regina quickly changes the subject to boring small talk. Like bank statements and oil changes and what happened on *Cheers*."

Anna laughed. "That's a ridiculous plan."

"Ridiculous plans work all the time," Gina said. "Just watch."

Forty-nine

Spring Quarter: Benchmarks & Requirements

TO BE COMPLETED by Check-in Meeting #4,
TUESDAY, JULY 1

***Complete portfolio of 40 photographed pieces.

***Complete apprenticeship exit interview.

***Be prepared to tattoo paying clients on July 2, 1986.

MAY 27

D
on't kill me," Gina said. "But I have to cut out early today."

Dominic flicked a box cutter and sliced open a large cardboard carton. "How early?"

"Soon. My drawing class has a mandatory end-of-term picnic."

He reached in and pulled out a large metal contraption with a cord snaking from the side. Packing peanuts scattered across the floor. "There's no such thing as a mandatory picnic."

Gina had discovered otherwise. Anna had been suffering from wanderlust for weeks now, and they'd been planning a road trip for Memorial Day. Gina was packing the picnic lunch when Jeri called. *Where are you? You were supposed to help us set up. Don't forget your smock.* Gina had forgotten the baby shower. It was a clambake with fifty guests and Gina was tasked with face-painting children.

The fallout from her stupidity might've been a little milder if she could have brought Anna to the party. Catered food, wine, sunshine: not a terrible way to spend an afternoon. But that was forbidden, of course. So instead of eating lemon meringue in the sun, Anna listened to the laments of the Smiths while cleaning Maud Wagner's cage. The cottage was icy that night.

Gina had promised to make up for it today. This afternoon's picnic *was*, in fact, mandatory.

"You'll have to check with Rick, then," Dominic said. "He wanted to meet with you this afternoon."

She glanced into the office. Rick was sitting at Dominic's desk, surrounded by paperwork, a pen behind his ear. "Why?" she said. "Rick, are you the new boss?"

"No need to sound so hopeful." Dominic's shirt was now speckled with packing peanuts, clinging by static electricity.

Rick smiled. "I don't know, should I give it a shot?" He beckoned her into the office. She sat. "Well, Gina, have you done my laundry today? Please respond using *Mr. Alvarez.*"

"All your shirts are pink now, Mr. Alvarez, but yeah."

"And tell me how that portfolio's going."

"Still seven short." It was harder to find people to work on now that Anna wasn't allowed to shepherd volunteers through the door.

"When do I get one?"

Gina looked at him skeptically. "Are we still playing?"

"I mean it. I'd like a Pezadita Original."

She snorted. "I'm not putting my stupid doodles next to the artwork on you. Talk to me in the fall, when I'm a professional." She looked at the clock. "All right, boss. I have to go."

"In all seriousness," Rick said, "we have matters to discuss. Is this a private class picnic, or could I tag along?"

Having company might be good for Anna. She'd been quiet lately, sleeping too late for morning coffee because she was up until the wee hours, reading biographies with titles like *Dorothy Day: The Long Loneliness*. And she'd always liked Rick. "Sure."

He jangled his keys as Dominic tried fruitlessly to sweep the packing peanuts into a dustpan. Gina gave him a wave and followed Rick out the back door.

Anna was on the boardwalk in her red leather jacket, staring down into the river. Her hair was tied with two red ribbons, just like the day she'd picked up Gina at the shop for their first drawing session. A pair of swans paddled toward her.

"Now that we're safely outside," Gina said to Rick, "you should know this is not a drawing class picnic."

"Ni de pedo," Rick said.

"What's that?"

"Polite translation is *no kidding*. I hope you never have to lie to save your life."

Anna turned toward their voices, looking guarded. She pulled her jacket tight, tucking her hands under her arms.

"I have a surprise guest," Gina said.

Anna cautiously released one hand to shake Rick's. "How've you been?"

He wrapped her up in a hug. "La vida es buena. Agreed?" Gina saw Anna's face over Rick's shoulder; it was softening. "We miss you around the shop."

Anna raised her eyebrows. "We do?"

"*I* miss you. This one misses you." He patted Gina's shoulder. "She cries all day long and walks around hungry, because she won't eat anything but your delicious bread. It is a tragedy."

Anna smiled.

"Hopefully," Rick said, "we'll fix that soon." What was he up to?

Gina had imagined the arboretum as a sky-high forest, full of redwoods and tropical man-eating trees and hybrids in hot-tub-sized pots. In reality, it was just a park. A stately one, to be sure, with golf-course grass and flowering trees labeled with plaques—but just a park.

When they'd settled in on their picnic blanket, Rick cleared his throat. "Pezadita. I have to read you a letter."

Gina peeled the foil from her sandwich. "A letter from who?"

He took out an envelope. "Estimado Señor Alvarez. Es un gran placer invitarle a Usted reunirnos como Artista en Residencia—"

"Oh, come on."

"—al Proyecto Muralismo Renacentista por los meses de junio hasta diciembre—"

"Help a pasty Anglo, please."

When he announced "Cariñosos saludos, Rafaela Ramírez Mendoza," rolling the *r*'s like fingers drumming a bucket, Anna applauded.

"You know Spanish?" he said.

Anna shook her head. "You just seemed happy."

Rick turned to Gina. "They're inviting me to work on a project in Mexico City. There's a grant to bring artists from the States, shadowing Mexican muralists."

Gina's throat felt tight. "When?"

"I'm flying down in two weeks."

"Your aunt—"

"Is in remission," he said. "Remember?"

"Are you coming back?"

"Around Christmas. For a while. I want to check in on Tía before I move on."

She'd been so stupid, thinking someone like Rick would stick around at a place like Mulley's.

"What did Dom say?"

"The jefe wasn't happy, but he said, you know, *I can't stop you.*"

It felt like the energy in her body was leaving her, seeping down into the ground.

"I thought you were going to tell me something else," Gina said. She leaned back against a locust tree.

"What?" Rick said.

She'd had this wild, brief hope that Rick was taking over her apprenticeship. Stepping up in the shop, somehow. He was her mentor now, the only one left to coach her through the last few miles. Or so she had decided. Without really asking him.

"Nothing." She sat down on a patch of bare ground and picked up a stick.

"What are the murals for?" Anna asked, as if Gina were not sitting there suffering the loss of her only other friend.

Anna and Rick went on talking without her, and Gina drew in the dirt. Start with the beaky mouth. Fins like fringed wings; beady eyes.

She'd first seen this fish a few months before she met Rick, the week of her sixteenth birthday. She'd been working at the bait shop then, and maybe the boss felt bad for her, because his daughter Vanessa asked if Gina wanted to go fishing. Early in the morning, the two of them went down to a hidden bank, all tangled with blackberry brambles, and baited their hooks from a Folgers can full of night crawlers. To Gina, the surface of the water appeared still, but suddenly Vanessa grabbed a little net from her tackle box and scooped up a thrashing something.

Gina had never seen such a fish: the size of a lime, glow-green like a pack of Doublemint. It had a beaky mouth, fins like two fringed wings, eyes like glass beads. In short, it was wonderful. But Vanessa was already shaking her head. *Damn, look at that ugly thing.*

What is it? Gina had said. Vanessa knew all the fish—bass and bluegill and perch, every crab in the bay. But at this one, she'd shrugged. *People are so dumb. Somebody got rid of their aquarium and felt guilty flushing it. This water turns brackish downstream. It's going to die.*

Definitely going to die? Gina said.

Or if it lives, maybe it lays eggs, and then you've got an invasive species. Vanessa laid it on the ground and cast her line again. Gina felt grief-stricken for this creature, doomed to suffocate in the open air. She'd dug through the brush for an old jar to get the fish home, but all she found was rusted beer cans. The fish opened and closed its beaky mouth. Gina had only her notebook and a pen, and couldn't do anything but sit there and draw it while it died.

Vanessa never invited her to go fishing again, but Gina couldn't stop thinking about the fish. She searched the encyclopedias at school. That summer, she drew it again and again, and even with all the people coming in and out of the shop, nobody noticed or asked her about it—until the day Rick arrived. *Nice to meet you. Cool drawing. What kind of fish is that?*

I don't know. It showed up in Blue Claw from somewhere else.

That makes two of us, Rick said. *Maybe it can show me around.*

This whole time, she thought it was Dom making her feel safe. But it was Rick, too. This past year, maybe Rick most of all.

Rick and Anna were still talking as Gina drew in the dirt, dragging the stick in circles until she'd made a big zero of a fishbowl, deep as a moat.

"So with luck," he said, "I get the fire burning again. Travel, get inspired, start dreaming in Spanish like I used to. And maybe"—he glanced over at Gina and met her eyes—"maybe Pezadita steps up to fill my job. And then she gets the leverage to bring her friends around."

Anna, still unpacking the picnic basket, missed the moment—but Rick kept his eyes on Gina. He put his hand on his heart. Then he flashed his wrist.

¿De qué sirve?

Fifty

Gina's torso felt like one timpani-sized heartbeat. Rick's workstation was stripped, artwork gone, equipment in a lockbox, ready for him to leave behind. His plane would leave tomorrow. This was the last thing he would do in the shop: carry Gina's work away on his body.

She'd designed a new merit badge in his honor: Justicia.

"That's what you call 'justice'?" he said. "Trusting you with my leg?"

"Whatever, jerk. I meant your Oscar Romeo thing—"

"Romero. And justice would be practicing all over Mackie's leg." But all that day, Rick had shown off the drawing to anyone who walked through the door.

At the last minute, he said, "Pezadita, you know what? I love this merit badge. But I was wondering if I could get your fish."

"The ugly fish?"

"We've got history," Rick said.

"You're crazy." She took out her sketchbook. "But here. You have a hundred to choose from."

As Gina set up, Dominic stationed himself at the counter like an exam proctor, flipping through the Spaulding & Rogers catalog as if he wasn't watching her. She applied the stencil on Rick's leg, under a radiant Aztec sun, dipped the needle into the ink, and began. Rick was silent, letting her concentrate.

"Rick, you doing OK?"

"Euphoric."

She traced a curve. Crisp. Smooth. Dominic abandoned his magazine. "That's it. Good girl."

Her hand wobbled. "Damn it—"

"It's okay, Pez," Rick said. "You can cover a lot with shading. It's all good."

Yes, this one *would* be good, if Dominic could just keep quiet and let her focus. Rick's skin was like butter, the needle buzzed along with a steady hum, and as she worked, she felt her brain doing the same. A deep calm moved through her, like a flock of sparrows settling into a tree.

Stretch the skin. Trace the line. Wipe away blood and ink. Gina drew another perfect curve—incredible.

The phone rang. "Ignore it," Dominic said. "Keep going." It kept ringing. Gina stopped and shook out her hand.

"Stupid answering machine's on the fritz again." He jumped up and loped to the office.

"How are you doing?" Rick whispered. "Really?"

"Queasy."

"Ay, please don't puke on my leg—"

Dominic strode up the hallway. "I have to get Jeri to the hospital."

Gina stiffened.

"Too early, isn't it?" Rick said.

"Could be nothing." Dominic's jaw was tight.

Gina looked at Rick's leg, then back at Dominic. "Do you need me to come and—"

"No. Stay and finish." He grabbed his keys and left, bells clinking dully behind him. They watched him hurry past the front window and then disappear.

"She'll probably be fine," Rick said. "Mamí had false alarms. Every pregnancy. We all made it. They'll put her on bed rest."

"Yeah?"

"Sure. You good, Pezadita? You want to keep going?"

"I guess. Dom said to." Her chest hurt. After a minute, she picked up the machine.

After Rick's tattoo, Gina fled to the diner. Anna, tall and lovely in her dark red waitress dress, was taking someone's order. When she saw Gina, she waved her over to the counter.

A moment later, she brought Gina a cup of coffee. "Sit."

"Jeri's in the hospital."

Anna's eyes widened.

"Miss," called a bald man in the back. "Miss, I said Canadian bacon."

Anna put her hand on Gina's shoulder. "Hold on."

Gina waited, building a small tower with the packets of jelly. Two minutes later, Anna returned. "What's happening?"

"I don't know. Dominic told me not to come. I feel horrible. When they told me she was pregnant I didn't even want them to have this baby and now—"

A child started screaming in the back. A glass shattered to the floor. "Ugh," Anna said. "I'll be right back."

At the baby shower, she'd put her hand on Jeri's belly, and a foot pressed back against her palm. Gina almost lost her breath. Who was this, kicking away at her hand? She opened Jeri's copy of *What to Expect* to thirty-three weeks: no longer a shrimpish lima bean. Decidedly human, with real ears and eyes, floating in his private aquarium.

Gina's jelly tower toppled. She started again, this time fortifying it with marmalade. Maybe this was the closest thing she had to prayer—this simple, repetitive task, done with all her worry and hope.

Anna came back. "Third broken glass today. It must be a full moon."

"Can you sit with me? Just for a minute?"

Anna glanced across the diner, as if a jukebox might explode without her vigilance. "Why don't you draw? Draw me that tattoo I'm going to get one day. Hang in there one more hour; I'll finish my shift and we'll go."

"I don't even have my sketchbook. I left so fast."

"Take my notebook. My bag's on the coatrack."

Gina grabbed it and brought it back to the counter, but when she pulled the notebook out, a waterfall of papers and pamphlets spilled onto the floor. This day was cursed.

She gathered them up, recognizing the ones she'd brought home for Anna from Blue Claw Community—*Careers in Culinary Arts. Careers in Political Science*—shuffled in with others she'd never seen.

SANE/FREEZE CHICAGO: Antinuclear canvassers wanted.

TOKYO: Teach English, see the world.

CENTRAL AMERICA: Pax Christi, human rights fact-finding missions.

Anna had stopped talking about traveling lately; Gina suspected it was her fault. Most nights she came home from the shop frustrated and tired, and if Anna turned on the news, Gina didn't even sit with her on the couch anymore; she just went to her room. She didn't have the energy for the world that preoccupied Anna.

But it was a cagey thing to do, secretly collecting pamphlets, like you were going to take off in the night—like Stella in the bad times. A pile of brochures for Las Vegas, Great Lakes, Ocean City. *This house has bad energy, we have to go, we have to clear the air.*

One article was dated last week. *Flair for Publicity: Greenpeace, a Maverick Protest Group.* Written across the top, in Anna's hasty handwriting: *Phone for job openings?*

Anna ran past, looking weary and rolling her eyes. "Everybody wants Tabasco."

Gina tried to slide the papers into the front pocket, but they stuck on something. After that Pandora's box of pamphlets, what could be left in there?

An envelope. The return address gave Gina a zipper-pull of nerves:

NICOLAS EGGLI-PFISTER
House of Mystical Delights

Anna was all the way across the room, trying to soothe another irate customer.

To: Marianna Dellarocca . . . PLEASE FORWARD, postmarked January. Clever: he'd written to Anna at his own address, forwarding to the address he didn't know. Gina opened the letter.

Marianna,

I shall be formal to make up for your lack of courtesy. I opened my home to you. I saw extraordinary potential in you. I gave you employment, affection, and travel, and you have repaid me with rejection and neglect.

If you disappeared to pursue our tattooist friend, you needn't have. It could have been arranged. I can't imagine what tale you

*will spin to explain your departure, but if you have any decency it
will be the undiluted truth and you will inform her of my
ailments. When you move on to your next adventure, I hope
you'll give the poor girl a bit more notice than you gave me.*

Regards, N.

*Postscript. My health continues to be poor. And I am missing a
teaspoon, a cricket bat, and an apron. Please return them.*

Gina looked up. Anna was now dealing with the irate man's irate wife.

She pushed the letter into its envelope and massaged the base of her skull, where an ache was starting. *Inform her of my ailments?* Anna had never spun any tale to explain the timing of her departure; she just said she woke up and knew it was time to leave.

Which meant Anna might be the kind of person who habitually woke up and left.

Gina's pen drew agitated lightning bolts on Anna's notebook. What crazy carnival midway was she living on, that she'd lost her virginity to a middle-aged tarot card reader with mysterious *ailments* and fallen in love with a girl who couldn't decide between saving whales and joining the rodeo? A girl capable of concealing a letter like this?

All she wanted, all of a sudden, was Dominic. She needed to hug Dominic in his lumberjack shirt, smelling of cigarettes and Old Spice, like when she was ten and he was in trade school, home for a visit. Making her grilled cheese, drawing marker tattoos on her arms—he was the anchor. Always for her, never against her.

Rick was leaving. Maybe Anna would leave. But the Mulleys—even when they screwed up and fought and failed each other, at least the Mulleys knew how to hold fast.

Anna returned. "How's it going?"

Gina, silent, put Anna's notebook back in her bag.

Anna bent to look in her eyes. "Can I get you some food? You look pale."

"I have to go to the hospital," Gina said.

"You want to call first?" Anna pointed to the diner phone. Gina shook her head. "You're scaring me," Anna said.

"I just have to go." Gina stood quickly, dizzy spots clouding her vision, and barely felt Anna's hug. She was already looking out to the road, where the streetlights were snapping on.

Fifty-one

The hospital was a wash of light against the fortress-gray cloud cover of the sky. Walking through the glass doors to clean walls, candy stripers, and the smell of cafeteria minestrone brought Gina an unexpected sense of relief. All her memories of this place dated back to the days when her mother was hospitalized, when the weight of caring for Stella was lifted off Gina and placed onto adults, professionals, who knew what they were doing. Arriving at a hospital meant you weren't alone anymore.

Gina stopped at the receptionist's desk, where a *Get Well Soon* bouquet awaited delivery. "Jeraldine Harrison, please?"

The receptionist paged through a directory, but then Gina heard her name.

Dominic walked across the lobby, a few matted curls escaping his Mets cap. His lips were pressed tight, but whether this meant bad news or simply *I told you not to come*, she couldn't tell.

He looked tired, his eyes raw at the corners, stung pink under the cap's brim. He put his arms out. She ran to him, and he crushed her in a hug.

He smelled just the way she'd needed him to smell: every cigarette he had smoked that day, every hour of sweat. They stood there, Gina and Dominic, together—the way they should've been all along, before the pointless fighting, before every awful word. Dominic began to cry.

She'd never seen him cry before. He clung to her, head bent to her shoulder, and breathed a quiet, high-pitched gasp.

"I'm here," Gina whispered. "What's going on?"

Dominic's shaky exhale was hot in her ear. His tears wet her hair. "A boy."

Gina pulled away and looked into his face. "He made it?"

Dominic closed his eyes, face folding into grief, and shook his head. They fell into each other again.

Fifty-two

What a strange and awful thing—grieving a person who'd been so close to arriving, and now never would be.

It wasn't exactly that Gina wanted to cry; rather, it was an insistent *no* inside her. No, the story would not go this way. No, this human was not permitted to leave, not when she'd finally come to cautiously look forward to another Mulley in their lives. *What to Expect*, seven months of pregnancy: *Baby is two to four pounds, and can respond to light, sound, and touch.* He'd already been learning their voices, the buzz of tattoo machines, and the light of noonday. That was too much life to lose.

I need you to check on Mom, Dominic had said. *She wanted to come to the hospital and I told her it's not a good idea. She's hysterical. If you could just calm her down . . .*

Gina had been letting Stella calm herself.

Please. For me, Dominic had said. *So I can stay with Jeri.*

Gina hadn't been to her mother's house in months, not even when Stella started saying *Come over, I have a surprise.* Now she sat at the curb in the car she'd bought herself, looking at the place she used to live: red-shingled ranch, yellowed circulars in the driveway, moss streaking the roof.

Gina tried the doorknob and found it open. The only sound was the wall clock ticking, second hand stuck and twitching at the eleven. Gina flipped the kitchen switch; the bulb was burned out. "Mom?"

Room after room, empty. Stella's bedroom was a rumple of sheets. The bathroom was a sinkful of clutter and smelled of cigarettes and mildew. The living room sofa bloomed white with crumpled tissues.

"Mom, where are you?"

In the quiet, Gina heard static-flecked radio, a man's voice warbling *until the twelfth of never . . .* She followed the sound to the backyard, where Stella sat red-eyed, rocking in her wooden glider, a paper cup and a jug of Gallo wine on the cement patio. Gina clicked off the radio.

Stella stood and leaned into Gina, breath still catching. "They didn't want me there. He was my first grandchild. All I wanted was to hold him. Just once."

So familiar, the weight of Stella's head on her shoulder, the smell of Aqua Net and the poke of her earring. Gina could smell the wine on her breath. "They love you. You're a good mom." All the old lines. The trick was keeping her voice light, measured. "But Jeri's really sick."

Stella's breath quickened. "*Her* mother got to say goodbye. We knew she'd shut us out."

"Last week you loved her. You wanted Dom to propose."

"I should've believed her father when he told me the dirt on her, a woman who—"

"A woman who just lost her baby." Gina felt suddenly drained.

Stella's voice was icy. "Don't talk to me about losing babies."

Gina paused. In the trees, a host of cicadas began their rattle chorus, surging to a peak, dying like a wave.

If you were Stella, there was no middle ground. There was a river with Stella on one side, haplessly doing her best, and a handful of good people on the riverbank with her—until they inexplicably plunged into the river and swam away, to stand with Stella's enemies on the other side.

How scared a person must feel if they saw the world that way.

How tightly they'd cling if you took one step away.

But this was not a thing Gina could change—how Stella saw the world.

"I just wanted to hold a baby again." Stella began to weep, clinging to her paper cup. "Tell them to let me see him."

Gina didn't move; Stella grabbed her wrist, fingernails digging into Gina's skin. She raised her voice. "Gina, *call* them."

Ten seconds away from Stella's point of no return, when Gina used to drift off and wait until the shouting stopped. Instead, she looked her mother in the eye, put her hand on Stella's, and pried it off her wrist.

"Don't do that again," she said, quietly, firmly.

What was Gina's job right now? Stella was upset, but not in danger, unless she got behind the wheel.

"I'll be right back." Gina walked into the house, the screen door falling shut behind her.

The floor was sticky under her sneakers. She took Stella's car keys off the hook near the door, opened the kitchen cabinet, and hid them under a coffee mug.

A croak came from down the hall. Gina froze. A trill; a squeak.

She walked to her old bedroom, tense, cautious, and opened the door.

Unlike the rest of the house, the room was cleaner than she'd left it. The carpet was vacuumed; the stains were gone. The bed had been replaced by a crib, with a fresh coverlet, christening-gown white. Stella had prepared Gina's room for a visiting grandchild.

The source of the croaking stood in the corner. Two parrots perched in a large birdcage: one jade green, like the river thick with algae; one a cool gray, a February morning.

"Love you," crooned the gray one. The other one warbled something unintelligible in reply.

Gina watched them, baffled. Had Stella bought these to entertain the baby?

Or had she—in her loneliness—bought them for company?

Jeri *had* given Stella money last December: the five hundred dollars to repay Gina. But Gina had known, by the time February rolled around, that she'd never see that money. She'd predicted as much to Anna.

Seeing the evidence still hurt. At a moment when Gina's apprenticeship was about to end, when she desperately could've used that cash, she was watching two expensive birds—luxury purchases—grooming each other in the room she'd left. Gina thought she'd put the anger behind her, but it was stirring again.

Alongside the anger was a piercing sadness. All the months Gina hadn't been here, maybe Stella had sat night after night with these caged birds, repeating words of affection in hopes that they might echo back to her.

Gina leaned against the doorway, closed her eyes, and breathed. It no longer smelled like her room. And this was no longer her home. She turned and closed the door behind her.

"Love you," the bird was still croaking, as she walked down the hall.

Gina returned to the backyard. She would hug Stella and go.

"You saw the birds?" Stella rocked on the glider, sipping her wine. "One for me, one for you. That was your surprise. I kept asking you to come over and see, but you wouldn't."

Gina tried to absorb this. *One for me, one for you.*

"You always wanted a parrot," Stella said. "I still have a picture you drew. A letter to Santa."

It clicked.

This was Stella's best effort. She hadn't settled her debt—she couldn't risk cutting this tether to Gina—but she also hadn't given the money to some boyfriend. She'd tried her desperate best to find something that might make Gina happy. Something to connect them again.

But Stella was already moving on. "You didn't call Dominic, did you."

Gina, weary, pulled her car keys out of her pocket. She squeezed her mother's shoulder. "I have to go."

"Take their side if you want," Stella said, "but Jeri brought this on herself."

Gina paused. If Stella ever said that to Jeri's or Dom's face . . . "Please, Mom. Don't." She started walking away. "Good night."

"You get knocked up when you're young and there's no money," Stella said, slurring a little. "He says he's going to leave, you go to the neighborhood woman to take care of it. They always botch it. You're never the same."

Goose bumps rose on Gina's arms. She stopped and turned. "Who are you talking about?" she said, but this felt familiar, and she was afraid to hear the answer.

"She'll try half a dozen times," Stella said. "She'll lose them all. Unless she gets a miracle." She paused. "Sometimes you get a miracle."

Gina was mute. In the darkening yard, Stella's garden statues were lit clamshell-white in the back patio light, children fishing, cherubs kissing, lambs sleeping, all casting long shadows in the dead grass.

Ma, she could say, *miscarriages happen for all kinds of reasons.*

Ma, she could say, *abortions are in clinics now, not basements. They're legal. They're safe. You can still have babies.*

Or—Ma. Why didn't you tell me?

Was I the last one, or did you lose more?

Do you see it wasn't your fault?

"That would be awful," Gina said. "I'd feel terrible for anyone who went through that."

"She'll never forgive herself."

"Even if that was true," Gina said, "I hope she would. I would forgive her."

"You can't forgive her," Stella said. "Nobody can." She leaned her head all the way back on the glider until she was looking up at the darkening cloak of clouds.

"Yes," Gina said. "You can forgive a lot."

Fifty-three

Gina parked on Midway Street and slumped forward so her forehead rested on the steering wheel.

It was only eight, but she was drained. Marathoners had helpers to give them water, and boxers had cut men to fix their faces. Gina was alone, and she still had a night of work ahead.

But this was what Dominic had asked her to do. Hold fast.

She walked into an unusually crowded waiting room, so packed and loud that it felt like she'd stumbled into a house party. Mackie barked at her as soon as she walked in. "I'm drowning. Hurry and set up."

Gina walked over to the counter. "Where did they come from?"

"One big van. Take a look." He handed her a newspaper ad with a close-up of a woman's behind in Daisy Dukes, a heart tattoo peeking out from the bottom:

"Dominic could've given us a heads-up," Mackie said.

"His ads never worked that well before." She'd *told* him this was a keeper.

Mackie rubbed his eyes with his palms. He was in the clothes he used to wear before Jeri's dress code: a Coors Light T-shirt, a red-white-and-blue sweatband. A piece of toilet paper clung to a shaving nick on the back of his head.

Gina put the newspaper down. "I'll book appointments for the ones you can't do."

"Don't be stupid," he grunted. "They won't come back. We're not leaving money on the table. Set up your machine."

"What money? I work for free."

"Tonight you get paid." Mackie started breaking down his workstation from the last tattoo and setting up for the next. "If this shop doesn't start taking in cash, we're about a week away from the lights going off."

Gina shook her head. "He didn't give permission, I'm not chancing it. Not with all the shit they're dealing with."

"You want a repeat of that Thanksgiving disaster?" Mackie said. "Dominic left me in charge. You don't want to take your share, I'm happy to keep it all. But I'm not wasting this." He gestured at the packed waiting room. "Get your machine."

———

A nna called the shop at nine. *Where are you? What happened with Jeri? When are you coming home?* But people just kept arriving—the freshly tattooed calling their friends from the pay phone outside—so whenever Gina completed a tattoo, yet another head popped through the door.

It was almost midnight before she got home, famished and exhausted. Instead of warm lamplight and frying zucchini, she found Anna in the blue light of the eleven o'clock news, an empty cereal box next to her.

"Hey," Gina said. With every word after that, things got worse.

They went to the Queen Regina bed meaning to sleep and ended up talking, agitated, with all the lights on, as if that could make anything clearer.

"Do you really want to get into this now?" Anna said. "You're not in a good place, you're—"

"Don't talk down to me."

"You lost your nephew." Anna tried to hold her. Gina pulled away. "I'm trying to be compassionate. If you'd rather fight about how you read my mail—"

"What the hell was he talking about? Ailments? Did he give me some STD?"

"He's forty with a bad back, Gina. He's manipulative. He carries on like we were married twenty years and I left him battling cancer."

"What freaks me out is you never told me—"

"Maybe because I knew you'd freak out?"

"You have brochures for Tokyo!"

A breeze swelled the curtains. Anna's voice rose with anger. "I get that you see this beautiful future together, okay, fine. But what do I do? Play housewife?"

"Come on." But Gina felt a twinge of guilt. Maybe she had been picturing that, especially lately, with Rick leaving and a full-time job seeming possible.

Tattoo all day, come home to her loving girlfriend, a warm house, fettuccine alfredo—the perfect life.

"You knew I wanted to travel. I want more than just a job. I want what you have. Gina, I envy you."

"Stop it with the envy shit. You grew up with everything I didn't have."

"I envy your vocation." Anna stood and went to the window, lining up all the seashells and trinkets she'd gathered on the sill. "Look, I'd rather dream *with* you. I collect all these ideas, but your head's on pause till July. I just thought, what was the point hashing it out now?" She picked up the wishbone she'd saved, the one she always said they'd use to settle an argument. She gave Gina a strained smile. "Should we just go ahead and crack this tonight? So we can sleep?"

She couldn't joke this away. "I thought you were leaving me, like you left Nicolas. With no warning."

"This is different." Anna put the wishbone down. She looked exhausted. She flopped down on the bed and let her head sink into the pillow. "I wouldn't do that to you."

Gina lay next to her. "There's only so many places you can get work tattooing." Her head felt fuzzy. "And I can't leave them like this, now they've lost their baby and Rick is gone—"

"I wouldn't try to make you."

"But you're ready to go."

Anna didn't answer, just threaded her fingers through Gina's.

Gina brought Anna's face to hers and kissed her. Anna's mouth was cool like lemon water. After a second's pause, Anna relaxed into the kiss.

"I promise you," Anna said, "I won't disappear in the night."

Gina reached out of the bed and grabbed a red marker from her art box. She wrote across Anna's knuckles: HOLD FAST.

Fifty-four

Some good person should restore a submarine and convert it into a haven for grieving people. Peace in the Deep: stocked with tissues and lasagna, a respite from the needy world, safe in the embrace of the sea.

This thought came to Gina on Dominic's first day back at work. He looked like he'd been through a night of hard drinking. He holed up in the office, doing paperwork by the dull aqueous glow of one blue desk lamp, as if the glare of the overheads was more than he could stand. Gina left him alone for most of the day, but at dinnertime she ventured in and took the swivel chair across from him.

"How's Jeri?"

"What you'd expect." He looked down at his desk as if he'd never seen it before: the mess of ledgers, newspapers, catalogs. A copy of Gina's agreement was taped to his desk; he picked at the tape on the corner. "Things are kind of falling apart around here, aren't they?"

"Do you have half an hour?" Gina said. "I want to do something for you."

They went out the back door. She did not have a grief submarine, but was there anything more like it than a ride through a tunnel car wash? The pollen in the air had turned Dominic's Maverick from white to grimy yellow-gray, and people in despair should not have to think about things like that. She took his keys and climbed into the driver's seat. "My treat."

When they pulled in, Gina called to the man in the green jumpsuit: "We'll do the Super Wash." He waved them in. She cranked the window back up, eased the car onto the rollers, and put it in neutral.

Hoses spouted. Water hissed along the car's vinyl roof. When Gina was little, she'd always loved when Dominic took her to the car wash. It was their private amusement park ride, Pinocchio descending into the whale, down Monstro's hatch to find Geppetto.

"I know this week's been hell and back," Gina said. "But I wondered if we could do the exit interview a little early. Not today. When you're feeling up to it."

"Exit?" Dominic said, sounding surprised. "Where you going?"

"Maybe nowhere," she said. "That's why I want to talk to you. Anna wants to travel. But I don't want to run off if I could be useful here."

"Obviously you're useful," he said. "If it was up to Mackie, we'd never have toilet paper."

"What I mean is—with Rick gone," Gina said, "I wondered if you needed me to fill his spot."

Dominic looked listlessly out at the jets of water. "Haven't thought about it. We have to revisit the plan. We've been hitting some bumps."

"Maybe that vision isn't who we are," she said.

He shook his head. "I just couldn't hack it with the clients Jeri wanted. That's on me."

Gina drummed her fingers on her knees. "Remember last summer, when I promised I'd come up with ideas to help you?" It was getting dark in here, in the belly of the tunnel. She flipped on the interior light. "I was wondering—if it would be useful, maybe I could stick around and try doing some of them."

Stop saying *maybe*. Dominic didn't have to go around couching his thoughts in *maybe* and *Just wondering* and *If you don't mind*.

"What are the ideas?" He gestured at the cave of water fluming outside the windows. "We've got nothing else to do."

On a page buried deep in her sketchbook she had written: *What would make me stay at Mulley's?* Even with all her disappointment, even with Rick gone. She'd gone spelunking in her mind for any little ruby of an idea, any bit of excitement and purpose she'd felt this year. If Dominic said yes to any of these, then she could find a way to stay.

Go to conventions. Meet other women tattooers. They were far away, but they were out there. See if anyone could teach her to do mastectomy tattoos like Tía Andrea's; Long Island was rife with breast cancer. Become an expert at it. Connect with hospitals.

Stop trying to make the shop look upscale and just be good neighbors. Show people—by who they were, not their slick digs—that the Mulleys weren't dirtbags tattooing children with syphilis-infected ink. Stop trying to please Keith Yearly. Promote Phillips Electric and all the other businesses he'd undermined. Give out free coffee, like she'd suggested back in September, or have an art show by the river.

Let Gina create and post all that wild flash she'd dreamed of. Believe that if she was weird enough to love merit badges and hybrid animals, somebody else might, too.

She reached into the backseat for her leatherbound sketchbook, with the gold-embossed *G*. She'd taken her mess of ideas and organized them into a list: *Ideas for Mulley's.* She handed it to him.

Long moments passed. A downpour of water pebbled the roof. Nozzles shot stripes of pink and blue foam.

Finally Dominic gave the notebook back to her and flipped off the interior light. His voice was flat.

"It gets a little old," he said. "You playing armchair quarterback."

She bit her lip. "They were just ideas."

"*Be a good neighbor*? I don't give a shit about the rest of Blue Claw. They've given me nothing but grief. And speaking of things way outside your wheelhouse—"

"Fine," Gina said. "You're the one who wanted to see it."

He turned in his seat to face her. "I wasn't going to mention this today, but if we're clearing the air . . ." His top button had come undone, showing the bear tattoo growling out of his chest hair. "Two girls came in this morning and asked if Gina was still taking the coupon. You thought you'd just start charging customers while I was gone?"

Giant rollers came pressing down on the car's hood. They looked ready to pop through the windshield. She turned toward Dominic. "Did you bother to ask Mackie what happened? You told me I report to him. That was his call."

"There's moments I expect you to know better. You are not ready. I have a quality standard—"

The car jolted to a stop.

Dominic stared up at the windshield. Behind them, the big fringe still slapped the air, the curtain of water still flowed. But whatever rolled them along wasn't rolling anymore.

All the nozzles and brushes halted. The jumpsuit guy opened Gina's door. "Conveyor broke. Happens sometimes. Just wait out front."

Gina tiptoed through the tunnel, pressing as close as she could to the wall without wetting her clothes. Stray water drops fell from the ceiling. She clutched her sketchbook closer.

They emerged from the tunnel into the air, the sunlight blinding. There was a bench right out front, but a man was parked nearby, cleaning out his station wagon—tackle box, crab traps—and Dominic might succumb to machismo if there was another guy within earshot. Better to take the bench on the other side.

The walk had given her time to breathe. "So I should follow Mackie's orders, except when I shouldn't. It depends on circumstances, but you have no idea what these circumstances were. And you don't *want* to know, or hear my side of the story. Am I getting this right?"

He shook his head in disbelief. "You have a week and a half left on that apprenticeship agreement. No one promised you a job at the end. You should be begging me to keep you on."

She put her fingertips to her temples. "Do you know how many days I wonder why I'm still here? You don't listen to half of what I say. I finally find someone who cares about me and I can't even bring her around because you're so scared of Harrison. You want me to fall on the floor thanking you? When honestly I could've gone to Pirate Paul's a year ago—"

Dominic kicked the leg of the bench with the heel of his work boot. The sun was harsh on his face. "So that's your plan? Go to Paulie's? After we invested all this time and money in you?"

A minute more and he would hit his wall. She had to be careful. Inhale. Exhale. "I'm grateful for everything you've done for me." Gina leaned toward him, spacing out the words. "But a fancy salon is not the Mulley's where I grew up."

"Things change."

"Yeah, they do," she said. "And I could help them change again if you'd let me. There's a reason those girls came looking for me."

"Like you said, feel free to go to Paulie's."

She stared at him. "If I leave, you think I'm staying on this island?"

It surprised even her, to hear those words come out of her mouth, but it was true. Anna sure wasn't spending her life in this suburban purgatory. Rick was gone, and maybe he'd come back, but maybe not.

Dominic stopped kicking and leaned his head into his hands. His knuckles disappeared in his curls. "And go where? Tattooing's illegal in the city. You know that."

She'd never said the city. But if that's where he wanted to take this—

"That never stopped you. You apprenticed in Coney Island. You got that shamrock in the Village." She pointed to his arm.

"At my friend's apartment. Coney Island—you had to find us by word of mouth. I practiced on a ride operator named Smitty with nothing better to do. I wanted to train you better. But you know what, Gina?" Dominic's voice was rising. "If you think we don't respect you, then go on out there. If you want to risk getting arrested. Or robbed, or raped, or the shit kicked out of you—"

Gina sat gripping the bench. Over by the car wash building, the man detailing the Maverick halted his work, wax pad pressed to paint, and stared at them.

"Rick leaves, we lose the baby, and now you, too. Of all the selfish things you've ever done"—Dominic's boots made a rough crunch against the gravel as he stood—"this one wins the goddamn trophy."

Gina's brother turned away, his neat gray shirt clinging with sweat to his body, and stalked out of the lot, down the can-littered, brittle-brown road.

Fifty-five

Discipline. Pay for the car wash. Do not cry.

Drive Dominic's Maverick back to the shop. Leave keys on the counter. Do not cry.

Drive the Cricket home.

Now, in the sanctuary of the bed Anna had made her—now she could cry.

When the worst of it had passed, when she caught her breath, she stared into the shadowy green of the walnut tree outside her window.

The other night, Dom tuned the shop radio to baseball, an announcer interviewing Pete Rose, and Rose said: "I'd walk through hell in a gasoline suit to play baseball." Did she want to tattoo that badly? Enough to spend years of her life working with someone who'd say *You should be begging me*?

If not, what inferno was she willing to walk through? Face a raid? Get fined? Work out of an apartment; possibly work alone; risk all of Dominic's fears?

Gina crawled out of her bed, pulled her shirt off, and stood with her back to the mirror. She held up a hand mirror until she could see the figs on her upper back—one whole and one halved, scarlet at its core, with deep green leaves stretching outward toward her shoulders. The tattoo was completely healed now, no longer wet with fresh ink and blood, but part of her.

A tattoo wasn't just a decal on your body. It was something invisible made visible. A truth you'd kept to yourself that you were finally willing to have in the open, to be seen.

Maybe all Dominic's fears were real. Maybe not. She couldn't just pick up and get another job, but she could try it for a night.

Gina opened to the back of her sketchbook and pulled out a card. She dialed the phone number and waited.

Fifty-six

SATURDAY, JUNE 28

T he last time Gina had gone to the city was for her tenth-grade field
trip, herded straight out of a school bus into the grand halls of the
Museum of Natural History. This time, Anna loaded her down
with warnings: *Don't go to Times Square. Don't go to the Bowery. Don't ride
the subway alone. . . .* She'd never ridden the subway before at all. Eddie had
to show her where to buy a token to drop into the turnstile.

It was early evening, still light out, but in this world beneath the sidewalks,
Gina wouldn't have known midday from midnight. Kettle drums echoed
down the platform; men slept along the walls. The air was humid with the
smell of piss and wet newspaper.

Eddie still looked good—the black ponytail, biceps hefting his suitcase of equipment like it was an angel food cake. They stood waiting for the A.

"You never came back for that crescent moon," Eddie said. She'd told him the truth on the phone the other day—that she was related to Dominic, not Mackie—and all he said was *It did seem kinda weird that Dom was hovering over somebody else's sister.* "I tattooed one dot on your shoulder and then Dom hauled you out."

"Maybe tonight," Gina said. "If we run out of people to work on."

"Where did you hear about this gig? Pretty far from home."

"Some walk-ins." Fortunately, of those two drunk yuppies, the one with the party-planning girlfriend was not the same guy who'd been arrested on a DWI—although it seemed the consequences had not been long-lasting, anyway. When Gina asked Morgan if Preston was in jail, he laughed and said, *You know, it's remarkable. Sometimes those Breathalyzer results just . . . get lost.*

"Surprised your brother didn't want to do this with you," Eddie said.

Gina looked down into the dark chasm of the tracks between the platforms, watching a rat gnaw a grimy hot dog. "It's not his thing."

"And it's your thing?" Eddie smiled with one corner of his mouth, the same way he had that day at Paulie's. "Have you broken the law once in your entire life?"

The train arrived with a whoosh of hot wind and screech of brakes. Inside, thickets of graffiti bubbled and sprawled across the walls. She followed Eddie on, clutched the pole, and still nearly fell over when the subway lurched onward.

Off the train, up the stairs, out to the sidewalk, where she blinked into the golden-hour light. A rushing slurry of noise, a gray blend of cars and subway rush flecked with honking and jackhammering. Eddie navigated easily, talking as they dragged their suitcases through the maze of the city, but it was hard to listen; there was too much to take in. Scaffolding, pretzel cart, plywood plastered with show posters. The way people crossed the street in herds. Buildings so high their rows of windows disappeared in a flare of sun.

Finally Eddie stopped at a building with a tarnished 999 above the glass doors. Gina's stomach dipped as the elevator jerked upward. The numbers lit, higher and higher, and when the doors slid open, she found herself in a glass vestibule.

A man in a circus strongman's singlet was holding a boxy mobile phone and staring at his Filofax. He glanced at Gina's and Eddie's suitcases. "Jugglers?"

"Tattooers," Gina said. "We talked to Morgan Kenning."

"Ah. Yes," he said. "Speaking."

She studied him. He looked different since that night Mackie shoved his obnoxious friend out onto the sidewalk. "Did you grow a mustache?"

"I was subjected to the makeup artist." He rolled his eyes. "You're next. And Sondra fired her assistant yesterday, so apparently I'm in charge of orientation. Follow me."

They emerged from the vestibule into the open air. Gina's eyes widened. Colored lights and neon-bright circus bunting swooped pole to pole. Morgan led them past a black-mirrored bar with a neon sign above it: CIRCO ZONDRA. Gina tried not to trip as they race-walked across the rooftop over electric cords taped to the floor, passing black leather couches and a jewel-studded popcorn cart.

A breeze cooled the sweat at her hairline. All she wanted was to stop and stare. Above them, nothing but sky, deepening to violet, streaked with scarlet clouds. Around them, a kingdom of buildings, ten thousand windows lit up like sequins in a spotlight.

Gina opened her purse and pulled out the Ricoh point-and-shoot she'd grabbed from the shop counter. It was an afterthought, in case she tattooed anything portfolio-worthy; her ten remaining shots were precious, but she wanted to remember this.

As she snapped the picture, Morgan checked his notes and pointed to an open-sided tent in a corner of the rooftop. "You're stationed over there. Set up and then head to the fortune-teller's tent for costumes. Guests arrive, Madame Ringmaster calls you for your appearance, you bow, you work. And now"—he threw the clipboard on the nearest table—"I'm off to collect my promised dirty banana."

They walked to their tent to inspect the setup: two massage tables, heated cabinet with hot towels, table for work space, bright lights worthy of a photo shoot. "Swanky," Eddie said.

After unpacking, they crossed the rooftop to the fortune-teller's tent, which was furnished like some luxury version of Professor Marvel's wagon. Gina was staring at the coffee table, its surface a black marble Ouija board, when a man in a glittering miniskirt handed her an armful of clothes and pointed her behind a folding screen.

"Call me when you're ready to lace up the corset," he said. Corset? Breathing was hard enough already.

She walked out feeling like a circus doll, in colors bright as marzipan, garters like candy ribbons.

Performers lounged around the Ouija table. A burlesque dancer nodded hello, then went back to braiding the hair of a man with flame-tattooed arms. A lion-tamer dominatrix, whip at her waist, unscrewed a brass bullet from her necklace. She looked annoyed when Gina wriggled past.

"Sorry." Gina shrank into the fainting couch in the corner. Eddie squeezed in next to her.

The lion tamer tapped the bullet onto the table and a snowy pile of powder slid out. She pulled a tarot card from a silver box on the side table and used it to cut the powder into three lines. A police siren wailed from the street below.

Gina spoke in a low voice to Eddie. "Could we get arrested?"

Eddie laughed. "The cops aren't coming up here. Unless there's a fire or something."

"I'm extremely experienced," the long-haired man said.

"Who are you?"

"The fire-eater." The man bent to snort a line of powder from the marble table. "How did Sondra find you?"

"She's Ringmaster Zondra tonight." The lion tamer took the rolled-up bill from the fire-eater. Forceful bass echoed across the rooftop. Gina peeked through the crack in the tent flap.

And there she was—a flash of neon-green ringmaster's coat, pinched at the waist. Zondra had that look of aging TV stars, with their serums and surgery: she could've been twenty-eight or forty-five. She set her top hat and glass stilettos on the DJ booth and danced barefoot, alone, in the middle of the floor.

The lion tamer noticed Gina watching. "She studied dance at Bennington and ended up a Wall Street trophy wife. Now she's on a *journey*. To *find* herself again."

They'd been so aloof, but soon the circus performers were talking with the intensity of Greek oracles delivering revelations from the gods. Dark fell. Guests filled the rooftop. Cleavage and sequins, stilts and stilettos, explosions of taffeta.

A gong sounded, and all the lights went black. Sinewy music rose out of the darkness. "Welcome," purred a voice, "to Circo Zondra."

A spotlight snapped on to illuminate Zondra, who raised her baton. "Allow me to introduce your entertainment for the night. Madame Leonida!" The lion tamer strutted out, whip cracking. "Firemaster Björn!" The fire-eater followed. "Eduardo the Great Tattooer! And his assistant, Lydia, the tattooed lady!"

Gina's breath stopped short when she saw the crush of people now packed onto this rooftop, clapping and whooping as she stumbled up to Ringmaster Zondra's glittered podium. The spotlight was blinding.

"Live demonstrations all night, if you dare subject yourself to their artistry! And at the stroke of midnight"—Zondra put her hand over her heart—"they will tattoo the ringmaster herself." The crowd roared its approval.

When Gina and Eddie got to their station, a woman was already bending over the table, flipping up her cotton-candy skirt. Her bottom was smooth as a Corvette's curves, sun-tanned the golden brown of expensive whiskey.

"Ass by Jane Fonda," the woman said, coyly.

Eddie looked at Gina. "Lydia, could you please wash the glitter off our friend's derriere?"

What was Gina so anxious about? The woman wanted a rose, the same rose Gina had practiced drawing by the hundreds. She looked to the illuminated archway at the entrance, half expecting to see a compact man with curly dark hair pushing toward her. Dominic was not there.

Just do the tattoo. Spiraled center; stem; rose. The work calmed her down a bit.

As soon as Gina finished, a woman in a jester costume stepped forward. "I'm next."

"I just need to clean up," Gina said, and then her stomach dropped. She had left a huge, careless hole in her planning: she had no way to sterilize her contaminated equipment. A cardinal sin, and one of her first, most basic lessons. She'd brought a stash of new needles, but no clean tubes and grips; she'd been so stressed and distracted while packing that she'd forgotten.

She leaned over to Eddie. "How are you sterilizing tubes?"

"I packed extra."

"I screwed myself." Gina dug her fingernails into her palms. "I can't work."

"Does this look like a surgical unit?" Eddie gestured across the rooftop. "My boss used to dip his needle in alcohol and Listerine, run it for three seconds, and move along. We used the sterilizer to heat Chinese food. We all lived."

"There was no AIDS back then."

"They had other kinds of old-timey germ shit. Give everybody a new needle, spritz the rest with alcohol, you'll be fine. You can bend the rules for one night."

"Dominic would kill me." Gina looked up at the sky, so flooded with artificial light she could see only a few lonely stars. "I'll be back in five." She ducked into the costume tent, where the party noise was muffled and she could think.

She'd bent the rules when she tattooed with Mackie. It led to a fight that still made her chest hurt. On the other hand, what real harm had been done? The work had come out well. She'd realized how much endurance she had.

Eddie had given her some basic precautions tonight. She could trust him, or she could spend the night on the bench.

Gina made her way back. "You're not worried?"

"Nope." He adjusted his ponytail and looked up. "Next victim, please." The jester woman took a step toward him.

"I'll take her," Gina said.

F ive tattoos. Thirteen. Twenty. At one in the morning, Gina shook out her aching hand; for an hour she'd been saying *This is my last one*, waiting for the Ringmaster to appear, but nothing. "Whatever happened to the stroke of midnight?" she said. "My hand is numb." She'd long ago shot her last picture on the Ricoh, fingers crossed that even one or two would come out well.

A trio of women teetered over. Nobody was sober anymore—drowsy-eyed and giggly, yelling at their friends. Back home, anybody who came to Mulley's drunk or high and asking for a tattoo got a flat no.

The burlesque dancer wove her way through the crowd toward Gina. Her act complete, she was now roving the rooftop in little more than a pearl-embellished thong and starfish pasties. She hopped into Gina's chair. "Hello, pretty. Are you a prisoner here, or do you want to dance?"

"I don't dance."

The burlesque dancer smiled. "You just said my favorite words." She reached into her elaborate hair and pulled out a shell-shaped case. She popped it open and handed Gina a sea-green tablet embossed with a star. "Yours."

"What is it?" Even at the Cheshire Cat, the strongest thing she'd ever tried was weed.

Silver rhinestones framed the dancer's eyes. Her pupils were dilated, her cheeks flushed. She was stunning. "Bliss for sweet bunnies too scared to dance."

"I worked at a head shop. You can just tell me."

She laughed. "Ecstasy." Gina had never heard of it, but if she was going to be at this party, having this experience, she might as well truly have it. She wasn't doing Zondra's tattoo anyway. She was leaving that to Eddie. All she had to do was stand there like decoration.

She swallowed the tablet. The dancer ran her finger along Gina's cheek. "Find me soon." She slipped away.

Eddie looked over. "Not to be an after-school special, but that's some Russian roulette you're playing. People cut those pills with rat poison, meth, all kinds of shit. I don't feel like an ER trip."

Before Gina could respond, a tipsy woman fell into the chair. "Give me the bird! Freedom!"

A bare-chested man in silver pants came pushing through the crowd. "Hold up. That's my girlfriend."

Eddie took a good look at them both. "I don't know, man. She's really feeling the freedom tonight."

The man pointed at her tattoo machine. "How do you sterilize that?"

Here it came. Gina took a deep breath. "Machines don't need sterilizing."

"Even the parts that come into contact with blood?"

"We have an autoclave for that."

"I know all about autoclaves," the man said. "I'm a dentist. And I don't see one here."

"You do your job, I'll do mine," Eddie said. "We've got alcohol."

"You think that's foolproof against HIV and hepatitis, dipshit?" the dentist said.

Gina felt cold.

"Yes," Eddie said. "I think it is, Dr. Buzzkill. So I guess we have a difference of opinion."

"That's a difference of facts." The dentist tugged on his girlfriend's arm.

Gina watched them elbow back into the crowd. She leaned her head close to Eddie. "I'm packing up."

"Because of one guy with a stick up his ass?"

Gina's corset felt tighter. The lights flashed like knives and the speakers popped with a tinny beat so repetitive she couldn't think. *Jack jack jack your body, jack jack jack—*

She was starting to feel hot, and a little nauseated. Was this anxiety, or the drug kicking in? When the Ringmaster showed up, the spotlight would swivel their way. All eyes on Eduardo and Lydia. Dramatic music. Onlookers pressing in . . . "If I pack up, will you watch my stuff?"

"I'll be here till the grand finale," Eddie said. "But you don't have to quit just because—"

"Too much noise." Gina packed up fast and escaped to the black-mirrored bar for ice water. She ducked behind the fortune-teller's tent, a few feet from the roof's edge. Thank God. Space to take a breath. She leaned into the railing.

All around was the city, wide awake. The sparkling vault and dip of skyscraper canyons. The far-off Empire State Building. The glow of billboards and streams of ruby taillights below. The party fell away.

She stood for a long time holding that cup of water, letting ice cubes melt on her lips, letting the light of the city pour into her and fill her with radiant energy. It felt as if her whole chest was opening up toward this lightscape. For nearly nineteen years she'd wriggled around Blue Claw, like a little glow-in-the-dark fish. All the while, two hours away, everything glowed in the dark.

She and Anna could belong here. They wouldn't have to waste energy explaining themselves to anyone. This very night, she'd seen two women tangled up on one of those leather couches, ecstatically enjoying each other.

She was struck with sudden loneliness, a cold snap of missing Anna. Why was she clenching her jaw like that? She touched her face. The feel of her own skin was suddenly wonderful. The breeze came again, feathering her hair, carrying all the rooftop smells, cotton candy and cigarette smoke. Gina hugged herself. She ran her fingers along her arm, reveling in its remarkable softness, and the tingles on her neck became someone else's fingertips.

"Hello, bunny," said the burlesque dancer, sweet as warm milk. "Feeling anything?"

"Everything," Gina said. The bass of the music was the heartbeat of a goddess. The colored lights above the tent, the kaleidoscopic flicker of angels. She could've watched for hours.

"Of course you can dance. You're made of water." The dancer moved in close, face-to-face. She held Gina's hips and swayed them, until Gina was swaying on her own, like rolling waves. Gratitude flowed up in her, then a riptide of strong nausea. She closed her eyes. "Pull me in close," the dancer whispered, taking Gina's hands and moving them to the small of her back. The softness—what *was* this? Light whirled around the edges of the tent.

"I love it here," Gina breathed.

"We're all made of water," the dancer murmured in her ear.

The glow-in-the-dark fish of Blue Claw was dancing.

Until a man's voice barked: "Gina!"

Fifty-seven

So Dominic had found her.

Gina blinked and turned. None of the faces were his.

She was, however, face-to-face with a clown, several inches north of six feet tall, with a five o'clock shadow and green lipstick on his teeth. Gina recoiled.

"The tattooist said come back and hurry. He needs you."

Strange, flat calm. "Tell Dom I'll be there in a minute." She'd known what she was doing when she came to this party: walking away from an already burning bridge. Now they would make it official, that was all.

"Is your dom named Eduardo? He said it's an emergency."

No, Eddie, not now. She'd told him she was out. She wasn't leaving this heaven for the spectacle of Zondra's tattoo.

"She doesn't want to go," the burlesque dancer said. The clown shrugged and pushed himself into a dense pack of dancing people.

Gina hesitated. The word *emergency* echoed back like a siren in fog.

She jumped into the crowd after him. The limbs pressing against her body were overwhelming. It was like being trapped in an octopus tank. Finally she broke through to the other edge of the rooftop.

Ringmaster Zondra was in Eddie's chair, and she was hyperventilating. Eddie grabbed Gina. "Can you help her?"

Gina took a step backward. Fear crackled at the edges of that warm open feeling. "Get her a paramedic. What if she took the rat poison?"

"No, she's dead sober. She's just panicking. I thought another woman might calm her down."

"What do I know?" But already, just moments in, it felt like she knew this woman. Knew how to handle her fear.

Gina knelt. Zondra gripped her ringmaster's whip and gasped for air, looking up at the riot of lights, tears glinting. "Can't breathe," she wheezed.

A small crowd was forming. "Back off," somebody yelled.

Zondra's mascara bled smears down her cheeks, flecked with green glitter. Gina touched her back. The wheezing worsened.

Pretend she's Stella.

She dragged a chair up and leaned toward Zondra, who was now bent over in the chair, head between her knees, still gasping. Gina stroked her hand, trying to forget the people crowding in around them, watching, as if this were another sideshow.

"Hey." Warm, casual. "You're okay. My name is Gina and I walk people through this all the time. You got nervous about the tattoo?"

Zondra, still hyperventilating, didn't answer.

"No stress. Everybody's cool, nobody's even paying attention." She glanced up at the onlookers: a woman in a bikini of candy necklaces and a dude with glow sticks through his nipple rings. Eddie gestured them away.

"You have kids?"

"Ian," Zondra whispered. "Celeste."

"Such great names. I bet you're the coolest mom." The river of words was just coming, the lines she was so used to saying. Please let them be the right ones. "I'm not going anywhere, okay?"

Zondra's breath slowed. She was calming down. She kept her face covered with her hands.

"Actually," a man said, "I've got this."

She looked up to see Morgan waving her away. He took her seat and whispered in Zondra's ear. Eddie looked at Gina and shrugged.

Gina turned and made her way through the thinning crowd to the spot behind the fortune-teller's tent. Nothing but dark roof and empty railing. She scanned the rooftop; the burlesque dancer should've been easy to find, being mostly naked with that tall sweep of sparkling hair.

Gone. Gina looked out at the lonely city and the miles of lights.

Somehow Eddie was beside her again. She leaned into him and put an arm around his waist. He twitched, caught off guard, but then put an arm around her, too. It felt so good to be held.

"Did you want to stay and party?" he said. "Or try to make the next train?"

She had more energy than she could remember having in a long time. Now that Eddie's warm body was next to her, nothing sounded better than pulling him in closer, seeing what *his* skin felt like. He seemed like the most trustworthy person in the world. She turned toward him.

Then a word came to her: *No.* A second word: *Anna.* A crack of clarity like ice on her tongue. "My girlfriend will want me home," Gina said.

"Girlfriend," Eddie said with surprise. He drew back a little.

"I'll find Morgan," she said, "and get us paid."

Gina stood by the illuminated archway, a fresh four hundred dollars in her wallet, suitcase at her feet, no idea how long she'd been waiting for Eddie to get back from the bathroom so they could flee. She was back in her jeans, free of the corset and itchy taffeta, but her jaw was uncomfortably tight. She massaged it as she stared out over the city.

At two thirty in the morning, the skyline was still dazzling. In the building across the way, a woman smoked out of her open window. She was watching the city sparkle, too. If Gina lived here, she would never get tired of that view.

"What's your name?"

Gina turned. Ringmaster Zondra towered in her glass stilettos. Her makeup was repaired, hair re-coiffed, whip in hand.

"Gina Mulley." No fear. As if this was meant to happen, the entire night moving toward this moment.

"I was impressed with your poise tonight."

"Are you confusing me with somebody?"

"I don't get confused." Zondra's voice was cold as granite. She put out her hand. "You may call me Ms. Gardner from this point on." Gina shook it. "Thank you for your assistance earlier. My thirty-ninth birthday seemed like an auspicious time to face my phobias. I may axe my analyst tomorrow. We'll see."

"It was no problem," Gina said.

"Where do you work, Gina Mulley?"

"Mulley's Fine Art Tattoo Studio in Blue Claw."

"That seedy town on the way to the Hamptons? You're a long way from home."

Gina nodded. Did she look as flushed as she felt?

"Do you have administrative experience?"

"Some."

Ms. Gardner handed her a business card. "I recently let my assistant go. She lacked maturity. Perhaps you'd like to interview for the position."

Gina blinked. Just like that, she was a record needle dropped into a perfect circular groove. Everything was exactly as it should be. Everything made sense.

"A typical day might involve arranging travel details, assistance with social events . . ." Ms. Gardner gestured toward the rooftop. "Relieving the nanny if I'm running late. Et cetera."

Eddie returned from the bathroom. He stood behind the ringmaster, suitcase in hand, staring restlessly up at the archway.

"What is your current salary?"

"I work two jobs. About two hundred a week."

"I can raise that to three hundred."

Gina was trying to keep her expression neutral and professional, but with this last sentence, she felt her face open up in wonder. So much for poise.

Ms. Gardner bent toward Gina, as if to speak confidentially. Unlike everyone else at this party, her breath did not smell of alcohol and her pupils were not dilated. Her speech was entirely measured. In fifteen minutes, she had regained complete composure.

"I understand this job may sound less than romantic if you've been pursuing your art full time."

Eddie, pacing behind Ms. Gardner, tapped his watch.

"But I can give you entrée into a world you won't encounter in Blue Claw. My former assistants—those who left on good terms—now work at MoMA, Jacob's Pillow, and the Public Theater. You will network with extraordinary people. I expect to fill the position quickly. Consider it."

Ms. Gardner shook her hand again, and as soon as she released it, Eddie swooped in. "Thank you," Gina called, as Eddie pulled her toward the elevator.

The train whipped east. Out the window, the charred knot of clouds over the moon was breaking, pulling away strand by strand, a lunar striptease.

This rooftop offer was her wide-open, sky-size door.

Last year Dominic's most ambitious idea for her was a florist-shop job an hour outside their hometown. This ringmaster woman looked like she could tug any filament in the web of New York City and conjure whatever she wanted. All Gina had done was be herself, and Zondra had seen her and sought her out and said *Join me.*

This would answer Anna's travel itch. Manhattan: a piece of everything in the world, palace of every possible curiosity; it would be impossible for someone like Anna to grow bored or sad or lonely here.

"Why would you leave Mulley's?" Eddie said. "There's nobody better than Dominic. Paulie would say the same thing."

"It got ugly," Gina said, "working with family."

"Last summer at Paulie's, you looked like you'd walk on hot coals to get that job."

"I didn't think I could be happy doing anything else."

"All the same," Eddie said, "I'd sleep on it."

"Okay," Gina said. "Fine. Play devil's advocate."

"You hit the jackpot, getting a year with Dominic. Taking on an apprentice is a crapload of work and a big risk. You invest all this time and then somebody might do exactly what you're thinking of. Screw you, have a nice life."

"Where's the *screw you* in that? I'm going to finish everything I promised him."

Eddie shrugged again and yawned. He closed his eyes.

Fifty-eight

SUNDAY, JUNE 29

The journey home lasted either four hours or twenty minutes; Gina wasn't quite sure. After the Jamaica train and the Hicksville train and the Blue Claw train, finally she arrived at her little rust-speckled car, lying in wait at the station. The warm bath of feeling had evaporated. Exhaustion hit in little dits and dahs like Morse code, her eyes dropping closed and then snapping open. She pulled up to the cottage at dawn.

Anna was already awake, bent over some task at a card table under their walnut tree. Strips of morning sun banded the front yard, hemming in the scrap of shade where she sat. Smoke from a stick of incense corkscrewed up into the branches.

At the sound of the car door, Anna turned and waved limply.

Gina walked over to the table. "What are you doing out here?"

"The fresh air felt good. And the light." The table held a couple of cutting boards with strips of pepper, coins of carrot, diced tomatoes. "I'm chopping veggies. I needed to think." A newsletter sat next to the vegetables, wrinkled with pink dots of tomato juice.

Gina pointed to it. "What's this?"

"You first." Anna set the knife down. "How was the party?"

Gina sat down on the browning stubble of their grass and unlaced her boots. "I never saw anything like it. Sex and coke and people kept sticking money in my garters and . . ." Beautiful Anna sat there like a milkmaid in a painting, and Gina felt a stab of guilt, thinking of the burlesque dancer. She yanked off the boots. "They offered me a job."

"No way."

"The woman who threw the party needs an assistant. Three hundred a week." Gina breathed deep. "We could actually get out of here."

Anna moved on to a carton of strawberries, slicing them into a bowl. "And what about tattooing? You'd just give it up?"

"Not forever." The words felt hollow. Hard to imagine how she would get back in, once she'd gotten out. "I'd still be doing artsy things. I'd be with you. We'd have an adventure."

"The Village is getting pricey. But . . ." Anna looked up into the tree's spidery branches. "I could see us on the edges. A teeny little studio. Christmas lights on the fire escape."

A flood of relief. "I'll call her today." Wind rushed the tree and a few green walnuts came sailing down. Gina picked one up, rubbed it, and breathed in the citrus smell. "How was your evening?"

Anna sliced another berry. "Slow night at work. Put some oatmeal in the crockpot, watched *The Day After*." Gina needed to sneak that video back to the library before Anna renewed it again. It was getting stressful, nuclear bombs going off in the house all the time.

Anna put her knife down. She looked at the newsletter on the table, then at Gina, and took a breath. "What if you had to go the city without me? Just for a few months?"

This was so strange that there was nothing to say in response. Gina tilted her head, waiting.

"Do you remember I told you about the Nevada Test Site? Where they set off all the nukes?" Anna reached for the newsletter. "There's going to be huge demonstration this fall. Last night I talked to the founder of a new Catholic Worker house in Las Vegas. She told me about this thing called the Nevada Desert Experience, Franciscans and Buddhists doing vigils for peace . . ." She pressed nervous thumbs along the newsletter's creases. "I think this is it."

Gina stared. "Which part?"

"All of it. I just want to live there for a while."

"And do what?"

"Whatever good I can."

"You just said you could see us together. You think the Catholics want your girlfriend along?"

"We don't have to *stay* at the Catholic Worker. We'd camp until we found an apartment. If you come, you could tattoo in Vegas—"

"For how long? Three months? Six?"

"What if we just see how it goes?"

"I can't just walk into a tattoo shop and get work," Gina said. "Do you understand how cutthroat this business is? You set up in somebody else's territory, they might kick the shit out of you." She grabbed a dropped strawberry and ripped bits from its leaves.

Anna looked close to tears. She put her hand on her chest. "I need to clear the air in here. Can you picture the desert?"

The wind shifted and pushed the incense smoke toward Gina, a thick myrrh smell, too strong. She turned her face away.

"All that big open sky," Anna said. "Actually doing something about the things I have nightmares about. Suddenly I can breathe."

"Then what's all this for?" Gina waved her hand at the vegetables. "What's left to decide?"

"Whether I could really go," Anna said, "if you wouldn't go with me."

Gina stood, went inside, and slammed her bedroom door behind her. She dialed the shop.

Jeri's crisp voice: "Thank you for calling Mulley's Fine Art Tattoo Studio! We are located at . . ."

Finally, the beep. "Dom, I'm sick. I'll see you tomorrow." It wasn't even a lie. Gina was so tired she was nauseated, her voice raspy from shouting over music all night. She changed into an old T-shirt and got under her sheets; she wanted to sleep and dream of nothing. The prism pendulum in the window splashed the ceiling with colored light.

Anna knocked and came in.

"I need some time," Gina said. "You know there's no ocean in Nevada? No bagels or pizza or—"

"I don't want to be an almost-Marianna."

Gina rolled over. "What does that mean?"

Anna went to the window and flicked the pendulum with her finger.

"Everybody loves the Anna part of me." The prism swayed, upsetting all the scraps of rainbow, making them chase circles around the room. "Nicolas did, for sure. Anna cooks delicious things just for you. Anna listens and tries to be helpful. Anna's quirky just like you, and thinks you're fascinating and charming and sexy. But there's all these other parts of me gasping for air. I want to be a whole person." She leaned on the windowsill. "I grew up in the city. It's not some exotic place for me, like it is for you. I could see us happy there one day. But if I can't go and take a deep breath, part of me is going to suffocate."

Flecks of rainbow were all around them, slowing, quieting.

"I don't want to be an almost-Marianna," she said.

Fifty-nine

Gina slept. Hours and hours, shades down, sheets damp, while Anna padded around the cottage and then left for her diner shift. The place fell silent until Gina woke in the late afternoon and knew what she had to do:

Go back to the beginning.

Back to her bench on the docks of the Bifurc River, behind the shop. Go to the place where she'd been one year earlier, staring into that filmy water for three days, wishing for inspiration and a glimpse of an ugly fish. When Dominic said *You have to strike out on your own* and *This is just a pile of nots.* When she'd wished for a fortune-teller to walk through the door of Mulley's Tattoo and make everything clear.

She dropped off her roll of film at the one-hour Fotomat, parked behind the shop, and collapsed on the bench. It had sprouted new graffiti since her last visit. Gina pried off her knockoff All Stars, pressed her toes into the sparse grass, and put pen to paper: *WHAT TO DO NOW.*

Everything was so much simpler when she'd wanted just one thing: to be a tattooer at Mulley's. It was amazing how much she'd wanted that, how quickly she'd scribbled her name on that contract without even reading it, so certain she would trade everything away to work by Dominic's side.

Running off to Nevada felt like the same thing all over again, except this time, she'd be trading everything to be with Anna. This idea of tattooing in Vegas while Anna protested at the test site—one look at the map took it off the table. Those places were ninety miles apart, the same distance as Blue Claw from Manhattan, and that was assuming Gina even wanted to work in Vegas. She knew for sure, after last night, that she didn't want to tattoo at any shop with standards as lax as the ones Eddie had allowed. That dentist who lit into them was right; she could've been spreading disease on that rooftop, and it was irreversible now. She would never allow herself to work like that again. If she spent all her money to move to Vegas and Eddie's casual attitude turned out to be the norm, she'd be stranded.

Could she really let Anna go to Nevada without her, though? It was one thing for someone like Anna to love someone like Gina when there were no other options around. She could see something beautiful in anyone. But out in the world, in some fascinating activist community, Anna would quickly gravitate toward someone else. If Gina didn't go to Nevada, they'd be broken up by Labor Day.

But if she wasn't tattooing, what would she do out there, with no education, no résumé? The same kind of jobs she'd done in high school. The desert equivalent of a bait shop.

Ms. Ringmaster Zondra Gardner had a point: she'd meet people in the city who would never walk into Mulley's, art professionals who could toss her opportunities she couldn't even imagine. And it turned out the city *wasn't* a sinkhole of certain death. When you emerged from a subway station, you *didn't* get simultaneously robbed at gunpoint and arrested. Had Gina really loved the city, though—or did that sea-green tablet love the city? Could she trust anything she'd felt after she swallowed that? Of course Manhattan looked alluring from a rooftop, surrounded by fire-breathing performance artists and drag queens. But if she went to work for Ms. Gardner, she'd take dictation and shuttle kids around and maybe get screamed at for ordering fifty pounds of the wrong color glitter.

And like it or not, Eddie was right: She'd badgered Dominic mercilessly for this apprenticeship. What did it say about her that after a year's investment, on the doorstep of a full-time job, she was thinking of quitting tattooing? Was she the kind of person who would abandon her brother the same week he'd lost his son?

Although, it felt like Dominic had abandoned her months ago. Was she the kind of person who'd keep on sacrificing for someone who didn't even *see* her anymore?

Gina closed her eyes, breathing in the smells of detergent from the laundromat and bread from the bakery. She leaned back on the bench, trying to gather herself and dissolve the static. No matter what she said yes to, she was saying no to some other important thing. What did she want?

Fingers brushed her shoulder. "I'm here," a man said.

She jumped, startled, and twisted around. The sun was a nudge above his shoulder, blinding.

"Perhaps you're running late?" Nicolas sat down next to her. He was smartly dressed, chocolate brown pants, pin-striped like the blackened grooves on an old copper lamp. "The front door is locked. What luck I parked here and happened upon you."

Of all the days.

"Shall we go inside?" he said. "For my appointment?"

She hadn't thought of it in months. A jittery feeling was coming over her, both guilty and wary. "I have to cancel."

Nicolas looked amused. "Sternli. You're being coy. If you wanted to cancel, you wouldn't be sitting here."

"To be honest?" Gina looked off at the murky river. "I completely forgot."

He sat on the bench beside her. "I suppose I should have kept my hopes in check," he said, with a note of resignation. "The callousness of the young. *With empty hand men may none haukes lure. For wynnyng wolde I al his lust endure. And make me a feyned appetit—*"

"What?"

"Chaucer. The words of a heartless woman. A bit of money and she'll endure a man's lust." Nicolas looked melancholy, holding her eyes. "She'll even pretend to want him back."

She stood. "What do you mean, heartless?"

"Good night, Gina Mulley." He stood and turned toward his car.

He didn't get to walk away telling that story. "I'm not heartless. I've had the month from hell. I'm exhausted."

"Sternli." He paused and turned. "What happened?"

My best friend at the shop moved away. My brother lost his baby, I tried to be helpful, but he threatened to fire me. I'm having trouble with Anna, which I can't tell you about because you don't know I'm with Anna. I ended up on a rooftop tattooing stockbrokers in nipple clamps, and now I can't decide between taking a job with a ringmaster or moving to Vegas with my lover so she can become a radical nun.

"Things," Gina said.

Nicolas walked back to her, reached out, and caressed her face. She recoiled.

"What can I do?" he said.

What could he *do*? There was nothing he could do.

Wait. There was something he could do.

Gina reached into her back pocket and pulled out her wallet, stuffed with every precious dollar she'd earned last night—half of the Circo Zondra payment and all her tips. She counted out a hundred. "You can take your deposit."

Nicolas put his hands in his pockets. "Sternli. I'd infinitely prefer an hour of your attention to a handful of grubby bills."

"I'm giving it back." Debts tied people to each other. She was leaving nothing unfinished today—no unchecked boxes, no unpaid debts, no almosts. Gina held the money out.

"Enough of that." Nicolas kept his hands thrust in his pockets. "Now. If you'd like some guidance—"

"I don't."

"Just a moment ago, you were meditating on a question." This would have been more impressive if her notebook wasn't opened to the page scribbled with *WHAT TO DO NEXT.* "And as I tell my clients when they find themselves lost . . ."

If she left the money there, he'd have to take it. What if she just walked away? Could she do that? Gina dropped the cash on the bench. She pulled her sneakers back on, turned away from the water, and headed back toward Midway Street.

Nicolas followed.

Dear God, he was leaving it on the bench? A hundred dollars. That was two weeks' rent. Almost a month of groceries. One foot in front of the other.

"You're discarding your money for some vagrant to pocket?" he said, sounding amused again.

"It's your money." Twenty large pizzas. Almost a hundred gallons of gas. Don't even look.

"In any case," Nicolas said. "As I tell my clients—"

"I'm not your client." Gina stopped at her car, pulled a duffel bag from the backseat, and continued walking briskly.

He matched her pace, delivering his river of insights, as if they were just out for a stroll: "Sternli, would anyone who cared about Gina Mulley want to see her stuck here with her ungrateful family? No! We want her to board a plane, travel the world, try her hand at shamanic tattooing at a mystical mountain retreat center. We want Gina to realize, finally, that she is *above* cleaning toilets—"

"No one's above cleaning toilets," she said. "It's part of being human." She opened the door of the laundromat.

The woman at the counter nodded at Gina. "How you doing, honey." Gina always thought she looked a bit like Stella—frank voice, feathered hair.

Nicolas followed Gina in, still talking as she unzipped her duffel bag and loaded the washer. "Sternli, I want more for you," he said. "What is life for, if not tasting all the experiences we can? And you were one of my peak experiences last year."

"I'm not an experience." Gina shoved an armful of towels into the machine.

"I'm sorry?"

"I'm not an experience. I'm a person. A whole person." She stuffed in a handful of Anna's red lingerie, hoping he wouldn't recognize it. She slammed the machine shut, inserted her quarters and detergent, and sat down on the bench.

Nicolas rolled his eyes. "Do you know the word *semantics*?"

Her annoyance was giving way to anger. She *did* know that word, and this *wasn't* semantics. If you treated someone like a whole person, and not just a new experience for your collection, then you didn't write their lines for them, pressing them into your bed muttering *Let me have you.*

"Gina." He leaned in, took her hand, and spoke in a low, warm voice. It was the voice from his violet brocade couch; the four-in-the-morning voice, murmuring how pears came to be trapped in bottles of liqueur; the voice that said *Let us embark.* "Why are you behaving as if I'm leaving?"

Fear began to creep in again.

She pulled her hands away from his and planted them in her hoodie pocket. She nodded up at a sign behind him, above the register. Her voice felt shaky.

"You are leaving," she said. Nicolas looked up at the sign. NO LOITERING.

"Is this guy bothering you?" the woman said to Gina.

They answered at the same time—Nicolas rolling his eyes, *Certainly not*, as Gina said, firmly: "Yes."

Nicolas looked at the woman. "We're just having a conversation."

"No," Gina said. "We're not."

He sniffed, as if suddenly unsure what to do with himself. In the silence, washers gurgled, dryers tumbled. Finally he picked something off the floor and dropped it in Gina's lap. "Send my regards to Marianna."

Gina's heart was racing, but she made herself sit there coolly, calmly, holding Anna's red underwear, until the door slammed behind him.

Sixty

I t took Gina a good half hour to steady her nerves, but when Nicolas was safely gone—no silver convertible in sight—she walked to the Fotomat and picked up her photos. Then she tossed her laundry in the dryer and let herself into the tattoo shop, locking the door behind her.

Nicolas was imagining a movie for a character named Sternli, but that wasn't her name. He had a pocketful of experiences he called *Sternli*, but Gina was more than those things.

She was more than Dominic's *G*, the helpful kid sister and sidekick.

She was more than Stella's miracle baby or Queen of Almost.

As much as Rick loved her, she was even more than Pezadita.

So maybe the question to ask before *What to do now?* was actually *Who am I now?* As Anna wanted to be a whole Marianna, what would it mean to be a whole Gina?

A question to ponder as she did her work this evening. She knew this much: a whole Gina finished what she started. The only items left on her agreement were an exit interview and a forty-piece portfolio. She was getting that album done tonight.

She spread her six months of photos on the glass coffee table. That first rose she'd tattooed looked clumsy to her now. One day, surely, the rest of these tattoos would look clumsy, too. But as she flipped through her Foto-mat stack, a few of the rooftop tattoos had turned out better than she'd expected: a crisply lettered *Carpe Diem*, a silhouetted skyline, a flame for the fire-eater. They were small but well made. She was pleased.

Among the party photos she found the picture she'd snapped of the roof-top view: the expanse of violet, the spires and rooftops of a city stretching to the sky.

Whole Gina didn't need to save the world, as Anna wanted to do, or even see all of it. But she was ready to see a little more.

She kept sorting through the photos. Six months of work.

A black-haired mermaid for a young guy who'd lost his black-haired mother.

An ornate key for a woman who'd been sober a full year.

An octopus for a man who just really liked octopi.

Gina was proud of these. She had so far to go, so much to learn, but she'd devoured every crumb of her scavenger education. She'd labored over these tattoos, and enjoyed that labor.

Another thing she'd learned this year: whole Gina relished this work.

And here was the photo of the wing-finned trancefish she'd tattooed on Rick. That day had been such a sucker punch of awfulness. With Jeri at the hospital, she hadn't been able to bask in that moment with him. Seeing the photo was like getting some of it back. Fins like fringed wings, bright eyes, an electric citrus green, looking so much more alive than it ever had in her high school notebooks—as if it were waiting to come to life on someone's skin and swim out of the shop. *I was hoping we'd get one more deep talk*, he'd said. *I'll miss you, Pez.*

I snuck a surprise in your bag, she'd said. *You can look on the plane.* She'd spent an hour choosing a new sci-fi novel for him.

What a coincidence, he'd said. *I'm leaving something for you, too. A treasure hunt when I'm gone.* But their goodbye was so hurried and distracted, and the rest of that night was so wrenching, she'd forgotten he'd even said that. She'd never looked.

Gina slid the trancefish photo into the album and poked around the shop. Nothing in her workstation drawer. Nothing in the cabinets, in Rick's old drawer, in the office.

In the closet, though—in the peanut butter jar where she used to keep her change—she found a rolled-up letter. Underneath the jar was a package wrapped in brown paper:

FOR PEZADITA.

Gina, Pezadita, mi hermana,

Like I said, I wish we had time for one more deep talk. They always get my gears turning for days. I guess I have to settle for a letter.

Pez, I just keep thinking about that question: Does our work do any good? Sometimes we do these tattoos like Tía's, but other days it's a GAS, GRASS, OR ASS tattoo that Johnny might not think is so hilarious ten years from now. And all the while this cranky viejito is in my head heckling me, "Hey cabrón, there are families in this world scavenging in garbage dumps to stay alive. You just spent an hour of your life tattooing Daffy Duck on somebody's nalgas. What good are you?" Cranky old man has a point, and I guess that's why I'm getting on a plane tomorrow. To learn from this muralism movement and see what art can do for a community. When your job is making art, you know . . . ¿De qué sirve?

My gut tells me you're going to find some other answers to that question, though, the longer you work. I would really like to hear them when you do. So I'm leaving you some stationery. You got pretty good at international mail last summer.

I also noticed you like to collect business cards. Maybe it's time for la artista to get her own. See package. And if you decide you'd rather be a plumber or a biologist, these cards will also work for bookmarks and shot glass coasters.

Don't forget to write, Pez. We'll have a good deep talk through the mail.

Abrazos, Rick

Gina unwrapped the package. She'd never had her own stationery, let alone with her name on it. And business cards on fine, creamy stock:

GINA MULLEY
TATTOO ARTIST

She carried them to the waiting room and stared at her name, paired with that title.

She missed Rick so much it hurt. But she didn't have to continue on this path just because he gave her these cards, any more than she had to obey the slip of paper in a fortune cookie. She knew this about Whole Gina: she didn't want her fortune told anymore.

And yet—her name on that business card looked right. If Dominic were like Rick, she could stay here and make that happen. Why couldn't he see their work like this, as a force for good? This place could glow like a beacon. So much was possible here.

But Dominic wasn't Rick; Dominic was Dominic, with all his rulemaking and caretaking and all his love and failings; he knew who he was and he wasn't changing anytime soon. She could grieve for what they might've done together, but she couldn't cling to it anymore. Sine proprio.

And Gina was Gina, and who was that? Maybe every fierce wish she'd had this year, everything that felt wrong and everything that felt right, was an inkling of an answer.

Maybe Whole Gina was not a particular constellation of job and geography and lover and home, but a way of being.

Whole Gina was still weird and awkward, probably, but chose to speak. Could listen deeply and was worth listening to. She was not afraid of doing the right thing, even if it made a scene or cost the favor of a powerful person.

Whole Gina stayed awake and alert. She didn't trancefish through the hard parts.

Whole Gina, it turned out, could love someone and make them happy. She didn't want Anna to go—part of her worried that she'd never find anyone else who made her feel this alive, let alone who felt the same about her. But maybe if Anna had seen something lovable in her, then someone else could, too.

Whole Gina did her work for the pleasure and satisfaction of it, and definitely for buying groceries, but not for pats on the head. She would pour out a whole trophy full of pennies and pink champagne if one day she could help a person like Tía Andrea heal.

If Whole Gina had ambitions of working at a New York City gallery, it would make sense to run errands for Sondra Gardner. If she thirsted for work with global consequences—or if she craved marvelous, unplanned adventure—then it would make sense to wander the desert with Anna. But those weren't her dreams.

Gina Mulley, Tattoo Artist. She wanted that. But Mulley's Fine Art Tattoo Studio didn't need a Whole Gina; they just needed a worker bee. All the work and wishes in the world wouldn't change that.

The vision she'd had by the river last year, then—was any version of that still possible? She could still see it clearly:

Working in a tattoo shop, her machine vibrating in her hand, a living thing.

Her drawings on the wall, crisp and bold.

A woman in the chair, freshly tattooed with a cresting wave, sky-blue as hope itself, saying *I love this,* and Gina saying *Thank you*—just *Thank you.*

A community of people who felt at home in the space she'd made.

The space she'd made.

Sixty-one

JULY 1

egina, I love you. Go out with a bang.

Gina was standing at the back door of the studio, digging around for the key in her jeans pocket, when she found the note. It was folded with a sprig of wild mint tucked inside. She was still smiling when Dominic walked up.

He gave her a half hug around the shoulders; they went in together.

"What's on your schedule today?" He said it so casually, but they both knew. It was circled red on the calendar.

Gina peeled the apprenticeship agreement off the wall. It was flooded with green highlighter, every item except two. She handed it to Dominic.

```
***Complete photo album of 40 portfolio pieces.

***Complete apprenticeship exit interview.
```

"Do we really need an exit interview?" he said.

"I'm finishing the list." Gina sifted through the acetate stencils until she found the old Sailor Jerry anchor. "And I need one last tattoo. I want you to supervise."

Dominic sat down at Rick's empty workstation as Gina washed her hands. "Who's it for?"

She wiped down her workstation and laid out a paper towel. "Myself."

He put his hand on her arm. "Gina, you have thirty-nine pieces in your portfolio. Let's call it done."

She kept setting up. Ink cups. Razor. Green soap. "It's important to me."

The standard colors for that anchor were red and black, but Dominic didn't comment as she mixed her pigments in the little cups—the searing orange of a hot coil, a moody violet she'd gotten from Sally the Viking. She propped up her foot and shaved a patch above her knee.

"Look, I get it. It's a rite of passage. My early work's all over my thighs," Dom said. "But this is nerve-racking, watching you."

Gina shrugged and took the stencil and dusted the charcoal outline onto her leg. Dominic picked up a pencil and paper from the barren lunar surface of Rick's old countertop and doodled a tight grid of dots. "I have to tell you something."

She looked up.

"I'm sorry about the car wash." His dark hair fell over his forehead. "This isn't an excuse. But I don't know what's happening to me. Since the baby, I feel like—I'm not in my own body. Like I'm remote-controlling it from somewhere else." He kept penciling dots. "I can't focus, I can't hear people when they talk. I don't even know what I said to you. I think it was bad and I—Gina, I don't know what to do."

"I don't know, either," she said.

Dominic pressed the pencil so hard that the point collapsed, scrawling a stray mark.

"But I love you," Gina said. "And I've done things like that, too."

He turned the pencil over and erased the mark. "That's all I had to say, I guess. You go on."

Gina picked up the machine and did a test run on her skin. Bearable.

As if he'd been waiting for the buzz of the machine before speaking, he said quietly: "I love you, too."

She nodded, dipped the needle in ink, and pressed her foot to the pedal. That moment when the vibration began was her meditation bell now, all her attention distilled into that one patch of skin. When he started talking again, she almost didn't hear him.

She paused the machine. "What?"

"Is the anchor going to say 'Hold Fast'?" he said.

She smiled. "No." She wiped the blood from her skin. The stenciled anchor said SINK OR SWIM. She traced out the first three letters, and then she went her own way: SINE PROPRIO.

Satisfied, she spent a pleasurable quarter hour filling the anchor with color to the brim. The needle droned. Her skin stung. She shaded a gradient of glow all around it, like the anchor had sucked up a sunrise.

When it was finished, she pointed to the camera. "Take a picture for me?"

Dominic did it. "That's forty?"

"That's forty." She tore off a piece of plastic wrap to bandage the tattoo.

"How many total?" he said. "To get those forty you liked?"

"Two hundred seventeen."

"You've worked your ass off."

"Are we starting the exit interview?"

Dominic paused. "Sure."

Gina finished cleaning and sat down in the waiting room, where she'd put the typewriter on the coffee table. He sat across from her.

"I never did an exit interview and I don't know what you're supposed to say." He leaned forward. "So here goes. We've been through a lot of shit this year. But I want you to stay."

"Why?"

"Because you're an asset here. I didn't think you'd last a month, and here it is, July. It's not always the hotshot talents who end up doing the best work. It's the people who come at it with humility and devotion, and that's you. You're doing solid work, maybe masterful work one day. And I want you here."

"You're allowed to just come out and say *I'm proud of you*."

"I *am* proud of you."

She cleared her throat. "Here's the deal. I love this shop. I know you think you want me here. But I don't know if you really do."

Dominic drummed his fingers on his knees. "I just said I do."

"You want part of me here. Almost all of Gina. There are parts of me you'd rather keep quiet. And I can't."

He massaged his temples, which meant he did not want to get on this subject. "You're talking about Anna." At least he wasn't walking away.

"Not just Anna. Everything I'm supposed to be quiet about." All the words she'd been keeping in her head broke free and poured out. "When you tell me to make the coffee and stay out of the conversations. When Keith Yearly is straight-up attacking Lamar's business and cheating your neighbors and you don't even open your mouth to say *Dude, that's not right*. When a customer insults Mexicans and you let it slide. I used to think you kicked out the bikers with white-power patches because you thought it was wrong. I love you and I want to believe that. But now I wonder if you just didn't want the fights."

Dominic looked frustrated. "I get no credit for all the times I have listened to you? How many diner conversations, how many—"

"Even when I do get to talk, nothing happens. The guy who snuck half-naked pictures of me got away with it. He's never going to get caught."

"I dropped the ball on that. I know." He rubbed his face. "But that is not the same thing. Business is complicated."

"If that's the business we're going to run, I don't belong here." Gina pressed the asterisk key. It clacked against the paper, leaving a little star.

"You're telling me you don't want to be a tattooer?"

"No. I love tattooing. It feels like a calling. But I don't belong *here*."

"I don't know if I belong here, either," Dominic said.

It felt like her car hit a dip in the road out of nowhere. "What?"

"I don't know if I want to keep this shop open."

"I thought keeping it open was the whole idea," Gina said. "With the investment, and Harrison, and Jeri."

"Do you know why I opened this shop?"

"You got tired of that back room in Coney Island."

Dominic shook his head. "I said to myself, Mom's a wreck, I'll do this until Gina graduates high school. Then I'll get her out in the world and figure out what next. But next thing you know I got two other guys on payroll, and one of them's got an aunt with cancer. More people to be responsible for. Then Jeri comes along with her big vision and her dad wants return on investment. Then a baby's coming. Now you want me to be some crusader for justice, or whatever the hell—"

"Not a crusader," Gina said. "A good friend."

"You know what I want to do? Right now, this very second?" He paused. "Go home and build myself a private workshop."

"What kind of workshop?"

"I don't know. Making clocks, for all I care. Some kind of tinkering I can do by myself, sell my work through the mail, and everybody will leave me alone." He stood and stretched, his illustrated arms reaching for the ceiling.

"Is this normal for an exit interview?" Gina said.

"Turns out I suck at interviews," Dominic said. "Look. This is never what I wanted for you. I used to daydream that you'd move to Connecticut and be an art teacher, and I could shut this down and be on my way. I don't love tattooing the way you do. It's a job I'm good at. But if you have an offer at Paulie's, or in the city, anywhere but here, you should go."

"What does Jeri want to do?"

"Nothing's changed for her. She wants a successful studio and a family. I'll stick out the game for her until she calls it on account of rain."

Gina nodded. "You didn't ask me what I want."

"What do you want?"

She pushed her notebook across the table at him.

She couldn't pull this off yet, of course; she didn't have the business skills or the mastery of tattooing. But one day—years in the future—she could. A shop that felt like home. A place where people were listened to. A place where they came to heal and feel like works of art, like Andrea had.

"Please believe me," Dominic said, "you don't want your own shop."

"Not now. In a few years." She pointed to the drawing. A vow: "I am going to tattoo here one day."

"So are you staying or not?"

For the time being, Gina still needed a teacher. Not a protector, not a provider and permission giver, but a teacher.

"I finished what I promised you," she said. "I want to stay long enough for you to finish what you promised me."

She sat down at the typewriter and clacked out three lines, one percussive letter at a time. He sat next to her.

INDEPENDENT CONTRACTOR AGREEMENT

Between Dominic Mulley and Gina Mulley

To be revisited every three months

"Item one," she said.

    ***We will speak to each other respectfully. Any issues
    will be taken seriously and handled professionally.

"Yes," he said. "Fine."

    ***PROFESSIONAL DEVELOPMENT: Dominic will schedule
    regular, dedicated time to mentor Gina. Gina will be
    allowed time to attend at least one convention.

"What if I don't have time for a convention?"

"It doesn't say *you*," Gina said. If she could take a train alone, she could take a bus alone. She reached for the magazine where she'd bookmarked the convention ad. *West Coast Tattoo Expo V. January 1987, Los Angeles.* Kari Barba was going to be there. So were Vyvyn Lazonga, Jacci Gresham, Shanghai Kate Hellenbrand, and surely other women tattooers—the ones who hadn't made it to magazines but were honing their craft, just like she was.

She resumed typing.

    ***TERMS: Gina will work on the same terms as other
    Mulley's tattooers: 60% of payment for each tattoo
    retained by artist, 40% to Mulley's Tattoo.

   ***CLEANING RESPONSIBILITIES will be shared among
   tattooers.

"Ha," Dominic said. "Mackie's going to bitch. But fine."

   ***Mulley's Tattoo and its investors may not interfere
   with, comment on, or restrict Gina's personal life.

Dominic cleared his throat. "A little passive-aggressive, don't you think? Sticking it in the agreement?"

"No," Gina said. "I don't think it is."

"What am I supposed to do about Harrison?"

"The right thing."

"What if I can't agree to this? Not just won't, but can't?"

She looked down at her new tattoo. *Sine Proprio.* It already felt like it belonged there.

Sixty-two

SEPTEMBER 23, 1986

D id you decide?" Gina said.

Anna was sitting in the Mulley's waiting room, holding open the botany book. "For Regina, the queen of throwing things." A grape leaf.

Gina laughed. "Stop. That's what you want to take to Nevada?"

"Not really." She flipped to another page: Wild mint. "This."

"You sure you want mint? It means 'virtue.'"

"Also," Dominic called out from the office, "it's weird."

Sassy banter. This was progress. Since the day Dominic signed her new agreement, he'd kept his word: not a complaint, not one sarcastic aside about Anna's visits to the shop. Gina was pleasantly surprised.

All the same. "Stop eavesdropping," she called back.

"It's *wild* virtue," Anna said.

"Okay, wild virtue it is," Gina said. "Hang out while I draw."

G ina was finally fulfilling her promise, and just in time: in a few days, Anna was boarding a bus for the huge October 1 demonstration converging on the Nevada Test Site.

What came after that was hazy—Anna felt confident she'd meet *someone* at that protest who could help her find a job out there—but in the meantime, she had a tent, a few contacts in the Nevada activist community, and all the money from selling her Buick, and she seemed at peace.

They'd agreed to try it until New Year's: three months of Anna adventuring in Nevada. Three months of Gina staying in Blue Claw and absorbing all the knowledge she could, training with Dominic at Mulley's Fine Art Tattoo Studio, taking another class at Blue Claw Community. Three months of a long-distance relationship, letters and interstate phone calls, before they even talked about what came next.

But then, in January, a pilgrimage. Gina would board a westbound Greyhound, first to Nevada to pick up Anna, then on to Los Angeles for the convention. She'd sent in their check and registration forms last week. Paperwork submitted. On time.

It was a good plan, they agreed. It really was. But now the day had come to give Anna her tattoo—a day Gina had expected would feel victorious and satisfying, a milestone crossed. Instead, it felt like the day she'd tattooed Rick. A blessing given reluctantly, a soggy handkerchief waved at a departing ship.

Maybe *this* was adulthood: making the best choice you could, and then coaxing yourself to make peace with it.

An hour later, after Gina had drawn three different versions of that wild mint—*It's good*, Anna kept saying—she positioned the transfer on Anna's ankle.

Gina tattooed a dash and stopped. "Is that okay?"

"Yes. Stop worrying." Anna was breathing evenly. And after a while, a familiar peace did come: Joan Jett on the radio, *crimson and clover, over and over*, the flow feeling of the work doing itself almost without her, Gina there only to keep her hand steady. As the minutes passed, the world disappeared, even Gina herself disappeared, and nothing was left but the wild mint, sprouting line by line.

She'd been writing a letter to Rick, adding a little each day. *Dear Rick, How are you, my friend? I'm making a new list. HOW TO FACE THE FUTURE WITHOUT A CRYSTAL BALL.*

She'd started the list when she found herself drifting back to her old habits—pulling a trancefish, spacing out to hide from hard moments. The other day she caught herself anxiously doodling the classic knuckles tattoo, HOLD FAST, as if those hands could hold Anna here. Sometimes Anna seemed so fired up about her journey that Gina worried she wouldn't be missed at all.

How to love without grasping?

Gina picked up her shader, dipped it in green, and imagined she could infuse this ink with love. *Marianna, take this on your travels. Carry it in your skin, snug against the nerves. The ink will fade; you will change; so will I. But whenever you see this tattoo—wherever you go, whatever you decide—remember this love goes with you.*

Half an hour later, Gina wiped the skin clean and gave Anna a gentle smear of ointment.

"Finished," she said.

It was the size of a teacup's mouth, so fresh and wet it could have been plastered there by a spring rain. Twin leaves of mint sprouted on Anna's ankle, glowing green.

Gina took the afternoon off, and they went in search of Anna's favorite hot dog truck. It had moved to another neighborhood, a strip of public beach on the Great South Bay.

This felt like a day for extravagance. They bought the variety platter: a chili cheese dog, a sauerkraut-and-onion, mustard-and-relish, and a classic ketchup, served up with chips and a can of root beer.

The September air was cool and fresh, faintly brined. They carried the food out to the beach and set it on a picnic table. Gina straddled the bench; Anna tried to get comfortable without bumping her new tattoo. The ocean stretched out before them, shadow-blue and winking with whitecaps.

Anna started in on the mustard-and-relish. As Gina took her first bite, cupping her hand to catch the dripping chili, she felt rich. All the food she cared to eat, in the company of a person who felt like home: a year ago, she wouldn't have believed such abundance was in her future.

For a few minutes, they ate without talking, content to listen to the waves. Then Anna spoke.

"I'm going to miss you," she said. "So much that I don't let myself think about it. I'm going to get on that bus, and once we pass New Jersey it's going to hit me all at once."

"I needed to hear that," Gina said. "You seem like you never worry."

Anna snorted. "You should see inside my head," she said. "Part of me can't wait to get to the desert. But part of me wants to skip ahead to New Year's when we're together again. I just want to know how this turns out. Now I have sympathy for all those crazy people who paid for readings at the House of Mystical Delights."

"I was thinking the other day"—Gina reached out and brushed a crumb off Anna's sleeve—"if I try to fast-forward too often, or zone out when things are hard, I'm going to wake up on my ninetieth birthday and wonder where my life went. I don't want to miss it. So I've been playing a game with myself."

Anna licked a smudge of mustard off her thumb. "What's the game?"

"First," Gina said, "I imagine I actually *am* ninety. My bones hurt, my eyesight's going, my tattoos are faded, but I have a little cottage and it's been a good life. So"—she took a swig of soda—"I decide, as a last hurrah, I'm going to spend my savings on a vacation."

"To where?"

"To *when*. It's a time-travel vacation."

"When do scientists invent that?" Anna took a bite of the sauerkraut-and-onion dog.

"Sometime between now and when I'm ninety," Gina said. "Just listen. The rules are: it's a one-time-only trip to some other year in your life. You don't get to change anything, it's already written. You just wake up in your past, in your younger body again, and relive one season of your life."

"And what season do you choose?"

Gina ran her fingers along the wood grain of the picnic table, the carved initials gritty with sand. "This one. The fall of eighty-six, when I'm working and taking classes, and you're going to Nevada, and I'm already missing you. So as I sit here in this nineteen-year-old body, I'm really ninety, and for some reason I chose this particular season, even though it feels all up in the air and in between."

"Why would you choose *this* time?"

"Exactly," Gina said. "That's why I have to pay attention. It might be disguised as some little unimportant moment. So I can't trance out, or I might blow right past it."

Anna looked thoughtful. "And you actually find those moments?"

"Every day. Even the hard days," Gina said. "Try it. Find one."

"Mine's easy for today." Anna touched her ankle, just above her tattoo. "You doing this for me."

She handed over the last bite of the mustard-and-relish dog; Gina took it. Delicious.

"What's yours?" Anna said.

Gina gestured at the hot dogs, the ocean, Anna herself. "All this."

"If I knew you were traveling back seventy years to get here," Anna said, "I could've arranged a better dinner than hot dogs."

Gina smiled and looked out at the bay; the tide was rolling in. "This is enough."

She gave Anna's hand a squeeze, stood up, and walked alone toward the water's edge. Fire Island was a scribble in the distance, dividing sky from water.

Beyond that, the open Atlantic.

A bit farther, beneath those waves, a world of coral reefs and caverns, octopi and whales, and fish that glowed in the dark.

Enough. More than enough. A wave skimmed up to meet her, and Gina bent to rinse her ink-stained, relish-sticky, sand-flecked hands in the beginning of the ocean.

Acknowledgments

Thank you to the Bennington Writing Seminars community, Bennington College, and its generous faculty, past and present, especially Alice Mattison, Rachel Pastan, Sven Birkerts, David Gates, April Bernard, Tony Eprile, and Roland Merullo. Cheers and love to all the Junie Levins, most of all V. Hansmann, and our writers' group for so many years of pizza and conviviality.

This book was shaped, like a piece of sea glass, over twenty years, with the help of many friends who commented on drafts and shared knowledge. Special thanks to Angela Herring, Courtney Hill, Lorian Tu, Heather Jacobs, Elizabeth Lee, Erica Marsh, Monica Hubbard, Shannon West, Ka Damon, Alli Poirot, Sarah Jey Whitehead, Narayani Sharp, and most of all Kira Watson, my first agent, who coached me through a year of transformative edits and continues to bolster my spirits to this day. Brother Mark D'Alessio introduced me to the idea of sine proprio. Tracy Moavero was the activist mentor who helped shape Anna's ambitions. And warm thanks to one of my first readers, my high school comrade Nicolas, who was tickled to have an unsavory psychic for a namesake, but who—other than his Swiss heritage—has absolutely nothing in common with Nicolas Eggli-Pfister.

Deepest gratitude to Rubén Degollado, author of *Throw* and *The Family Izquierdo*, who lent his cultural and editorial expertise, brought Rick and

Tía Andrea's dialogue to life, and suggested the title of this book. Without you, there would be no Pezadita.

An ocean of thanks to my agent, Chad Luibl, and my editor, Jeramie Orton, for bringing this book into the world. You are both whip-smart, heart-of-gold human beings. Gina's story is stronger and more daring because of you. My heartfelt gratitude to Pam Dorman. I couldn't ask for a better home for Gina than Pamela Dorman Books.

I made it through the last ten drafts because of artist-writers Sarah Lybrand, Sofia Titvinidze, and Jodi Jeanson Hunt. Thank you, loves, for all the work bees and childcare swaps, brainstorming sessions and readthroughs, and times of consolation and celebration.

Dad, Sandy, Megan, and Sam: So much love. Thank you for your joy.

Charlie and Milo: I love you with every fiber of my being. You've cheered for me since you learned to throw pennies in fountains. I will always cheer for you, too, and for the work of your heart. The last chapter of this novel is for you.

To Rob, and to my mom, Joan Gervais: You are people of few words and great love. I could write another book about how much I love you and how each of you helped me persevere, but you're also modest and wouldn't like that, so I'll just say:

A Note on the Research

Thank you to the all the tattoo artists who generously shared their stories and expertise with me: Lynn TerHaar of Dutchman Tattoo, who opened the first woman-owned shop in Suffolk County, New York (Artful Ink in Bohemia); Kelly Gelling, current owner of Artful Ink, and Victoria Ohman, who tattoos there; Michelle Myles at Daredevil Tattoo on Manhattan's Lower East Side, which is both a working studio and an excellent tattoo museum; Eric Ziobrowski; Stacey Sharp; Mick Michieli-Beasley of Dragon Moon Tattoo in Glen Burnie, Maryland; Marc Gold of Top Hat Tattoo in Rocky Point, New York; and Marvin Moskowitz, third-generation tattooer, whose father and uncle, Walter and Stan Moskowitz, opened the first tattoo shop on Long Island.

To Marguerite, now at SnapDragon Ink in Delhi, New York one of the first women to tattoo on Long Island: My love for this art form began when I was six years old, sitting on the floor of Peter Tat-2 in Hempstead as you tattooed my mom. Thank you.

I'm also indebted to the following resources: Huck Spaulding's 1988 manual, *Tattooing A to Z: A Guide to Successful Tattooing*; *New York City Tattoo: The Oral History of an Urban Art*, by Michael McCabe; *Bodies of Subversion: A Secret History of Women and Tattoo*, by Margot Mifflin; the audio documentary *Last of the Bowery Scab Merchants*, by Walter Moskowitz; the documentary *Color Outside the Lines*, from director and producer Artemus Jenkins and executive producer Miya Bailey, exploring the work of Black tattoo artists (including the legendary Jacci Gresham); and *Smile Now, Cry Later: Guns, Gangs, and Tattos—My Life in Black and Gray* by Freddy Negrete, which offers a glimpse into the Chicano roots of black-and-gray tattooing.

The West Coast Tattoo Expo V is imaginary, but Kari Barba, Vyvyn Lazonga, Jacci Gresham, and Shanghai Kate Hellenbrand are real artists who—along with many other groundbreaking tattoo artists, too numerous to list here—helped pave the way for women in the field.

Finally: It goes without saying that much has changed in tattooing since 1985, particularly regarding safety and cleanliness. The best place to get a tattoo today is a reputable shop that—unlike my fictional Mulley's of the 1980s, or Mackie tattooing out of his apartment—is licensed by a local or state health department. Contemporary tattoo apprentices also need a far greater level of artistry than the humble sketchbook drawings I created for this novel, and undergo training for much longer than Gina did. If you're considering this line of work, I highly recommend listening to every episode of the podcast *Tit for Tat Chat*, by "lady tattooers" Zoe Bean and Betty Rose, which cheerfully demolishes any glamorized ideas about the daily life of a tattoo artist.